Miss O'Malley's Maine Summer

Miss O'Malley's Maine Summer

Thomas E. Coughlin

Fitzgerald & LaChapelle Publishing, LLC

Written, produced and printed in the United States of America

ISBN: 978-0-9666202-4-5

Cover Model: Kara Flynn, the Irish-American cover girl, hailing from
Lowell, Massachusetts

Cover Design: Lisa Atkins, Pelham, New Hampshire

FIRST EDITION
Second Printing

Fitzgerald & LaChapelle Publishing, LLC
814 Elm Street, Suite 401
Manchester, NH 03101
Ph: (603) 669-6112   Fax: (603) 627-5888

Dedication

For Edward F. Coughlin

Dad, for my Irish blood and for being
there for what feels like—forever.

Acknowledgements

Dick Varano and Billy's Chowder House, the Plummer Family for the use of their magnificent house and property, Lori Schofield, Betsy Chase, Nicole D'Amato, Sean Coughlin, Bob and Ruth Ann Cullinane, Sarah Windle, for the use of the ladder in May, and again in September, Dennis Canney for finding me Kara, and Peter Mars, my dearest friend and editor.

1

RED HAIR SWIRLED WILDLY around the young woman's face as a persistent ocean breeze gusted over the water's white caps and up onto the shoulder of land above the sea. The twenty-year-old paused atop the grassy collar at the end of the beach and gazed out over the quarter-mile long expanse of sand and crashing surf. With currents of fresh air buffeting her face, she took in the extraordinary vista. Perched fifty feet above sea level, the redhead was pleased to see she was alone. In summer it would not be unusual to find dozens of visitors in this place, largely on vacation or holiday, speckling the shoreline atop colorful blankets. However, it was the last day of April in Ireland's County Donegal and the stream of tourists that make their way to the northwest corner of her country was, at present, only a trickle.

Layla O'Malley was a pretty girl, fresh faced and pleasing to the eye. Her deep, auburn hair framed perfect, alabaster skin, save for a sprinkling of freckles that danced across the bridge of her nose. Closing her eyes, she jutted out her face, letting the invigorating breeze take hold and blow her hair horizontally. An impending journey was about to steal her from this place. However, for the moment, she would allow her senses to take in all that her beloved beach at Glencolumbkille offered. Moments later she focused her eyes on the pathway before her and began the descent to the sand below.

Arriving thirty seconds later at the edge of the swirling Atlantic, Layla stepped out onto a patch of beach where the sea had deposited sand from a previous high tide. There, the twenty-year-old set herself down, legs folded beneath her, and looked out at the incoming action from the waves. At this moment, her thoughts raced frantically through the collection of issues confronting her, not the least of which was her transcontinental plane ride the next day to Boston, Massachusetts. It was fair to say that Layla O'Malley of Glencolumbkille had lived a sheltered life, able to count the times she had left the county on one hand with single ventures to Dublin and Belfast among these limited excursions. However, tomorrow she would be flying in a jetliner, seven miles above the ground as best she could estimate. It was thoughts like these that brought her back to this special place a final time before her departure.

Peering out over glistening water, Layla contemplated the series of events that brought her to this crossroads in her life. It was less than a year since an American couple appeared at the O'Malley's front door. She arrived home from work that day to find her parents and two strangers engaged in lively conversation at the kitchen table. She quickly learned that a distant relative, a fifth cousin as best anyone could determine, had tracked down relations from the 'old' country. A year earlier, Brian Kelly had received a genealogical survey of his family's history as a gift from his wife on his fortieth birthday. Armed with these details, he managed to trace a limb of the Kelly family tree up to County Donegal and ultimately to the door of Eoin, Finula, and Layla O'Malley. Brian and Margaret Kelly stayed in the area around Glencolumbkille for three days, treating the O'Malleys to dinner in Killybegs on two consecutive evenings. On the final day of the American's stay in Donegal the tourists were treated to a homemade Irish dinner at the humble home of their newfound relatives. It was while breaking bread on this final evening that Brian had first brought up the notion of having his young cousin come to the United States and work for the season.

Six months had passed since that dinner with the Kellys from America and the wistful thought of flying over an ocean and working in a strange place was no longer a daydream. It was about to play out. It was now when the young woman began to question the wisdom of her decision to accept her cousin's invitation to spend the spring and summer working in the United States along the coast of Maine. Over the cold, gray winter her spirits were buoyed by the prospect of expanding her horizons beyond the boundaries of her rock-strewn county. In the months leading up to her departure, Brian Kelly had managed to extinguish her parent's fears relating to their only daughter's planned absence. Mr. Kelly promised on more than one occasion to guarantee the safety and well-being of his young cousin. Layla would be comfortably and safely lodged in a private cabin on the premises of her cousin's motel operation and live day-to-day under the watchful eyes of Mr. Kelly and his immediate staff. Over time Layla's parents had come to accept their daughter's scheduled time away as a critical ingredient in her maturation process. Now, with her *Aer Lingus* plane ticket and passport laid out on the surface of the kitchen hutch, Layla knew time had grown short and this adventure, the first of its kind in her short life, was about to begin.

Sitting atop a modest bank of sand and observing the slow advance of the surf, the redhead's imagination took hold of her. Time spent alone over the cold, winter nights had brought on blissful thoughts of future encounters with any number of American men. She enjoyed meeting and dealing with Yanks on holiday from the United States. However, all too often, time in their company was usually far too brief to conjure up anything approaching a friendship. But, that was about to change, she thought. She did not anticipate returning home until mid October. The upcoming work adventure would span nearly half a year, more than ample time to sow the seeds of a meaningful friendship, or perhaps something much, much more.

Following a peek at the surging, ocean water in front of her, Layla fell backwards onto the firm sand, stretched her arms outward, and gazed up at a scattering of white clouds as they gusted by against the blue sky. In little more than twenty-four hours she would be soaring over clouds much like these. This thought sent a wave of anticipation and fear through her. She remembered the countless times she walked home in darkness, glancing up at the stars and blinking lights of some aircraft forty thousand feet above. Often times she had tried to imagine the individuals on those flights and their destinations. Now, after six months of anticipation and planning, Layla O'Malley was about to follow in the path of the very people she had tried to visualize on so many occasions and on so many dark, starry nights.

The pretty redhead was nearly a half hour into her good-bye visit to this magical beach when a surge of cold, ocean water made contact with her outstretched hand, jolting her up to a sitting position. She opened her eyes to behold a near circle of seawater. Immediately jumping to her feet, she retreated back from the oncoming tide in the direction of the dune that formed the back wall to the beach. Layla, always the fanciful romantic, took the development as a farewell of sorts, the beach water at Glencolumbkille acting like a jumpy, spinster aunt, anxious to hustle a guest away who had outstayed her welcome. Layla turned and trudged through the soft sand at the rear of the beach, taking a moment to glance back at the advancing tide every few seconds. There was still much to do with preparations for the following day's flight. Reaching the bottom of the hill from which she had descended a half hour earlier, she raced to the top of the stony steps and turned back a final time. No doubt, her idle thoughts would bring her back here over the coming months. Her eyes took in this special place, absorbing details of the cresting waves and far hillside. Finally, she whirled in the direction of the road and began the walk home.

The O'Malley residence, a humble two-bedroom cottage, was no more than a kilometer away. The house, with its slate roof and whitewashed exterior, was another reason why Layla's visit to the United States could not have come at a better time. This cottage, home to the O'Malleys from before Layla's birth, was owned by a Mr. Neal Connolly of Killibegs. Just after the Christmas holidays, Mr. Connolly informed her parents that he was entertaining the idea of putting his property up for sale. However, before taking any action, he promised to give the O'Malleys first refusal on the house. The family, excited at the prospect of owning their first home, had run the numbers and found themselves short on the down payment portion of the transaction. However, they had been given until the end of the year to come up with the necessary cash and Layla was sure she could save enough money in Maine over the summer to close on the cottage.

The walk back to the house led her past a number of modest dwellings much like her own and up a gentle hill. Glencolumbkille was not a gentrified Dublin suburb, not in the least. It was a small community where every face seemed to be a familiar one, except in May through September when most people on holiday arrived. The walk, seaside to front door, took no more than fifteen minutes. Arriving at the front step she pushed in the heavy, bright green painted door, and entered the hallway.

"Is that you, love?" called out her mom from the kitchen.

"Aye, I've come back from the beach," the twenty-year-old called back while slipping off her sweater.

"Da's taken the car to the village to pick up something special for dinner tonight," said Finula O'Malley while joining her daughter in the living room. Finula was a woman of modest stature, barely over five feet in height and petite. Her ordinary, plain face looked out from beneath a scramble of frizzy, black hair. "I'm afraid the reality of the moment has just caught up with him all of a sudden. It's finally penetrated his thick scull that he's going to be losing his daughter for the next six months."

"You do know I'm going to miss you both something awful," confessed Layla, seated at one end of the family's couch.

"Your mind must be racing to beat the band, with the trip to America finally here."

"It's a wee overwhelming," confessed the young woman as she popped nervously to her feet. "And I shouldn't be just sitting around when there's still packing to do." Layla sailed across the room, planting a kiss on her mother's cheek before scurrying up the stairs.

From outside her bedroom window came the sound of deceleration from a vehicle. For thirty minutes she had been pulling clothing from bureau drawers and from off hangers in the adjacent closet. She peeked out through window curtains and caught sight of her father emerging from the car. Within seconds Eoin O'Malley was unloading two bags of groceries from the back seat and stepping over the lawn in the direction of the front door. She glanced back at her bed where a collection of casual wear lay strewn across its surface. Immediately, Layla broke from the room and raced down the stairs in the direction of her father.

"Daddy, let me help you with that," she said behind a wry smile. "And what's a man of your advancing years doing carrying a couple of heavy objects as these?" The man knitted his brow.

"And that'll be enough of this 'old man' nonsense from you," he answered in mock anger. His daughter removed a bag from his cradled arm and walked toward the nearby kitchen. The husky man with disheveled, red hair followed his daughter from the hallway.

"Am I the only one who's beginning to have second thoughts about this whole idea of Layla working in the states?" asked the man in a voice intended to carry throughout the house. "Our daughter is about to fly off to another continent and stay under the watchful eye of a man we barely know. For all we know this Brian Kelly could be a drug dealer or some underworld racketeer."

"I never heard such rubbish," answered his wife appearing in the far doorway. "First of all, Mr. Kelly's me kin—not close kin, but kin. Secondly, he and his wife didn't strike me as anything but good, honest people. Eoin, you know as well as me that you're only starting this because you see this precious thing about to test her wings—and you know you're going to miss her terribly." Layla glanced up at her father and flashed him a sad smile.

"Da, it's only six months. I'll be home in no time." The man nodded in begrudging agreement, the trace of a tear suddenly visible in the corner of his eye.

"I'm just afraid you'll meet some Yank who'll promise you the moon and the stars and that'll be the end of us back here."

"Eoin, stop talking like an eejit," snapped Finula, wrapping her arm around her daughter's shoulder and drawing her near.

"It's not like I'm going to the states for a good time, not with the house going up for sale at the end of the year and us not having money to close on it. It's going to take any extra money I can make to come up with the down payment—extra money I could never earn down at the welcome center. Mr. Kelly says I can make more than enough money waitressing at that chowder house place in Wells Beach. No Da, I'll be back with enough American dollars to close the deal on the house. That I promise." The pretty redhead stood motionless in the kitchen between her parents as the enormity of the situation took hold of all those present. "I'll be flying into Shannon next October and think of what a grand time it will be when I step off the plane and we set eyes on each other again," Layla exclaimed, reaching out to them both.

Layla O'Malley's last evening at home before her departure played out much like the American wakes of her ancestors one hundred and fifty years before. An American wake was the name given to the gathering of family and friends of a traveler prior to his or her journey across the ocean to the United States or elsewhere in search of financial salvation. It was labeled a 'wake' because of the overwhelming likelihood that the adventurer would never be set eyes on again by those assembled. So it was in the O'Malley house that night where too few expressions of optimism and joy were exchanged by the family. Young Layla retired early on this night, knowing she and her father would be on the road by six o'clock the next morning. With red hair strewn about the surface of her pillow, the twenty-year-old lay awake for a period, transfixed at the prospect of being thousands of miles away and in a strange land when next she put her head down to rest.

11

THE BEDROOM WAS STILL blanketed in darkness when the tender squeeze from a hand brought the girl out of a deep sleep. Layla opened her eyes to the sight of mother standing over her. The woman's expression said everything the girl felt compressed deep within her. The painful time of good-byes was nearly at hand.

Making her way down the stairs toward the kitchen her eyes picked up on the two pieces of luggage resting by the front door. Everything was in order for her pending departure. On the kitchen table sat a bowl of steaming porridge and a cup of tea. She entered the room, joining her mother at the table. Mrs. O'Malley raised her eyes from her own cup and forced a bittersweet smile in her daughter's direction.

"I suspect that will be the last drinkable cup of tea you'll be getting till we get you home in October," called out her father as he burst into the room.

"And I suppose the Americans don't have a teabag among them," answered Layla.

"I suspect you won't be finding Bewleys anywhere in Maine—or in Boston for that matter," he roared. "It appears the good Lord has given us a fine morning for the drive to Shannon. There's a fresh breeze off the water and I think I'm seeing a hint of the sun on the horizon." His conversation came off as forced, seemingly intended to draw everyone's attention away from the matter at hand. Finula lifted her eyes up to her husband, then immediately returned them to her daughter.

"Layla, you'll be in me prayers every day till you appear back in our doorway," she uttered.

The family remained huddled over their last, collective meal for six months for the next twenty minutes while the redhead reassured her parents. She reminded them of her mission: the accumulation of enough American dollars to purchase, at long last, the house.

"Under the watchful care of Ma's own kin, Mr. Kelly of Wells, Maine or somewhere in New Hampshire, I still haven't figured that out yet, I will work me fingers to the bone and return with me pockets stuffed with American dollars. And who knows, I might very well convince some rich, Irish-American that it's time he returned to his ancestral home and settle down in County Donegal, and make an honest man of him." Mother and father laughed and rolled their eyes as the girl swallowed the last of her tea and reached for her mother.

"I will call home the minute I arrive in Maine," she promised, pecking the woman on the cheek.

"It's a blessing I have to be at the laundry today, that it is. I wouldn't want to have to watch you get on that plane and disappear from us up into the clouds," said the woman as she returned her daughter's affection.

"Give Mr. Kelly me best."

Eoin O'Malley pushed himself away from the table and silently exited the room. Seconds later he reappeared in the doorway slipping on a jacket.

"Better we be getting on the road," he announced before turning away, walking down the hall, and fetching her luggage. Layla extended her mother a final hug before leaving the kitchen and grabbing her coat from a hook in the hallway.

"Ma, I hope you don't mind being called too late but I will be talking to you before me head hits the pillow tonight. Reaching you from the United States of America…and how amazing is that?" The redhead slipped a plaid coat over her shoulders and made for the front door. She turned and flashed her mother a final smile before jumping in the front seat of the car beside her father.

"You be careful driving, Eoin," called out Finula as the car pulled away from the house.

The vehicle drove away through a silent row of cottages in the village. Streaks of morning light were just breaking through the cool, morning air, illuminating the nearby eastern face of Slieve League, the two thousand foot mountain that stood crouching over the western end of Donegal Bay. Layla took in every detail of the terrain, from the mountains to the desolate peat fields, committing her homeland to memory as the car motored in the direction of Killybegs, the town where her mother labored in the laundry. It was well over two hundred miles from her front door to Shannon Airport, a ride that would take father and daughter over much open road but also through congested cities like Sligo and Ennis. For this reason, Eoin had allowed considerable time in the event of the unexpected, prolonged delays from traffic congestion or roadwork, not to mention mechanical difficulty with the automobile. The truth was, neither of the O'Malley's vehicles were late models or totally dependable. The flight from Shannon to Logan Airport in Boston was not scheduled to depart until nearly one-thirty. By his best estimate, father and daughter should pull into the terminal at ten-thirty.

The drive this morning proceeded relatively close to plan. In the town of Donegal the two stopped long enough to fill the car with petrol and purchase coffee for the road. In western Ireland of 1998 even open roads between cities were largely of the two-lane variety. The anticipated congestion in the city of Sligo never materialized. However, it was replaced by an extended delay in the town of Knock when the combination of the stream of visitors to the holy shrine there and the transport of a modular home along heavily traveled and narrow N17 caused movement to come to a standstill. Eventually, under the directive of a mildly irritated garda, Eoin and the other southbound motorists found themselves directed up onto the sidewalk for a distance of one hundred yards.

"This is why I had us out the door so early this morning," commented Eoin as the car finally cleared the area of congestion and picked up speed. "Now Layla, it's eejits like those bogtrotters back there moving that house during morning drive that makes it necessary to give yourself so much extra time. This way the eejits can do what eejits do and we still have plenty of time to catch your flight."

It was just beyond eleven fifteen when the O'Malley car pulled into the general parking area of Shannon Airport. Eoin scrambled from the vehicle, unloaded the luggage, and escorted his daughter to the entrance of the international airport. He watched on soberly as his Layla presented her ticket to the Aer Lingus attendant. The man looked on, taken with the poise of his only child. She seemed like a different person from the young woman who sat quietly at the kitchen table hours before, taking in each and every bit of advice her anxious parents tossed at her. She gave off the appearance of a polished, young lady, an experienced traveler setting out on another transatlantic journey. He watched from the edge of the terminal as the twenty-year-old handed over her luggage, turned, and made her way toward him.

"That was easy enough," she exclaimed, reaching her father as he stood leaning against the wall. "I have me boarding pass and they've told me what gate to go to when the flight's scheduled to take off."

"I can stay with you here as long as you want. Whatever suits you. But, I'll not be watching the plane lift off and fly up into the clouds. I have a long ride back to the house and I'm thinking I might stop at the shrine at Knock and ask the Blessed Mother to give you a safe trip."

"Da, that's a brilliant idea. If you leave in short order you might even make it home before ma. You might want to catch a bite once you're out of the airport."

"So you don't mind me leaving you here?"

"Oh, of course not," she answered, reaching out and embracing her father. Following a prolonged hug she separated herself, only to notice moisture welling up in the man's blue eyes.

"Now Da, what's this? I told you…I'll be back in no time. Try to think of the craic they'll be when I come home in October and we can sit down together in the kitchen, no—when I come home and take you two out to dinner in Killybegs. We'll celebrate me return and the purchase of the house. God, it'll be a grand time." Eoin pulled his daughter to him.

"I swear I love you more than heaven and earth. Your mother, too. Be careful over there in the states, watch the drinking, mind Mr. Kelly, and don't you be trusting any of those young, American men."

"It's them you should be worrying about, not me. I'll get to mass every Sunday and stay out of the company of hooligans and slappers. I promise, Da." The man pushed his daughter to arm's length, kissed her on the cheek, turned, and made his way through a set of automatic doors and out of the building.

***

Layla opened her eyes to the sound of the steady whir from the plane's engine and a smile from the female flight attendant standing a few feet from her in the aisle.

"Can I interest you in a beverage of any kind?" asked an extremely attractive woman with black hair and deep, blue eyes. Layla motioned in the negative and turned to the window. Sliding the shade upward she peeked downward and thought she could make out a jagged shoreline through the misty cloudbank.

"Hello ladies and gentlemen, this is your captain. We are currently cruising at thirty eight thousand feet. If you glance out the window, passengers on the right side of the plane should be able to make out Newfoundland. Our flight path will take us over Nova Scotia, the Bay of Fundy, then along the coast of Maine to Boston. At the moment we are slightly ahead of schedule and should land at Logan Airport in approximately one hour," squawked the voice from over the aircraft's intercom. The twenty-year-old gazed dreamily out the window, a sense of relief descending over her. The long journey over open ocean was behind them, she thought. Again, she trained her eyes on the stretch of shoreline far below. It seemed incredible to imagine but she was flying over a whole, new continent, new to her anyway. Glancing down at her watch, Layla noted that it was nearly six o'clock. Barring car trouble, her father would be home by now, and her mother. No doubt they were discussing her and surely how quiet the house was without her.

"You'll want to be changing the time on your watch before you get off the plane," quipped the elderly woman seated beside her.

"Aye, of course. Do you know what the time would be?"

"Five minutes to one, child. You'll want to be turning your watch back five hours." The elderly woman had a sweet quality about her. She was an American. "This makes the sixteenth year in a row that I've visited your beautiful country," she added.

"Sixteen years, you say! You must surely like it there," chirped Layla.

"Yes, my husband and I began our annual trips in 1982. I lost my Paul six years ago but I've kept up the visits on my own ever since," she confessed, extending the girl a somber smile. Layla reached over and squeezed her hand. "It's funny, I never feel closer to my Paul than when I'm back in Ireland. We made so many fond memories there, and so many old friends I can go back and visit. My children think I'm crazy for going back, year after year. They don't understand." With that said, the two grew quiet, shifting their eyes in the direction of the projection screen where a British comedy was in progress.

"I've come over to work," blurted out Layla, not content to let the banter die on a solemn note. "I'll not be staying in Boston for long. Me cousin will be picking me up and driving me up to Maine. I'll be working there for the next six months."

"You Irish have to be the friendliest people on earth," exclaimed the woman, the sentiment seeming to come out of thin air. "I'm not Irish myself. My Paul had the Irish blood in him. But I've fallen in love with your country and the people."

"Well, as you probably know, the Irish are quite fond of Americans, too. I remember, growing up and a young thing in school, Mr. Gallagher, he was me teacher, teaching us in history class how the Irish people probably would not have our independence if it weren't for all the help the Americans gave us during the struggle—that being there's so many Irish in the states from immigrating there during the hard times and the struggle." The elderly woman was about to comment on Layla's statement when the plane dipped through a wave of turbulence, sending up a restrained chorus of oohs and ahhs.

"Until that little dip this whole flight's been smoother than a drive to Killybegs," the girl exclaimed. The woman laughed, closed her eyes, and let her head fall back onto her head cushion.

Layla found herself drifting in and out of a light sleep over the next thirty minutes. More than twelve hours had passed since she had been rousted out of her warm bed back in County Donegal. However, a general change in sound and a sense of speed from within the cabin suggested that the flight might be approaching its destination. A glance out the window told her that the aircraft had lost altitude from that of a half hour earlier. At present the attendants were scurrying the length of both aisles, searching frantically for any remaining uncollected plastic containers or meal trays.

"All seats in the upright position," commanded what appeared to be the senior member of the team of stewardesses and in a voice carrying a distinct, Dublin accent. Layla refocused her attention downward where the whitecaps on the water were now plainly visible and the only land in sight was a scattering of small islands a thousand or so feet below. The jetliner continued to glide closer to sea level. Layla glanced sideways to see the kindly woman in the next seat peeking over her shoulder.

"We seem to getting very close to landing and all I'm still seeing is water!" exclaimed the girl.

"Oh child, it's always that way. The runway is right on the water. We'll be setting down just fine," reassured the woman. Seconds later, with the sound of the jet's engines roaring through the cabin, the choppy water below gave way to terra firma and the detailed markings outlining the dark runway. The Airbus set down with a pronounced jolt, followed by a distinctly different sound from the plane's engines, no doubt intended to slow the forward speed of the aircraft. Layla peered out the window for her first look at the United States of America while the Aer Lingus jetliner taxied its way in the direction of the terminal. It was not long before passengers around her leaped to their feet and began removing carry on luggage from the compartments over their heads. Instinctively, Layla rose to her feet and ducked her way out into the aisle.

"Have a wonderful stay up in Maine," said the sweet lady from the seat below. "Me, I always take my time and wait until most everyone else is gone." Layla reached down and squeezed the woman's hand, flashing her a bright smile. It was a full five minutes before the crowd of passengers, congregated in the aisle, began streaming toward the front of the aircraft. Exiting the body of the plane, the twenty-year-old picked up on the lilt of the Irish dialect being spoken by a family. She fell in behind this group, not completely sure of what to do in the airport on arrival and surmising her responsibilities would be identical to these other Irish residents. The young woman's strategy proved to be an effective one. After following the Irish family through customs she made her way downstairs behind them to claim her baggage. There she stood by a conveyer belt, watching hundreds of pieces of stranger's luggage pass by her with one eye and peering around the immense room for any sign of her cousin with the other. All around her there was the reuniting of families and friends with hugs, kisses and handshakes. Layla carried her luggage away from the crowds of people and conveyer belt and out into an open hall. There, she pushed her bags against the near wall and sat atop them. In front of her, individuals hurried by in both directions, most not so much as casting her a glance. Her eyes darted from face to face, anxiously awaiting the appearance of her cousin. She attempted to not appear out of place or overwhelmed in any way, but this was the exact feeling taking hold of her. At the moment, all she knew with exact certainty was that her best course of action was to remain in this place and hope her cousin Brian had not forgotten her.

Twenty minutes had passed when her roving eyes picked up on two young men across the terminal. Her attention was drawn when she realized that she was the object of some scrutiny on their part. Casting her eyes downward, she was still able to ascertain that she was the clear object of their discussion. Seconds later a wave of fear curled up within her stomach as the two began shuffling across the terminal in her direction. Both males were black, dressed in loose-fitting, baggy clothes, and sporting dreadlocks.

"Hey little mama, what are you doin' sittin' here all by yourself?" called out the shorter of the two. Layla looked up into their eyes. They did not appear to be more than seventeen or eighteen years of age.

"I'm waiting for me cousin to pick me up. He should be here any minute."

"Shee-it. What's that accent you got? You from England or somethin'?" asked the second youth, smiling menacingly into her face at close range. Layla felt herself pinned against the wall as the two youths closed in, now invading her personal space.

"Gentlemen, I see you've come to the rescue of my little cousin," called out a voice from over the young mens' shoulders. They whirled around only to be confronted by a tall, rugged looking, middle-aged man sporting a two-day-old beard. "Thanks for keeping my princess company while I drove up and down every one-way in the Back Bay." The youths stepped back from the girl, eyeing the confident stranger cautiously.

"Sure man, it's the least we could do," responded the shorter youth as they began a methodical walk to the other side of the noisy terminal. Brian Kelly stepped forward, lifting Layla to her feet and grabbing hold of the two pieces of luggage. Her cousin towered above her, standing no less than six inches taller than her. She did not remember him being as imposing looking on his visit to County Donegal the previous autumn.

"My apologies, kid. I got turned around but good on the other side of the tunnel. There's this thing called the *Big Dig*. It was as if I'd never seen the city of Boston before," he confessed, smiling down sheepishly at his cousin. Layla reached her arm around the man and pulled him to her.

"No, Mr. Kelly, you were brilliant. I don't know what those two hooligans were planning on doing with me." Brian howled with laughter as he guided the girl toward an exit and the adjacent parking garage.

"I have a suspicion they didn't have any idea what to do with you either," he answered, half under his breath.

Less than fifteen minutes after being rescued from the plane terminal, Layla was staring out the window of her cousin's truck as it emerged from a half-mile long tunnel and back out into natural light. Around her was the chaos of widespread road construction, definitely on a scale exceeding anything she had seen at home. Her cousin had grown quiet, intent on processing the information on each and every road sign in front of them.

"Layla, keep your eyes open for a sign for Route 95. That's where we want to wind up." The twenty-year-old focused her eyes on the road ahead even as vehicles sped by the pickup with seemingly no regard for their safety.

"Jaysus, it seems dense having everyone driving on the wrong side of the road," the girl blurted out.

"Dense, huh? When in Rome, do as the Romans do. You're going have to get used to it, princess."

"Do the people drive like this, like eejits I mean, up in Maine?" she asked.

"Not for the most part," he answered before reaching over and pointing to a sign in the distance. "Looks like 95 north to me, and that's where we want to be." Glancing back occasionally through the rear window, Brian cautiously eased the vehicle into the inside lane and waited on his exit to appear. "Okay, now things should start to improve. After all, it's Friday afternoon and all of the corporate deadwood is trying to sneak out early for the weekend."

As predicted by her cousin, the pickup was soon able to distance itself from the congested, inner-city traffic and the two found themselves cruising northward, leaving the towering, concrete buildings of downtown Boston to slowly disappear in the rear window of the vehicle.

"So, how does it feel being here in the USA? First impressions, please," ordered Brian.

"Tis a bit much. And it's glad I am that me cousin was here to take care of me," admitted Layla in a tone drenched with relief.

"That's what I promised your mom and dad, and that's what you'll get. My job is to get you back to County Donegal in one piece."

"Are we going to where I'll be staying this summer?"

"That's exactly where we're going. We've got to get you settled in, unpacked, and, oh, on the phone to your folks to tell them you got here safe and sound."

"You know, Mr. Kelly, I'd be knowing scarcely a thing about the house you'll be having me live in."

"Layla, stop with the Mr. Kelly thing. It's Brian, or cousin, or a variation of the same—but drop the Mr. Kelly, please." The redhead agreed before falling silent, content to stare out the passenger window and take in the landscape. In time her eyes were drawn back to within the cabin of the pickup and specifically onto her host.

"This whole day—just being in the truck with you—and herself being on the other side of the ocean, it just seems to be not real, as if I was dreaming. But a dream it's not. Am I right?"

"Tis not a dream," he answered, quickly picking up on one of her foreign expressions. "Here's how I see things playing out: Once we reach Maine we'll hop onto Route 1 then peel off and take the scenic route. I'll take you up through York and Ogunquit and show you some of the scenery. When we reach Wells, I'll let you unpack, or at least start, put a call through to your folks so you can tell them what a dump I have you living in, then we'll finish up the evening by going out to dinner—my treat." The girl smiled over at her cousin then resumed taking in the Massachusetts countryside through the passenger window.

The two had traveled northward for some time, content to half-listen to the light rock music from the radio. It was only when the Ford made its way onto the bridge spanning high above the Piscataqua River and linking New Hampshire to Maine that Layla's eyes opened widely and she emerged from her dreamlike state. Seconds later a billboard by the side of the road announced their whereabouts in no uncertain terms: Welcome to Maine, The Way Life Should Be.

"And didn't we just drive into New Hampshire only a wee bit back in the road? Tis a wee state!"

"Not that wee, cousin. It has a wee coastline and that's where we were passing. It also has mountains and everything but most of it's inland. It's not that small. That's where my wife and I have our house. I'll be taking you there, eventually. However, what we will do today is drive a few miles east to the coast and head home by way of York and Ogunquit." A few miles later, the road running like a corridor between the two lines of pine trees bordering Route 95, Brian steered the pickup onto an exit. "I'll take you through York first. One of the things that'll look really different from home is how we have our houses built so close to each other compared to how it is in Ireland. It's not as developed as you go further north in Maine, but here in York County, every foot of shoreline counts."

"Brian, it's going to be very different here. I hope I can fit in and don't come off like an eejit."

"Don't worry so much about fitting in, Layla. Just be yourself and people will love you—take my word for it." As the vehicle made its way along a roadway crowded with shops, offices and homes, Layla took this time to survey her cousin. It was scarcely an hour since Brian Kelly had found her sitting nervously in the airplane terminal hallway. Somehow, though, this American, a stranger despite some common ancestry, had already done away with most all of her anxiety. Her cousin had a ruggedly handsome face framed by a head of dark, brown hair with a quantity of silver running through it, particularly visible near the temples. She knew he was in his early forties and this was underscored by a trace of laugh lines extending from the corner of his eyes. Picking up on her scrutiny, he shot a glance in her direction.

"What's going on in that pretty, little head of yours?" he asked.

"And sure it's nothing—nothing at all," she answered, not prepared to confide in him her observations.

The twenty-year-old had just shifted her eyes from inside the cabin to the roadway when the pickup cleared a forest of mobile homes planted on both sides of the road. At that moment their proximity to the Atlantic Ocean became fully apparent. The bright, afternoon sun hung brightly in the western sky, lighting up the blue water now visible off to the right of the vehicle.

"This is Long Sands up ahead. In the summer this is wall-to-wall people. But now, with the water freezing and all, it's mostly just joggers and retired folks out for a walk. That changes big time after Memorial Day."

"When is that?"

"I'm sorry, I forgot. You're Irish. It's at the end of May. But what I really want to show you is about a mile from here," acknowledged Brian. The Ford brought them the length of the mile long beach before he turned up a marked incline and onto a road that closely bordered a neck of land protruding out to sea. Layla peered out through the passenger window, catching glimpses of the sea between the majestic homes.

"That big building there on the right, that's the Lighthouse Restaurant. I swear, that place has the best view of the ocean from its dining room than any other place I've ever been," said Brian. "See it, it's right there," he added, extending his arm across the girl's face and intentionally obliterating her view. His gesture brought an eruption of laughter from the redhead that rapidly spread to her cousin. Layla did not hesitate to pick up on the man's playful gesture. Lunging across the cabin of the pickup, she pushed his head back against the headrest, but careful not to block his view of the road.

"Oh, Brian, that house there on the left, gorgeous it tis. Do you think herself will be in position to purchase it by the end of the summer?"

"Herself! I love the way you Irish say that whole herself–himself thing. No, I don't think there's any amount of overtime to get you there." A moment later the Ford pulled into a circular, parking area. Layla quickly realized that they had reached the end of the neck of land and water was now visible on three sides of them. However, foremost in her line of sight was a small, rocky island due east of the promontory, less than fifty yards from their position. Atop the craggy spit of land was an impressive lighthouse and personal dwelling, the two structures occupying the better part of the island's total surface.

"That, my crazy cousin, is one of the most photographed places in all of Maine, or even New England for that matter," exclaimed Brian, pulling the truck into a parking space and turning off the engine.

"And does anyone live out there?"

"Not since the eighties, I'm afraid. The federal government pulled the plug on that then. They called it a cost cutting, budgetary measure. There was a military family living out there but they were recalled. They mechanized everything. This is the same government we hear about spending ten thousand dollars for a toilet seat, but they couldn't afford to keep *one* family out on the island watching over the lighthouse," lectured Brian.

"That sounds kind of sad," added Layla, her eyes transfixed on the beacon a short way out to sea.

"Want to get out for a couple of minutes?"

"That would be grand." The cousins emerged from the pickup with Layla making her way down a series of rocky ledges to the edge of the water. Brian did not follow, content to lean on the side of the truck and take in the surroundings from this elevated perch.

"Will I have a view like this out me window?" she called up to him.

"This is nothing compared to the view from the twenty-four room house I'm putting you up in, cuz," he answered while looking out to sea.

"And will I have servants, Brian?"

"Only two, my wife has me operating under a tight budget." The redhead scrambled giddily up the rocky face of the ledge and ran to her cousin.

"And how far are we from Wells?"

"Just a couple of towns away. Shall we be off?" Brian asked while gesturing his young charge into the pickup.

Her cousin exited the parking area and drove the vehicle through a series of secondary and winding roads. For her part, Layla went back to curiously peering out the window.

"Everything is built on top of the next," she exclaimed, clearly taken aback by the proximity of each house to its neighbor.

"The land is very valuable along the coast so very little is allowed to go to waste," he explained while they motored through a densely, populated neighborhood. Shortly after emerging from the crowded rows of vacation homes, they were back within sight of the ocean. "Ten minutes ago we drove by Long Sands. Now, this is Short Sands. I'm taking you this way so you'll know where everything is—should you get a call from one of your servants, and they need a ride home."

"Ahh, yes—the servants," clowned Layla.

"Seriously though, you may not have all the time in the world to be visiting places up here, and this is an easy way to sneak in a little sightseeing."

"No Brian, I'm happy to take the scenic route to the house. And don't be thinking otherwise." Their route brought them through a village where shops were coming to life after the cold winter. Layla's eyes drank up attractive storefronts with names like Whispering Sands, Garfield's, and a large building that boasted of its world famous saltwater taffy. Brian slowed the Ford to allow his cousin to take in her surroundings. Up the street from what appeared to be the epicenter of the small, vacation community hung the marquee to the village's movie theater, its letters spelling out "Opening Soon."

"We'll be hopping on this little, winding road about a mile ahead. It reminds me of some of the roads in Ireland, particularly around Dingle, except it's not as narrow as the roads there," he explained.

Minutes after leaving behind the coastal hamlet at Short Sands, Layla and Brian were cruising along the back road linking the towns of York and Ogunquit. The roadway wove its way over rocky terrain, playing tag with the nearby Atlantic while it rose and fell between homes that literally clung to the hills adjacent to the foaming sea.

"Something's missing here," called out the girl as they passed a sign marking the entrance to The Cliff House.

"What?"

"Yer sheep! Where's yer bleedin' sheep?" The comment, delivered intentionally in a thick, Irish accent, caused Brian to burst into laughter.

"We have no bleedin' sheep—at least not like you folks have!" he exclaimed, giving his cousin a playful push on the shoulder. "Well, someone is certainly beginning to relax after her long trip over the Atlantic," he added behind a wink.

"It's the company...and good craic. I just hope *me* servants are as entertaining as *me* cousin," said Layla, reverting back to the thick accent.

"Just don't go holding your breath until those servants show up at your front door." The comment brought a smile to the girl's face. An instant later she was humming an unfamiliar tune at a level just loud enough to be heard. This went on for the next minute or so, causing the conversation inside the vehicle to fall into a lull.

"While you and your wife were visiting last year, did me Da tell you about our family being direct descendants of Grace O'Malley?"

"Isn't that the famous pirate queen?"

"Tis, and we are nothing less than direct descendants of the great woman herself," bragged the girl. A smile broke across the man's face as he shot the girl a skeptical look.

"Pretty good with a sword are you?" Brian asked.

"Aye," she answered, her face half-covered by strands of red hair. "Tis in me blood."

It was not long before the two found themselves behind an elderly driver, reducing their speed to less than twenty miles per hour. Outside the cabin of the vehicle the weather appeared to be deteriorating with clouds eliminating any direct sunlight, and wisps of fog creeping onshore and visibly moving inland. It was Brian who decided to break a prolonged silence.

"So cousin dear, aside from saving money to bring home for the purchase of the house, do you have any other objectives or goals set for yourself over the next six months?"

"Well, for sure, saving for the down payment on the house is me number one goal. And I suppose I would be lying if I didn't say that meeting a nice American boy while I was here hasn't crossed me mind from time to time," she answered.

"God knows you'll be meeting plenty of guys at Billy's this summer. I'd say there's a good chance that a few might tickle your fancy."

"You can be sure that I'll not be running around like some cheap, little slapper. That you can be assured of," she answered emphatically. The forcefulness of her statement brought a chuckle from Brian.

"I'm very glad to hear that. You do know I promised your parents that I'd not only watch over you while you are here but also that I'd make sure you made it to mass every week."

"And I can't believe they'd even question the likes of herself on something like that! Did they think I'd change who I was just because I was in the states!"

"Don't get upset now. They just care about you and want to be sure we don't corrupt you over here. They've probably been watching too many American television shows and think we all have the morals of the lowlifes in L.A. and New York City. You know Layla, it's amazing the crap that gets on television. What really bothers me is that I think a lot of the people in Europe and other places think all Americans think like the dirtbags that work in the television and movie industries. Man, if this country was like the way it's portrayed in the movies, we would have gone to the dogs a long time ago," stated Brian behind a sideways glance.

"We do have a lot of your shows on our telly."

"All you get to see is what people in Los Angeles, and New York, and maybe Las Vegas are like. Thank God we're a lot more than the sum of those parts. Hey, we've arrived in Ogunquit," exclaimed Brian as the pickup veered past a sign for Perkins Cove and continued up a road lined with shops and luxury motels. "Next stop—Wells, Maine, and the home of one Layla O'Malley for the next six months."

As the set for the play that was to be her life for the next six months drew closer, Layla felt the nervous anxiety increase within her. They had reached the heart of Ogunquit Village. She had expected this place with the strange sounding name to somehow bear a resemblance to the town of Donegal back home with its wide city square enclosed within a walled encampment of retailers, banks, and hotels. However, Ogunquit appeared to consist of an elongated parade of commercial buildings extending northward along Route 1.

"Was Route 1 the first road built in the states?" she asked of her cousin.

"I doubt it, but I'm not sure. It does run from the northern coast of Maine all the way down to southern Florida. That's quite a distance." The girl nodded but continued to gaze out the passenger window. "I'm going to give you the option of going straight to the complex where you'll be living, or take the scenic route in. Trust me, Route 1 is not the scenic route," he added.

"The scenic route would be grand," she answered.

The pickup motored northward until, with some exaggerated fanfare from the driver, it crossed the town line and entered Wells. The air outside the vehicle had become increasingly laden with fog. When a set of traffic lights came into view Brian quickly announced that they would be turning right, due east, and heading one mile to the ocean. Traveling along a well-kept, residential neighborhood, the man shot his cousin a mischievous glance.

"So she's looking to meet a nice, American boy while she's here working among us," he said sarcastically, as if speaking to an invisible, third person somewhere within earshot. Layla shifted her eyes in his direction while a comical smile spread across her face. "Well, you'll be meeting none of that sort up here in Maine. There'll be plenty of no-accounts, losers, phonies, sanctimonious clowns, underachievers, dime store Romeo's, and pompous windbags—but nice American boys—I don't think so."

"You mean there'll be no dossers, bowsies, boyos, eejits, gobshites, Joe Soaps or mulchies?"

"God, whatever those are, they sound really disgusting!" he confessed.

"And trust me, they are," she answered, turning away from him and peering out over a landscape of long grass and marshland. Presently, the sea was nowhere to be seen. However, the roar of the crashing surf was now invading the cabin of the vehicle. Reaching a stop sign, the pickup came to a complete halt, turned, and accelerated northward. From inside the truck, the young woman watched as they passed what seemed like an endless line of oceanfront homes, partially obscured by the misty fog that, at the moment, silently hung up and down the coastline of southern Maine.

"Some of the houses along here are absolutely gorgeous," she confessed.

"I hope you're referring to the majestic ones with the magnificent, wrap-around porches and widow's walks," quipped Brian.

"Not necessarily." She pointed toward an immense structure standing three stories high and dominated by an outside deck with ornate images carved into the railings.

"Do you like that?" The girl nodded yes. The man wrinkled his nose, his eyes returning to the roadway.

"Now when I see that house what I see is some egomaniac throwing up whatever he thinks might impress his neighbors, and make him look like the *big man on campus*. No Layla, my little Irish princess, what I see is a tasteless tribute to someone's overblown ego. The problem is, I'm old enough to remember the perfectly simple and wonderful cottage that sat here before this massive eyesore went up. Bigger is not always better."

Layla pondered over the words from her cousin. She was gaining much insight into the man who would be, for lack of a better word, her guardian in this new country. Then, abruptly, the pickup left the line of oceanfront houses behind and made visual contact with the ocean. Within seconds the vehicle was skirting gray, foaming surf as the road made contact with the open sea. For the next mile the twenty-year old was able to finally visualize this place named Wells Beach and the intimate, almost precarious relationship it had with the Atlantic Ocean. What she saw were beach houses aligned in close proximity to the sea, separated only by a two-lane road and a manmade, stone barrier. At this hour the sea water stood shoulder-to-shoulder with the wall with spurts from the wave's action flying over the cement barrier every few seconds, carrying with it seaweed that now littered the roadway in front of them.

"Our houses down here on Wells Beach sort of play a game of chicken with the ocean," he quipped as his cousin peered out the passenger window. "When there's a bad storm we just have to pay the price." A short distance ahead the Ford turned onto a gravel road and Brian motored to the end of it. "On the left here is the tiny cottage I bought back in the eighties. I was quite content here until Maggie showed up a few years later. The cottage is small, and quite unpretentious, and this does not suit her." Layla looked first at the yellow cottage, then to the open marshland that surrounded it.

"Is this where I'm to be staying?"

"No, I rent this out on a weekly basis during the spring and summer. I told you, you'll be up closer to me, on Route 1," he explained. "I just wanted to show you this little place because it's close to my heart. A couple of years back Maggie bought a place right on the ocean. That's about a mile from here on Atlantic Avenue. I'll show you that another time."

Brian turned the vehicle in the driveway, then rejoined the road running adjacent to the ocean. Layla now extended herself, taking in the unfamiliar surroundings with eyes wide open. Following a left turn that pointed the pickup away from the open sea, the Ford gradually picked up speed.

"Young lady, up ahead on the right-hand side of the road is where you will be laboring long hours over the coming weeks and months. Layla O'Malley, I give you…Billy's Chowder House." The redhead focused her eyes on a dark, shingled building sitting by itself in the middle of the marshlands. It seemed a strange sight, resting apart from all other structures in the midst of acres of undeveloped landscape. At present, it sat eerily alone in the fog, like a great barge that had lost its way at sea and come aground here and now.

"'Tis nothing like I imagined," she blurted out.

"We're almost home. Next stop—your twenty four room house." The Ford accelerated past Billy's, traveling a half-mile and rejoining Route 1. Following a short pause at the intersection, the pickup headed north a short distance before turning between a break in an extended, stockade fence. At the rear of an expanse of plush lawn sat a large, white house."

"Is that me twenty-four room house?" Layla called out.

"That little thing! Not even close." The truck circled behind the house and came to a stop by the back entrance. "Before I take you to see your place, I want you to meet someone," said Brian matter-of-factly as he stepped down from the Ford. He guided his cousin onto the porch and through the door marked, 'OFFICE.'

"Millie, I have that little hooligan from Ireland that you wanted to meet," sang out Brian. It took only a moment before the sound of footsteps could be heard approaching from the far side of the first floor.

"Hooligan is it? Where is our little visitor?" called out a woman's voice. Then, a gray-haired woman emerged from the kitchen and into the lobby. She approached Layla without even a moment's hesitation and placed a hand on each shoulder. The woman appeared to be around seventy years of age and radiated a grandmotherly quality. Her skin was lined and subordinated to a pair of piercing, blue eyes. "I'm Millie, and I've been looking forward to your arrival for six months now," exclaimed the woman while staring deep into the girl's eyes. Layla returned the affection, reaching her arms around the stranger and initiating an embrace.

"Brian's told me so much about you. Tis like you were family before I set eyes on you," confessed the young woman.

"I can have a pot of tea ready in five minutes," offered Millie, extending Layla to arm's length and inspecting her more closely.

"I could go for that," chirped Brian from across the room. "How about you, cousin?"

"Aye, if it's not too much trouble."

"No trouble at all, none at all," declared Millie. She turned and shuffled in the direction of the kitchen. "We'll have a nice chat over tea. Brian, why don't you see Layla to her cottage and let her drop off her luggage. That should give me just enough time to bring the water to a boil." The cousins agreed and made their way back to the pickup.

Brian reached into the cargo area and removed both pieces of luggage in a single motion. Beckoning to his cousin with a head gesture, he led her behind the nearby motel building and up to a small cabin. Layla watched as her cousin made his way onto a narrow, screened porch and dropped the suitcases down on the wooden floor. Layla looked on patiently as he tried unsuccessfully to open the door.

"I would of sworn I left this open this morning," he declared following a final, futile attempt. "Wait here for a second. I'll go back to the office and get a key from there." Brian threw up his hands in frustration and made his way past his cousin, retracing his steps from the main building. Layla took this opportunity to take in her surroundings. Fifty feet away and down the slope from the cabin was a swimming pool, still covered from the winter. It was situated in the center of a large lawn. Beyond the pool the land continued its downward slope. Unfortunately, any terrain a distance beyond the swimming pool was, at present, covered in dense fog. She would have to wait and see the full extent of the view at another time. Turning to the door, she was able to make out a few details inside by peeking through a window. Gazing into the darkened room, she picked up on a couch pushed against the near wall and the picture of a nineteenth century schooner hung in a dated frame facing the doorway.

"You're probably wondering where the other twenty-three rooms are," commented Brian, returning with a key to the front door.

"And where will I be having me servants sleep?" The man laughed, shook his head, and proceeded to insert the key and throw open the door. Layla stepped around her cousin and got her first, meaningful view of the interior of the cabin. The walls and floor were pine. Additionally, the open ceiling revealed more pine boards in the construction of the roof. She glanced at the surrounding living space, little more than her bedroom back home. However, this glorified studio apartment was furnished and laid out to fully utilize every square inch of living space. At present she was standing over a sleep sofa, in good condition and deep maroon in color. It faced across the room to a medium-sized bureau that supported a small television set. A combination unit sporting a fridge, sink and electric burners was nestled in one far corner while the other corner was home to an undersized dining set. Not coincidentally, the table and chairs had been placed adjacent to a pair of windows that, no doubt, provided a view of the landscape beyond the swimming pool. The redhead shot her cousin the briefest of glances, remained silent, then crossed the room and surveyed the small bathroom. It consisted of nothing more than a dated, porcelain sink, toilet, shower stall, and medicine cabinet. Layla turned from the room and locked eyes with Brian.

"And herself is expected to live here for six months?" she asked, sporting a stern expression and moving back into the main room.

"Layla, it has all the comforts. You didn't think I was serious when I went on about the twenty four..." She reached him in mid-sentence, throwing her arms around the man.

"Brian, I love it so much I think I'm going to cry," she called out, applying a bear hug and burying her face into his chest. Her embrace was followed by what sounded like sobbing.

"Oh, for crying out loud—you're kidding, right?"

"No, I am not. This wee cottage is grand I say! Yes, grand is what it is. And isn't it me first place all by meself." She looked up into her cousin's face, tears visible in the corner of both eyes.

"So you aren't disappointed?"

"And sure, I'd be dense if I didn't take to a place like this."

"Good, I'm glad you feel that way, because it's about to get better. Didn't you wonder about the ladder leaning against the far wall?"

"To reach the articles you'd be storing above the privy?"

"Muttonhead," he answered in his best Irish brogue. Pushing Layla to one side, he took hold of the ladder and finessed it to the far side of the room. It was then that she noticed the open space above a section of ceiling and extending out over the porch.

"Climb," he ordered, directing her to ascend the ladder. She followed his instructions and cautiously climbed upward until her head cleared the base of a sleeping loft. There, tucked under the beams supporting the roof, was a full-sized mattress and accompanying night lamp. Beyond the end of the bed was a rectangular window facing out over the grounds and swimming pool.

"Oh, have a gander at that," said Layla, clearly impressed with the sleeping arrangement.

"Up with ye," barked Brian, again clowning with the brogue. She lifted her feet from the ladder and hauled herself onto the mattress, quickly making her way to the window.

"I'll bet there'll be a grand view from here when the fog lifts."

"The best in the entire complex," he remarked. "Oh, and by the way, this little place has a lot of history. I stayed here my first summer in Wells…way back in the seventies and before you were born. Also, my step-daughter, Jenny, stayed here for a whole summer not all that long ago. So, it has a lot of family history. Anyway, I'll put your bags inside the door, and why don't you join Millie and me for tea in about five minutes." Layla called down in the affirmative and listened as her luggage was deposited on the floor below and the door was closed behind it. Rolling over onto her back, she gazed up at the wooden slats and beams of the roof that rested only a couple of feet above her head. She closed her eyes and thought back to her house in Glencolumbkille. It seemed unimaginable that she had slept in her own bed the prior night. So much had transpired and such a distance had been traveled since she lifted her head from the pillow this morning. She rolled back on her stomach, pulled back the curtain, and looked out over the swimming pool and into the dense fog. She longed for the clouds to lift and to see the extent of her view from this private spot. For the first time she felt the tiredness that would certainly provide a sound night's sleep in a few hours. But first, there was tea with her hosts, a call home to Da and Ma, and dinner with the man she was growing more fond of with each passing minute, Brian Kelly.

III

L AYLA FELT HERSELF slowly emerging from an indeterminable period of sound sleep, her return to consciousness the result of a bright ray of light streaming through the rectangular window and into her face. Her eyes flickered open to see the curtain behind her head partially drawn and sunlight horizontally streaming into the sleeping loft. It was morning, she thought, her first in the United States. The redhead snatched at the curtain, returning it to the center of the rod and eliminating the direct light responsible for her awakening. In an instant her thought process began replaying the events from the previous day: the sad good-bye to her parents, the long plane flight between continents, her drive to Maine in her cousin's pickup, her first sight of this cabin, tea with Millie and Brian, the call home to County Donegal and her parent's voices from three thousand miles away, and finally, dinner with Brian at a restaurant named Alisson's in a gorgeous place called Kennebunkport. Layla reached out her arms, letting out with a yawn. Struck with a thought, she rolled herself over onto her stomach and pulled back the curtain. Her blue eyes instantly focused on the panoramic view her cousin had mentioned the previous evening. It was a crystal clear morning and she was now able to take in the panorama visible from her window. Beyond the swimming pool was a landscape of green and blue: the long, sloping lawn gradually leading into a vast area of green marshland that extended for well over a half-mile and only interrupted by a few corridors of sparkling, blue water. Beyond this idyllic exhibit of nature extended a horizontal finger of land crowded with cottages and houses and ending at a harbor that shimmered and sparkled like an animate sapphire. Finally, serving as a backdrop to this wondrous explosion of natural color was the mighty Atlantic, spanning from just beyond the distant homesteads to the far line of the horizon.

"Sweet Jaysus!" she said aloud, slightly in awe of the view from her bed. Following no less than a full five minutes of gazing out over the magnificent landscape, Layla pulled the curtains and returned to lying on her back. She looked up at ceiling beams that rested no more than two feet from the tip of her nose. Reaching up, she inspected the wood and meditated on how close her face was to the shingles nailed onto the opposite side of these pine boards. She considered her proximity to the roof and how it would sound lying in bed during a significant rainfall. *God, how I love this little place,* she thought. Acting on an impulse, she kicked off the bed covers and maneuvered her way to the ladder. Brian had already advised her to descend the ladder in the same manner as ascending it. Turning her back to the room below, her foot found a wooden step and shortly thereafter her bare feet made contact with the cold, hardwood floor. The twenty-year-old let out a shudder and looked up at the clock. It read eight thirty-five. The room was bright as sunbeams shone in through the two, easterly facing windows. She turned to the sink and began filling a pot for tea. She had inspected the cupboard the evening before and knew there were approximately a dozen tea bags and a small jar of instant coffee there. As the water flowed into the pot a song her father had sung to her the evening before her departure came into her head. She smiled and burst out in song.

"Oh, I'm going back to Massachusetts,"
"Something's telling me I must go home."

She turned from the sink and took a step toward the kitchen table. Raising her eyes from the room and through the far window, she caught sight of a young man frozen in his tracks, paint can and brush in hand, staring in at her. Dressed in only her panties and a bra, Layla let out with a howl.

"Janey Mack! And what do you think you're gawking at you muck savage?" Outwardly flustered, the boy quickly made his exit, disappearing behind the motel building. Layla rushed to the windows and hurriedly closed the Venetian blinds. Pulling open a bureau drawer, she rummaged through an assortment of garments before pulling out a blouse and pair of jeans. Once dressed, she made the rounds and closed the remaining blinds within the unit. This accomplished, the redhead collapsed on the couch and remained there until the whistle from the teapot prompted her to action. Although convinced she would have to drink her tea without milk, a check of the mini fridge below proved fruitful, a one-half gallon of milk, three cans of soda, and a stick of butter were part of the cottage's inventory. Brian, it seems, had thought of everything.

Forty-five minutes after her encounter with a stranger at the window, and following a hot cup of tea and a good, warm shower, Layla marched across the grounds to the office. Pushing open the door, she found her cousin busy behind the front desk, entering data into a computer. He did not appear to even lift his eyes from the monitor.

"How was your first night's sleep in the US of A?"

"It was grand, everything was grand until I caught some muck savage peeping through me window this morning," she shot back.

"That would have been Billy," responded Brian nonchalantly.

"Tis nice to know the little savage has a name."

"And I'll tell you this my cousin dear: He's been taught a lesson, and a painful one at that."

"You're coddin' me," she answered.

"No, our little Billy has been summarily discharged."

"Sacked?"

"And he'll be nursing a broken face for a week or two on top of that."

"Brian, you didn't?"

"When a man descends that low, and with a blood relative of mine, well, there's hell to pay."

"Brian, it's not like he laid a hand on me."

"And wasn't it pathetic watching him beg for his job. I told him I didn't care about his three children and his sickly wife. I told him that just before I gave him his first kick in the arse. The first of many I must say." The redhead approached the registration desk, laying her arms down and staring soberly into her cousin's eyes.

"I wish you'd give him his position back. I'm getting a terrible feeling from all this," she confessed in a deferential tone. He turned from his work and looked his cousin straight in the eye.

"Billy works around here part time. He's a little slow, but absolutely harmless. He came over here about an hour ago in an absolute dither. It took me a half-hour to calm him down and tell him everything was all right. According to him, you weren't naked or anything."

"Aye, I had me knickers and a bra on."

"He'll be seeing as much at the pool this summer. However, I did impress on him that he couldn't be staring into cottages anymore. Are you okay with that?"

"And he hasn't lost his position?"

"Absolutely not. I have him working down at the far cottages the rest of the day."

"That's grand."

"Oh, and Layla, I'll be having blinds hung in the cabin no later than this afternoon. I can't believe I let you stay in a unit without blinds," said Brian in a contrite manner.

"There'd be blinds already there," she admitted sheepishly.

"And are you saying that some eejit was parading around in her cottage dressed in nothing but her knickers and a bra – with her blinds flung open?" he asked in his mock brogue.

"Aye, I'd be the eejit." He shot her an understanding smile, whirling his chair back into position to resume his work.

"Anytime you want breakfast, the kitchen here is open to you. You do know that, right?"

"Thank you, Brian. Thank you for everything."

"I'm heading home to New Hampshire later this evening. You're free to join me. We'd be back Monday morning to take you to Billy's. I'll introduce you to Dick and get you going with your new job."

"Actually, I'm more keen on moving about Wells for the next day or two. You know, to get me bearings."

"That's understandable; no problem. I'll give you a rain check. Just keep in mind, you're a pretty girl and with that red hair you'll turn a few heads. Don't be hooking-up with the first jerk that smiles at you. We had this discussion. You're over here for a reason: to save some money for that house back home."

"Trust me, Brian, I'll not be losing sight of what I'm here for."

"Don't be afraid to set your standards high."

"I will not."

"Oh, and before I forget, there's a bike out in the storage shed that's yours to use."

"And sure you're too good to me," she responded, batting her eyelashes comically.

A fresh breeze blew in from the marshlands, prompting Layla to glance up from the novel she had balanced on her chest. She had curled up on the couch a few minutes earlier after borrowing a book from the main house. A feeling of utter contentment had descended upon her. She was not sure if it was the product of the cozy cottage surroundings, her cousin's hospitality, or perhaps it had something to do with the absolute independence now present in her life, but something was elevating her spirit and she embraced her situation at this time and place. On impulse, she bounded to her feet and scurried up the ladder to the loft. Spreading herself out over the mattress, she pulled back the curtain and stared out over the Rachel Carson Wildlife Sanctuary to the Atlantic Ocean nearly a mile away. The seawater sparkled off in the distance and her mind harkened back to something Brian had said during their drive north from Boston. He told her what a wonderful adventure she was setting off on. He said her job guaranteed that every day she would meet new and interesting people, perhaps more different people in a single month than she had met in her entire life. He had preached, as more mature adults were prone to do, that she would only be young and absolutely free once in her life, and to grab hold of this opportunity and live it to the fullest. But what had really fueled her imagination and anticipation was a single statement he had made with his eyes locked on her own: that every day she awoke and went to work could be the day she turned a corner, or opened a door, or entered a room, and laid eyes on the most appealing man she had ever seen in her entire life. That was the wondrous thing about life, he had said. Brian stated that he fondly remembered when it happened to him nearly twenty-five years before. She was not sure if he was referring to his wife, she assumed as much, but had not questioned him on the matter.

Layla propped up her head with one hand and looked off to the north, beyond the harbor, to a distant neck of land extending out toward the horizon. Brian had said something about seeing all the way to Kennebunkport from this window and she reasoned that this was what he was referring to. However, her mind did not stay focused on the topography for long. Now, she was playing with ideas of a more personal nature. The anxiety associated with the long plane ride, the initial meeting with her cousin, and her housing questions had been put behind her, leaving the twenty-year-old to contemplate on more pleasurable things. As she saw it, she had reached the ripe, old age of twenty and still had not experienced a sensation approaching romantic love. She reached this conclusion through observation, namely the ecstatic behavior of those fortunate enough to be immersed in a smooth running love affair and, by comparison, the tortured demeanor of the unfortunate man or woman suffering from rejection from the object of their affection. Layla was sure that no member of the opposite sex, at least from the assortment she had been exposed to, had the capacity to prompt pleasure or pain on the scale she had witnessed in others. She prayed that this was not because of something lacking in her but only because the right man had just not crossed her path to date.

Her arm growing sore from propping up her head, the redhead rolled onto her back and stared up at the center beam less than two feet above her head. With no specific activity planned for this day, she was free to entertain any thoughts that washed into her consciousness. It was still relatively early on this Saturday and she decided to go out and meet the world half way. Layla carefully descended the ladder, slipped on a pair of sneakers, and made her way back to the office and her cousin.

The door to the office flew open and Brian looked up to see Layla making her way toward him.

"I'd like to take you up on that offer to borrow a bicycle," she called out. The man reached behind him and pulled a set of keys down from a nearby hook.

"The little brown one—that's the one that'll open the storage shed just across the driveway. The bike you want is the green one hanging from the two hooks on the back wall." He tossed the ring of keys to his cousin. She failed to catch them and they fell to the floor with a bang. "Fortunately for both of us, that was not a stick of dynamite," he added with a chuckle.

"And Brian, how would I be finding the nearest Catholic Church?"

"That'd be St. Mary's on Eldredge Road. When you're bicycling down Mile Road toward the beach, look off to the right. You'll see the steeple up above the trees. Just bike in that direction. They'll have the times of the masses out front. I know there's a four o'clock mass. *And tisn't it grand hearing me cousin talking about going to mass,"* added Brian, dressing his sentence in a thick, Irish brogue.

"And would you be mocking me?" Her question brought the man to his feet. He walked around the desk and applied a hug, enveloping the petite redhead.

"It is truly wonderful having you here with us," he whispered to her. That second the phone rang and the mood of the moment was broken. Brian left Layla, scrambling back behind the desk to answer the ringing telephone.

"And let's see if you are not tired of the sight of me by June," she answered before exiting the office and leaving her cousin to attend to business. The storage shed was only a few steps away and within seconds the oversized, wooden door swung open, spilling light into a large, windowless room. On the far wall hung a green bicycle, one of five grouped together at the other side of the shed. Layla lifted the bike from two hooks extending outward from the wall and rolled it out of the building and onto the driveway. Her first attempt at mounting the full-sized two-wheeler found her legs coming up short of the pedals. Jumping back to the pavement, she adjusted the seat downward to its lowest position and tried again. This second attempt proved successful and she wasted no time shoving off. It took her less than a minute to pedal the bike to Mile Road and begin the easy journey due east toward the Atlantic. The first stretch of road was a downward incline, causing her to press on the brakes to keep her speed under control. However, soon she had reached the marshland and flatter terrain, her legs pumping the bike while her orange-red hair blew horizontally like a flag in a gale. At the halfway point on her junket the twenty-year-old slowed while crossing a bridge that spanned a deep, watery leg in the estuary, then rolled to a near standstill as the bicycle passed the front door of Billy's Chowder House, her future employer. Her blue eyes scanned the entranceway to this solitary structure in the midst of the spacious marshlands, thinking she might catch the briefest glimpse of a fellow employee. She did not. Instead, her eyes latched onto two elderly women as they grappled with the front door. An instant later, tires whirring on the pavement below her, she passed the restaurant and its parking lot and rolled closer to the beach area.

Layla felt a rush of wonderment wash over her as she reached the chain link fence that crowned the parking lot and separated it from the sandy beach below. It was a shoreline pockmarked with ledges of rock, washed smooth by the action of the advancing and retreating tide over the centuries. She dismounted the bicycle, leaning it against the iron fence, and focused her attention on the individuals, largely couples, who populated the expanse of sand below her. The sight of these men and women, many holding hands or engaged in some manner of embrace, caused her to reflect on her circumstances. Layla stared out over the vast Atlantic Ocean, pondering on the great distance separating her from the other side of the massive body of water and her parents who would be sitting down for dinner in just a couple of hours. No doubt she would be in their conversation, their eyes darting from the others to the empty chair pulled up snug to the kitchen table. She already missed them. She wondered if she, too, would be walking the beach in the months to come, her arm wrapped around a young man, speaking of her dreams and hearing out his own. Resting her chin upon arms crossed atop the fence, the young woman thought of how different this beach was from her own back in Glencolumbkille. There was no grassy hilltop to peer down at the sea from in this place. Here the terrain was flat, and every square foot covered with tar and cement. Layla had not been resting comfortably in this spot for five minutes when a van pulled into a parking space just behind her and a half dozen young men spilled out of the vehicle and onto the sidewalk, a myriad of cat-calls and sarcastic statements filling the air around her. She took this as a cue to hop back on her bicycle and explore further down the coast.

"Hey red, don't leave on my account," called out one of the brood, a fellow with a flat face, close cropped hair, and wearing a sweat shirt reading, 'Property of Ohio State.'

"And don't you be worrying about me, biffo. I'll not be changing me plans for the likes of you," she retorted, rolling the bike off the sidewalk and out into the parking lot. Her response ignited a round of laughter.

"Man, I love that accent," chimed one of the boys before the lot descended the stairs *en mass* for the beach.

Layla pointed the bicycle southward and headed in the general direction of Brian's small cottage. Aside from getting more familiar with the town of Wells and its beaches, she also needed to locate the church. She had failed to pick out the steeple during the bike ride down Mile Road as Brian had suggested. Engrossed in a leisurely ride through a neighborhood lined with fine, oceanfront homes, her attention was captured by a sign reading 'DEPTULA LANE.' This was the road where Brian had shown her his cottage, she thought. She made a sharp right onto the gravel road and pedaled no more than a hundred yards to the end. Dismounting the bicycle and letting it fall onto the green lawn, she climbed up onto the large deck that flanked two sides of the cottage. From here she had an open view of much of the marshland. An extended arm of the estuary, a waterway, snaked by the edge of the property. It was a beautiful and quiet place, home to a few beach cottages and an assortment of wild birds. Layla turned to the south and surveyed a white steeple springing up through the tree line on the horizon. This, no doubt, belonged to the church that Brian had spoken of.

The deck was furnished with a lounger and a set of table and chairs. Layla made herself at home, falling back onto the lounger and breathing in the warm, fresh air. The temperature was in the mid-sixties, seasonably warm for a spring afternoon in early May. She lay back, her eyes closed, allowing her other senses to take in the bounty nature was serving up on this day. Her face grew warm as the rays of the sun beat down on her. However, it would only take a few seconds of this natural bliss to trigger a reaction. A moment later the redhead jumped to her feet, as if prompted to action by an attacker. The direct sunlight to her face reminded her of the possible consequences: a marked increase in the number of freckles dotting the bridge of her nose. She would have none of that, she thought. She pulled the lounger a few feet up along the wooden deck, bringing it to rest in a shaded area. This accomplished, the redhead collapsed back onto the furniture and resumed her thoughtful repose. It was after this maneuver that the mood of her meditation grew more solemn. For the first time in her life the young woman was experiencing an emotion called loneliness. The backdrop was perfect: the air surrounding her was quiet and still, except for the low, methodical roar of the ocean. The marshlands almost seemed asleep, void as they were of all movement. Amid all this, vehicles silently progressed up and down Mile Road like phantoms, the sound of their motors muted by the half-mile distance. Her feelings baffled her. Back home she embraced moments like this. Unlike most of her friends and acquaintances, she did not require the constant company of her peers. It was not unusual for her to pack a lunch and a book and go off into the bogs the better part of a day or climb the mountainous terrain around Slieve League for an afternoon of reading and meditation. Somehow, though, this was different. In Glencolumbkille there was always the knowledge that waiting at home on her return was her mother and father. Now, here in a foreign country, there was only Brian Kelly to turn to, a distant blood relative whom she only met in earnest the day before. It was this alienation from all human beings on this foreign continent that certainly accounted for the emptiness within her.

Deciding not to let her spirits spiral downward any further, the redhead sat up and made haste for the bicycle. She looked off toward the southern horizon and got her bearings set on the church steeple. Layla followed up by pushing the bike forward and mounting it in one movement, setting out for Eldredge Road and St. Mary's Church.

Layla spent thirty minutes locating Wells' Catholic church, committing the schedule of masses to memory. Following a decision not to retrace her trail back to the complex, she forged onward and rejoined Route 1 a half-mile up the road. Now, bicycling along the busy interstate, she made note of a number of local businesses and landmarks. From time to time she became confused by the flow of traffic. This was to be expected. For all of her life until the previous day, automobiles had always driven on the left side of the road.

However, for the next six months she would have to adapt to a nation that mandated driving on the right.

It was barely an hour after leaving on her self-guided tour of Wells, Maine when Layla directed the bicycle between segments of the stockade fence at the Atlantic Coast Lodge and coasted to a stop at the back door of the main building. The redhead hopped from the bike and immediately scrambled through the back door and entered the office. Hearing the door open and close from the next room, Brian appeared in the doorway.

"Where are they?" he asked, looking behind the girl and out into the yard.

"And who would they be?"

"The gang of bachelors who must of gotten a look at my gorgeous cousin and are, no doubt, in close pursuit."

"Then sure I must have given them the slip 'cause there's not a man to be found out there." Layla sauntered across the room and collapsed onto the couch. Brian swiveled his chair ninety degrees until he was facing his cousin. "I visited your cottage—the one at the end of the wee road."

"I'll have to show you where we keep the spare key. That way you can get in out of the rain if you need to," he said, surveying the twenty-year-old closely. "Is everything okay?"

"'Tis fine. In good form, I am."

"Level with me now," he answered, sounding insistent.

"Well…if you must know…I had a bout with a case of the blues earlier on, down at the cottage. 'Tis nothing."

"When you say the blues, what exactly do you mean? Are you lonely?"

"Aye. I'm missing me parents something brutal."

"That's understandable—and I'll bet they're missing you terribly, too. Right now you don't know anyone, Layla. That'll change once you start work on Monday and you start meeting people—people your own age. People are going to take to you—the guys in particular. Inside of a week or two you'll have your new friends and I'll probably hardly see you."

"'Tisn't so."

"No, it's okay. Cousin, you're here to work and save up some money, and experience something of the United States. You're not here to hang around with your forty-two-year old cousin all day. However, for the first week or two I want you to feel welcome hanging around all you want. I know what loneliness feels like. It's no joke."

"I can't believe it came on me so quickly."

"Let me toss this out at you. It's not even one o'clock yet. If you want, why don't you call your folks again and tell them you're missing them. They'll probably like hearing that."

"You wouldn't mind? I say that'd be grand. I'll pay you back for the call the moment I get me first wages."

"No–no charge. Just keep the call to ten minutes. Then, later, if you're still down then why don't you come back to Bedford with me. You can see Maggie again, and you have a couple more cousins, my son and daughter, Brendan and Colleen, to meet.

"No, I'll not be barging in on you and your family at home."

"Maggie's already said she wants you to come over and visit as soon as you can. We'll just be making it a little sooner than anticipated. I'm getting off at five. Just be ready then."

"No Brian, I'll make me call to Ma and Da and that'll be grand," she insisted.

"If you change your mind, and you have until five o'clock to do so, just let me know."

"And can I go in the next room to call over to Donegal?"

"So you can call me a bleedin eejit without me hearing it?" he heckled, reverting back to the brogue. Layla let out with a hoot.

"And sure there's no putting anything over on you, biffo," she clowned, elevating her brogue to another level.

"Okay, let me have it. What exactly is a biffo?"

"And sure you don't want to know," she answered, her face blushing red.

"No, come on. You've called me that a couple of times now."

"I've only meant it in the nicest way," she explained behind an innocent smile.

"Out with it cousin. It's the least you can do—with me covering the cost of an unscheduled call back home." Layla approached Brian and threw her arms around the man, burying her face into his chest and out of sight.

"Now you know I love me cousin dearly, don't ye?"

"Out with it, red." The girl laughed nervously into his chest.

"Biffo—big ignorant fecker from Offaly," she mumbled half under her breath.

"I've got a feeling you cleaned that up a little for me," said Brian, placing a kiss on the top of her head.

"I'll be off to make me phone call home now," she called out, pulling away from the man and scurrying into the nearby kitchen. She ran to the phone that hung on the far wall of the room, half expecting Brian to follow. However, it was only a few seconds before she picked up on the sound from his keypad back in the office. She paused before picking up the receiver, then retraced her steps across the kitchen and back into the office. His back was to the door as he inputted data into the computer, his eyes locked on the monitor. The redhead tiptoed up to behind his chair and planted an innocent peck on his cheek. "I say this bogtrotter would be lost right now if it weren't for her cousin, the Yank. Thank you, Brian—for everything." She watched as the man shook his head.

"It's going to be one hell of a summer with you around," he exclaimed before resuming his work.

Layla was hard at work in her closet when she heard rapping at the door. Before she could completely disengage herself from her organizing project, Brian had stuck his head inside the room.

"Last call for New Hampshire. I'm heading out until Monday morning," he announced. She looked up and read the clock. It was ten minutes past five.

"That's all right Brian. I'll be fine. Give me love to Mrs. Kelly and the rest of the family, and tell them I'll be over to visit in no time at all."

"Have it your way…but, of course, I'm going to dress this whole thing up like we have a real uppity Irishman visiting over here, and she thinks she's too good to join us in Bedford."

"And sure, would you really do that to little ol' me?" she asked, batting her eyelashes and putting on a pathetic face.

"Absolutely, it's amazing what we biffos will do… given the opportunity." Layla laughed and waived him off. It was clear that getting her cottage personalized to her needs was her top priority at the moment "Hal's in for a few hours tonight. If you need anything, just go over and ask. He knows who you are." With that said the door closed and she was left to her own devices until Monday morning.

Layla let out with an extended sigh of relief as she flicked off the power to the vacuum cleaner. That was it: her clothes had been neatly hung and put away in the bureaus, the furniture had been dusted, the bathroom completely cleaned, and now every square inch of floor space had been vacuumed. She climbed the ladder to the storage area above the bathroom and returned the vac to its proper place. Strolling to the refrigerator, she pulled a can of soda from inside the door and wandered out onto the porch. It was early evening and the sunlight shone from the western horizon. Shadows from the cottages and the motel building were elongated, extending halfway down the spacious lawn that ran to the edge of the wildlife sanctuary. The estuary below had refilled with tidewater and left a line of blue through the green marshlands. However, her attention was captured by the thickly clustered buildings that dominated the extension of land a mile east of her on the finger of sandy soil called Wells Beach. For it was there that a collection of random windows, not more than a dozen, were ablaze like yellow diamonds from the nearly horizontal light boring in from the far, western horizon. Layla stood transfixed, raising the soda to her lips periodically but maintaining eye contact with the imagery. It was as if the tiny peninsula was a jeweled bracelet, she thought. She watched knowing that the radiant phenomenon would soon vanish. The twenty-year-old stood motionless for the next two or three minutes until the sun disappeared behind a narrow stretch of clouds, not to return on this evening.

At dusk a cool breeze coming in off the Atlantic dropped the air temper-ature and sent the young woman inside the cabin. She collapsed onto the couch and glanced around the room. Layla felt a sense of accomplishment. There was an order about her living quarters and she knew she was at least partially responsible for it. The redhead yawned, throwing her head back and contemplating her circumstances. She had come upon good fortune. It was a wonderful existence, this period in her life she was about to embark upon and it struck her what a remarkable act of generosity made it possible. As the petite redhead maneuvered the ladder across the room and against the lip of the loft, she thanked God for sending her American cousin into her life.

IV

LAYLA MANEUVERED her way through the assembly of worshippers as she pushed toward the lobby and the two exits. The mass had been crowded, thanks to the return of some of the summer residents. She smiled at anyone who happened to make eye contact while moving to the back of the building. It was there that her bicycle, or perhaps more accurately, Brian's bicycle, was resting. She had now experienced her first American mass and was somewhat amazed how similar it was to the ones back in Donegal. Layla had sat alone in church, something she was unaccustomed to after joining her parents every week at St. Kieran's. Mounting the bike in a single fluid motion, the redhead set off toward the sea, preferring the slightly longer route back to the complex because of the superior aesthetics.

The girl coasted in from Route 1 and up to the main house. Brian would not be back for another twenty-four hours but she was in need of human company. Entering the office, she found Millie attending to the needs of a guest, an elderly woman who was going on about having first stayed at the lodge just after the end of World War II. Layla gestured to the silver-haired woman and stepped back out onto the porch. It was a lovely morning with a few majestic cloud formations set off against a bright blue sky. Leaning forward against the porch railing the pretty redhead counted the vehicles parked in the motel doorways. A scraping noise from wood on concrete caused her to glance sideways and notice a young man in paint-splattered clothing working at the rear of the storage shed. Surveying him more closely, she was sure it was the individual whom she had caught glancing through her front window the morning before. She scrambled down the short flight of steps and crossed the parking area, walking up behind the young man who stood perched fifteen feet above her on a ladder, generously applying white paint to the side of the building.

"Tis grand to see you didn't lose your position after that wee episode at me window yesterday," she called out to him. The boy appeared sixteen or seventeen years of age with an innocent, round face and blond hair.

"My position? I don't understand what you mean."

"Your job. You know—you didn't lose your job after I hollered at you yesterday." The boy turned around and glanced down, making eye contact with Layla. He became visibly shaken.

"Oh, it's you. You know I'm very sorry about that from yesterday—and Mr. Kelly said it was okay so long as it never happened again –and…and told me I could still work here…"

"'Tis all right. I just came over to say I was not mad and not keeping a knot in me britches over it," she came back in a reassuring manner. Layla picked up on what Brian had said about the young man. There was a sweet, simplicity about him that set him apart from most others. "Well, I won't keep ye from your work," she called up before turning and heading back to the main house.

Layla reached the front door to the office just as the World War II woman was departing. The two exchanged smiles before the redhead walked to the check-in area and threw her head down playfully on the oak desk.

"You wouldn't have an egg to spare, would you—for a wee girl with the hungry horrors?" The statement caught Millie by surprise, sending her into a gale of laughter.

"Hungry horrors is it? I swear, I haven't heard that expression in twenty years! Hungry horrors—my word, my mother would say that to me when I was a girl. Haven't you any food in the cottage?"

"A wee bit, but I didn't have any before I went to mass this morning. It's something I learned from me grandmother, fasting in the morning before communion," she explained.

"You've already been to church?"

"I took me bike, or should I say Brian's bike, to the nine o'clock mass this morning. 'Tis good exercise from here to St. Mary's."

"That is so nice to hear…a girl your age who still keeps holy the Lord's day," said the silver-haired woman, an approving smile suddenly present on her face. "If I can get a few minutes rest from our guests I'll whip you up something. Have any preferences?" asked Millie.

"I'll not be asking for you to wait on the likes of…"

"Nonsense girl, what would you like? It's the least I can do for a good, Christian girl like yourself."

"Well, if it isn't any bother then a bowl of porridge and maybe a couple of eggs dropped on some toast would be grand," answered Layla sheepishly.

"I'm guessing a little Quaker Oatmeal will pass for porridge, and the other will be a snap," answered the woman as she stared approvingly at the girl.

The matronly woman walked back into the kitchen followed by her Irish visitor. In a matter of minutes the pot of oatmeal was steaming on one corner of the stove while eggs were being prepared on another. Layla did her part by boiling water for tea. Breakfast was on the verge of completion when the door in the next room opened, calling Millie back to the front desk. The twenty-year-old took over, spooning out a bowl of oatmeal and dropping a couple of three-minute eggs on wheat toast. By the time Millie rejoined Layla at the kitchen table her meal was half gone. The seventy-year-old found a cup of tea steeping for her. Layla took a bite from her plate and addressed her new friend.

"I've been running over something in me mind and it would do me a lot of good to ask the question," she said, looking seriously across the table. "The truth is…I feel a wee bit desperate asking you this but tis playing on me mind." Millie knitted her brow and beckoned the girl to continue.

"Tis me experience—and God knows me parents have said as much—that you have to be very careful around persons who come off as too nice. And sure, I've seen as much at home, I have. It's just that me cousin has been very good and thoughtful towards me…and I was thinking that maybe herself should be careful, if you know what I mean?" The redhead looked up into the woman's kind eyes.

"Brian Kelly may be the most honest and decent man I have ever met in my life. Do you hear that? You have absolutely no reason to have second thoughts about your cousin's motives. Period! End of discussion." Millie dropped her eyes and took a sip from her cup.

"You're probably thinking me to be a malignant, little mulchie…asking something like that of me own cousin."

"No, of course not. I'm not sure what a mulchie is, but it probably isn't too good by the sound of your voice. It's just that I've known Brian for nearly twenty years now…and outside of showing a little too much temper once in a while, he's one of the finest human beings you will ever meet." Layla reached over, setting her hand down on the woman's.

"Tis good to know." The woman took another purposeful sip from her cup and rose to her feet. For a moment she seemed a little perturbed by the young woman's questioning but rapidly shrugged it off and turned for the door. Layla looked up from her meal, already questioning the wisdom of her inquiry. Reaching the doorway, Millie turned and glanced back at the girl, a playful grin breaking out on her face.

"And do you think if there was anything wrong with your cousin…a great looking chick like me wouldn't have brought it out of him over the years?" cracked Millie behind a wink and a smile.

"And you won't say anything to Brian now, about me being such an eejit?"

"Of course not. It'll just be between us girls."

Patches of dark clouds began to appear on the western horizon as Sunday afternoon wound down. Layla stayed close to her new home on this day, doing little more than running a handful of errands for the office. Thirty minutes before the sun would disappear behind the nearby buildings on Route 1, Layla strolled down the grassy lawn to the edge of the wildlife preserve. From there she could glance over at Billy's Chowder House, about a quarter-mile away, and consider the new chapter in her life that would commence the next day. However, it was also from this quiet spot that she thought back to her parents in Donegal, and the beach at Glencolumbkille. It would be dark there now, she thought, and perhaps chilly enough to have peat burning in the fireplace. Only two days had passed since her arrival to the United States, but she already missed the smell of the peat.

The hint of pink illumination along the eastern horizon told Layla that Maine would soon be awakening and the formal start to her career as a restaurant waitress would commence. Already her stomach tingled with excitement and anticipation. Her eyes trained due east, the girl watched the gradual lighting process in the far sky. The extended finger of sandy terrain that was Wells Beach slowly became visible. Between the crowded echelon of buildings that lined Atlantic Avenue advanced a single pair of vehicular headlights. The vision of the beams of light appearing and disappearing between the houses was hypnotic, setting off a series of possible scenarios in the girl's head. Was this some married woman's lover retreating from her bedroom before the sun shed light on their indiscretion? Then again, perhaps it was something as simple as a lobsterman leaving for his boat and a long day of labor out to sea? The pretty redhead, wide-eyed and focused on the two, tiny orbs of light, considered these possibilities until the vehicle silently disappeared behind a tree limb a hundred yards down the hill. In spite of her best efforts not to, she found herself entertaining thoughts of her possible inability to function as a waitress. She quickly drove these negative thoughts from her mind. Rolling onto her back, she stared up at the ceiling beams and thought of her parents. They would be at work at this hour. She estimated it was about five-thirty here, making it ten-thirty in County Donegal. Brian would be back from home in a few hours to escort her down the road to Billy's Chowder House. Layla thought of her conversation with Millie the day before, and her question regarding her cousin's trustworthiness. She prayed Millie would not repeat her words to Brian. Glancing over the top of the pillow, she picked up on a sliver of light. The redhead returned to her stomach and spied the first glimpse of direct sunlight peaking over the faraway horizon.

Layla was seated on the porch, her feet up on the wooden rail and a cup of tea in her lap, when Brian rounded the corner of the motel and approached cottage fourteen. Lifting her eyes from the rim of her cup, she greeted her cousin with a timid smile.

"So cuz, are you ready to join the ranks of the great, American workforce?"

"I'm as nervous as a long tailed cat in a room full of rocking chairs," she answered before taking a long swallow from her tea.

"No big hurry; take your time," reassured Brian, reaching the door to the cottage. "Everyone back in New Hampshire sends their love." The redhead scrambled to her feet and retreated inside, only to emerge from the tiny building a few seconds later. She pulled the front door shut and tested the lock. That accomplished, she hustled to Brian's side and waited on his direction. With an exaggerated signal of his hand she was instructed to follow him to the truck. With barely a dozen words exchanged they were exiting the driveway and on their way to the restaurant. Stopped in a line of traffic waiting on a green light, the girl glanced across the cabin of the Ford. It was good to have her cousin back, she thought. She had missed his company.

"I will just take you in the restaurant and we'll leave you off with Dick Varano—you know, the owner. I think you're going to like him."

"Will I be working with him most of the time?"

"I doubt it. I think mostly he's upstairs or maybe in the kitchen. You'll be out on the floor." Brian glanced across at his cousin and noticed a trace of apprehension etched on her face. Lifting his hand from the front seat, he extended his arm across the bridge of her nose.

"Oh look, there are geese swimming around out on the estuary," he declared, clowning again as he had on the ride from the airport three days earlier. The gesture brought a hearty laugh from the girl.

"Tell me I'm not going to make an eejit of meself," she asked.

"You're no eejit, cuz, not at all. A biffo, maybe, but not an eejit." Layla nodded her head in mock acceptance and took a deep breath. He slowed the Ford and turned the pickup into the far end of the parking lot.

Brian escorted the twenty-year-old up an outside set of stairs on the side of the building. After applying a couple of raps to the door a voice called out from within. Seconds later the two were standing before a man with a head of thick, dark hair and a broad smile. Rising from his desk he extended a hand to the Irish girl.

"I'm Dick Varano…and you must be Layla. I know that because you've come a long way to work for me." He shifted his eyes upward to Brian. "And you, well…I know who you are," he stated lightheartedly.

"Hand delivered, one Layla O'Malley, County Donegal's number one waitress and now a member of the team at Billy's Chowder House."

"Number one waitress is it! And sure I've never worked a day in me life at it," confessed the redhead in her Irish lilt.

"To be honest, I saw Layla here doing more busing than waiting on initially…knowing she had no experience and all. But in the last twenty-four hours I've gotten word that three Lithuanian girls I was supposed to have here all summer will be staying home at the university and I'm really short of people to start the season. Layla, we're putting you on the fast track. You'll be shadowing one of the other girls for the first couple of days, you know, to pick up on as much as you can…then, you'll be on your own."

"Ahh, that takes a weight off me mind. You say I'll have a wee time to adapt."

"Absolutely," answered the man while extending his hand to welcome her to the team.

"And that's probably my cue to take a hike," chirped Brian. Reaching down, he applied a hug around the girl's shoulders and turned away.

"I'll be giving you a full report when I get back to the house tonight."

"I'll make us some tea when you get home," added Brian. "Oh, will you need a ride?"

"Tis a short walk. I'll be fine," assured the girl, giving her cousin a reassuring smile as he exited the office.

Following only a few minutes devoted to paperwork in which Layla signed off on a few American employment forms she did not completely understand, Dick brought her downstairs into the restaurant. She entered the front door behind her new boss and immediately saw there was some construction in progress. A few feet in front of her and at the end of a short hallway was what appeared to be an addition to the building. Aside from the work in progress Layla observed two distinct dining areas, a room to the immediate right and another to her left at the end of a corridor. It was barely eleven-thirty leaving the dining rooms quite empty. This afforded Dick an opportunity to introduce his new employee to the three young women assembled in the hallway in front of the greeter's station. He stepped between two young women huddled close together on a bench. The two were introduced as Vickie, a long-legged brunette with beautiful, deep brown eyes and a mouth set in a permanent, seductive pout. Her friend, whose name Layla understood was Susan or Susanne, was blond, attractive, and sporting a deep tan that, no doubt, required some degree of maintenance in a climate like Maine's. Both young women extended Layla a cursory, but polite, hello before returning to their private conversation. The third waitress seated a few feet away in semi isolation showed a little more interest in Layla's arrival, flashing the redhead a wide smile and rising to her feet.

"And this is the old pro you'll be shadowing for the first couple of days. Tami Webster, I want you to meet your shadow for the next day or two. This is Layla O'Malley who comes to us all the way from Ireland," announced Dick. "I want you to show our new girl here everything she ever wanted to know about waitressing but was afraid to ask." Following a period of polite laughter Layla joined the Webster girl seated on the bench.

"And Dick, that ends your participation in the process. I'm sure you prefer being upstairs crunching numbers," said Tami, exhibiting a certain comfort level with the owner of the restaurant. With that said the man flashed his newest employee a reassuring smile and made his way back to his office.

"And sure you must be put out having to have me parading behind you for the next couple of days?" asked Layla.

"Put out! You've got to be kidding. I was starting to feel like a fifth wheel around these two over there. I've been kind of odd man out. But now I'll have you, Layla, to keep me company and to gossip with," answered the petite blond behind a playful grin. "Oh, there's a few other girls, Lori Schofield, Nicole D'Amato and Betsy Chase, but they're all off today."

"That Vickie—tis a beauty she is."

"And boy don't she know it," came back Tami in a whisper. "Wait till you see how some of the male customers fall all over themselves around her. Last year—this is at least her third year working summers—she had this guy who always, always, left her a fifty dollar tip."

"You're joking!"

"So help me God," exclaimed the girl in a low voice while raising her finger to heaven.

"What kind of an eejit would do the likes of that?"

"And he was married," added Tami in a whisper to the ear.

"Sweet Jaysus!" exclaimed Layla, raising her voice high enough to prompt Vickie and Susanne to abruptly stop in mid-sentence and glance over at them.

It was only a few minutes before a steady stream of customers ended the bonding of Layla and Tami, and the redhead found herself walking in the footsteps of the experienced waitress. Tami was assigned tables in the oldest section of the restaurant simply referred to as the dining room. After leaving menus and soliciting an order of beverages from a pair of couples seated there, the tiny blond led Layla through a pair of swinging doors and into the kitchen. At that time introductions were made and Layla met the head cook, Adam Dillon, a middle-aged man with a serious face and piercing, green eyes. An assistant to Adam, Billy Sousa, made a point of approaching Layla and sizing her up, running his eyes up and down her trim body while offering only the weakest of welcomes. Billy was a tall, lanky kid of no more than twenty-five years of age who wore his close cropped, jet-black hair under an oversized cap. The last person to make an appearance in the kitchen and, therefore, be introduced to Billy's newest waitress was the expediter, Dave Newcombe, an overweight man with a smooth, round face atop a massive, imposing body. Layla learned at this time that an expediter was the individual in the kitchen who is responsible for bringing all the elements of a meal together on the plate. The bus boy, Willy Samuals, was not scheduled to punch in until one o'clock on this day. She learned that she would be working closely with all of these people and that they could prove to be valuable allies, or conversely, terrible enemies in the months to come.

"Billy can be a real jerk if he gets into one of his moods," advised Tami after the two young women exited the kitchen. "It'll never get too bad as long as Adam or, of course, Dick is around. Now, it goes without saying that Billy and everyone else is as polite as a minister around our precious Vickie."

"And sure we couldn't have anyone or anything cross our beautiful, little swan, could we?" answered Layla, picking up on her new friend's sarcasm. The blond let out with a burst of laughter, seemingly happy to see her pupil already shared her sentiments.

The day passed with nary an incident or uncomfortable moment with Layla literally testing her wings in the final hour, handling the table of two regular customers with only the slightest level of supervision from Tami. At nine o'clock Dick Varano approached his new Irish waitress and called an end to her first day of work in Maine, complementing her on a job well done and asking her to report the following day at eleven.

It was quite dark on Mile Road when Layla set out on the one-half mile walk back to her cottage on the grounds of the Atlantic Coast Lodge. During the hectic summer season from Memorial to Labor Days, Mile Road would normally have a steady stream of vehicular traffic and a few people on foot at this hour. However, it was early May in the Pine Tree state and Wells still retained much of the quiet sleepiness it accumulated over the recent, frigid winter. For Layla, the walk alongside the marshlands was not intimidating in the least. Back home she had walked along roads far darker than this and without the benefit of the wide shoulders on either side. She remembered, on occasion, walking through bog fields with friends when the only light came from the Milky Way overhead and the only reference point might be the pin-point of light visible from the window of a faraway homestead on the side of a distant hill. Here, illumination from commercial enterprises spanning the length of Route 1 provided ample light to guide her footsteps even though that light was nearly a half-mile away. So it was on this evening that the energetic European made short work of her hike, passing through the stockade fence lining the front of her cousin's holiday resort not much more than ten minutes after leaving work. Staying on the paved driveway, she passed behind the main house and spied Brian speaking with a couple inside the office while the visitor's car idled a few feet away. She glanced down at the automobile's license plate and saw it was from Pennsylvania. She had hoped to speak to her cousin and update him on her day but decided to leave the man to his work and retired to her cabin instead. After only a few minutes resting on the couch in front of her television, she was reminded of how tired she was from a full day's work. It was only twenty minutes after flicking on the lights in the cabin that Layla climbed the ladder into the loft and slipped between the sheets.

When her head made contact with the pillow on this evening she had no way of knowing that the next day would bring two men into her life who would alter it over that summer and on into the future.

$\mathcal{V}$

LAYLA DIRECTED HER BICYCLE onto the sidewalk and over the short bridge as she approached the restaurant for her second day of work in Maine. Rolling the bike around the building and out of sight, she started for the front door only to be intercepted by a voice from above.

"I'm afraid you're going to have the shortest training period on record, Layla. But from what everyone's been saying about you, I don't think you've got a thing to worry about." The redhead gazed up at her boss, shielding her eyes from the sun.

"And does this mean I'll be keeping me own tips now?" she asked, a trace of excitement in her voice.

"Yeah, that's right…less ten percent for your bus boy," he answered, relieved to hear no hint of apprehension in the Irish girl's voice. "You might want to shake a leg. Susanne's not coming in until four and we're a girl short," counseled the man before ducking his head back into the office.

It was only seconds before the young woman burst through the front door and made her way to the locker. Returning to the main floor, she learned that she was assigned to a row of tables in the 'back bay' room. These were the least busy tables and often where locals were seated. These tables had no water or harbor view, something visitors and tourists placed considerably more of a premium on than townies whose landscape was dominated by water. Layla was happy to see Tami working the other side of the room and flashed her a big smile on the first occasion their paths crossed. The redhead had not even exchanged words with her new friend when a man was escorted to one of her tables. A woman she had not been formally introduced to yet was acting as greeter at the moment. The woman, smartly dressed and appearing to be in her mid-thirties, spotted Layla and approached her.

"It's a tradition. The new girl gets Johnston—sort of as an initiation. Don't hold it against me," she whispered, then made her way out of the room and back to the front desk. Layla, somewhat confused by the message, glanced over at her occupied table and sized up her first customer. William

Johnston's appearance and demeanor could best be summed up in a single word—stern. The stocky man sat glaring down at the menu, his eyes scanning it under a pair of bushy, white eyebrows. Appearing about sixty years of age, his skin was parched and wrinkled, no doubt the result of working out of doors. His clothes were soiled and showed the signs of prolonged wear. She approached the table while the man continued to pour over the luncheon menu, as if considering it for the first time. When he failed to raise his eyes to her after ten seconds the girl spoke up.

"And sure everything looks so good, it must be a chore just choosing one thing," she said, not able to come up with anything else and wanting to grab his attention.

"What are you, a comedian?" Johnston snapped while glancing up at her for the first time.

"Ah no, just a bit of a dosser, but no comedian."

"What's that accent, I hear. Are you a Scot by any chance?"

"Sweet Jaysus, no. I'm from Donegal, I am," Layla answered proudly, a wide smile breaking across her face.

"Catholic?"

"As Catholic as the pope." He frowned up at her and let out with a growl. "I was born and raised in Portrush. I came over to the states in my twenties."

"And a lovely town I'm sure it is. Would you be an Orangeman?"

"I am," he replied, casting her up a suspicious expression. "Why do you ask?"

"No reason; none at all. And would you be ready to order?"

"Large bowl of chowder—with extra crackers and a Bushmills and ginger."

"Ah, and that'll be grand. But you did know that there is only one size bowl?"

"I don't want you bringing me my chowder in one of those small bowls," he snapped.

"And sure—that wouldn't be a bowl at all, would it? That'd be a cup."

"What are you, some kind of wise guy?"

"Nothing of the sorts. I was just pointing out something so that there was no chance of getting your order wrong. The truth is me good sir…you're me first. And you know what they say about your first: you never forget your first," explained the girl before shooting the man a mischievous smile.

"I'm your first?"

"Me first customer," she answered. The man did not return her smile, choosing to end the banter and affix his eyes on a newspaper spread out on the table before him. Seeing she was not going to coax any more conversation from him, she made her way to the kitchen and set the order in motion. The bank of tables by the windows was Tami's responsibility this Tuesday and she was already making haste to keep up with the customer's needs. When Layla and her new friend did pause briefly in the hallway, Tami was quick to prepare her friend for a bitter reality.

"Don't be too disappointed or upset when Johnston doesn't leave you anything. He's like that with everybody," she cautioned.

"And sure the poor creature is probably living hand to mouth," said Layla sympathetically.

"Like hell he is! He's an old bachelor who still has the first dollar he ever made. Don't you go and feel sorry for that old miser," cautioned Tami, tossing Johnston's table a sarcastic snarl.

If Layla had any ideas about bringing down the wall of indifference around William Johnston, they were hastily abandoned on this day. All efforts to draw the stone cold Anglo into friendly conversation proved futile. So it was, following close to an hour of minding to her first customer in the state of Maine, the redhead found nothing in the way of a gratuity on the table. Fortunately for her, Dick Verano made note of her bad fortune and finessed two of the restaurant's most popular customers into her section, guaranteeing his rookie, Irish waitress some meaningful tip money to carry her into the afternoon. By two o'clock the rush of luncheon customers was ebbing and the waitresses were able to catch some down time between visits to their respective tables. Just as on the previous day, Vickie and Susanne worked in close proximity in the front dining room. Layla and Tami were standing idly by the doors to the kitchen when a glance into the front room caused the animated redhead to stop in mid-sentence.

"And would you know who that man at the table by the wall would be?" she asked as she stared at a table occupied by three men and a woman.

"The guy with the slightly long, black hair?"

"Aye."

"Philip Trask. He's a local sculptor. Well, local...out of Boston."

"Oh, sweet Jaysus—he's beautiful he is," blurted out Layla, unable and unwilling to take her eyes off the man. Philip Trask was a professional of approximately thirty years of age with a strikingly handsome face and a sophisticated bearing. The remaining individuals at the table were young professionals like him, well dressed and poised.

"And does he come in often?"

"Quite a bit–maybe once a week," answered Tami, a little puzzled by her friend's curiosity about the customer.

"He's another one of Vickie's regulars. He does make a point of asking for her." Layla continued her trancelike stare into the front room, seemingly unable to remove her eyes from the image of this stranger. "Layla, just so you know in advance, there's good and bad news on the availability front. Philip is very much a bachelor but limits his socializing to his friends and acquaintances from back in Boston. Every once in a while he'll bring in some runway model type from Massachusetts... but that's it. He's never even made a pass at Vickie, and God knows she's made it clear the door was always open for one. Personally, I think he's a bit of a snob."

"There'd be few gorgeous men who don't know how gorgeous they are," came back Layla in a soft voice.

"Layla–order up," cried out a voice from the kitchen, bringing the Irish girl back to the tasks at hand.

"I'll be wanting to know everything there is to know about that one," she confessed, turning from her friend and making her way back to the kitchen.

"I hope we're not getting in the way of your socializing out there," wise-cracked Dave before turning away and following up on another matter. Layla did not answer, knowing she had allowed herself to be distracted.

Following five minutes of dedicated attention to her customers, Layla made her way back to the reception area and rejoined her friend on the bench. The redhead comically sidled up to Tami, their backsides coming in direct contact atop the hardwood surface.

"And now, back to the matter at hand, more facts on the handsome Mr. Trask," quipped Layla. Tami shook her head.

"I don't know too much more. Vickie might know."

"Oh, ask Vickie and have the man know I've already set me eyes on him... and may begin stalking him at any hour of the day or night," complained Layla.

"Oh, there's Betsy Chase. She must be in visiting. She's a local. If anyone can tell you about the guy, she can." The two, young women approached the desk and discreetly pulled their fellow waitress aside. Tami knew the woman had worked at Billy's for a number of years and probably had some knowledge of repeat customers.

"Betsy, our little, Irish rookie here was wondering if you had any general information on Philip Trask you might be willing to share with her?" Layla flashed Betsy a blushing smile and waited on a response.

"Well, he has his studio over in Kennebunkport... but he does a lot of his work at his family's house up at Moody Point. You can't miss it. It's almost directly across the street from the Grey Gull Inn."

"And information of a more personal nature?" coaxed Layla.

"Don't waste your time, honey. He's a snob of the first order. He runs around exclusively with his friends from Boston. A couple of years ago he had a Barbie Doll up here with him all summer. I don't think anything came of it because I haven't seen her around in close to two years. But as far as dating waitresses, well, forget about it—it ain't going to happen." Layla nodded and thanked the woman for her frankness. She glanced back over at the handsome stranger's table and saw him in the midst of an animated story, his hands orchestrating the flow of the tale in the air around the foursome gathered there. Layla and Tami returned to the bench. Layla remained standing as her friend dropped down onto the hardwood. By remaining on her feet she was able to peer into the next room, committing the handsome sculptor's fine features to memory. She remained in place for a full five minutes, her eyes shifting back and forth between her friend seated below and the table in the next room. For the time being, the eyes of Philip Trask did not leave the company of his friends and even momentarily scan her way.

"Layla, if you could see your face right now," advised Tami. "Be careful around this guy, he seems to be just bowling you over. I've seen girls go down this road before. You don't want to go where that road'll take you," she cautioned.

"And don't you be worrying about me," she answered, her eyes transfixed on the proceedings at the Trask table in the next room. She watched discreetly from behind a support column as the artist with the black hair dominated the conversation at his table, supplying three-quarters of the narrative.

"Oh, I knew there was something I meant to tell you. While you were busy earlier with old man Johnston, Dick hired and introduced a new dishwasher who'll be starting tomorrow. His name is Wesley and I couldn't help but notice that every time you flitted in and out of the kitchen his eyes stayed glued on you. Dick literally had to say something to him to get him focused on what he was saying. He was that distracted by a certain redhead."

"So that's how it is," she answered defensively. "The little bogtrotter would be well advised to take her mind off of the high and mighty artist and maybe set her sights a little lower—like on busboys and dishwashers. Is that what you're trying to tell me in so many words?"

"You're taking it the wrong way, Layla. I didn't mean anything by it."

"I'm sure you didn't. I know your me friend and you want only the best for me." With that said she glanced back to the front room to catch Philip Trask and company rising from their table and making their way toward the front door. Feeling slightly self-conscious standing by herself in the reception area, Layla joined Tami on the bench. The gentrified foursome went out of their way to wish Vickie a good week and moved toward the front door. Layla watched as Mr. Trask fell to the rear of the group. Then, in what appeared to be an unconscious gesture, the sculptor's head turned in the direction of the two waitresses seated against the wall. It was in that moment that he first set eyes on Layla O'Malley. In an automatic response, the redhead flashed the man a sweet smile. Her gesture seemingly caught Trask by surprise. He answered it with the absence of any response. A second later he was through the door and descending the stairs.

"Is it me imagination or did the man look at me like I was something he'd just scraped off his shoe?" she asked.

"What an uppity ass."

"And don't I feel like the eejit…smiling at him like a ninny."

"Girlfriend, don't waste your time even thinking about this guy."

"Now what was it you were saying about a dishwasher who had eyes for me?"

"Wesley—his name is Wesley."

"And this Wesley…would you say he is a handsome lad?"

"He has a nice face. Though, he does have an acne problem."

"Oh, and I'm sure the hot kitchen this summer and some time around the Frylator will do wonders for that," blurted out Layla, causing both to burst out in a fit of laughter.

The wildlife sanctuary surrounding the restaurant was shrouded in darkness as Layla made her way to the side of the building and unlocked her bicycle. It was nearly ten o'clock and she was the last waitress to punch out of work. Traffic on Mile Road was practically nonexistent as she pedaled eastward the one-half mile up to Route 1 and her cottage. This night was darker than most with a thick blanket of clouds blocking any light from the moon and stars. Her thighs burned as she pedaled the last few yards, finally breaking the incline and onto Route 1. Layla hugged the side of the road for the next hundred yards and coasted into the complex and toward the storage shed. In the distance, the sound from the horn of the evening train out of Portland cut through the still, night air.

With the bike secured and out of the elements, Layla made her way across the yard and toward cottage fourteen, her American home. Lights were visible through a second story window in the main building and also in the office. She was not sure if her cousin was working and began debating whether to drop in for a visit.

"Were you planning on dropping in to chat, or are you too tired?" The voice had come out of the shadows from atop the porch.

"Brian, you scared the living daylights out of me," she blurted out, straining her eyes to make out the man standing no more than twenty feet from her.

"I was just grabbing some fresh air when I heard you thrashing around in the shed. At least I thought it was you."

"Oh no, a visit would be grand. I would have come by last night but you seemed very busy and I didn't want to be a nuisance."

"Come on kid, join me for a soda. I'll bet you've never had a Moxie, have you?"

"A what?"

"A Moxie. It's Maine's very own tonic…I mean soda."

"Is that what you drink?"

"Sometimes, you know, along with Coke and orange and everything else. I'll open us a couple of cans." Layla hopped up the stairs and into the office while Brian disappeared into the kitchen, returning with the beverages. "So how was your second day of work?"

"Oh, it was grand, it was. I'm already working on me own—we being short of help at the moment. Anyway, I've just got to share me good fortune with someone." She reached into the pocket of her jeans and produced a small wad of bills. "T'irty t'ree dollars in tips on me first day working by meself."

"How much did you say? Did you say turdy tree?"

"T'irty t'ree... t'irty t'ree dollars." Her cousin roared with laughter while he opened both sodas, finally handing her the can over the front desk.

"There are just some things you should try to avoid saying with that brogue of yours, Layla, and one is thirty-three." The redhead knitted her brow, mimicking anger, and took a sip from her can.

"Janey Mack!" she exclaimed after swallowing her first mouthful. "It isn't what I expected."

"Give it a chance. You'll get to like it. Now, I take it you're satisfied with your tips."

"I am... and considering tis not even close to the busy season. I'm quite satisfied. Oh, and the t'irty t'ree thing. Numbers are the only words I find meself dropping the h's from. Tis always been that way. At least I don't do it on all me words like so many of us do back home." Brian just smiled down at her, visibly enjoying her company.

"I can't remember if you told me. How much money do you want to go home with to help your folks buy the house?"

"Eight t'ousand dollars."

"Ouch! I'd say you better keep your nose to the grindstone then," he suggested.

"Aye," added the girl before taking another swig from the can. Layla let her head fall back onto the cushioned couch, closing her eyes and taking a deep breath.

"Oh, before I forget, Maggie wants to know when you might be coming over to New Hampshire and visiting. You can always visit us at the Atlantic Avenue house this summer but she wants you to see the house in Bedford."

"And sure the American Kellys have cottages coming out of their you-know-whats, they do. Nothing like the poor, Donegal O'Malleys who will have to work their fingers to the bone this summer for a solitary one."

"I apologize if I came off sounding like a braggart," confessed Brian.

"Oh, no cousin, no need for that—not with you giving me that grand little cottage, and a place to stay for nothing and me bicycle to ride to work everyday. You'll not need to apologize to the likes of me." The room grew quiet. From outside came the sound of an automobile engine as a guest returned to the complex following an evening out.

"I'll ask Dick for a weekend off before the busy season," she said, her voice cutting through the silent room. "I'll go home with you, Brian, and meet with everyone back in New Hampshire."

"Maggie will like that—having you with us at the house for a couple of days. She hasn't seen you since last year in Glencoloumbkille."

VI

L AYLA WAS PULLED from a relaxing sleep by a swirl of cawing and chirping birds occupying the tree limbs along the property. Pulling back the window curtain just above her pillow, she peered out over the estuary and harbor below to see the sun brightly illuminating the surface of the ocean a mile away. The redhead let out with an extended yawn, reaching her hands to beyond the edge of the mattress. She shook the sleep from her head and tried to remember the day of the week. She closed her eyes and inventoried her week. It was Thursday, she thought. Tomorrow would mark two weeks in the states. It was chilly in the loft on this morning. She remembered turning the baseboard heat off the night before. The cottage had retained much of the heat the prior evening from the sun beating down on it throughout the day. She inhaled and extended her bare foot from beneath the bed covers, the sole of her foot making contact with the top of the ladder. She thought how nice it would be if she could call out to someone to fetch a hot cup of tea. She pulled her foot back under the covers and closed her eyes for a moment.

It was a full ten minutes before the twenty-year-old crawled to the bottom of the bed and peeked down into the living room. The clock hanging on the wall above the television set read five twenty-five. It was earlier than she expected. Nonetheless, her desire for a hot cup of tea drove her out from under the covers and down the ladder. After filling the kettle and turning up the heat she slid into her jeans and threw on a heavy flannel shirt. With the water still far from the boiling point, she opened the top drawer to her dresser and removed an envelope. From inside, she counted out three hundred and fifty-five dollars, her accumulated savings thus far. She was pleased with her progress in putting away money for the purchase of the family home but this had been overshadowed in the last few days by other events. It had been over a week since she had talked to Brian in private. Over the past few nights it was Millie on duty in the office when she had returned from work. Layla flicked on the television for the weather forecast and began preparations for her tea when she noticed through a break in the Venetian blinds a figure pass by the cottage and down the hill toward the pool. Upon closer examination she could see it was her cousin, apparently out for an early morning stroll. Turning to the door, she stopped in her tracks as the whistle atop the teapot began to sound. Returning to the stove, she turned down the burner, slipped into a pair of sandals, and made her way onto the porch. Incredibly, Brian had already disappeared from sight. She stepped out of the cottage and down the lawn, sure her cousin could not have gotten far. Halfway to the swimming pool she observed him sitting at the far side of the pool, his back leaning against the wooden, picket fence. Following in his footsteps, she came up upon him, his eyes glued to the horizon as he sat motionless.

"Could I bribe ye with a cup of tea if you'd let me join you for a few minutes?" she asked. He turned in surprise.

"You're certainly up early this morning," he commented. "You can join me with or without the bribe."

"And how would you be having it?"

"Two sugars—and a little milk." Layla turned and scampered up the hill. It took her less than five minutes to return to his side, a pot and two cups of tea balanced on a tray. She placed the setting down on the grass between them and prepared the beverages.

"I'd just be in need of a friendly voice and face," she confessed.

"Something wrong at work?"

"Tisn't work so much as personal things. Oh, and before it slips me mind, would it be okay to call me folks from the office overnight tonight? The time difference really makes it a chore calling them at a reasonable time—given me work schedule. I have the money to pay ye now and it would be grand to hear me parent's voices. I'd be wanting to ring them at about one-thirty."

"I'll give you one of our extra keys to the office and you can wander over and call whenever you want to. How's that?"

"Oh, that'll be grand." Layla lifted her cup and carefully swallowed her first mouthful of the hot beverage. Brian, too, had begun sipping from his cup, his eyes all the while trained on the horizon.

"I take it everything has been satisfactory with the cottage."

"Oh, it's grand. One thing though…I could do with another rug. If you don't have one to spare then herself could pick one up."

"You would like another rug? What, you don't like the one in there now?" quizzed Brian.

"Oh no, tis fine. But I could do with another." Her cousin took his eyes from the horizon and peered down at her.

"You'd like a second rug to go over the one already in there?"

"Aye. Tis cold in the morning still and I don't want to be leaving the heat on till July." He shook his head and drew another sip of tea from the cup.

"Am I missing something here, cuz? How is a rug going to make things warmer except maybe for your feet when you're walking on it?"

"I'm thinking about when I'm up in the loft and I can throw it over me." He stared down at the girl, a dumbfounded look plastered across his face.

"Wait a minute. Wait a minute. I think we're talking about two different things. Could you mean blanket when you say rug? You mean what you cover yourself with in bed—over the sheets, right?"

"Aye."

"They're called blankets here—not rugs—you little eejit," laughed Brian, reaching down and tousling her hair.

"And would you have a spare from the main house herself could borrow."

"Of course. Wow, you had me going there for a second. So, what exactly are these personal things you might want to talk over with me?" he asked, attempting to get the conversation back on a more serious note. Layla nodded her head and sat back against the fence. She hesitated before speaking, as if trying to organize her thoughts.

"I'd be losing me best friend from work tomorrow. Tami's gotten a position in Providence and won't be at Billy's after tomorrow. She's been a good friend and who I've spent most of me free time with since getting to the states. I'll be missing her something brutal after she's gone." Her cousin reached across and applied a one armed hug.

"It's one of life's hard lessons…good people moving in, then, too quickly, out of your life again. You just have to hope and pray there'll be someone else to fill their place in a short while. Wouldn't it be great if the eejits would move out of our lives as quickly as the good people?"

"Aye," she responded, staring out toward the distant Atlantic Ocean.

The two sat a few moments in complete silence, each savoring the taste of their tea and presumably reflecting on their lives. From the harbor below came the distant sound of a lobster boat engine turning over.

"Sounds like someone's getting a late start this morning," commented Brian.

"Late?"

"Yeah, those guys are usually out there at the crack of dawn." Layla nodded and turned her head.

"Would you be interested in hearing how your cousin made a complete fool of herself?"

"I don't know. Would it make my cousin feel better to talk about it?"

"It would."

"Go ahead then kid, I'll just listen."

"Well, for a little while now I've had me eyes on a lad who comes to Billy's on a regular schedule. His name is Philip Trask."

"The artist guy?"

"Aye, he's a sculptor. So, from the moment I set me eyes on this beautiful man, I began trying to come up with a way of meeting him, and letting him know I exist. I learned from me friends at Billy's that this will not be easy. This is because the only way to meet the man would be to wait on his table...and doesn't he ask for Vickie all the time and no one else. Well, yesterday doesn't Mr. Trask come in with his high and mighty friends and it's Vickie's day off. So herself not being the village idiot, I bribe Betsy to sit Mr. Trask and his friends at one of me tables...and Betsy knowing I'll return the favor as soon as I can does just that."

"And I'll bet the poor man has no idea he's being stalked by my lovely cousin, does he?"

"I should hope not. So here I am with this opportunity to make a favorable impression on Mr. Trask and don't I come off like some dimwitted scrubber."

"Wow, scrubber huh, that doesn't sound too good. Okay, what happened?" Layla took an extended sip from the rim of her cup before looking up at the man pathetically.

"As I was saying, with Vickie not on duty I was given Mr. Trask's party of four. When I approached the table I literally could feel me hands shaking—I was that nervous. I gave them all their menus and asked if anyone cared to order a beverage. They did...and everything seemed to be going smoothly enough. It was the closest I'd been to this gorgeous man...and didn't he have skin as smooth and clear as a baby's."

"God, I already hate this guy and I've never even set eyes on him."

"Hush now, Brian. So here it was—with me bringing them their drinks and twice I catch Mr. Trask looking up at me and smiling. That's when I start taking their orders, and each of them as finicky as the one before, asking for everything just so. The last at the table to order is Mr. Trask. He uses a couple of big words on me and someone at the table says something about me being lost and not understanding what he's saying."

"May I just say that I don't particularly like these people...and I don't even know them."

"Anyway Brian, it was at this juncture that I made a complete eejit of meself. With the whole table looking up at me, I stared down at Mr. Trask and said, thanks...and have a nice day. Their mouths all dropped open in disbelief and Mr. Trask says: You are coming back with our order, aren't you?" Her cousin dropped his head and held back a laugh. "I'd become so flustered me mind wasn't working right! Thanks...and have a nice day, I said, like I was bleedin' planning to go home and take a bath and leave them just sitting there."

"What did they say?"

"Mr. Trask just stared up at meself...like he couldn't believe his ears. You are planning on returning with our food, I hope, he says," she repeated. Brian lifted the cup of tea to his lips and withheld laughter.

"You know Layla, it's actually kind of cute. They probably gave you a little good-natured ribbing for the rest of the meal. That isn't so bad. Besides, you gave them something to talk about over their chowder."

"Oh, you're right about the ribbing but I'm not sure it qualified as good-natured."

"You've set yourself apart from the other waitresses," he suggested, attempting to put a positive spin on the embarrassing moment.

"Oh, set apart I am—there's beautiful Vickie with the long, tan legs and beautiful face—and there's the white-as-a-sheet eegit from Ireland standing next to her. Be sure to watch the eegit very closely or sure she'll walk off with your order and go home to take a bath or something…leaving you to starve," blurted out Layla. The redhead placed her cup of tea back on the tray and balanced her face atop her propped up knees.

"You really care about this guy, don't you?" Brian asked, his voice taking on a more thoughtful tone.

"Brian, I've never felt anything in me life like what this man makes me feel. I just have to set eyes on him and me stomach tightens and I can feel meself shake."

"Well, for starters, it's not like you're not attractive enough for the guy. You are a very pretty girl, and you don't have to play second fiddle to Vickie or anyone else. So don't let looks deter you from pursuing this guy, okay?" She nodded yes.

"I know you're probably thinking I've put me head in the clouds and long-ing after a man who's successful with money and a fine reputation. I know I'm a bit mad to think that someone like him would even look at me twice, let alone want to get to know me. But I can't help it. I've never had eyes for anyone like I have for him. I've never felt anything like this before. I find meself thinking of him constantly…and it hurts to go any time without just seeing him. But now, I know there is no way to overcome the silly article I made of meself already…and probably no chance to change the impression I made on him already."

"No kid, don't think that way. Where there's life, there's hope. You might just get a second chance."

"And haven't I been racking me brain to come up with a scheme…but anything I come up with has me throwing meself at him…and that's never a good idea."

"How about in your prayers? Have you been asking the Big Guy for help in making progress?"

"Oh, I couldn't be praying for something like that!"

"Why not? You can ask for anything…and doesn't the Lord tell us to just ask."

"Have you ever asked for something like that?"

"I used to do it all the time. Think of it this way: Wouldn't Mr. Trask be better off in the company of a nice, Catholic girl instead of running around with those phonies you say he's always with now?"

"Aye."

"Then you'll be doing it for him as much as for yourself."

"And doesn't the Lord already know what ideas I've had in me mind at night when I put me head on the pillow and think of Philip Trask?"

"Yes, I suppose he does. So my little cousin has been entertaining thoughts about a member of the opposite sex. Well cuz, welcome to the club…and trust me, it's a very big club. He'll understand."

"So you're saying I should pray for help in me desire to grow closer to him."

"Exactly. Ask Him with everything you got. In your daily prayers, at mass, when you take a walk on the beach…ask Him to intercede. And if it's not going to do you any real harm, I'm pretty sure He'll come through for you." Layla stared up at her cousin, a thoughtful expression spread over her delicate, female features.

"And wouldn't it be grand if He saw fit to lend me a hand."

"It's not beyond belief that He will. However, I just want you to remember that old saying—be careful what you wish for, you might get it." She broke out in a broad grin and reached down for her tea. From all appearances, the encouragement from her cousin had spawned a degree of optimism in the young woman and outwardly lifted her spirits.

The two cousins sat comfortably against the fence surrounding the swimming pool while the sun inched deliberately upward from the eastern horizon. Billy's Chowder House was visible from their position in the middle of the spacious lawn, prompting a question from Brian.

"Is the new room open yet, the one at the back of the building?"

"'Tis scheduled to open in June," she answered. "They'll be moving the bar out there." Her cousin nodded and closed his eyes. "When I came down to join you a short while ago I was meaning to ask you what brought you out so early."

"Oh, I've got a lot of driving to do in the next couple of days, and an emotional trip I make every year…and I was just out here to get myself psyched up for it," he explained.

"And what kind of trip would that be?" The girl thought she detected a shroud of sadness descend over Brian as he peered eastward into the distance.

"I'll be going up to Quebec to visit a couple of people…and to visit a graveyard like I do every year about this time."

"You lost someone?"

"Yes, a long time ago…someone I loved very much."

"It was a woman…aye?"

"Yes, and we were going to marry after she finished her education. That was many years ago… moving in on twenty. She lost her life saving a little boy from a car out of control. I was down here on the property when the call came from Canada. Millie found me and I rushed up there—but she was gone before I could reach her. Now I go up and visit Angelique's parents and spend the night…and spend time with her at the grave site," explained Brian. Layla reached across to her cousin, placing her head on his shoulder. "You know, it's at this time of year when my thoughts go back to her and I miss having her. I seem to have these remote caverns in my mind and when this time of year comes around I find myself exploring them, revisiting memories of our times together and trying to fathom the world she's in now, and if I'll ever join her and see her again."

"I'm sorry for being such a busy body and asking questions of you."

"No, it's okay."

"Does Mrs. Kelly know?"

"Oh yeah, it's no secret. She always makes a few comments but she's sort of accepted it by now," he answered.

"Tis romantic when you think about it. I just hope a man will love me enough some day to go through what you do—if I should die before him, I mean." Brian nodded his head, a weak smile etched on his face. Nothing was said for a few moments, each content to sip on their tea and enjoy the early morning in silence.

"Now Layla, can I definitely tell Maggie that you'll be visiting—like for a couple of days?"

"Aye, maybe the first weekend in June if you can manage it. That means it won't interfere with your Memorial Day."

"Good. I'll schedule it here at work. It'll probably be my last weekend visit home until after Labor Day."

VII

L AYLA PULLED THE DOOR to her cottage forward, tripping the lock and securing her residence for the day. Security was important. Inside the tiny cabin was nearly four hundred dollars in accumulated tips. Turning from the door, she peered out over the swimming pool and rolling lawn. The sky was overcast and a light fog hugged the harbor below. Nonetheless, the redhead decided to take the bicycle this day, Monday, May eighteenth. This would be her first day without Tami, she thought. She rounded the corner of the motel building and caught sight of her cousin on the back porch of the office. His back was to her as he carried on a phone conversation. She had not seen him all weekend.

"And look at the little skiver trying to sneak off with my bike," he called out from above.

"And sure you've got eyes in the back of your head, you do," she replied. "And I'll have you know I'm no skiver—me who's worked for two weeks straight without a day off." He turned and surveyed his cousin.

"Has he proposed yet?"

"And who would that be?"

"That Trask guy. Why? Have you already got your eyes on someone else?"

"I haven't seen the man in nearly a week. Maybe today. Oh Brian, I'm needing to be asking another favor of you. Could I avail meself of the washers and dryers downstairs? Me clothes are getting a little manky."

"You've got a key, Layla. You don't have to ask."

"Thank you so much."

"Are you sure you want to take the bike?" he asked as she made her way toward the shed. "They're calling for rain this afternoon and tonight."

"Aye. I'll try to store it out of the rain. Don't wait up ma, I'll be grand." She threw her cousin a whimsical kiss and made her way into the storage shed. Seconds later she was pedaling up the driveway and starting her five-minute ride to work.

Layla cleared the front door of the restaurant a short time before eleven o'clock. Her arrival prompted Vickie to momentarily lift her eyes from the day's menu specials and extend her a listless hello. Dick was downstairs from his office talking to Susanne and a girl Layla did not recognize. The twenty-year-old made her way into the kitchen where she punched in and hung up the light jacket she had thrown over her shoulders back at the cottage.

"You're not the newest kid on the block anymore, Layla," called out Adam Dillon from his desk at the back of the kitchen. "Christ, we're going through waitresses like paper towels," he added, no doubt referring to the new girl out front. She still felt a little uneasy hanging out with the men in the kitchen so she quickly found her way out front. Wandering in the direction of the new back room, she surveyed the progress made by the contractors over the last few days. No doubt this room would soon be open and it was clear to her that this would be the dining area of choice for most of the customers the coming summer. The twenty-year-old was again assigned tables in the back bay, giving Vickie and Susanne the large majority of the lunch crowd.

With her section of tables empty of customers and the settings in place, Layla returned to the front hall to take a breather on the bench and join the other girls. On arrival she found the new girl seated alone at one end of the bench while Susanne and Vickie gossiped at the other. Ignored by the gossipers, Layla meandered toward the new girl, waiting on any sort of acknowledgment. In the next moment the brunette raised her eyes and extended a shy, hesitant smile. She was a pretty girl with large, dark brown eyes set in an oval face. However, her patented pretty face was offset by a weight problem, her frame carrying thirty-five or forty excess pounds.

"You're replacing me best friend. Saturday was her last day," announced Layla.

"She wasn't fired or anything was she?"

"No, nothing like that. She was offered a position down in Rhode Island befitting her education…that's all. Now I'm without me friend," explained Layla while dropping herself on the bench beside the girl.

"I barely know a soul here myself," acknowledged the heavy set brunette. "Susanne will be showing me the ropes while I shadow her but she doesn't seem too interested in striking up a friendship, or even a conversation."

"And what would your name be?"

"Donna. Donna Pento."

"Well Donna Pento, I'd be Layla O'Malley—straight off the boat from County Donegal—except no one comes over that way anymore. I'm only here for half a year, working here for Dick and trying to save some money. Now you might want to keep that in mind, should you find money starting to burn a hole in your pocket. You can feel free to pass anything extra along to this poor, Irish lass sitting here before ye." Donna's eyes lit up, pleased by the sense of humor of the outgoing young woman seated beside her.

"I was wondering what kind of accent you had. I get confused between Irish and Scottish accents."

"And where would ye be staying in the area?"

"I'm sharing a cottage with two of my college friends up on Route 1, not too far from the Hayloft Restaurant."

"I can't place where you mean. Is it near the top of Mile Road here?"

"No, it's more toward Ogunquit."

"And did you bicycle in this morning?"

"No, I drove. I have my brother's car right now. He's stationed in Germany and he's letting me use his car until he gets back."

For the next few minutes the two young women exchanged information, each interviewing for the position of workmate, a confidant, and trusted ally of the other. The steady stream of words between the two was interrupted a few minutes later by a call from behind the front desk.

"Layla, I just seated a party in your section. You might want to attend to him," called out Vickie who had assumed greeting duties sometime in the last half hour. Layla reached over and squeezed the new girl's hand.

"Enough craic for the time being. Tis time to earn me pay," she said, hopping to her feet and making for the back room. She proceeded down the hall, a pitcher of water in hand, and made her way into the largely empty back bay. There she eyed William Johnston seated alone at a table along the wall. His face was twisted almost in a grimace as he fidgeted with the contents of his wallet. His clothing appeared particularly grimy and soiled, his white shirt showing the effects of a hard morning of work. He did not appear to see his waitress as she made her way towards him.

"And how is my absolute favorite customer today?" Layla sang out, causing the man to abruptly raise his head.

"So they stuck you with my table again, did they. You must be making enemies here for that to happen."

"It's nothing of the sort, Mr. Johnston. I'll have you know I had to wrestle a girl to the floor and threaten the poor creature with a good beating just to have you seated here with me and not somewhere else."

"Don't you be feeding me that rubbish."

"Rubbish you call it. Truer words were never spoken and I only wish there was a Bible close by for me to swear on it."

"Can I talk long enough to place my order?"

"Only if you can remember what you are," she answered, folding her arms playfully across her chest.

"Remember what I am? What in the name of God are you talking about?"

"Now don't you be bringing God into this. What's this? You don't remember what you are?" The man rolled his eyes and glared up at her in defiance. "You's me first—me very first customer."

"A large bowl of chowder—with extra crackers, and a Bushmills and ginger."

"With extra crackers what?" Layla asked.

"What?"

"What comes after extra crackers?" she prodded. The surly man glared up at her.

"I could report this to your boss."

"And sure you wouldn't."

"And why not?"

"Cause you's me first. Now, what comes after extra crackers?"

"Please, damn it! Are you happy now?"

"Aye, let me put your order in this minute," she exclaimed, turning from the man and making for the kitchen.

The amiable redhead returned a few minutes later with the man's lunch and beverage. The man's eyes left the table and made contact with hers.

"You know missy, if I wanted to be badgered and prodded by a female I would have married years ago," he stated, his tone less severe than minutes earlier.

"And if it's help you wanted finding a good woman, then sure I could be of assistance to ye," answered Layla behind a sheepish grin.

"Sweet Jesus, you're the last person on earth I need poking their noses in my life! Off with you now and let me enjoy my lunch in peace." She pressed her hand down on his soiled shirt and applied a tiny squeeze to the shoulder.

"Don't you worry, I'll check back in with you in a few minutes." She whirled around and hurried back to the front of the establishment where she found Donna seated quietly at the end of the bench.

"I notice you're wearing slacks, Layla, like me. The other girls are already in their shorts. I'm overweight as you probably noticed and the prospect of people leering at my fat legs all summer is a turn off, particularly if I happen to be standing next to Vickie or someone."

"I'd be feeling the same way."

"Why? Your legs can't be fat."

"Not fat…but as white as a virgin bride's gown, they are. Tis the Irish curse."

"I'd trade you in a minute," confessed Donna, looking her friend up and down.

"And have you had a problem with the scale all of your life?"

"No, just since midway through high school. That's when I gained the weight and I've been unable to shed the pounds ever since."

"I'd say that it's a shame it is. With your beautiful eyes and complexion, I could see you as a rival for Vickie if we could shake off a few of these pounds.

It's probably nothing more than some bad habits you picked up. I could work with you if you'd like—keep you on the straight and narrow as they say. Why don't you start by weighing yourself tonight, if you can, so we can measure any progress down the road." Layla jumped to her feet. "I should be checking in with Mr. Johnston. The poor creature's out by his lonesome in the back bay."

"Vickie and Susanne were making jokes about him when you were out there. Is he a difficult customer?"

"Oh, he's all right. He's as tight as a camel's arse in a sandstorm, but he's all right," joked Layla as she left for the back bay.

Approaching the gray-haired man, she was greeted by a lifted glass and a request.

"Another Bushmills and ginger," he called out with the bravado of a pirate ordering his first whiskey after six months at sea. The redhead twisted her face into a disapproving scowl.

"I'm starting to think that that level of alcoholic content cannot be good for your health, Mr. Johnston. I don't want yourself getting like me uncle Seamus. Now there's a tale you don't want to hear."

"You're right, I don't." Layla pulled out the chair across the table and seated herself.

"Me da would say that me uncle Seamus would 'lick his drink off a scabby leg,' he would. This description caused Johnston to break out in an involuntary laugh, shaking his head in disbelief.

"I'm not your uncle."

"Herself is just saying that a little moderation when it comes to the hard stuff can't do any harm. Maybe we should be thinking of something a little better for your system. What if I have them build you a nice pint of Guinness? Don't they say it's actually good for you, and sure won't you be helping out the economy back in the republic."

"The last blasted thing I need to be worrying about is the economy back in the republic! Missy, I'd say you're getting a little too familiar with me and a little too big for your britches. I'll have my usual—a Bushmills and ginger."

"You're me first and I care what you put in your body. Humor me, Mr. Johnston," she asked with a trace of manufactured desperation carried in her voice.

"You're going to drive me to another establishment with this nonsense of yours," he threatened.

"And sure you couldn't stay away from me and this place if you tried," countered Layla. The man shook his head in frustration, overgrown strands of white hair falling over his eyes.

"And would you care for any dessert with your pint?"

"Bring it, you damn little pest. No dessert, just a pint."

"And I'll see if they can draw the shamrock on the foam like they do for me da in Killybegs," she added triumphantly.

"Sweet Jesus... at least spare me that!" Johnston cried out.

"Okay then, we'll skip the shamrock... this time."

On arrival back by the front desk, Layla saw that Donna was absent from the long bench, having returned to shadowing Susanne. Vickie was seated behind the front desk, her head buried in the newspaper. She put in Mr. Johnston's order for a pint and took a seat at the far end of the bench, resting her head back against the wall and closing her eyes for a moment.

"If you're tired now, just think what it will be like in July when it never slows down," came a voice from a few feet away. She opened her eyes to see Adam Dillon, the head cook, standing just outside the door to the kitchen, a can of soda cupped in his hand.

"Tisn't the work so much as a terrible night's sleep," she replied. The man brought the soda can to his lips and took a sip.

"A lot of good reports about you, Miss O'Malley, circulating out in the kitchen." The middle-aged man sounded quite sincere.

"And is that all you lads out back have to do is talk about the likes of me?" Her words brought a crackle of laughter from him.

"Wow, it's been a while since I've been called a lad. Miss O'Malley, you've made my day." The words scarcely out of his mouth, the man disappeared behind the swinging, kitchen doors. Layla smiled inwardly, happy to hear the positive report from a man she respected.

"Layla, your pint is up," called out a voice from behind the bar. The red-head jumped to her feet and fetched Mr. Johnston's beverage. Walking down the hall to the back bay where the grizzly lobsterman sat alone at his table, she was pleased with how her relationship with this long ago immigrant from Northern Ireland was developing. Upon reflection, she realized she had taken social and workplace liberties with this crusty character. Somehow, through all the silliness, the man had put up with her outrageous meddling and even gone along with it to some extent. Mr. Johnston's eyes lifted from his plate as Layla arrived at the table and placed down the Guinness. He shot the waitress a glance then peered down at his drink.

"Didn't you say they'd be a shamrock in the foam?"

"Aye... and sure didn't they forget to put one there. Well, no bother, herself can just try tracing one out with the tip of me finger." She reached for the glass of stout and stopped. "And now I'd be trying to remember if I washed me hands after me last visit to the ladies room. I make a habit of it as a rule, but I do remember being in a hurry. Oh well, tisn't life a gamble anyway. Now let's see if I can get those three leafs just right," she said, deliberately extending the tip of her finger toward the glass. His hand came down on her wrist, arresting its advance toward his beverage.

"Next time...I'll have it that way next time," stated the man though a chuckle. Layla smiled.

"Good man yourself, that'll be grand Mr. Johnston. I'll leave you with your pint and check back again in a few hours—I mean minutes."

Layla was pleased to see her new friend seated on the bench when she returned to the front area. She playfully sidled up next to the brunette, looping her arm around Donna's shoulder.

"Have they posted your schedule yet?" she asked. "Maybe we have some time off together to do something."

"I don't know. I mean—I just started." Layla bounded to her feet and made her way into the kitchen where schedules and the time clock were located. Walking up to the listing of weekly shifts, her attention was grabbed by something a few feet away. There among the employee's coats and jackets was a single red rose, the stem placed through the hanging loop of her windbreaker. Stopping in her tracks, she stared on in disbelief for a moment before turning back to address any onlookers among the kitchen help. There were none. She walked over to her garment and curled fabric around the flower, shielding it from sight of any passersby. Slightly taken aback, she returned to her friend in the front room without further scrutiny of the schedule.

"So, am I on the schedule?" asked Donna while Layla deposited herself next to her.

"No, I don't think so. It may take a wee time for us to have some free time together," said the girl blankly, her mind racing with questions and possibilities behind the single rose. In seconds a rational explanation popped into her head. Perhaps a generous impulse on the part of Dick had prompted him to buy each of the girls on duty a flower. It was possible, she thought. But, if that was the case, why hadn't anyone else mentioned it or perhaps found a way to wear it on their person?

"Has any one of the other girls spoken of receiving a rose today?"

"A rose? What do you mean?"

"Oh, nothing...just some silly thing that came racing into herself's mind," she explained. The statement brought a chuckle from Donna.

"You called yourself, herself?"

"Aye and why wouldn't I?"

"No reason, I guess. It just sounds funny, that's all. You sound funny saying that." The slender redhead sprang to her feet and addressed her new friend.

"Funny is it? Like a clown maybe! Maybe you think I'm just here to amuse you—like a clown in the circus? Oh, there's the Irish girl, here to amuse Donna Pento. Layla, the pathetic, little Irish clown." The explosion over, she glared down at the brunette. Donna's eyes had already grown wide in astonishment as she stared up the young woman. She attempted to speak but only could utter a short series of garbled syllables. It was then that the twinkle returned to Layla's eyes and a broad grin broke out on her face. "The movie *Goodfellas* and the *Joe Pecci* character—you have to have seen it!" Donna breathed a deep sigh of relief.

"Please don't ever do that again," she implored, bringing a roar of laughter from Layla.

"Hello…has someone forgotten their table in the back bay?" called out Vickie from behind the front desk.

"Sweet Jaysus—Mr. Johnston."

Layla hustled to the far room just as the lobsterman was rising from the table.

"Mr. Johnston, I'm so sorry for leaving you alone back here so long. I ran into something in the kitchen that put me back on me heels," she explained.

"Never mind with your chatter. I just want to get my bill paid and I'm still waiting on the tab," grumbled the man without so much at a glance down at his waitress. Layla placed his itemized slip on the table.

"And you wouldn't be upset with me, would ye?"

"It's really of no consequence to me how you carry on so long as I get my check and get back to my boat."

"And you must know by now, tis me who'll be taking your money and making your change. Now if you'll just hold your horses and set back down, herself will do that right now," explained Layla. She placed her hands on the man's arms and guided him backward. Following her lead, Johnston collapsed back onto the chair. "And I'm still waiting on whether you're upset with me for forgetting you out here."

"It's okay. You needn't make a federal case out of it," said the man calmly. Layla took the man's twenty-dollar bill and counted out his change. With the exact change on the table beneath them there came a pregnant pause. "No one around here seems to realize that tipping is quite different back home than here." The redhead stared down at him out of the corner of her eye, a crooked smile spread over her face.

"And sure, we aren't back in Portrush, or Killybegs for that matter, are we Mr. Johnston?" The lobsterman shook his head before grabbing his change and rising to his feet. "And may the lobsters literally jump into your boat the rest of the day," sang out Layla as the man strode for the exit.

"It'd be a hell of a trick. The boat's in for the day." With that said, the man disappeared down the hallway.

Layla returned to the bench and Donna a few minutes later. It was midafternoon and the pace was slow. Sliding in next to her new friend, she saw that the girl had a large piece of fudge balanced in her hand.

"What's this?"

"One of our customers brought in a small tray of fudge. I think there's still some up at the front desk."

"Never mind that. What happened to your diet? You know, the diet I'll be working with you on."

"It's just this one piece," explained Donna.

"Do you, or do you not, want to be the girl that boys will think is a fine bit of stuff?"

"Of course I do."

"Then you must get serious. Now, give me that fudge." She reached out her hand and snatched it away. Hustling to her feet, she made her way through the swinging doors to the kitchen.

The redhead returned to her friend a minute after leaving her, her hands empty.

"Did you give it away?" Donna asked while her friend dropped onto the bench beside her.

"I went up to the lads in the kitchen one at a time and asked them to close their eyes and open their mouths."

"And did they?"

"Each and every one. And aren't men all complete eejits when a young girl asks them to do anything? I broke off a piece of fudge and popped them into their mouths. And sure, I could have been taking lint from me pockets and they would have done the same."

"It's cause you're a pretty girl—a slim, pretty girl."

"And Donna, you being me new friend, sure, we'll have all the lads opening their mouths and closing their eyes for you before the end of summer." The two, young women broke into laughter at Layla's prediction.

***

Memorial Day came early in 1998, the solemn holiday celebrated on May twenty-fifth. This meant that Layla's only planned visit to her cousin Brian's home in New Hampshire would fall over the last two and a half days of the month. Layla glanced at her watch and did the math in her head. It was twenty-five minutes past one o'clock. Brian would pick her up at three for the start of her only scheduled weekend off for the season. Since arriving at the start of the month she had visited the Kellys at their beach house on Atlantic Avenue, but on these two occasions there had only been time to share a few anecdotes and sip on a can of soda. However, that was about to change. Layla would be spending the entire weekend with the Kellys of Bedford, New Hampshire, dining at their table and sleeping in their bed. On this day she had once again caught tables in the back bay. She was making change for a warm, elderly couple from Pennsylvania when she caught sight of a familiar, hulking man being escorted into the room. It had been some time since William Johnston graced the dining rooms of Billy's Chowder House but he had returned.

"I'll be right over, Mr. Johnston," she called out before checking back to the kitchen on the status of another table's meal. Making her way in the direction of the kitchen, her progress was interrupted by Susanne.

"Oh Layla, don't get your nose out of joint about having Johnston palmed off on you again. He asked for you specifically. I know it's Donna's turn to catch him but, as I said, he asked for you." She waved off the woman's explanation, indicating she had no problem with the assignment and hastily returned to the kitchen.

The redhead left the kitchen with a tray covered in plates and a glass of fresh water. Of immediate concern was the delivery of entrees to the table by the window. Layla chatted with the party of three while placing their meals before them. After learning that the one individual who ordered lobster was a veteran at removing the meat from within the shell, she excused herself and approached Mr. Johnston from the rear.

"And what's this I hear about a certain Orangeman asking for a certain pathetic, little, Catholic girl from Donegal?" Layla asked in a whisper delivered from over his shoulder.

"The best of a sorry lot," he answered, his voice sounding as if the words were escaping his mouth over a bed of gravel.

"And sure is it that, or could it be I remind ye of another lass from Donegal... maybe a lass from your youth that you met in Killybegs? Could that be it, Mr. Johnston?"

"Could you just take my order and dispense with the foolishness," grumbled the man but with none of his former hostility. She gave his shoulder a playful squeeze before circling his chair and addressing him face to face. "The large chowder with extra crackers and a Bushmills and ginger." The redhead rolled her eyes.

"You do know the terrible rut you are in... you with the same lunch day in and day out."

"And the same waitress to boot."

"Aye, the same waitress; the same dull waitress."

"A little nuts in the head, but dull you ain't," answered the lobsterman, his voice dropping off at the end of the statement.

"Let me put your order in and I'll come back and tell ye about me weekend," she called out as she made her way out of the room.

The twenty-year-old returned with food for another of her tables before catching her unlikely confidant up on her planned weekend in New Hampshire with her extended cousin's family.

"When you mentioned plans for the weekend, I almost assumed you had found yourself a feller," said Johnston as the girl flitted by him, refilling water glasses around the room and making sure her tables were being properly attended to.

"No, nothing like that. Unfortunately for me, the only man I have eyes for thinks I'm a bloomin' eejit and that's only if he knows I exist at all."

"Oh, he'll come around. Give it time...a pretty girl like you."

"That's what me cousin Brian says but I don't see it happening, but thanks for the kind words," she added.

With all of her tables under control, Layla returned to the front desk and caught sight of Donna resting on the bench, her legs stretched out in front of her. Judging it would take a few minutes before Mr. Johnston's lunch was ready, she sidled up to her friend. Donna was bubbling with excitement.

"Oh, before I forget—great news. I stepped on the scale this morning and I'd lost four pounds from last week! Do you believe it?" Layla gave her friend's arm a shake.

"Our bicycle riding down to Ogunquit and back is working me friend. And sure you'll be just a willow of a girl before too long, you will."

"And something else Layla—something you've been wondering about for a little while now."

"Out with it, you," ordered Layla in comical fashion.

"It concerns who left the rose on your coat that day..."

"Out with it you malignant, little scrubber or I'll eat your head off in front of the entire restaurant," she threatened, now totally comfortable kidding with her friend of less than two weeks.

"It's the dishwasher kid. What's his name? Wesley?"

"Aye, and wouldn't that make sense. Me friend Tami told me the lad had eyes for me back when I first started. Well, I've got to be honest. This word comes as a relief. I actually began to worry that it might have been Mr. Dillon who left the flower—and him being a married man and all—well, that wouldn't have been good at all."

"Why would you have thought it was Mr. Dillon?"

"Oh, it's just that he had come out of the kitchen and spoken to me a little earlier that day. That's all." Layla reached inside her slacks and removed a hanky. A second later she was removing a trace of excess makeup from above Donna's left eye. "Oh, and didn't I just have a brutal thought run through me head."

"What?"

"Well, what's going to happen when you lose all the weight you're going to lose and wear shorts like everyone else in here? You, with your tan, will want to be showing all the lads that you're a fine bit of skirt. And then, there'll be herself, with me white legs still hidden under me slacks, and looking like the solitary eejit."

"Well, to be honest Layla, I've been seriously considering wearing them whether or not I lose the weight. It's not like I'm going to be the only one in the building with a few extra pounds on them," answered her friend as Layla hopped to her feet and went back to the kitchen in search of Mr. Johnston's lunch.

Layla glanced down at her watch after bidding Mr. Johnston a good weekend. It was ten minutes before three o'clock. The plan had Brian picking her up at the restaurant's front door and transporting her to New Hampshire. Knowing she would be assigned no more customers, she walked back toward her section to set Mr. Johnston's table before extending good-byes to her fellow employees. Reaching his small table by the wall, her mouth dropped open. A folded dollar bill was tucked beneath his beverage glass. The redhead slipped the bill into her front pocket and prepared the table, a smile of satisfaction covering her face. Two minutes later she was standing at the front desk in front of Vickie and Susanne, the dollar proudly displayed before them.

"My gratuity from Mr. Johnston," she stated proudly.

"You're kidding!" Vickie called out as if hearing news she had just won the lottery. "Here, give it to me. This should be framed." In one swift movement, Susanne snatched the dollar from Layla's hand and giddily went in search of a small, unused frame kept in a drawer at the bottom of the front counter. Layla made haste to follow the young woman and retrieve the bill.

"You'll do nothing of the sort. You'll not be making sport of that man," she insisted, plucking the dollar back and stuffing it in her pocket.

"Oh, for God's sake, I'll give you a dollar in its place if that's what's bothering you."

"You'll not be making sport of Mr. Johnston," answered Layla.

"If Dick ever caught you pulling something like that he'd have your head on a platter," injected Betsy Chase who had come upon the small fracas. This counsel from a third party on the matter of the dollar bill provided resolution to the dilemma. After bidding the trio of women a good weekend, Layla searched out Donna for a hug, finding her in the kitchen. She approached the brunette from the rear and draped her arms over the girl's shoulders.

"I'll be returning Sunday night or early Monday morning. I'll ring you as soon as I'm back so long as it isn't an ungodly hour. Don't forget: diet soda only and no sweets, and bicycling every morning—all the way to Ogunquit—all the way to Perkins Cove. Are you hearing me, lass?" she whispered in her ear. Donna whirled around and hugged her friend.

"Call me as soon as you're back," instructed her friend.

"You two dikes want to give it a rest," snapped Billy Sousa. "I'd like to keep my lunch down if you don't mind."

"Oh Billy, and here I was about to give you a long, wet kiss...and there you go and kill the mood," came back Layla, bringing a chorus of laughs from the rest of the kitchen staff.

"Any time paddy, any time," he answered. He followed his words with an exaggerated licking of his lips. The redhead gave her girlfriend a final embrace before moving back through the swinging doors and out of Billy's Chowder House. Outside the building, she was taken with the dark, overcast sky. Having no desire to stand in the doorway, she took a few steps in the direction of the bridge that spanned the Webhannet River on the west side of the restaurant. She expected her cousin at any moment and made sure he would have no problem spotting her. The twenty-year-old had not been on the side of the road for more than two minutes when a swell of voices rose from between the vehicles in the parking lot. Layla glanced back over her shoulder to see Philip Trask and his usual circle of friends moving toward the entrance to the chowder house. In spite of a conscious effort not to, she caught herself staring at the handsome sculptor as he joked with his companions. She stood invisible to the group until the young woman in the collection of friends spied the redhead.

"Hey red, you will seek cover in the event the clouds should open up in the next few minutes?" hollered over the gentrified metropolitan-type dressed completely in white. Layla went to shout back at the woman, then remembered her antagonizer's status as paying customer and held her tongue. Instead, her eyes shifted from the slender socialite to Philip Trask.

"Don't take anything she says seriously, miss. She's just learned her grandparents have further restricted her trust fund and she's been unbearable all day," called out Mr. Trask. Layla smiled back at him, unable to utter so much as a word of acknowledgment. Only seconds passed before the foursome cleared the front door and disappeared inside the building. She took a deep breath, continuing to gaze in the direction of the handsome sculptor. "He had not remembered her name," she thought. She was sure she had introduced herself to him and the rest of the table on that one occasion she had waited on them. It saddened her that he had not committed her name to memory. She was playing with possible reasons to re-enter the restaurant, just for the opportunity to set eyes on Philip Trask for a few more seconds, when a Ford pickup truck coasted onto the edge of the parking lot. Brian had arrived to pick her up and take her to New Hampshire for the weekend.

It had been over a week since Layla had sat down with her cousin and shared a conversation. Over the Memorial Day weekend she observed how busy his workday was and purposely stayed clear of him. However, seated across the front seat from him, she felt more akin to the man than she had anytime to date.

"A bit of bad news from the home front, I'm afraid," he said, breaking a half-minute of silence.

"And what would that be?" she asked, genuine concern detectable in her voice.

"You're still not going to meet Jenny or Brendan this weekend. They're hiking up in the White Mountains and not due back until next Wednesday. I'm sure it's nothing personal. However, you'll finally get to meet Moira, our little Irish house guest, cook, nanny, college student, cleaning lady, and anything else my wife can dream up for her to do."

"Now, she's employed by Mrs. Kelly?"

"She's more than an employee now. She was Colleen's nanny when she was a baby. We're paying her way through college and giving her room, board and a stipend to stay on and help with the house until she graduates."

"And where does the creature hail from?"

"Doolin, in County Clare." Layla nodded her head in acknowledgment. Presently the two were traveling south on Route 1, just before the village of Ogunquit. The twenty-year-old glanced over at her driver. She felt remarkably comfortable around this man, not just because they were related by blood, but more due to his disposition and maturity.

"Would you mind if I asked you a question about the family?" inquired Layla.

"No, go ahead—shoot."

"Herself is a little confused about you and Mrs. Kelly's older son and daughter. Are you Jenny's father and is Mrs. Kelly Brendan's mother?"

"No on both counts. Maggie May had Jenny when she was in high school. I knew her back then but I wasn't the dad. Brendan, well, he's mine only— mine, and a woman named Linda Turcotte who now lives up in Kennebunk. She just moved back to Maine a short while back. She lost her husband about three years ago. Layla, the truth is, the story behind Brendan is a confusing one, very confusing. But, I am his dad. There is a physical resemblance. Now Jenny…she's a dead ringer for her mom."

"Mrs. Kelly is a beautiful woman, she is." Brian glanced over at his cousin and smiled.

"Aye," he said in jest, copying Layla's typical way of responding in the affirmative.

The pickup had reached the town of York by now, motoring southward toward the border of New Hampshire.

"So my little, Donegal beauty, how are things progressing in your personal life these days?"

"Me new friend Donna is working out just grand. I can confide most anything in her and we are already spending time together away from work. She is a little on the heavy side so I'm working with her on that, bicycling in the morn, and we'll have her looking fine in no time."

"Are you over that sculptor guy already?"

"There'd be nothing happening on that front at the moment, in spite of me asking the Lord every morning, noon and night for help. He's still the only man I've had eyes for since I got here, and hasn't it been a month."

"When's the last time you called your folks?"

"Wednesday morning it was, and you be sure to tell me when it shows up on your telephone bill."

"How are they doing?'

"Grand—they're grand. I was able to tell them how me savings have gone over a t'ousand dollars. Imagine that! A t'ousand dollars."

"You did it again. A t'ousand dollars?"

"I told ye, it's only when I say numbers. I can't remember to pronounce it right," she admitted, prompting Brian to lean across the front seat and tousle her red hair.

"You're going to make it kid…eight grand before you go home." She flashed him a wide, satisfied grin and looked straight ahead at the road.

The sun was high in the sky over Route 1 as Brian drove his cousin southward. The air on this Friday was heavy, early evidence of the humidity that would likely blanket the region much of the next three months. When Layla caught her cousin peering over at her out of the corner of his eye, she flashed him a grateful smile.

"You know Layla, it might be good to go over a few do's and don'ts to keep in mind when you're at the house. Now, I love my wife madly but she is a very opinionated woman. On top of that, she loves to argue a point. So, with that in mind, you'd be wise to stay away from certain topics. First, she loves to give me a little good-natured razzing about religion—but that's only with me. So don't worry about anything along those lines. What you have to avoid bringing up, or reacting to, is politics. Maggie is very conservative, and she despises Bill Clinton. So, whatever you do, for the sake of peace, quiet and harmony at the house, don't be bringing fat boy up or reacting to anything she might say. In all likelihood, nothing will be said, but just in case," warned Brian, his tone warm but serious.

"Mr. Clinton is admired by many in Ireland. Do you feel the same way your wife does?"

"It's funny, I've never liked the guy but, then again, there are a lot of politicians I can't stand. I never used to carry around the hostility my wife does. I just figured he was like so many of the others—a bunch of smarmy phonies who say whatever they think will get them elected. That was before he pulled that crap down in South Africa where he received Holy Communion."

"Received the Holy Eucharist! Mr. Clinton's not Catholic, is he?"

"Of course not. As I see it, fat boy just saw a chance for a photo op—yes, the cameras were flashing. In other words, Clinton saw nothing wrong with degrading another person's religion—as long as he thought he could gain some political advantage from it. That's about as low as someone can sink in my eyes. I mean, I was brought up to respect other people's religion, and hopefully, I always have. Anyway, after that stunt in Africa, I came around a lot closer to Maggie May's idea of the guy than before."

"And you're sure this happened?" Layla asked.

"Cousin, it happened." She took a deep breath, visibly processing her cousin's words. "By the way, I'm hoping to take you down to Lowell to meet my aunt and uncle tomorrow. That way I can also take you around town and show you where I grew up."

"That sounds grand," she answered.

"Oh, and I have to warn you, Colleen is talking about you sleeping in her bedroom with her. Apparently, she views you as a peer. My four-and-a-half-year-old views you as her peer," repeated Brian. "Of course, we can come up with an excuse to get you out of this. We have a guest room at the end of the hall upstairs."

"No, it sounds like a bit of fun—meself and Colleen."

"I'm also thinking we should call your folks over the weekend from the house, and let your parents talk to Maggie May and Colleen."

"Brian, I know ma and da would love that, they would."

The sun was still high in the sky, the time being just after three-thirty, when the Ford turned off Route 1 and made its way onto the highway. Most traffic in the immediate area was heading north in the opposite direction, either somewhere else in Maine's York County or, in some instances, miles north to Camden or Bar Harbor. Inwardly, Layla marveled at the fact she was so relaxed, in spite of the fact she would be spending the next two or three nights in a strange house and surrounded by individuals she barely knew with the exception of Brian. The cabin of the pickup was quiet, causing her mind to stray back to home in Glencolombkille. She tried, as she often did, to picture where her parents would be and what they were doing at that exact moment. She imagined them both seated in the living room in front of the television, her mother knitting and peering over the top rim of her reading glasses at the sound of anything worthy of her absolute attention. It was now over a month since she had laid eyes on her mother and father and she missed them terribly. It was of great consolation to hear their voices every week on the phone, to receive news from back in County Donegal, and to hear them proclaim how much they missed her. However, none of this was a replacement for the reassurance of a single embrace from her father or the warmth embedded in a smile over the kitchen table from her mother. These sentiments must have bore witness on her face because a cursory glance by Brian over at the redhead caused him to break the extended silence.

"I hope you're not letting the prospect of sleeping with Colleen dampen your spirits. You probably haven't slept in a bed with a wet spot in a while, have you Miss O'Malley?" Layla's face broke out in a smile.

"Don't be mad, Brian, that hadn't even crossed me mind," she answered.

"But now that you bring it up, is the little lass…"

"Don't worry…don't worry, it's been over a year since my little princess has had an accident. And I told you, we'll come up with an excuse for you to have your own room."

"I'll not hear of it. If me little cousin thinks enough of me to want me to share her bed, who am I to say no."

The pickup was making good time in the journey to Bedford. They had already crossed the bridge high over the Piscataqua River, delivering them into New Hampshire.

"May I ask you a slightly personal question, Layla?" The twenty-year-old reacted to the words from her cousin, her jaw visibly dropping open.

"Aye."

"Now, I wanted to ask you this way back on the day I picked you up at the airport, but I figured it might sound a little strange."

"Go ahead Brian, you can ask."

"Anyway, I couldn't help notice the first time you got in the truck and a few times since…I couldn't help noticing the scent you wear. It's quite wonderful, and quite unique. I mean, I've been inhaling fragrances off of women for forty years now, but I can't remember anyone before wearing your scent."

"And sure there's a good reason for that, there is," she answered. "That fragrance is me own—taught to me by me grandmother."

"What is it?"

"First, ninety-five percent of it is a common, lavender cologne. They sell it everywhere in Ireland. But, when I was a little girl, me grandmother took me up high into the hills surrounding Glencolombkille and showed me a specific kind of wildflower—a wildflower with a strong, strong, wonderful smell. Me grandmother showed me how, when the pedals of this flower are added to lavender cologne and let to steep, it creates a wonderful, new scent. Tis the scent you smell from me."

"And no one else wears this?"

"No, not even me ma. Tis mine alone…and thank you for noticing."

The clock on Brian's dashboard read four forty-five when the vehicle left Route 101 and turned onto Joppa Hill Road. The Ford rattled its way over multiple bumps in the country lane as it slowly ascended toward what would be Layla's temporary home over the next two days. Behind them, her and Brian's luggage rumbled from side to side in the cargo area, causing the girl to glance back more than once before the pickup eventually reduced speed. She caught her cousin staring out the right hand side of the cabin and shifted her eyes in the same direction. There in the distance, slightly elevated from the roadway, was a stately, white, colonial home resting at the far end of a horseshoe driveway. At the rear of the main and probably original structure was a sprawling addition extending back in the direction of a line of mature pine trees.

"We're home," proclaimed Brian, turning the Ford between two granite pillars and up the driveway.

"Have a gander at that!" uttered Layla, her eyes focused on the front of the house.

"Okay, step one in keeping Keogh in a good mood: park the truck in the garage or out of sight behind the house. She doesn't like our neighbors knowing I drive around in a older model pickup truck."

"And who would Keogh be?"

"That's Maggie May's maiden name. It's one of my many pet names for her." Brian decided against the use of the garage but did park the vehicle alongside the far end of the house, well out of sight of any passersby. Emerging and jumping down from the cabin of the Ford, Layla caught an unobstructed view of the Kelly's back yard, including its large swimming pool.

Brian escorted his cousin around the house and up to an impressive front door. Pulling a ring of keys back out of his pocket, he manipulated the lock to the heavy, wooden door and swung it open. Seconds later, the two were standing in a thickly carpeted and matted entranceway.

"Why doesn't anyone in this house love their daddy?" the man called out, his voice loud enough to carry up the stairwell no more than fifteen feet away. From above their heads came the sound of frantic activity, culminating in the scurry of tiny feet. Seconds passed, then a small, blond figure appeared at the top of the stairs.

"Don't move," ordered Brian before sprinting up the stairs and enveloping his daughter a moment later.

"How's my Jelly Bean?" he asked, lifting his daughter shoulder high and descending the stairs with her. Layla looked on as the child giggled playfully into her father's ear. Reaching the bottom of the stairwell, he walked casually toward his cousin.

"Hello Colleen. Do you remember me?" Layla asked. The four-year-old nodded yes but did not speak. Instead, the girl cupped her hand around her father's ear, shielding her words from the visitor.

"Why don't you ask her yourself?" questioned the father.

"Are you really my cousin?" Colleen asked timidly.

"Aye, I am."

"Are you really staying with us at the house for a while?"

"I am."

"If you want, you can stay with me in my room. I have a big bed and there'll be plenty of room for us." The words barely out of the little girl's mouth, her father whispered something in her ear. A look of utter shock filled the little girl's face.

"You don't really still wet the bed, do you?" Colleen asked in astonishment.

"And sure your father's telling a fib, he is."

"Cause you're awfully big to still be wetting the bed," the child declared. "But, I'd still let you sleep in my room with me, but only if you promise not to wet the bed," the four-year-old stated, spelling out the conditions of her invitation.

"Do you know your cousin's name?" asked Brian of his daughter. She took a moment, then answered confidently.

"It's Layla, and she comes from Ireland where Moira comes from."

"That's right. You're a smart girl, Colleen," added Brian, planting a kiss on the child's head. The four-year-old promptly wiggled in her father's arms, indicating she wanted to be put down. Back on her own two feet, she extended her hand to Layla and escorted her toward the stairwell.

"Colleen, bring Layla up to see your room, and take her down to say hello to Moira. I'll go get the luggage from out of the truck." Layla glanced down at her tiny hostess who countered with an angelic smile, the kind only produced by the absolute innocence of a young child.

It was well beyond six o'clock and the kitchen in the Kelly house was alive with activity. Moira toiled in the kitchen, joined by Brian, Layla and Colleen. The foursome hovered over a dinner of haddock and baked potatoes. However, the culinary activity had, at least temporarily, taken a back seat to clowning as Brian added random amounts of seasoning to the items on the stove and in the oven. An explosion of laughter from the kitchen permitted the lady of the house to arrive home undetected, allowing her to appear in the doorway behind the group like a ghost materializing in a dark hallway.

"Kelly, you're home ten minutes and you have the place sounding like a frat house on New Year's Eve," crowed Margaret Kelly, standing in the doorway attired in a smart business suit. Layla's eyes scanned from her cousin to his strikingly attractive wife.

"Don't you mean sorority house? I'm a little outnumbered here in the gender game," he answered. She conceded the point and approached her husband, pecking him on the cheek before making her way toward their guest.

"It is so good to have you here," said the woman, albeit with a formality that drained much of the warmth from her words. On instinct, the redhead crossed the kitchen, applying a hug and planting a kiss to the woman's cheek. "Thank you so much for having me here," Layla whispered discreetly in her hostess's ear.

"Tell mommy who's going to be sleeping with you tonight," injected Brian. The four-year-old flashed her mother a triumphant smile.

"Layla is—and she's promised not to wet the bed."

"Colleen! Don't be saying something like that in front of our guest," insisted Margaret, visibly taken aback by her daughter's indiscreet statement.

"Relax Maggie May, it's our little, running joke," advised her husband behind a lighthearted wink. Layla reinforced her cousin's explanation by reaching across the kitchen table and giving Colleen an affectionate hug.

"Okay then, I have a suggestion," voiced Margaret as she approached Moira at the stove. "I'll step in and assist Moira with dinner and why don't you three make your way into the dining room and set the table."

"Brilliant," exclaimed Brian, borrowing an expression from his Irish cousin. Layla circled the table, scooped up Colleen and nudged her male cousin out of the room. The three made their way across the hallway where Brian retrieved china from behind glass in a heavily ornamented hutch.

"So Kelly, what's on the itinerary for you and Layla tomorrow?" called out Margaret from the other side of the hall.

"I thought I'd take her down to Lowell and show her where I spent my childhood... walk in the footsteps of greatness. I'll call the tour, "Brian Kelly, the Early Years."

"Ten minutes of that and she'll be jumping off of the city's highest bridge," wisecracked his wife. "Why not stay a little closer to home and show Layla around Manchester?"

"Oh please Keogh, give us a break here. What are we supposed to see, aside from panhandlers and fleabag lawyers? Would you like that Layla, spending quality time with lawyers?"

"Spend the day with solicitors?" questioned the young woman.

"Yeah, that's what my loony wife is suggesting. You see, the city is infested with them. You can't avoid them," stated Brian, projecting his voice so his wife could hear him. "Now if we go to Lowell, there's the museums, the national park, the historic buildings, and, of course, the 'Brian Kelly, the Early Years' tour."

"Wait until I get you behind closed doors, Kelly," she warned, suddenly arriving in the dining room with a platter stacked with dinner rolls. Moira arrived in the room a few seconds later with a pitcher of ice water. When the Kellys returned to the kitchen together, Layla took the opportunity to speak to the Irish girl from County Clare in private.

"Is this leading to a squabble do you think?" Moira laughed under her breath and shook her head.

"No, not at all. It's how they communicate with each other... back and forth, back and forth. Don't be letting it bother you. And sure, sometimes I think it's their form of foreplay. They'd be in good form tonight." The redhead breathed a sigh of relief and smiled back at the girl.

"I'm going to sit right next to you, Layla," piped up Colleen, suddenly feeling left out of the proceedings.

Brian and Margaret reappeared in the doorway moments later, both carrying trays. They set about covering the table with the evening's meal.

"So Kelly, it's been over four days since we spent any time together. Which of your fantasies about me have sustained you this week?" The question caused Layla's eyes to widen, slightly shocked by the nature of the question in front of a guest. "No, don't tell me… I'm taking a long, hot shower and you're the bar of soap?" Her husband laughed, shaking his head in disbelief.

"That is so high school," he responded, pretending to dismiss her.

"Or was it the one where you come back from a long trip and find me sleeping in your bed, a helpless street urchin seeking shelter from the bitter cold on the outside?"

"Sorry Keogh, but if I remember correctly, that's your fantasy, not mine." The attractive woman lifted her eyes from the table, a devilish grin breaking across her face.

"Then it must be the one about the beautiful, medieval queen and her obedient slave boy," she stated. Brian's head turned in her direction, his eyes locking onto hers.

"All right Keogh, back off," he answered, her words having struck a nerve. With that, the two broke into a synchronized laugh, the couple clearly sharing a secret in the way only husbands and wives could do. Layla took in the banter and the unspoken communication between the two. She was not sure why, but she liked what she saw. Behind the chiding and name-calling was, in evidence, a comfortable bond. "Are we almost ready to eat?" Brian asked.

"Why doesn't everyone take a chair and I'll bring in what's still on the stove," answered Moira with a certain authority. The family members took their places with Brian at the head of the table. Colleen slipped her fingers through Layla's hand, seating her between herself and the setting reserved for Moira.

The evening meal spread out before the family, Brian made a request of their guest.

"Layla, would you do us the honor of saying grace?" The young woman looked over in surprise at her cousin but complied.

"Dear Lord, thank you for the food on the table and for our good health. And thank you particularly for this opportunity to spend some time with the Kellys, and keep Brendan and Jenny safe as they climb through the mountains. Amen." She ended her prayer with the sign of the cross before opening her eyes. The family was already in the process of serving itself, save Mrs. Kelly. She stared across the dining room table at the twenty-year-old, her hypnotic blue eyes clearly expressing approval.

The mood in the room was lighthearted on this evening. On those occasions, and there were more than a few, when Colleen looked away from her meal peppering Layla with questions or comments, her father would sneak a dinner roll from her plate and claim it for his own. After managing to pilfer two from the youngster she finally caught on and gave her father a stern lecture on the evils of stealing.

"Oh Maggie May, I thought of you the other day. Well, not you in particular, but the circle of people you work and socialize with."

"I'm not sure I want to hear this," she answered.

"No, you'll want to hear this. It's a Bobby and Perez story." The woman closed her eyes and shook her head.

"Layla, have you met Brian's childhood friends, Bobby and Perez?"

"I don't think so."

"If you don't think so, then you haven't. I think it's safe to say that once you've met them you won't forget them."

"Careful Keogh, they're clients."

"You had to remind me."

"So, as I was saying before my wife rudely interrupted, last week the boys and I were having lunch at Congdon's…"

"You didn't come down to Billy's and have lunch there with me?" Layla asked.

"Cousin, cousin, variety is the spice of life. Damn, will I ever get this story out?"

"Go ahead Kelly, we're all listening," reassured his wife.

"Oh, for Layla's sake…a little background."

"For the love of God just tell the story!" snapped Margaret.

"Bobby and Perez own a lawn and property maintenance business out of Kennebunk. They are near and dear friends of mine from my distant youth."

"I'm not sure 'distant' captures the enormity of how long ago your youth was," wisecracked his wife.

"My friends run this business—have done well with it—and have become respected members of the business community." His spouse rolled her eyes but withheld comment. "Now, it seems that one of their customers, a demanding little, weasel lawyer from Kennebunkport as it turns out, is eight weeks late with his payment and they find it necessary to make a house call, cause invoices and phone calls are just not getting it done. So they pull up to the house on a Saturday and knock at the door. First, this gutless, little, corporate weasel sends his wife to the door to tell them that her husband is too busy to speak to them. But, they won't leave. They tell her they're not leaving until he speaks to them. They will stand out on the porch until he decides to grace them with his presence."

"Oh, that must have made the woman's day," commented Margaret. "Under even the best of circumstances these two do not dress up a neighborhood, and I'm being kind."

"She delivers the message, and probably tells this clown to get his ass to the door. Anyway, the boys don't have to wait more than a couple of minutes before the weasel joins them on the porch. Bobby always does most of the talking and he reminds the guy that he's very past due. Now, here's the part that reminded me of your corporate friends and associates, Maggie May. The guy tells them that the reason he's so far behind on his payments is because he's barely been able to make the maximum contribution to his 401(k) and, therefore, other things have just had to wait. Perez just looks at the guy, not quite sure what the hell he's talking about. Bobby's fuming, but stays calm on the outside. He leans over and whispers into Perez's ear, explaining to his partner what the pompous clown in front of them is saying. Now, think of it: this self-absorbed, yuppie puke has no concern with paying his bills so someone else can put bread on the table for his family or pay his rent. All this scumbag cares about is keeping up with some write-off on his tax return. Isn't that incredible?"

"Those are your people, Brian, your typical, tree hugging, granola eating, politically corrected, liberal pukes. Maine's infested with them. No doubt, they're New York and Massachusetts transplants. These are the same hypocrites who preach about compassion and the redistribution of wealth, as long as it's not out of their pockets," preached Margaret. Brian shot his cousin a subtle glance, a reminder not to engage his wife in political discourse.

"My people?"

"Anyway, what happened?"

"Well, Perez listens to what Bobby says and goes into a tirade. First in English, then to Spanish, then back to English again. Bobby pretends to hold him back, like a baseball player keeping a teammate from slugging an umpire. Then Bobby says to Perez, "Stay away from the truck." That's a signal to Perez to start walking toward the truck. The lawyer's standing there not knowing what the hell is coming down and Bobby goes into his good cop-bad cop routine. Bobby pretends to be afraid for what's about to happen but never says what's in the truck. With the attention of both men now turned toward the truck, Perez hefts a six-foot pike pole from the truck bed and appears to examine it for weight as he turns to look back at the lawyer. The lawyer's eyes widen, and without hesitation he finally says he can write them a check. I mean, who wants all this playing out in their front yard—their wife and kids maybe watching through the window. In the end, the boys got their money, and probably lost a customer. But then again, who wants a dirt-bag like this for a customer?"

"What is a pike pole?" Layla asked, her interest piqued by the story.

"A garden tool like a rake or a shovel. Nothing really threatening. The point was to make the clown panic and wonder what could be going through Perez's mind."

"They do know that they could just go to small claims court and collect the money that way, don't they?" Margaret asked.

"Much slower process, and a lot more time consuming. Besides, I don't think they liked their chances up against a lawyer in court."

"Good point," conceded the woman. "Oh Brian, guess who's going out with a young man for a day at the ocean tomorrow?" Brian looked down the table and detected a mild blush spread over Moira's face.

"Give me a hint. Is she from Doolin by any chance?" The brunette smiled and nodded yes. "Well, it's about time. I was beginning to think the men around here were all losing their eyesight."

"From all reports, a date over to Rockport and Gloucester."

"We're not calling it a date, just time spent getting to know each other better."

"I take it he's from school."

"Yes, we share a finance class with a dozen others."

"And what about you, Layla? Have you started seeing anyone yet over in Maine?" inquired Margaret.

"No, I'm leaving me options open, I am." She held her breath, wondering if Brian would speak up and mention Philip Trask. He did not. "One thing's for sure, I won't be taking up with just any Joe Soap who comes along and shows me any interest."

"Smart girl," added Brian behind a wink.

Most of the evening was spent in the living room with the television contributing for little more than low, background noise. Conversation dominated the people's time together. Layla was surprised by her hosts' interest in Ireland and County Donegal in particular. Colleen nodded off to sleep a short time after eight-thirty, her head in her father's lap. Moira excused herself about an hour later, explaining she wanted to get a good night's rest for her long day of exploring the Massachusetts coast the next day. When Brian caught sight of the nightly news flashing on the TV screen, he checked his watch and suggested an end to the evening. Layla and Margaret agreed and with Colleen tucked into her father's shoulder, they made their way into the hall and up the carpeted stairway to the second floor. The foursome paused in front of the master bedroom. Layla reached out to Margaret, giving thanks again for having her over the weekend. The elegant woman returned a hug, this time with more enthusiasm than she had only hours earlier in the kitchen. The redhead planted a kiss on the woman's cheek and separated herself. Layla turned to Brian who looked down on the two approvingly.

"And to you, me cousin, I say to you, goodnight slave boy." Husband and wife burst out laughing in unison.

"Good one," declared Margaret.

"I'm moving you to a smaller cottage the moment we get back," threatened Brian, unable to camouflage his surprise. He reached down and passed his daughter into Layla's arms.

"And sure I doubt if there is a smaller cottage in all of Maine," she answered.

"May my daughter turn your overnight into a living hell," he declared, shaking his head in disbelief and following his wife's lead into the bedroom.

The queen-sized bed provided ample room for child and adult. Layla lay beside her young, distant cousin, their faces only six inches apart. Thus far she had enjoyed her time in Bedford, even more than she had anticipated. Amazement was the only word she could come up with to describe the warmth and trust extended to her by the Kelly family. Here she was, still almost a stranger to Mrs. Kelly, sharing a bed with their only child. The redhead studied the young girl's face. She would probably grow to largely resemble her mother, she thought. Following a few minutes of close scrutiny, the child's eyes blinked open and focused on her sleeping partner.

"You know what's cool about having you sleeping with me, Layla?"

"I don't know. What?"

The tiny girl grew serious. "Sometimes when I wake up in the middle of the night and the wind's blowing outside, and the room's dark, I get afraid that a monster might be in the room with me."

"And sure we all felt like that when we were wee ones like yourself."

"But with you here with me in bed, and my daddy sleeping in his room with mommy, I'm not a bit afraid," she confessed.

"And well you shouldn't be." The child showed a contented smile, staring deep into her older cousin's eyes. The little girl yawned, started to close her eyes, then froze.

"Now you do know where the bathroom is if you need to go in the middle of the night," she asked.

"Don't you worry Colleen, I'm grand," answered Layla, amused at the notion that the girl could not separate reality from the clowning of adults.

VIII

ON SATURDAY MORNING the Kelly household was buzzing with activity. Moira arose at six thirty and immediately began primping herself for a day along the coast of Massachusetts. Brian made a point of meeting the prospective beau at the door at nine o'clock, playing the role of the protective father and taking measure of the young man. Anthony Fournier, Moira's male friend, seemed like a genuine soul, although somewhat ill at ease from the scrutiny placed on him by his female friend's employer. Brian shook the young man's hand before wishing them both a fun day. His employee of nearly five years told him not to stay up and worry should they run late, reminding him she had her own key. Brian remained standing in the driveway as the compact car pulled away from the house and cruised out of sight.

Margaret expressed her joy over breakfast at the prospect of having the house to herself all day. Colleen would accompany her dad and cousin to Lowell, giving the professional woman uninterrupted personal time to spend reading, working out or perhaps by the pool. At ten o'clock, Layla and her cousins hopped into the cabin of the Ford and headed south to Lowell, Massachusetts.

Apologizing to his houseguest no less than three times for any inconvenience, Brian began the day trip to the city of his birth at St. Patrick's Cemetery with a visit to his mother's grave. He had lost his only real parent twenty-six years before, the rapid passage of time still eliciting assertions of disbelief from him from time to time. From memory of other visits to the quiet place, he paced off a distance from a nearby elm tree until the trio stopped over a marker reading, 'Elizabeth Kelly.'

"This is my closest link in the chain that connects me to you," said Brian to his Irish cousin. Layla closed her eyes, seemingly in prayer, and stood quietly by her cousin. Colleen, growing fidgety, wrapped her arms around her father's leg and questioned why they were loitering in this place. The brief, solemn interlude at this quiet, green place ended in a simple gesture. Kneeling down over the tombstone, the man kissed his fingers and ran them over the granite stone. In the next instant, the three were walking back in the direction of the Ford.

Brian let out a sigh of relief when two empty parking spots came into sight. They were downtown in Lowell and only a hundred yards from Kearney Square, the epicenter of the city. Layla peered out over the dashboard at an impressive structure showcasing multiple pillars on its front face and an array of carvings laced across the exterior.

"That, my child, is where I graduated from high school," he announced, no shortage of pride in his voice. The trio emerged from the pickup and locked up. In the next instant Colleen was hoisted up onto her father's back, her mode of transportation set for the duration of the visit. Layla was direct-ed to leave the sidewalk and proceed down a walkway that brought the three visitors to a meeting of watery channels. On closer examination she was able to establish that a large portion of the flowing water was passing through manmade waterways.

"This is not some wonderful gift of nature, these canals here. Behind us is the Concord River," Brian explained, pointing to shallow, slow moving water a hundred feet away. The water right below us here comes from the Merrimack River and it's come a distance. Layla, do you have any idea how this canal got here and why?" She shrugged her shoulders, indicating she did not. "Irish immigrants, kid, they did a lion's share of the work back in the eighteen hundreds. Think of how deep these things are, and as we walk around and see how many miles of canals there are, think of how many back-breaking hours must have gone into it."

"Was this all dug by hand?" the Irish girl asked while staring across at the network of interlocking waterways.

"No, I'm sure they had shovels," answered her cousin, not one to let a potential straight line go to waste.

"Oh, so they did have shovels. And sure that makes it a lot less impressive than I first thought," she said, unwilling to let her cousin escape with the final witticism. He shook his head and chuckled.

"It looks like slave boy has his hands full around the likes of you," he admitted. Layla purposely brought her shoulder in contact with him, the bumping action further evidence of the bonding continuing to grow between the two.

The three continued to walk alongside physical evidence of the country's industrial revolution, tangible proof of a time of growth, exploitation and hardship. Layla glanced downward at immense granite slabs—retaining walls for the unnatural, manmade flow of water—and thought of the men who toiled to put them there. Perhaps they were men from County Donegal. Men long ago buried in a foreign land, far from the burying places of their mothers and fathers. Men worked not so unlike beasts of burden so that their sons and daughters, grandsons and granddaughters might succeed in the land of opportunity. The redhead lifted her eyes from the canal below and found her cousin staring thoughtfully in the direction of a nearby modern building.

"'Tis something about that place that's put your mind somewhere else," she observed, causing him to return his thoughts to the here and now.

"Nothing to do with that building... just this place. I just have this vivid memory of my mother bringing me here once, all the way from Centerville, to see a giant fire. The Rex Bowling Alleys were in this huge building on that site over there. I remember my mom looking at the flames as they shot through the roof of a monstrous building and getting real sad and saying that a Lowell institution had been taken from us and would never come back."

"And did you ever bowl there?" Layla asked.

"No, I must have been too young. But I remember watching my mom and some of her friends from work bowl. I was really, really young. I seem to remember pin boys down at the end of the lanes resetting the pins and motioning to my mother and her girlfriends. I can't believe this is all coming back to me. Stuff like this always happens when I come home to Lowell."

"'Tis grand to be able to bring back thoughts from your childhood like that."

"Daddy, can you buy us some ice cream?" asked Colleen following an extended period of silence.

"Not right now, Jelly Bean, but on the way home."

Layla and the Kellys proceeded up Merrimack Street toward an impressive building in the distance, a structure with a steeple reaching skyward and ultimately perched with an eagle. The building, which Brian identified as city hall, was still in the distance when he coaxed Layla onto a side street.

"This is where I went to high school for three out of my four years," he stated. "I went to school for one year in Manchester, New Hampshire... and that's where I met your mommy, Colleen."

"Janey Mack! It looks like it goes on forever," exclaimed Layla.

"There's a whole other building on the other side of the canal. That wasn't there when I graduated. Oh, I knew there was something else in the neighborhood I wanted to show you." He directed Layla onto still another side street. There, wedged in between the back of retail outlets and a restored nineteenth century building sat a house of worship. "Saint Joseph's is where my mom would go when she really needed a prayer answered. This church isn't like all the others; it's open all day. We can go in right now if you'd like." The twenty-year-old nodded yes and followed her cousin inside the shrine. With Colleen lowered to the ground, the three climbed the stairs and entered the lobby to the church. "Now when my mom would come here years ago, she'd be praying for things like putting food on the table or how she was going to come up with the rent money that month. She swore, and God knows this woman didn't make a habit of lying, that her prayers were always answered... always," said Brian.

"And you think I should be asking Him for a way to meet Philip Trask?"

"Why not? Granted, it's not as important as what my mom was asking for—food and shelter—but it's important to you. You do believe, don't you?"

"Aye."

"We can go in and say a few prayers. There's no harm in that."

"I could always pray to St. Jude, the patron saint of hopeless cases," added Layla.

"What's this hopeless cases garbage? Layla, you're a very attractive girl. It's not like we're asking for this Trask guy to fall hopelessly in love with a leper!" The redhead laughed through a discernible blush and signaled for them to enter the church.

Inside and surrounded by silence, they prayed. Colleen mimicked her father, kneeling in the pew, her hands folded in front of her. Shortly after, Brian signaled to the young woman to walk ahead and inspect a particular statue. She rose to her feet and approached the visual representation of a man of God. She knelt close by the statue and sat quietly. After a few minutes of prayer and meditation, she rose to her feet, dropped a donation into the receptacle, and lit a candle. Following a short prayer over the flickering flame, she rejoined her cousins at the back door and exited the church.

"What do you think? Was that a sign?" Brian asked. Layla shook her head in disbelief.

"A statue of St. Jude, the patron saint of hopeless cases. 'Tis a wee bit odd. I've never seen a statue to the man before," she admitted.

"Before we go over and spend some time with the Clarkes—and have a great lunch—I want to just walk a little ways and try something out," said Brian. Colleen shimmied back up onto her father's back, calling for her dad to break out into a gallop. A few minutes later they were scurrying across a busy street and entering an area dominated by standing stone tablets, all containing inscriptions. Layla soon learned that they were in a park dedicated to a local writer, Jack Kerouac. The inscriptions on the stone tablets were the words and thoughts of this Lowell native, his words chiseled into rock to preserve them for the nearest thing to eternity that anyone could come up with. Layla meandered from tablet to tablet, scanning the words of this pop culture icon.

"Look, Maggie Cassidy—Maggie, just like your wife—except you call her Maggie May," she stated whimsically. Brian smiled and broke into a trot, his daughter still piggybacked on him, in the direction of a nearby canal. Layla followed close behind and joined them as they peered down into the dark, slow moving water below.

"Layla, did you know that thanks to her mommy, and Brendan, and Jenny, our little Colleen here can swim like a fish. In fact, she may be the best four-year-old swimmer in all of the US of A."

"Is that a fact," answered Layla, now staring into the little girl's face with exaggerated admiration.

"Last summer I beat Moira in a race at the pool—down and back," trumpeted the little girl. "And this year I'm going to race Jenny and Brendan, and I bet I'll win," she boasted.

"Okay, that's grand, beating the likes of them. But do you think you could beat your cousin Layla?"

"How good are you?"

"Me swimming is in a desperate way. It's terrible I am."

"Then maybe we can race in the pool when we get home today?"

"Why wait? We've got water right here," proclaimed Brian. The little girl looked down into the dark, mysteriously slow moving water.

"Here?" Colleen asked. "With our clothes on? There could be alligators."

"And sure we'll race them too," added her cousin, upping the stakes by tenfold. The intelligent little girl examined her cousin's face, then her father's, searching for a clue to whether or not the grownups were being serious. Layla was first to give the gag away, bursting out into a fit of laughter.

The afternoon visit with the Clarkes went well. The trio arrived at the house at the stroke of one. It was Colleen and Layla who shared the spotlight on this day. Playing to the attention heaped on them by Jimmy and Martha Clarke, the two lit up the house with laughter and energy. Informally scheduled for a couple of hours that morning at the Kelly kitchen table, this social call on the man and woman who took Brian in after his mother's death stretched out to well after five o'clock. Layla noticed her male cousin's withdrawal from the activities early on. He seemed content to sit back in a corner chair and silently take everything in. She wondered if perhaps he might not be thinking back to a time when he was the child on the premises, his energy generating much of the social interchange and activity in the room.

The living room was left cluttered with games and toys, items brought down from the attic and their own son and daughter's childhood, when Brian, Layla and Colleen eased their way into the front hall and toward the door. Colleen, carrying a vintage Barbie Doll, seemed least anxious to leave. It was Layla who gently nudged the four-year-old toward the door, leaving Brian to extend final good-byes. His aunt was first to give him best wishes, thanking him profusely for the opportunity to meet his Irish cousin. Then, uncle Jimmy, his eyes moist from the abundance of joy given off by his young guests and the alcohol content of four beers, embraced his nephew.

"Brian, I swear I would sacrifice ten years off my own life if I could only give your mother an hour with that sweet angel of yours... and for her to meet that beautiful and charming, Irish cousin of yours. You are a blessed man, Brian."

"I know uncle Jimmy, I know." He extended the man a short embrace and turned for the truck.

"I hope you don't mind if we drop by a few times this summer—up in Wells I mean."

"Absolutely not. Let me know ahead of time. I'll make room in my schedule for you," promised Brian from the truck.

The pickup eased out of the driveway and the three visitors headed back toward Bridge Street, their time in Lowell drawing to a close. In a rear seat, Colleen clutched her Barbie, her eyes taking in every detail of the doll.

"Do you have any idea how proud I am of you two?" Brian asked rhetorically.

"Oh, come on," answered Layla.

"No, I mean it. You made those people's day back there."

"Well, it's not like it came at any great sacrifice. I had a grand time. When they brought Colleen and I upstairs and we got to bring down all those toys. It's hard not to act enthused when you look in that one's face and see her grinning ear to ear, happy as a clam."

"Okay Jelly Bean, what do we do now?" asked Brian while turning to the back seat. "Didn't I promise you ice cream this morning?"

"Yes daddy, you did."

"It's off to Dracut, and some Richardson's ice cream," he announced.

"Sweet Jaysus, me arse is already twice its size from this morning after that lunch, and now you're talking ice cream?"

"You're in the US of A now, baby doll—eat till you explode," he cried out. He turned the Ford northward and headed out of town. It was only a short drive up Route 38 to Dracut and an ice cream stand called Richardson's. "This is in keeping with the theme of this day, namely, my youth. You see, this ice cream stand has been here a long time. I remember back to when I was nine years old. I had just made friends with this older guy—older, you know, twenty or so. I had held his jacket during a fight and we had sort of bonded. He was new in town and had no friends, so even a nine-year-old jerkoff like me was better than nothing. At least, in me, he had someone to talk to. Anyway, he told me that I could drop by his apartment every once in a while to see if he needed any errands run. So, one summer day, I came by his apartment unannounced to see if I could run errands and maybe earn a half a buck or something. He was in a good mood that day for some reason, maybe because he had made a few bucks himself. He let me in the apartment and asked me where he can get good ice cream, not the store bought crap. I told him about Richardson's because uncle Jimmy and aunt Martha would sometimes take my mom and I out for a ride and get ice cream there. Then he asked me if I wanted some ice cream. Remember Layla, this is back in the nineteen sixties before child molesters and degenerates were everywhere. I said yes to the ice cream idea, thinking he had a car. He didn't have a car! So me and Perez walked all the way out to Richardson's for a frappe that day, and all the way back."

"That's not the same bloke you were talking about last night who had to go collect his money with a shovel, is it?"

"Oh yes it is. Tis the same bloke," he answered, adopting an Irish brogue for comic effect.

"And sure, you're one who holds onto his friends."

"Old friends are the best—tried and true blue. It was the walk that day, in the heat, an hour out and an hour back that was important. The ice cream was secondary. It was learning about one another that was important. I got sore legs and a free frappe that day, and Perez threw in a dollar for future work. A dollar actually bought something back then. Anyway, we've been friends ever since." The truck passed through a set of traffic lights and shortly after cruised into the parking lot for Richardson's Dairy. "So you see Miss O'Malley, when I come back to Lowell to visit and make the rounds around town... there's more going on than meets the eye. Sometimes it's more than just really good ice cream."

IX

IT WAS EARLY SUNDAY EVENING and Layla's stay at her cousin's Bedford home was drawing to an end. She and Brian would be on the road no later than seven the next morning. At the moment she was waiting on Moira. The Kelly's domestic was downstairs in the laundry room. To occupy herself, the redhead was reviewing artwork and family photographs hanging in the hall. Layla had volunteered to give the Irish girl from County Clare a hand putting together a simple meal of homemade soup and sandwiches on this evening. Walking the hallway toward the back of the house, she scrutinized three or four Wyeth prints, artwork foreign to her but pleasing to the eye. Just before the back door she came upon a beautifully framed photograph of the family members. Following a cursory examination she was able to conclude that the photo had been taken inside the pool area and fairly recently. She deduced this from Colleen's appearance. The little girl, appearing front and center in the picture, was no less than three years old at the time the photograph was taken. Her eyes passed from Brian to Margaret, then stopped on the image of her cousin, Brendan. Layla had not expressed this to anyone, but she was disappointed upon learning that both he and Jenny, Margaret's daughter, would be absent from the house over the weekend of her visit. She had learned from Brian that they were infrequent visitors to the oceanfront house at Wells Beach, leaving Layla to reach the conclusion that she would, in all likelihood, return to Ireland in the fall before meeting either of these two young people. Brendan, she thought, bore some resemblance to his father but with more classical features. Jenny, like her mother, was a beauty, the mother-daughter resemblance being startling.

"And sorry I am for keeping you waiting," crowed Moira, appearing through the doorway from the cellar.

"What are they like, Brendan and Jenny?" Layla asked.

"They'd be in love, them two. They're easy enough to get along with. It wasn't always that way though. Brendan, when he first came here… Brendan was a malignant, little hooligan, he was. I think it was Brian who put him in his place…it's hard to say. But he's fine now," she explained.

"And what time did you wind up getting in last night?" questioned Layla.

"Oh, late it was. And didn't I have a grand time. Layla, we just talked and talked and the day flew by. Oh, it was a grand day."

"Well, you let me know how I can help with supper. It's the least I can do."

"There'll be nothing to it; maybe help with the sandwiches. I'm just reheating chicken vegetable soup from last week. I made enough to feed an army on Thursday and now I think we'll be finishing it off." The women were interrupted at this point in the conversation by the approach of Margaret.

"Layla, after dinner I'd appreciate a few minutes of your time. Maybe I can help you out with something," she stated. The twenty-year-old answered in the affirmative and left for the kitchen with the girl from County Clare.

Layla looked up at the bedroom clock as she forced the last piece of clothing into her overnight bag. Across the room, Colleen was sound asleep, the victim of a long day beside and in the family swimming pool. Remembering Mrs. Kelly's request from earlier in the evening, she made her way from the room and down the hall where she found Margaret at work in her home office. She stood in the doorway until the attractive woman raised her eyes from the reading material spread across her desk. Immediately, the woman removed a pair of glasses from the bridge of her nose, pushing them to the side in one, rapid motion.

"If you're not too busy, I thought I'd speak to you on that matter you wanted to discuss," said Layla. The woman's face reflected a moment of confusion before acknowledging her young guest's request.

"No, this is a perfect time. Come in, come in." Layla pulled up a chair, positioning herself directly across the desk from Mrs. Kelly.

"When you three were in Massachusetts on Saturday I took it upon myself to pick up a few things for you at the mall."

"And sure you didn't have to do anything like that."

"I did it because of something Brian mentioned to me on Friday night. He said you were a little uptight about wearing certain outfits at work, because of your fair complexion and not wanting to go out in the sun too much, something I can readily understand." The redhead fidgeted in her chair, not sure what to expect from the woman at this point. "Layla, I'd like to make a suggestion to you. Would you hear me out?" She nodded yes. "You have a wonderful figure and it seems to me a shame to keep it covered all summer. So, what I'm suggesting to you is abandoning whatever you're wearing now, slacks or pants, and replacing them with a pleated skirt. I've been to Billy's enough times to know the shade of green their uniforms come in and have picked you up three to bring back with you. You're a size six, right?"

"Aye, size six."

"I've also picked out hosiery that will complement your skin color and play off of the skirts." The woman rose from behind her desk and snatched a bag from the table along the far wall. "Take this back to Wells with you and give it a try when you're comfortable with the idea." Layla, sitting quietly in the chair, opened the bag and visually examined the merchandise inside. "And don't be afraid to look a little different at the restaurant. You will look fabulous in this outfit...and, who knows, it may become your signature outfit. None of the other waitresses are wearing a skirt, are they?"

"No ma'am, herself will be the first." Layla stood up to leave.

"By the way, did Brian mention anything to you about passing me on a little of that wonderful perfume you wear?"

"No, I don't believe he did."

"Typical...typical for him. He said it was your own concoction. Is that true?"

"Aye, tis only cheap lavender cologne mixed with some of the wild flowers that grow along Slieve League."

"Well, whatever it is, it's wonderful."

"Stay right there, Mrs. Kelly. I'll be right back." Layla bounded from the room, returning a minute later with a small, blue bottle. "Tis me traveling bottle, but you can have it. I have more back at me cottage." Layla circled the desk and embraced her hostess. "In case we leave too early tomorrow...too early to say good-bye...I wanted you to know what a wonderful time I had visiting here." Margaret Kelly returned the hug, planting a kiss on the young woman's cheek.

"Take care of yourself, young lady, and don't let my husband get away with anything," she ordered.

LAYLA REPORTED TO WORK on Monday and found herself the lone waitress outfitted in slacks. Over the weekend, Donna had mustered the courage to convert to Bermuda shorts and based on customer and her peers reaction, or lack of one, decided to stay with the decision. The work pace was hectic on this Monday. Vickie was obliged to return home to Massachusetts to attend a funeral, leaving Billy's short of wait staff. It was after two thirty before Layla and Donna managed to grab some time together on the bench.

"Did you miss me at all over the weekend?" Layla asked of her friend.

"Oh, were you gone somewhere?" Donna replied. The friends shrieked aloud with laughter, causing a few customers to stare over at the twosome. "Poor Wesley was walking around with a long face, thinking his Irish princess had gone home without saying good-bye. He perked back up, though, when I told him you were only in New Hampshire for the weekend and would be back on Monday."

"You're pulling me leg—about Wesley I mean."

"No exaggeration Layla; he's got it bad for you."

"I mean the poor creature's never even spoken to me."

"He's really shy to start with, and on top of that he's probably intimidated by you."

"Intimidated you say! Cause here I am walking around with me nose in the air—looking down on everyone and everything in me path," she clowned.

"No, that's Vickie's job. Oh, I know what I didn't tell you. I lost two more pounds over the weekend. I'm sticking with the plan just like you told me to."

"Oh, that's grand. Shall we go out and celebrate with a banana split or something?" Behind them the door swung open and William Johnston entered the room. Layla watched as the man was pointed toward the newly opened lounge. He deferred, choosing instead to be led toward the back bay. Thirty seconds later Vickie returned, indicating to Layla that she had a customer.

"Well, I see you've finally returned and joined the rest of us working people," Johnston roared as Layla approached the table.

"Working people you say...and you sitting there with hands as soft as a baby's arse," she countered. The lobsterman laughed and stared down at his well-worn, dirty hands.

"You've got a mouth on you missy; I'll give you that," he answered. She placed down a menu and poured ice water into his glass.

"And did you not want to be seated in the new room, closer to the bar and your blessed Bushmills?"

"No, I've got everything I'm comfortable with right here in this old room." Johnston turned his attention to the menu, staring long and hard beneath a pair of bushy, untrimmed eyebrows.

"A large bowl of fish chowder with extra crackers and a Bushmills and ginger."

"Sweet Jaysus, are you ever going to order anything else?" she crowed in mock exasperation. "I'll put in your order, Mr. Johnston, and bring you back something I picked up for you while I was in Massachusetts. Tis in me pocketbook in the kitchen." She returned a minute later hiding something behind her back. "Close your eyes why don't you," she suggested. The man complied. "Now open them." Johnston opened his eyes and looked down upon a bright, orange coffee cup resting on the table in front of him. "An orange cup for me favorite Orangeman in the world." The lobsterman lifted the cup, pretending to closely scrutinize it.

"You bought this for me?"

"Aye, at the Catholic shrine to Saint Joseph in Lowell. Tis a Catholic cup. It was blessed by a saint, Saint Layla of Glencolombkille, patron saint of eejits and bogtrotters," she answered behind a perfectly straight face. "And sure—every time you take a drink from the cup another Catholic is taken into heaven."

"That may be the only way any of that crowd will get there," joked the lobsterman.

"Oh, I didn't like that crack one bit, I didn't. I think we'll be limiting you to just one Bushmills and ginger today...then switching you over to Guinness. I've been cutting you some slack the last two weeks or so, but that's over now. I won't be playing the sweet, little mulchie for you anymore, not after that crack," she stated through an exaggerated glare.

"Did you really go out and spend money on this cup?"

"No, I was only coddin' with you, Mr. Johnston. The closet back at me cottage had too many coffee cups and I was just thinning out the herd. But, as they say, tis the thought that counts."

"Well, thank you young lady; thank you very much."

Checking the wall clock above her head, Layla pushed down her card and heard nine thirty-five inscribed on it by the machine. Her first day back on the job after the long weekend away had garnered her over seventy-five dollars in tips, including a two-dollar gratuity from the blustery Mr. Johnston. The redhead passed out a series of hasty good-byes to staff members and shot for the front door, anxious to return to the cottage and cuddle up on the couch. Exiting the building, she was confronted with a steady downpour, the weather having apparently deteriorated sometime in the last few minutes. She circled the building in a trot, finding her bicycle harnessed to its stand and dripping wet from the precipitation. Following a short struggle with the lock she managed to pull the bike free and begin her wet trip up Mile Road to Route 1.

After rattling the bicycle over the adjacent bridge she sped ahead up Mile Road, the brightly lit Route 1 a half-mile before her in the distance. It was a night like so many back in County Donegal, the skies opening up and pelting water on the ground all around her. Dropping her eyes to the pavement just in front of her, she pumped down on the pedals, not lifting her head to measure her progress toward the illuminated roadway at the top of the modest hill. She heard a vehicle approach from the rear, then pass her with an accompanying spray from the puddles of water collected on the street. It was a miserable night for a bicycle ride, she thought. Finally, after no small effort on the final incline, she crested the hill and turned northward. Only seconds passed before she turned between the stockade fence at the Atlantic Coast Lodge, literally coasting the remainder of the way by the motel building and to cottage fourteen.

With her bicycle now safely undercover on the cottage porch, Layla stripped off her wet clothes and dried herself with a towel from the bathroom. It was still a few minutes shy of ten o'clock. She clicked on the television, then changed her mind and shut it off. She needed the quiet of the tiny cabin for a while after the long day of interaction with others. It was the middle of the night back home in Glencolombkille, she thought. She drew a mental picture in her mind, a picture of her parents sound asleep in their bedroom. Running the math in her head, she realized that this was her fortieth day away from home. She had spent the equivalent of a whole Lenten season away from Glencolombkille and her ma and da, she thought. She missed Ireland, but the time seemed to be passing by at a decent pace. Layla rose from the couch, tossing the afghan to one side, and knelt down at the radiator. She turned the knob until the metallic tick told her the heat was coming up. It was a cool night for June, she thought. She placed her sneakers, literally drenched from the bike ride from work, directly in front of the electric baseboard. Outside, the rain had been joined by a blustery wind. She let out with an involuntary yawn. She was growing tired. She maneuvered the ladder back to beneath the loft and climbed the stairs, her bare feet still wet from the bike ride home. The redhead crawled forward to the head of the bed and slid open one curtain. Blackness dominated the view from the small, rectangular window while water droplets pelted against the pain of glass only inches from her face. Rolling onto her back, she listened to the persistent rain as it pattered on the roof above her head. She nodded off to sleep having no way to know that her life would take a meaningful side journey in the next twenty-four hours.

XI

LAYLA'S EYES FLICKERED open to the sound of wind curling through the eves of the cottage and the steadfast flutter of raindrops buffeting the roof and sides of the building. The watery onslaught from Mother Nature had not let up all night, waking the twenty-year-old more than once. On one occasion she was called from a dream, causing confusion on her part when she opened her eyes and was confronted with pine ceiling boards and not the familiar surroundings of her room back home. The dark clouds, spread like a shroud over the southern coast of Maine, left the room in semi-darkness. Climbing to the foot of the bed, she peeked down to the main floor and to the clock above the television. It was nearly seven-thirty. She had managed to get in over nine hours of sleep, something that pleased her. After forty days and forty nights in the sleeping loft she was now able to scale the ladder with absolute ease. She did, and was preparing tea only seconds later.

With tea on and the radio tuned to a local station for a weather update, Layla stepped across the room and pulled a bag from the closet. Inside were the articles Margaret Kelly had purchased for her. She removed one of the green skirts and a pair of pantyhose from the brightly colored bag before stashing it back out of sight. This was the day, she thought, she would emerge from under her dreary slacks and present herself, for better or for worse.

At ten forty-five that morning and with rain teeming down, Layla darted from the cottage and sprinted to the office in the main house. The door flew open and the redhead hustled inside, already dripping from the effects of the ten second run from her porch.

"Is there any way I can put upon you for a ride to Billy's?" she asked breathlessly. Brian detached himself from a stack of paperwork and scrutinized his visitor.

"Is this something new?" he asked, motioning toward his cousin and her outfit.

"Aye, it's something Mrs. Kelly picked up for me. I'm wearing it today for the first time."

"And how do you plan on keeping the boys off of you?"

"Aw, go on with ya. I'm just sporting a new look so not to look like a sad sack next to the other girls."

"Well, my little Irish princess, you've hit it right out of the park with this outfit. Who would have known? Why have you been hiding this great little figure of yours all this time?"

"I haven't. Didn't I give your yardman Billy quite the eyeful that first morning here?"

"Oh, that's right. Billy got an eyeful through your window. Maybe he just felt a little hesitant about passing on the word, me being your cousin and all!"

"What about the ride, Brian?"

"Not a problem. How soon?"

"In about thirty minutes?"

"Fine." He reached into a closet behind him and produced an umbrella. "Here's a brand new invention you might get some use from." The man passed her the umbrella over the front desk and returned to his paperwork. "And sure would you be needing some instruction on how to open it... or for knowing which end to put yourself under?" He spoke in an exaggerated brogue.

"Someone's forgetting who the biffo is and who it isn't," she answered on her way back out into the deluge.

Layla sat fidgeting beside her cousin as the pickup rolled down Mile Road toward Billy's Chowder House.

"I'm going to stand out like a girl up the pole at a single's dance, I am," declared Layla as the windshield wipers sloshed back and forth in cadence.

"What in the name of God does that mean?" Brian asked.

"Up the pole—pregnant," she answered.

"Oh, I get it... up the pole... single's dance. Cute, kid, cute." Brian stopped the pickup at the edge of the driveway and gave the girl a confident smile. "Now I'm limiting you to bringing home no more than two, male love slaves. Two, I can house in the storage shed. Any more than two and we'll have to drown them in the pool and bury them at sea. Is the Irish princess following me?"

"She is. Two love slaves and then I stop taking applications." He leaned across the cabin of the pickup and pecked her on the cheek.

"There's nothing to be uptight about." He gestured her out the door and she complied, opening her umbrella as her foot hit the pavement. She stood in place as the Ford circled a hundred and eighty degrees and rolled back up Mile Road. Layla, remaining dry under the umbrella, walked deliberately toward the front door. She was about to reach for the doorknob when the driver's door to a vehicle parked sixty feet away flew open and a male half appeared from behind the wheel. She stopped in her tracks, recognizing the vehicle, a red sports car, of Philip Trask. Her eyes grew wide as the man lurched forward, emitting an agonizing wail. On instinct, she walked toward him. Nearing the car she was able to identify Philip Trask. The man, his upper body slumped down over his knees, was now moaning quietly as he peered down on the pavement.

"Is there anything I can be helping you with?" she asked in a soft voice.

"No... I am very, very sick to my stomach right now and I do believe it'll be coming up any second," he said, managing to force the words out between deep breaths.

"Might you want to bring yourself over to the marsh and away from your car," she suggested.

"I am so goddamn dizzy all of a sudden," he answered.

"Here, hold on to me now," she instructed. She leaned her umbrella against the vehicle and reached down to him.

"You're going to get soaked," he observed.

"Don't you mind." Layla reached down, hoisted him to his feet, then walked him deliberately toward the border of the parking lot. Five feet from the edge of the pavement he brushed her away, dropped to his knees, and proceeded to vomit onto the ground. The twenty-year-old looked on as the young man purged his stomach through a series of excruciatingly violent upheavals. The process was brought to a close by three unsuccessful lurches from the stomach, the last bringing on a protracted moan.

"You'll be needing to get home and get some bed rest," she counseled.

"I'm supposed to meet someone here for a business meeting."

"And sure you'd be wise to reschedule that." Trask made an attempt to rise to his feet unassisted but staggered immediately, requiring Layla to step forward and anchor him. This action empowered her to take charge of the situation. She directed him back to the car as the moderate rainfall briefly intensified. Armed with the names of the man's business clients she proceeded inside and left word at the front desk that Philip Trask would be forced to reschedule his eleven forty-five appointment due to illness.

"What, did you take a dip before work?" Vickie asked sarcastically of Layla as she stood at the front desk, her clothes soaked to the skin. The redhead tossed her the evil eye but withheld a reply, content to return to the parking lot and the aid of Mr. Trask.

When she reached his car, a Pontiac Firebird, a few seconds later, the man was behind the wheel. She pulled open the door and placed her hand on his forehead.

"Sweet Jesus, you're burning up," she called out. He turned and looked up at her. His eyes were half drawn and unfocused.

"I think I'll be taking the wheel," she announced with authority.

"No one drive's my car but me."

"In a pig's arse!" The redhead reached down and hoisted him from the driver's seat. Upright, but on unsteady legs, he was marched around the vehicle, then deposited in the passenger seat with a resounding thud. Returning to the other side of the car, she dropped down into the driver's seat. "Now let me get me bearings here, because everything is backwards from what I'm used to." She glanced over at Philip Trask and found him with his eyes closed. Taking only two or three minutes to become familiarized with the dashboard, she turned the ignition key and started the engine. Within seconds she was within the stream of traffic on Mile Road.

"Mr. Trask, wake up. You're going to have to give me exact directions to your house." His eyes lethargically half-opened. He turned his head in the girl's direction, limply raising a finger.

"Take a right up here onto Webhannet. It's across from the Grey Gull." This effort seemingly drained his entire bank of energy because in the next second she observed his eyelids closing again. They had only driven a few hundred yards south when Trask unexpectedly lurched forward, spewing vomit over himself, the dashboard, and eventually Layla.

"Oh, and isn't this nice," she muttered under her breath.

"What the hell kind of a bug have I picked up?" he cried out, wiping the upwash from his shirt and onto the floor of the car.

It was no more than a quarter of a mile up the road when Layla caught sight of the house. Her need for directions from the man was no more than a ploy. Weeks before, on Betsy Chase's directions, she had bicycled by the house and surveyed the property. However, at the time, she had held out little hope of ever visiting the summer home of Philip Trask. The Trask driveway more resembled an early twentieth century road. Layla turned the car through the opening in a wooden fence and past a 'PRIVATE ROAD' sign. The road leading up to the green-trimmed, white house bordered a spacious lawn on one side and a moderate drop down to a rocky shelf of boulders and the blue Atlantic Ocean on the other.

"Is there anywhere in particular you'd like me to park the auto?" she asked. Philip shook his head no and reached for the door handle.

"Here now, I'll give yourself some assistance." Disgusted with his circumstances, he shook her off with a wave of the hand. However, his bravado was to be short lived. Rising to his feet in a single motion, he stumbled backwards against the car before crumbling back into the passenger seat and a small pool of his own vomit.

"Oh Christ, there's something really wrong with me; I know it."

"You buck eejit, you. You've got the flu and nothing more. It's for sure you're burning up with the fever. We'll get you to bed and pump some liquids in you. You'll be grand in a couple of days."

"That's easy for you to say. You don't have everything spinning around in your head like a top."

"Shall I take you into the house or shall we keep arguing out here in the rain?"

"If you would, I would really appreciate it," answered Philip, growing weary with the war of words. Philip Trask was no more than a couple of inches taller than Layla. He reached back into the vehicle and plucked the keys from the ignition, depositing them into a front pocket. Finally, Layla reached over and lifted the man to his feet.

Initially, things proceeded according to plan as the two stumbled over a patch of lawn and up onto the screened porch. However, reaching the front door, they realized a house key was needed to get them inside. Philip fumbled unsuccessfully for the next few seconds in an attempt to pluck the keys from his front pocket. His form-fitting pants and the dampness provided by the precipitation created a problem that he was unable to overcome in his current, weakened state.

"Would you get them?" he asked, motioning to his front pocket. Layla stepped back and looked the man up and down.

"And tell me you haven't put us through all this just for the thrill of having me hand moving inside your pockets," she jested. He closed his eyes and took a deep breath. "No, I suppose not," she added. The redhead leaned her charge back against the building and plunged her hand deep into his pocket, coming up with the set of keys on her first pass.

"It's the small, gold one," he said listlessly. Inserting the key, the lock clicked and the dated, wooden door swung in. Retrieving the man from the porch, she moved him inside gingerly while surveying the interior of his home. The inside of the house was dominated by knotty pine walls and furnished with dated furniture from the mid-twentieth century. To the right was a first floor bedroom.

"Would that be your room?"

"No, it's not. My room is upstairs…and if at all possible I'd like to be in my own bed tonight, and for the duration." Layla nodded in agreement and spotted the set of stairs leading to the second floor. The stairwell was narrow and steep with room for no more than one person to pass comfortably at a time.

"You can lead but with me right behind ye all the way. If you should feel yourself growing faint, you're not to worry, I'll be sure to step out of the way and let you fall." She waited on the man's reaction to her humor. It did not come. His illness no doubt clouding his thought process, he nodded in perfect agreement and began the trek up to the second story. Just beyond the halfway point she felt his body grow increasingly limp. Wrapping her arms around him from the rear, she pushed him upward the last few steps until they reached the landing.

"Here on the left—my room's on the left," he muttered. With Philip Trask in tow, Layla turned through an open doorway into a medium-sized bedroom, dominated by a queen-sized bed against the far wall. The room was meticulously kept with light streaming in through an irregularly sized window to the left of the bed and a second facing southward.

"Just let me get into bed, and open the windows for some cool air," he ordered. "I don't care if we get rainwater in the room."

"You'll not be lying in any bed with your clothes stinking of puke. Sit up here and peel your clothes off…shirt and pants," she ordered. Trask fell half-heartedly back onto the mattress, unbuttoning his shirt a moment later. She stepped out of the room, searching for a bathroom and some soap and water.

"Is there no bath up here?" she called over from the adjoining bedroom, a room splashed in pink and clearly female.

"No, there's only one bath in the house and it's downstairs off the kitchen," he called back weakly. She scurried down the flight of stairs and returned a minute later with a damp face cloth. She found him still sitting on the edge of the bed, his posture not unlike that of a propped up corpse.

"Trousers, too…trousers, too," she insisted, pushing him backwards onto the mattress and unbuckling his belt. "Now, you can take it from here. I have no interest in fiddling with your trousers or manky underwear. Wait! First let me wash what's left of your morning breakfast off of your face." She ran the damp, soapy face cloth over him with motherly authority.

"Oh God, I think I'm getting sick to my stomach again," he muttered.

"And sure, there can't be too much left in you. I'll run downstairs and find a basin to put next to the bed. When I come back I want you under the covers and your clothes on the floor. Are you making sense of me?" Trask nodded in the affirmative and Layla went in search of a receptacle.

Following a brief search, she climbed the narrow stairwell, a large, porcelain pot in her hand. She turned into the bedroom and found Philip in bed and under the covers. Beside the queen-sized bed was a pile of discarded clothing, a pair of navy blue briefs atop the heap. Trask himself was spread out motionless, the sheets pulled up to his neck. She approached the head of the bed and placed the pot down on the floor. His eyes popped open for a second, then closed.

"When I open my eyes the whole room starts to spin, and that's what could bring on more vomiting," he whispered. "There's still spinning when I close my eyes; it just isn't as bad."

"I brought you up a pot in case you need to purge again." She reached out, placing her hand on his forehead. "You're running a brutal temperature, you are, particularly for daylight hours. Is there a doctor or someone I could call?"

"Our family doctor is out of Boston," he answered, his eyes remaining closed.

"Would you feel better if I gave him a ring and ran this by him? There's no questioning that you've got a bad dose of something."

"That's probably a good idea. There's a Boston phone book downstairs right under the phone. I know my mother has all the emergency numbers written in on the sleeve. His name is Curran; just look for Doctor Curran and a Boston number. His office is on Beacon Street."

Layla glanced up at the dated kitchen clock as she placed the receiver back on its cradle. It was a few minutes past one. She took a moment to explore the bottom floor of the house. Stepping back through the living room she came upon a sprawling expanse of windows and floor space. It had all the ingredients of an all-purpose room including easy chairs, convertible sofas, a writing table and bookshelves. On closer scrutiny the twenty-year-old was able to deduce that this piece of the living quarters had been, at one time, an extension of the porch. Layla walked to the ocean side of the house and gazed out at the gray Atlantic. The rain had let up, now little more than a heavy mist as best she could fathom. She felt a smile crease her face as the image of a young Philip came to mind, jumping on the furniture and asking to play outside by the edge of the sea. Turning from the row of windows, she walked from the room and proceeded to the stairs. She plodded upward to the second story and re-entered his bedroom. His eyes were closed. She crept up beside him.

"I just got off the phone with Doctor Curran. Are you hearing me?" His eyes opened and he gestured for her to continue. "I hadn't planned on speaking to the man himself—perhaps his nurse—but it seems the Trask name carries a little weight with it back in Massachusetts."

"We've been with him for years," whispered back the man.

"I told him how you had a bad dose of something and rattled off your symptoms. He seems to think you've picked up a specific strain of the flu. There's a couple going around but he seems to think you've got the worse of the two."

"That's me, nothing but the best."

"He told me to tell you that it's something you'll just have to ride out. He thinks you should start feeling better in seventy-two hours or so. That's three days." He shot her a look, seemingly insulted by the translation of hours to days for his sole benefit. "His only concern was the temperature, and he wants me to monitor your fever for the next twenty four hours, just as a precaution."

"There's a thermometer in the medicine cabinet in the bathroom," he muttered listlessly. Layla remained seated at the edge of the bed, staring down at the man whom she had agonized over for the last month. He reopened his eyes, questioning why she had not already left in search of the thermometer.

"We might want to sort something out first, before we take your temperature, I mean," she stated seriously. He gestured her to continue. "The doctor's only real concern with ye is the body temperature thing. He's insisted we take an absolutely accurate measurement, with no margin for error." The man's eyes widened. "He'll not be wanting your temperature taken orally, or under the arm." Philip Trask stared directly into her eyes then waived her off with a violent movement of the arm that must have sapped the last of his strength. "Go on with ya. You can't be disobeying the doctor's orders." She placed her hands on his forehead. He let out with a long shiver, followed by a pathetic moan. "It's a bad dose of something you've got, and we can't be playing games with it," she declared with resolve. "There's a world of difference between a one hundred and two temperature and a one hundred and t'ree temperature."

"A hundred and what temperature?"

"Don't ye mind," she snapped back at him before leaving for the downstairs bathroom.

Philip Trask had already nodded back off to sleep by the time the redhead appeared in the doorway of the bedroom.

"It looked as though no one had used this thing in a while once I was finally able to put me fingers on it, so I washed it off real good in scalding, hot water and alcohol. Who's to say the last bloke to use it hadn't had special instructions himself," she mused aloud, bringing her patient back to consciousness. She strutted across the bedroom, seating herself on the far side of the bed. Layla brought the palm of her hand back to his forehead. "'Tis no question you're burning up; 'tis only a question of how hot?"

"I keep waiting for you to break down and say that this is some sort of gag," he admitted, noticeably laboring to speak.

"And if you have the slightest notion I'm playing you for the eejit, then I could drag ye down the stairs and we could ring the doctor's office, so you could hear the words straight from the man's mouth," blurted out the redhead.

"No, no...I couldn't survive another trip up and down those stairs," he conceded. Layla dipped the thermometer back into its holder, then extracted it and shook it in the air in front of her.

"And doesn't this whole matter remind me of something from me childhood back in Glencolombkille," she stated. "Sure, I remember me parents discussing it in the living room with company. A strange case it was."

"Is it warm in this room... really warm?"

"Not really. Anyway, there was this family, the Crowleys, and didn't their little baby start running a fever not so different from your own. Well, they were faced with taking the lad's temperature just as we're facing the same here. So, Mrs. Crowley sets to getting a reading and don't the baby start to fuss. As luck would have it, the front doorbell rings and isn't she called to the door, leaving her biffo of a husband to mind the child."

"I'm not sure I want to hear the rest of this story, if you don't mind," admitted Trask but with no success.

"Mrs. Crowley returned to her baby only to find her brainless husband examining the poor little thing's arse, and crying out the thermometer's slid up the laddie's hole. They ran around the house in a panic for the next hour, waiting and hoping the baby'd return it."

"I hope they called a doctor," mumbled the man.

"I'm sure they considered that, but they didn't. Instead, they put a call in to Father Cleary, and sure wasn't the good man there, by their side, in no time flat."

"Please tell me this story has a happy ending," implored Trask, the moisture from his perspiration darkening the pillowcase by the side of his head. Mercilessly, she continued without a clue for her audience.

"It wasn't long before the holy man became flustered, not having the slightest idea of what to do. You see, me Protestant friend, there is no patron saint you can turn to for losing a thermometer up a baby's arse…or, at least, the good man did not know of any. In the end, the town turned to prayer, and a few novenas were said for the child's future health and welfare."

"What happened to the child?"

"Aw, he was grand. You see, a month after the wee lad's miracle of a recovery, Mrs. Crowley found the thermometer between the cushions in the couch during her housecleaning. The baby's idiot father must have dropped it there between mouthfuls from his bottle of beer while watching over the poor, little creature." The handsome, black-haired man shook his head in disbelief and withheld comment. Layla reached over and swept his moistened hair back from his face. "And about now you're probably feeling sorry for yourself, and what this blasted flu had done to ye. Well, I'm telling you, it could be worse. You could be the Crowley baby and have an eejit of a father to take care of you. Now…open," she instructed, directing the thermometer up to his lips and slipping it under his tongue.

Rising from the edge of the mattress, Layla sauntered to the door and turned back. Philip Trask, unable to speak with the thermometer protruding from his mouth, had affixed his eyes on her.

"I must be calling Dick at the restaurant and tell him I won't be making it in at all today," she announced. "I'll check your temperature when I'm done with that business." Layla shuffled downstairs and went for the telephone. The dated, rotary phone rested on a copy of the Biddeford phone book. The twenty-year-old fanned through a few pages and found the listing for Billy's Chowder House. Within seconds she was waiting at her end of the line while Betsy tracked down Dick Varano. Her fidgeting by the phone stand was soon interrupted by the sound of her employer's voice.

"Layla, get me up to speed. How soon will we have you back here? We're busy as hell and understaffed with you out there playing nurse."

"Dick, I'm in a difficult position here with Mr. Trask. The doctor's said he can't be left alone until his fever breaks, and we don't know how high it might go when the sun goes down tonight."

"Are you telling me there's no one else he can get to come over?"

"That's what he says." A silence came at the other end of the phone that gave her reason for concern.

"I'd like you to come by my office a little bit early tomorrow. You will be here tomorrow I take it."

"Aye, Dick, I promise ye that," she blurted out. "He's a very good and important customer he is."

"That's not the point, now is it?"

"No, I guess it's not," she answered weakly.

"Remember, my office in the morning," he said, reminding her of their meeting.

"Will you be sacking me?" Layla asked timidly.

"If I were letting you go I wouldn't wait till the morning."

"I'll be there at ten forty-five, I will."

"See that you are." She heard the receiver go down at the other end of the line and knew she had tried her boss's patience. She had not been entirely truthful with the man when she had claimed that there was no one else to stay at his bedside.

Layla returned to her patient five minutes later carrying a pitcher of ice water. The bedridden man's eyes were closed and only reopened when her backside came down onto the bed beside him, bringing him out of a state of semi-consciousness.

"I'd like to see you putting away one of these every couple of hours or so," she stated, a reference to the clear glass pitcher. The redhead reached out and removed the thermometer from his mouth.

"It looks like a hundred and two and a half. That seems high for a daytime temperature."

"It feels warm in here," he remarked lethargically.

"It isn't, at least from my perspective," she added, pouring ice water into a glass and placing it on the table by the bed.

The girl looked up from a magazine as a fresh, ocean breeze blew the white, lace curtains horizontally by her ear and over her head. She was spread out on a couch in the all-purpose room, surrounded by a dozen open windows. The rain had stopped and the smell of the clean, sea air permeated the space around her. Layla had decided to let Philip get his rest and retreated downstairs. Now, with a half-dozen back issues of *Down East* magazine scattered about her, she grew restless. Dropping her feet from their perch on the coffee table, she strolled out to the kitchen. The clock read five minutes past four. Realizing she had not communicated a word back to her cousin, she picked up the phone book and looked up the Atlantic Coast Lodge. In seconds the phone was ringing.

"Atlantic Coast Lodge," sang out a familiar voice.

"Brian, tis Layla."

"I know, I know, you'll be needing a ride," he said hastily.

"Aye, but not till the morning."

"Morning! Okay cuz, what's up? And this better be good."

"You will never believe where I am."

"Out with it."

"I am down here no more than t'irty feet from the ocean, playing nurse-maid to none other than Philip Trask." Her statement was met with silence. "Did you hear what I said?"

"What do you mean playing nursemaid to Philip Trask? What does that mean?"

"It means I'm down here watching over him. He took violently ill in the parking lot at Billy's this morning. The doctor says he has the flu and needs someone with him overnight to monitor his temperature."

"And why is this you?"

"Just after you left me off this morning I saw him taking sick in the parking lot. He was supposed to meet someone for lunch but took violently ill beforehand. I went over and gave him a hand... drove him back to his house and all. Brian, he's got a bad dose of something."

"You left work and just went home with him?"

"He had no one. No one but me."

"What did Dick have to say?"

"I have to report to his office tomorrow before work. I'm sure he's going to eat me head off." The man let out with an extended sigh.

"Listen cousin, no funny business down there. Do you hear me?"

"Brian! How could you think such a thing?"

"Well, I know how you feel about the guy. That's all."

"Anyway, he's not in any condition to get off with," she explained.

"Layla, give a time and location to pick you up tomorrow morning."

"Nine o'clock would be grand, and I'll be standing close by the Grey Gull."

"Fine, and one more thing: Have you considered your situation right now and exactly what you've been praying for for the last month?"

"I'd have to be mad if I hadn't," she answered.

"That candle you lit at the shrine in Lowell... it's probably still burning."

"And Brian, would you be kind enough to drive back to Lowell and put it out? I won't be needing any more help along those lines."

"I'll get right on it," he came back sarcastically. "Remember, nine o'clock in front of the Grey Gull and no funny business. Understand?"

"Brian, he's half way to Saint Peter's gate."

"Good-bye cousin." She heard the click from the other end of the line and placed down her receiver.

Layla returned upstairs a half-hour later and found the water level in the pitcher approximately where she had left it earlier in the afternoon. Dragging a chair from the corner of the room, she placed it beside the bed and nudged Philip awake.

"Drink some of this water," she commanded, bringing the glass toward him. He struggled to raise his head from the pillow.

"Ooh, my God, my body is so sore. I think it's from the dry heaves I had back at the parking lot."

"Tis probably from a lot of things." He managed to swallow a third of the glass of water before collapsing back onto the pillow.

"I am so tired and weak. This is probably what people feel like when they're in last few hours of life, just slipping away."

"Listen to ye. You've got the flu and you need plenty of rest, and nothing more." He closed his eyes and let out with a sigh. Layla rose to her feet, circled the bed, and gazed out the window. "And did you hire an old man to come by and cut the grass?"

"Old man? What are you talking about?" he asked.

"There's an old man all dressed in black coming up the driveway, and sure he's carrying a sickle and looking up toward the bedroom window." Trask opened his eyes and glanced across at her, trying to process the meaning of her words. It only took a couple of seconds before he let out with a moan.

"I'm glad to see my sickness has done nothing to suppress your warped sense of humor," he said. "Most people would be showing a little compassion right now."

"Oh, and it's no compassion I'm showing! Well then, why don't you call some of those so-called friends I see you with at the restaurant? I could do with some reinforcements about now." Stepping back from the window, she walked toward the stairs.

"I don't even know your name," he called out as she reached the doorway. She froze in her steps.

"I told you me name."

"When?"

"When I waited on you a few weeks back."

"You can't expect me to remember your name from that far back, can you?" She turned back to him.

"I remembered yours," she replied, before descending the stairs.

Standing upon the front porch of the house, the redhead watched as the advancing tidewater washed over the field of rocks adjacent to her doorstep. It was early evening and the house's shadow from the lowering sun reached across the driveway and downward toward the Atlantic Ocean. It was amazing to her to think that this magnificent body of water before her extended three thousand miles to the base of Slieve League in Donegal. Stepping down from the porch and onto the road, she walked to the edge of the drop-off. Layla glanced down at herself. All evidence of residuel from Philip Trask's illness was gone, thanks to her efforts a few hours earlier. Her thoughts drifted back to Ireland and her parents. She would be returning to them in less than five months, returning to Donegal, and probably never setting eyes on Philip Trask again. The prospect of this brought on a painful feeling in her, hurtful to the extent of physical discomfort. She looked behind her, up to the window beside his bed, and longed to rest her eyes on him again.

Following a short battle to break them free, Layla emptied the metal tray of ice cubes into a bucket and marched upstairs. The house was growing dark with no direct sunlight making contact with Moody Point at this hour. Her entrance into the bedroom was met with no outward sign of acknowledgment. She circled the bed and sat herself down beside her patient. Philip appeared to be in a deep sleep. His coal black hair hung down over one side of his forehead. Tenderly, she brushed it back and surveyed his face. Incredibly, she thought, his perfect Anglo features held up under illness. She found herself wanting to lean down and press her lips to his. Summoning up a moment of strength, she drove this urge to the back of her mind and placed her fingers across his forehead. He was warm, she thought, perhaps even warmer than six hours before. She nudged his shoulder.

"You'll need to be coming around Philip. I need to take your temperature again," she explained. His eyelids flickered before opening.

"What time is it?"

"Somewhere around eight-t'irty. Open your mouth now, and let's get a reading." He followed her orders, allowing her to slip the alcohol tasting object beneath his tongue. Clearly weakened by his ordeal, he fought to keep his eyes open. "Would you be developing any sort of appetite?" Layla asked. He grimaced and shook his head no. She noticed that his eyes were trained on her, seeming to be taking in every detail of her face. "And what would you be gawking at? Do I have something hanging from me face?" Her words caused him to hold back a laugh. This was followed by a grimace. Two minutes passed and Philip Trask did little but stare at the woman watching over him. "Okay, let's see if you're dead yet," she sang out while reaching for the thermometer. She squinted her eyes and took an extended look at the reading. "It's up to a hundred and t'ree, it is. I don't like that." Reaching out, she laid her hand over his forehead. "And I'm not misreading the thing." Layla rose from her chair and removed two facecloths from atop the nearby bureau. The first cloth she packed in ice and laid it across his forehead. The second she dipped in the pail of ice, squeezed out the excess water, and reached for the man. His listless attempt to block her efforts were in vain. In one motion, she pulled the bedding down to Trask's waist and applied the cold cloth to his overheated body.

"Ohhh!" he cried out, his outstretched hand overpowered by the young woman's as she ran the cloth up and down his bare torso. She repeated this exercise for a short time before dipping the second cloth back in the frigid water and spreading it over his face. He ceased to offer any resistance.

"And what was running through your head back there when you kept staring up at me?" Layla asked. From beneath the outstretched face cloth came her answer.

"I was thinking that behind that outrageous deportment and morbid, sadistic sense of humor, there is a very pretty girl," he admitted. She felt her heart soar as she struggled to confine her euphoria.

"Oh, and I hope you don't think you're the first lad to tell me that," she responded, her thoughts spinning uncontrollably around in her head.

"Lad! You think I'm a lad? Well, I guess I should be flattered. Exactly how old do you think I am?"

"Oh, forty-five maybe...a wee bit younger than me da."

"Oh, thanks," Philip replied, sounding genuinely insulted.

"And sure, you know I'm just coddin' with ya."

"I'm thirty-one, and based on what you said a few seconds ago, I'm not the first to tell you how pretty you are."

"And sure didn't Timmy Brady once say he worshipped the truck that brought me manky knickers to the laundry." Philip contained a laugh, only to cry out in pain the next second.

"God, you've got a way with words," admitted the man before letting out with a groan. "I can't tell you how weak I feel."

"I want you to start drinking more water. That's what will bring down your temperature. Tis very high at a hundred and t'ree." He lay quiet for a moment, as if pondering the wisdom of his next sentence.

"I have never, ever been particularly fond of redheads," he admitted.

"That's because you've never, ever met the likes of me, Philip Trask," came back Layla emphatically. She rose from her chair and started for the door. "Now I want you to drink a pitcher every half hour till we bring your temperature under control."

"Please tell me your name," he asked, sounding genuinely sincere. She stopped and turned back to the bed. He had pulled the facecloth from over his face and was looking directly at her.

"Me name is Layla O'Malley and I'm from Glencolombkille in County

Donegal."

"You're only working here for the summer, aren't you?"

"Aye, and then I must go home."

"Thank you... for everything I mean."

"And sure, I haven't saved your life yet." He smiled. "And if it's all right with you, I'll be making use of the pink room across the hall tonight."

"That's fine. It's my mother's. She comes up and visits a couple of times every summer. My folks are divorced."

It was just after eleven o'clock when Layla retired to the pink bedroom. Across the hall, Philip was doing better. Two and a half pitchers of ice water and a series of ice-cold facecloths applied to the forehead had dropped his temperature slightly. Layla set the dated, wind-up Bulova alarm clock for seven and retired for the night. This would give her two hours in the morning to set up her patient for the day and still be on the road for Brian by nine o'clock.

XII

LAYLA WAS JOLTED UP to a sitting position and out of a deep sleep by the repetitive clanging from the alarm clock only inches from her ear. Reaching over, she fumbled to find the off switch before finally putting a halt to the ear piercing noise. The twenty-year-old closed her eyes and breathed in the refreshing ocean air streaming into the room through the iron mesh of the window screen. Seconds later her bare feet touched the linoleum floor and moved toward the small closet in the corner of the room. She had slept in a bra and panties and was now in search of something more substantial to wrap around herself. It came in the form of a pink robe hanging by itself from a single hook on the backside of the door. Stepping across the hallway, she stuck her head into Philip's room and found him semiconscious.

"Can I interest you in a cup of tea and maybe a slice of toast?"

"No food, please, and I know I've got some coffee downstairs. I'm not sure if we have any tea."

"No tea! And are the Trasks a band of muck savages?"

"Try the cupboard above the fridge. There might be some tea my mom left there." She nodded and turned to leave. "Oh, and mother...you look particularly nice in that robe."

Following a slow ascent of the steep stairwell, Layla turned into the bedroom carrying a tray crowded with breakfast.

"We will be having tea this morning, thank you. I've made toast for meself and included an extra slice or two in case someone gets hungry." She reached over, applying the palm of her hand to Philip's forehead. "You feel better than you did twelve hours ago," she announced. She poured the tea and added sugar and milk.

"I'm still dizzy but not as bad as yesterday, and, of course, weak."

"Now, if you'll be needing someone to get you to the bathroom, I'd suggest we do that now before I leave."

"Is there any way you could stay with me just one more day?"

"No, me boss will be eating me head off today at work as it is for missing yesterday. So why can't you call that brasser who told me to come out of the rain the other day? Something tells me she's not the hardest working woman on the planet."

"My friends are not the kind you might be accustomed to. They're social friends. We share a laugh."

"That makes them acquaintances, not friends. Friends are not just there in the good times."

"I suppose you're right."

Layla and Philip spent the better part of the next hour talking, about their work, families, and personal relationships. She learned that he did not own the house. His divorced parents owned the house. He learned the details behind her trip to the states and the importance of her savings program. At nine o'clock Brian drove to Moody Point and retrieved his cousin.

"It was grand of you to drive all the way down here for me," she stated as she stepped up into the cabin of the pickup. He rolled his eyes in a light-hearted fashion and pulled the Ford away from the side of the road.

"I must say, this is quite an accomplishment, Miss O'Malley." She giggled and tossed him a broad smile. "I'm thinking about our conversation just last Friday, and the utter hopelessness of hooking up with this guy. And now... this."

"Aye, tis quite amazing."

"Is the guy that sick?"

"As sick as a planeload of visitors to Lourdes."

"I was sort of only half humoring you when I urged you to keep praying for it," admitted the man. "I didn't see a snowball's chance in hell of you pulling this off."

"Oh ye of little faith," she sang out.

"And why am I taking you back to the house?"

"For me to take a shower and change. I have to be back at Billy's and up in Dick's office for ten forty-five."

Layla descended the stairs from her boss's office and hastily made for the front door. Entering the building, she was pounced upon by Donna who ushered her to the bench.

"Did you really spend last night with Philip Trask?" her friend asked excitedly.

"Aye, but only in the broadest sense of the word," Layla replied, shocked that the word of her time away was already public knowledge. "The man was flat on his back and dead to the world. It wasn't like we shared an evening over a candlelight dinner." Her friend sat quietly and waited on further details.

"You look really cute in the skirt and blouse," she added, glancing down at the girl.

"Thank you girlfriend. I've just spent the last ten minutes getting me head eaten off by Dick upstairs. I know I had it coming, and I told him as much. He said he might have sacked me if it weren't for the fact that customers are asking for me by name. When I said that was Mr. Johnston doing that he said there were quite a few more than Bill Johnston. I thought he was coddin' me but he insisted. So now it's up to me to put me nose to the grindstone and do me job. So why don't we get a copy of today's menu and the specials and study them together?" Donna agreed and they went in search of Adam Dillon.

"Oh, are you ready for this?" Donna asked excitedly. "I got on the scale this morning and I'd lost another three pounds!"

"Sweet Jaysus! How much does that add up to since we started this?"

"Nine pounds… nine pounds, Layla."

"We'll be losing you to Hollywood, we will. You'll be too gorgeous to be seen with the likes of me."

Layla scurried back toward the kitchen while her last party of customers made their way out of the building and into the parking lot. Donna had agreed to take on any last minute stragglers that Vickie might want to seat in her section. This left her free to punch out for the evening a few minutes ahead of schedule and bicycle down the road to see Philip. It was day three of his sickness and she expected him to be showing some real improvement, perhaps even be dressed, up and about. Excited, she pedaled frantically along the row of houses bordering Crescent Beach and then around the gentle arch of Fisherman's Cove. Reaching his driveway and the 'NO TRESPASSING' sign by the road, she sped in along the gravel surface until the bicycle tires rolled to a halt by the front steps. She looked through the windows, surprised the house was in darkness. She accessed the emergency key kept hidden on the porch and entered the house. Fumbling forward in the darkness, her outstretched hand made contact with a lampshade, allowing her fingers to feel their way down to the switch. In the next moment the living room was illuminated.

Layla quietly climbed the stairs, her sneakers allowing her to make no sound whatsoever. She reached the top of the stairwell to find Philip's room in complete darkness. She proceeded across the darkened room from memory, eventually reaching the man's bedside and turning on the lamp. She looked down to see him still buried beneath the covers, his three-day-old beard darkening his handsome face.

"Sweet Jaysus! I can't believe you're still lying there like a dying ninety-year old," she exclaimed in a loud voice. She placed her hand on his forehead. "Not a trace of a temperature and moaning he is like a whipped pup," she cried out to imaginary onlookers.

"I'm as weak as a kitten," he muttered. "I have virtually no strength, Layla."

"I have no strength, Layla," she repeated, mocking him in a less than masculine voice. He looked up at her and laughed.

"You are really something else," he said, staring up at her admiringly. She found a spirit of playfulness and exuberance gushing within her, no doubt brought on by the presence of Philip Trask.

"And sure are you mocking me, you sickly, little gobshite?" Layla followed up her words by mounting the man, pinning her knees to his ribs and holding down his arms by the wrists.

"Ohhh, God Almighty! I've barely eaten in three days. Take it easy," he pleaded.

"Oh, and wouldn't this be a good time to tell you who you're dealing with. I don't think I mentioned before that I was no less than a direct descendent of Granuaile O'Malley, Ireland's pirate queen. Back at the time of Elizabeth I there was another great woman who led men into battle, plundering and pirating on the open seas. Yes, a woman did this. And me da says that we are direct descendents of the great woman. Legend even has it that she had red hair like mine. So Mr. Trask, here you find yourself lying beneath a humble waitress, too weak to save yourself, and now you find out she's a direct descendent of a swashbuckling, pirate queen. I would say fate has dealt you a miserable hand here. Would you not?" The man lay transfixed beneath the weight of this young girl who only three days earlier was a complete stranger to him. He continued to stare up at her, the expression on his face bearing witness to the impact she was having on his mental state.

"Layla, would you kiss me?" She felt her heart literally pound inside her chest.

"What did you say?" she asked, wanting to hear the words again.

"Layla, would you please kiss me?" She did not answer him. Instead, she leaned forward and brought her lips down on his while simultaneously running her fingers through his full, black hair. Following two, uninterrupted minutes of bliss with their lips and mouths not losing contact with the others, she allowed herself to slump down onto the bed beside him. She lay beside him while his mouth explored her neck and delicate curve of her face.

"You smell wonderful. Do you know that?"

"I smell of the wildflowers around Glencolombkille, that grow there and on the side of Slieve League."

"It must be a beautiful place if it produced the likes of you," he answered.

"Perhaps we will be there together someday. That way, you can judge for yourself." They remained in a loose embrace for the next few minutes during which Layla drew his body closer, close enough to feel evidence of his heartbeat. Without warning, his hand slid down to her torso. It was abruptly stopped, her hand locking onto his wrist and robbing him of any movement.

"I just wanted to touch you," he explained calmly.

"There'll be no moving in that direction without me approval," she stated. She followed her reprimand with a final, light kiss to the lips before breaking the embrace and climbing to her feet. "'Tis late. Can I fix you anything before I head back to me cottage? I don't want to be pedaling around at all hours of the night."

"There's absolutely nothing left in the house," he reported. "Why don't you just stay the night?"

"I'll not be getting into that habit." She leaned down and kissed him a final time. "You could offer me the use of your car and I could bring you down groceries and make breakfast in the morning," she offered.

"I'd rather not—I mean, lend out the car."

"Suit yourself then," she answered, turning from him and making her way down the stairs.

The night air was cool as Layla bicycled the two miles from Moody Point to the Atlantic Coast Lodge. Her head was still reeling from the effects of her time in the embrace of Philip and from the feel of his lips pressed against hers. It was a dark night with no illumination from the moon and stars. By the time she reached Billy's Chowder House there were only two vehicles left in the parking lot.

The redhead let out a sigh of relief as the bike turned in between the stockade fence and onto the grounds of the lodge. Passing by the main house, she peeked over her shoulder and thought she saw her cousin standing in the office. Layla stopped and leaned her bike against the apple tree behind the building. Bounding up the steps, she opened the door.

"Sir, would ye like a spot of company?" Brian stepped out of the sitting room darkness.

"Oh, it's only you. And here I was thinking I had a late night rental," he answered.

"And sure is everyone turning their backs on me tonight?"

"I'm only kidding. You know that. Of course I'd like some company. Shall I put on the kettle?"

"Oh Brian, that'd be grand."

Layla sat across the table from her cousin, a pot of tea, milk and sugar cubes laid out on a metal tray between them. The complex's Route 1 sign along with the office were now in darkness. The building was silent, setting off the sound from Brian's spoon as it scraped against the bottom of his cup.

"If it's not a problem, I'll be using me key tonight to come in and call home."

"You know you don't have to ask, kid. That's why you have your own key." She nodded thank you and took a sip from her cup.

"I need to talk to someone cause me mind is racing out of control and I'm losing the ability to think straight," she confessed.

"Wow, there're only a few things that can do that to you."

"Brian, I'm feeling things so deep for someone that it hurts," she explained, her voice low and sincere.

"There's only one thing capable of doing that to you."

"Aye, and I can't believe something can make me feel so good, and scare me so much at the same time."

"It's the strongest emotion on earth, and we have no control over who we feel it for or how long we have to feel it. Scary stuff, cousin."

"Have you ever been in love with someone and had them not feel the same for you?"

"Oh yeah, it's called rejection and there's nothing to prepare you for it in advance or help you recover from it after the fact…only time."

"Well, I'm already thinking of having to go back home, and never seeing Philip again," she admitted.

"Things have a way of working out. Put it in the Big Guy's hands. Hell, He's already gotten you in the guy's house." Layla was about to mention the kissing and the time spent lying beside him in bed but wisely withheld any mention of it. "If things should ever progress with this guy and they start moving too quickly, I hope you feel comfortable enough to come to me first. I mean, this guy's been around…"

"And I'm just a twenty-year-old bogtrotter," she interjected.

"I'm just saying, don't be afraid to come to me for insight or advice. I know how guy's think, and I won't judge you or spread the word around. Okay?" Layla circled the table and hugged her cousin.

"I'd go mad without you, I swear."

Following her tea with Brian, Layla squeezed in two hours of sleep before her alarm went off, sending her back to the office. She made herself comfortable at the kitchen table then punched out the international phone number to the next continent.

"Hello," answered the familiar voice from three thousand miles away.

"Ma, it's Layla. Have I caught you two at a good time?"

"Oh dear, and didn't your father go to in to work early today, for the overtime. He'll be fit to be tied when he hears he missed your call," the woman explained. "And how are things going in the states?"

"Oh, they're grand. Me savings are over fifteen hundred dollars already, and we haven't reached the busy season yet."

"Well, that's very good to hear because your father's on pins and needles over this house thing."

"And why would he be any more than usual?"

"That would be because Mr. Connolly was approached by Sean Dolan about buying the house—offering to take it off of his hands immediately."

"And where would that eejit and his geebag wife come up with the money to do that?"

"The Dolans came into some money through an inheritance last month. He's interested in the house out of pure spite for your father."

"And where does Mr. Connolly stand on this whole matter?"

"Neal Connolly is an honest and fair man. He'll be giving us until the end of the year, as he promised, to come up with the deposit. After that, if we shouldn't come up with the money, he'll more than likely sell it to Dolan."

"Ma, you be sure to tell Da that his daughter has the matter well in hand."

"I will Love, and what about you? Have you had any time to do anything besides work?" Layla played with the idea of bringing up Philip Trask, but, decided against it.

"Last weekend I went down to New Hampshire and stayed with Brain and his wife. They had me sleeping with their little daughter and I even spent a little time at their pool," reported Layla.

"And what, may I ask, does their house look like?"

"It's grand. And don't they have a live-in servant, a girl from Doolin no less."

"And that wife of his... did she put on airs?"

"Actually, I like the woman. She bought me clothing while I was out visiting Massachusetts, and I can see she makes Brian happy. Yes, I had a grand time visiting with them."

"You know Layla, your father misses you something awful. He's not the same with you t'ree t'ousand miles away and across an ocean."

"And what's he going to do when I get married and move out?"

"Then, he figures, he can jump in the car and drive to Killybegs or Letterkenny and visit. Tis not like you'll be a continent away."

Mother and daughter went on for fifteen minutes before Layla called a halt to the conversation. She wished her mother the best and reminded her that she would return in less than five months. The complex was quiet this night as the girl tiptoed from the building and back to her cottage under a magnificent sky studded with stars.

On Friday morning, Layla joined Millie in the office, asking to use the phone. She placed a call down to the Trask house. Following four rings, the machine switched to a recorded announcement in Philip's voice, asking the caller to leave their name, telephone number, and reason for calling. The twenty-year-old complied and asked Philip to get back to her if he should need anything or want to talk. She left the office number of the Atlantic Coast Lodge as her own.

XIII

LAYLA OPENED HER EYES to the sight of the now familiar pine boards above her head. It was Monday morning and the start of another week. She extended her arms and let out with a yawn. Pulling back the curtain above her head, she looked toward the ocean and horizon and estimated by virtue of the sun's position in the sky, that it was about six o'clock. An instant later her mind was returning her to the same thoughts she wrestled with the preceding Sunday evening. She had not heard from nor seen Philip Trask since the previous Thursday night, the night of their romantic encounter in his room. Troubled by the passage of time without any contact with him, she had sought help the evening before from her cousin. He had counseled her not to go ahead with a plan to visit him unexpectedly at his house. When she had argued that the need to see him again was too great to endure, he had only underscored his advice all the more passionately. "Make him come to you," were his words and they were spoken without hesitation or any outward sign of doubt. An hour after leaving her cousin and in the privacy of her cabin, she burst into tears and wept for nearly half an hour, so great was the turmoil trapped within her. Now it was morning, and the relief from pain, that only sleep could bring, was over. The painful turmoil was back and she longed for the comfort of friendship at the restaurant.

Layla coasted into the parking lot of Billy's Chowder House in late morning and secured her bicycle by the back of the building. Reaching the front desk, she learned that she and Donna would work the back bay for lunch, which lifted her spirits. Making her way into the kitchen to clock in, she was verbally accosted by the unlikable Billy Souza.

"So paddy, what's this I hear about you spending the night with Philip Trask last week?"

"Ahh, and leave it to an eejit like yourself to make something out of nothing," she responded in a carefree manner.

"Never mind the chatter. Where do we stand with the chowders?" interrupted Adam Dillon and forcing the assistant cook to redirect his attention back on his job. Layla flashed the man a grateful smile while grabbing a list of the day's specials. She breezed through the swinging doors and caught sight of Donna spread out on the bench, her eyes closed.

"Me mate looks exhausted," called out the redhead, approaching her friend.

"My neighbors at the village I'm staying at are partying until all hours. They didn't quiet down until after four last night."

"And can't you call the garda and get some help with that?" Layla asked.

"The what?"

"Garda—the police."

"Yeah, I suppose."

"They've penciled us in for the back bay; both of us. We'll be working side by side, for lunch anyway."

"Don't tell me, Vickie's got the lounge again. Ever since they opened that new room, Vickie's gotten it four out of every five days. I don't think that's fair," complained Donna.

"And sure, we'll be fine. I haven't been given those tables yet, and I don't think I'm any the poorer for it," reassured Layla. "Now, wake up sleepyhead." She shook her friend's arm as she appeared to be drifting off.

"Let me fetch you some black coffee. We can't have you nodding off in front of the customers."

Lunchtime demanded a complete effort from the entire staff on this Monday. By twelve-thirty a waiting line had developed and the two, young waitresses went all out to keep the customers happy and the tables turning over in the back bay. Once the waiting line had subsided, Layla instigated a rivalry between two adjoining tables, promptly developing into a friendly yet boisterous contest involving the consumption of strawberry shortcake. It was activity like this that drew her mind away from problems of the heart. She actually found herself wishing that she could bring some of her customers back to the cottage with her in the evening, to help draw her mind away from Philip Trask.

She had just cashed out a pair of large tables and a cumulative gratuity of nearly thirty dollars when she looked up to see William Johnston being escorted to one of her small tables along the wall.

"And sure, me long weekend of prayers to Saint Layla, patron saint of biffos and bowsies, has been answered. Here is me own Mr. Johnston."

"And didn't last week you tell me she was the patron saint of bogtrotters?"

"You had better recheck your Bible, you. They'd be no saint assigned to bogtrotters. Those Jackeens in Dublin will have seen to that." The lobsterman gave out a polite laugh.

"There's no leaving you at a loss for words, missy," he declared, sitting himself down.

Layla playfully rolled her eyes as the transplanted Orangeman placed his repetitive order of fish chowder, extra crackers and a Bushmills and ginger, casting him a flirtatious wink before returning to the kitchen. On the walk out she was pulled aside by Donna, a serious expression creasing her pretty face.

"I thought you'd want to know that Philip Trask just came in with his usual crowd. They're out in the lounge." Layla felt her heart sink.

"And would you know if he asked to be seated anywhere in particular?"

"They asked for Vickie," answered Donna, her voicing tailing off to a whisper. Layla took a deep breath and proceeded to the kitchen, leaving the lobsterman's order. On her return back to the back bay, she shot a glance in the direction of the lounge and caught sight of Philip with his hand jokingly clutching Vickie's forearm. Turning from the scene, she slowly returned to her customers. Meeting Donna again in the hallway, she asked her to put in the Bushmill order for Mr. Johnston, not wanting to set eyes on Philip Trask or his friends. Donna agreed and Layla was spared the embarrassment of any direct contact with the man who was clearly avoiding her.

The redhead kept up appearances as she ushered a family of Canadian tourists from her station. The room was practically empty, the midday lunch crowd largely back to work or lying on the beach. After restoring order to a pair of tabletops, she meandered over to William Johnston. The man looked up at her from his newspaper.

"Is everything okay with you, missy?" Johnston asked. She flashed him an insincere smile and half turned from him.

"All right now; what's this serious face all of a sudden?"

"Oh, I just caught sight of someone that I could have gone without seeing." She stood over the table, her eyes now closed and a single tear running over her cheek.

"Oh, what's this?" asked the man as he spotted the single tear. He fumbled around the table before lifting the napkin from under his silverware and dabbing it on her face. The next second, the young woman was weeping, suppressed and barely audible, but still in tears.

"Come on now, no one's worth this," consoled the lobsterman. Layla leaned forward and rested the side of her face on his shoulder.

"You probably think I'm an eejit," she whispered.

"Nothing of the sort. Now you pull yourself together and show the world that you're stronger than this." She pulled back from the man and shot him a curious look, best described as an exaggerated pout.

"I'm sure you didn't come here today to be holding up the likes of me," she stated.

"Don't you think twice about it," he assured her, patting her hand as it rested on the table. "And how would that savings plan of yours be doing?" Johnston asked, attempting to take her mind off of whatever it was that was bothering her.

"I'm closing in on two t'ousand dollars. I've got a wee over nineteen hundred stashed away."

"You know, it's refreshing to see a young girl like yourself showing a little thrift these days. I didn't think any of you had it in you." Donna approached from behind Layla and delivered the lobsterman his drink.

"You know, I can't believe I'm letting this eejit even bother me. Clearly, he's an ingrate who has no interest in me or me friendship."

"Layla, if you want, I'll take care of any more business you have out in the hall or near the lounge. It's slowed down quite a bit and it won't be any trouble," offered Donna.

"I won't hear of it! I'll not be letting that gobshite put me or anyone else out of their way," she insisted.

"That's wise of you, missy. You can't be letting people of that mind know they've upset you."

"When mister high-and-mighty didn't return me phone call I asked me cousin Brian what I might do. He said not to call and show you're concerned. He said if the man felt anything for me then he'd call me back soon enough, but that I shouldn't come off as seeming desperate."

"Your cousin's a wise man," muttered Johnston before taking a sip from his drink. The waitresses took temporary leave of the dining area and meandered out by the front desk. Donna took a seat back on the bench while Layla checked up on Mr. Johnston's order in the kitchen. Walking across the floor, Layla resisted the temptation of catching a peek of Philip out of the corner of her eye and proceeded straight through the swinging doors. She grabbed the bowl of chowder, added to it an extra supply of crackers, and brought the lobsterman his lunch. Returning to the bench and her friend, she called out in a loud voice, "and sure you're getting as slim as me chances of dating Brad Pitt." Her girlfriend laughed.

"Four more pounds last week," she reported, before wrapping her arms around the Irish girl in a show of affection.

An elderly couple appeared in the doorway and was escorted by Susanne to one of Donna's window tables. Not wanting to be left sitting alone in the hallway, the redhead returned to check up on Mr. Johnston and see if he was in need of anything. Layla approached her lone customer at the moment, his eyes glued to the folded newspaper in front of him. He lifted his head at her approach, his lengthy, gray hair falling away from his shirt collar.

"Would you mind too much if I hung around your table for a wee bit?" He held back a laugh and motioned toward the other chair. "So, Mr.

Johnston, you never told me if you still had any family back in Portrush," she said, wondering if the man had any inclination to share any of his personal life with her.

"I have a sister. We're not on the best of terms," he blurted out.

"And why would that be?"

"We haven't spoke since the death of my mother."

"A squabble over an inheritance?"

"No, nothing like that. My parents were as poor as a church mouse. She got angry with me because I didn't go home for the funeral."

"And why was that?"

"You're a nosy little thing, aren't you!" exclaimed Johnston, in a voice best described as a dull roar.

"And sure if I didn't care I wouldn't ask."

"It was late spring and quite busy in the harbor. I couldn't afford to take the time away from the boat."

"And lucky it was for you that your mother didn't feel that way when it was time to raise you," she answered, her words visibly affecting the sixty-year-old man seated across the table from her.

"Right now missy, I think you're stepping a little over the line here," he admonished. In the next second Donna passed by and beckoned her friend back toward the hallway and front desk. However, Layla gestured her off, indicating she would join her in a minute.

"And how long has it been since you spoke to or wrote your sister?"

"Not since my mother's death; eight years it's been. She's in my will, and that's all she'd be caring about. I'm quite sure of that." The young redhead shook her head in disagreement and prepared her rebuttal before glancing up and noticing Mr. Johnston's eyes trained on something above and behind her. She turned in her chair to see Philip Trask standing over her, his haunting brown eyes making contact with her own.

"I managed to sneak away from the table at last. I'm sorry about not calling you back or getting in touch. I've been out straight."

"Oh, and I hope you didn't feel obliged to return me call. I just figured that not hearing from ye meant you were feeling better and I went back to me own business," Layla answered, forcing a light, breezy tone into her voice.

"Layla, listen, I'd like to make this up to you… for your time and effort down at the house."

"And don't you be giving it a second thought. You'd not be beholding to me for anything. It was the Christian thing to do and I'll have you not going out of your way for me at all. You've been through enough without thinking you need to repay me or something," she reasoned. Trask took a deep breath and rolled his eyes.

"Maybe I should get to the point here. The truth is, I'd enjoy taking you out, and I'd love to share a little more of your company."

"And you're saying this invitation is not because you feel beholding to me. Is that right?"

"Not beholding at all."

"Now, as it is, I work six nights a week. I'll be getting Thursday off this week."

"So then, will Thursday work for dinner and maybe a drive to Portland after?"

"Aye, and will I be sharing your company that night with your friends out there in the next room?" Philip laughed and shook his head.

"No…no friends on Thursday. Now, where shall I pick you up?"

"I'm living at me cousin's complex, the Atlantic Coast Lodge. It'd be directly across the street from Congdon's Doughnuts on Route 1. I trust you'll be able to find it. I'm in cottage fourteen. 'Tis next to the motel building." Philip smiled and half turned to leave.

"And shall I just stand around like an eejit all day and wait until you come? Or is there a time I can expect you?"

"Damn you. You have me coming off like a nervous teenager. Why don't we make it six o'clock?"

"That'll be grand. Six o'clock it is." The sculptor extended her a final smile, the well-practiced one he had trained on females for the better part of his thirty-one years, and made his way back to the lounge. Layla watched as Trask walked down the hallway and out of sight, then turned back to Mr. Johnston.

"Now was that the same man you starting bawling over just a few minutes ago?" The twenty-year-old blushed.

"Aye." Johnston pushed his empty bowl of soup across the table and snickered. "Now wait you, don't you be thinking I've forgotten what we were talking about before that one interrupted us. There's a matter between you and your sister that has to be sorted out. Do you know that me mother would never go to bed at night after an argument with me da without making up. 'Never let the sun go down on your anger,' she would always say. And here's you and your sister, going eight years without speaking."

"Missy, this is none of your business," insisted the lobsterman.

"Me, I know what your mother would have wanted, and it's not having her two children not speaking. I'll drop it for now, but you haven't heard the last of this from me. I won't let you rest until I know you're going home to Portrush to see your sister…for Christmas. Is that clear?"

"In a pig's ass you will," he answered. "Oh, and see to it I get a refill," he insisted, pushing his glass to the edge of the table. She surveyed him for a moment before responding.

"I'll fetch ye your Bushmills, but only because I'm in such good form, thanks to me date on Thursday." Layla spun around and stepped away.

"I can always stop asking for you when I come in," he called out to her.

"In a pig's arse you will," she volleyed back, exiting the room to the sound of the man's gravel sounding laughter.

Two hours had passed since the conversation with Philip, and Layla was still radiating from the prospect of an evening with the man. A temporary lull in customers sent her out to the parking lot for a few breaths of ocean air. Standing on the backside of the restaurant, she eyed the deep, green grass of the marsh as it framed the blue tidewater that licked the back of the property. Unexplainably, she felt the presence of another and turned. Behind her, standing eight or ten feet away, was Wesley, the dishwasher who was hired a short time after her.

"Tis nice to breathe the cool, fresh air," she called out to him.

"Yeah. After a couple of hours in that hot kitchen this is a real treat," answered the young man while moving tentatively in her direction. "I don't think we've ever been introduced or even said more than two words. My name is Wesley Wright."

"And I'd be Layla O'Malley." She reached forward to shake his hand. He appeared quite nervous and only applied a partial grip, catching only the ends of her fingers.

"Oh, I know who you are. Everybody knows who you are. You stand out."

"Tis the red hair. It doesn't permit you to simply blend in."

"Oh no, don't put your hair down. It's quite gorgeous," he admitted while awkwardly laboring over his words. "Actually, it's more than your hair that makes you stand out... even more than being so pretty. You just seem to put more into your job than the other girls." She laughed but did not respond. In that moment Layla picked up on nervousness in the lad, an uneasiness usually born of a fear of rejection. A second later she found out she was correct in her assumption. "I was wondering Layla, if we should ever have any time off together... if you would consider going out with me?" The words out of his mouth, he must have felt as if they hung in the air around them for an eternity. The twenty-year-old looked at him sweetly and placed her hand on his arm.

"And sure if I'm not flattered by your words, and under slightly different circumstances I'd be happy to go out on a date with a well-mannered, fine looking young man like yourself, but, the truth is, I'm presently hung up on another lad, seriously hung up on him, and I'm going to have to see how this all plays out before I can turn me attention to another." Her heart ached in that moment as the disappointment registered on Wesley's face. "But, I'm wondering if you'd be interested in joining me friend Donna and me mornings when we go out bicycling? It's for sure we'd love to have you and it's a good time to get to know each other better."

"I'd love that," he replied, his face brightening from the young woman's show of kindness. The redhead threaded her arm under his and started them back toward the entrance.

"If Dick should look out his window and see us down here, he'll be docking our pay. I'm already on probation for a stunt I pulled last week."

"You're on probation?" Wesley asked.

"Double secret probation, like the hooligans in the *Animal House* movie were," she added with a wink.

XIV

IT WAS LATE MORNING under a warm, June sun when Layla locked the door to her cottage and made her way to the office of the Atlantic Coast Lodge. There, she was pleasantly surprised to find both Brian and Millie working together on this day.

"The company must be doing especially well I'd say to afford to be paying both of you management types at the same time," observed Layla, entering the room and immediately collapsing on the couch.

"It's called a salary, one wage for a limitless number of hours, and that's how your slave driving cousin plans on working me into an early grave," muttered Millie, displaying her dry, Yankee humor.

"Quiet there, Mildred Pierce, and wouldn't you have had to drop dead back in 1977 for it to still qualify as an early grave?" Brian responded, flashing the woman a smile and scurrying into the next room.

"You'd better run after a crack like that," answered the silver-haired woman, pretending to be upset. "Will I put on some tea, dear?"

"Not for me, Millie. Actually I came over to see if you needed help with anything. I have the day off and I'm not expecting me date to arrive until six. So, I'm free to provide some inexpensive labor."

"Did you say date?" chimed in Brian.

"Aye. It'll be me first date with a Yank."

"Anyone I know, or have heard about?" Brian inquired.

"Philip Trask."

"Philip Trask, the artist?" Millie asked.

"Aye, the same."

"He comes from a very good family," said Millie, visibly impressed by Layla's potential suitor.

"Very good family... meaning they have money," cracked Brian from a chair in the next room.

"And that'll be quite enough from our friends out in the peanut gallery," replied the woman. "Don't you be listening to him. He's just jealous because he comes from Lowell and not Beacon Hill. Now Layla, what you have to be careful about is not letting yourself become overly impressed by the likes of Philip Trask and his fancy, polished ways." Layla, sprawled out on the couch, burst out in a melodic laugh.

"And sure, after you've seen a bloke sit in a puddle of his own vomit, tis no small task for him to be putting stars in your eyes." Her words brought a burst of laughter from the adjoining room. Millie looked curiously over at Layla, then out toward her boss. It was clear to Layla that her cousin had not shared the details of her experience the prior week with his close friend.

"Anyway, from what I've heard about that young man and the crowd he associates with, he could use a good, Christian girl like yourself to settle him down and get him on the right path," stated the woman. "And, he's from a good family."

"Come on Mill, just say what you mean: dazzle this guy, take his money, get a ring on your finger, and get him back going to church. Isn't that what you're trying to say?"

"She could be doing a lot worse things than getting a godless creature like himself back on the straight and narrow. I never said anything about money, mister know-it-all."

"And doesn't this remind me about something me da told me on more than a couple of occasions. He said, don't marry for money, but don't go courting where it's not present." Brian broke out in applause, expressing his appreciation for his cousin's tidbit of wisdom.

"That's even better than my old adage: don't marry for money, you can always borrow it cheaper." The words were barely out of his mouth when the door to the office pushed open and a middle-aged couple entered the building.

"Welcome to the Atlantic Coast Lodge, folks. I'm Brian Kelly, the owner. The stern looking woman behind the desk is Millie, our assistant manager and someone I'm deathly afraid of. And the redhead to your left who just abruptly jumped to her feet from the couch is Layla O'Malley, our resident lazy, good-for-nothing, who just lounges around all day tossing out witty, Irish sayings and looking pretty. Are you looking to rent a unit?" The man and woman chuckled in response to the unusual greeting, and walked to the front desk.

Layla sat fidgeting in the deck chair on her porch, waiting on the arrival of Philip Trask. For the first time since her arrival in Maine, she wore her favorite, single item of clothing, a form-hugging, white and red silk dress. Accessorized in white, two inch heels and an off white handbag, she felt quite comfortable in her own skin on this evening. A warm breeze was making it's way up the hill from Wells Harbor below, sending the wind chimes hanging at the corner of the porch into a random series of notes. The twenty-year- old listened for the sound of Philip's automobile through the beautifully chaotic sound from the chimes hanging only a few feet away.

Ducking her head inside the cottage door to check the time, her senses were suddenly assaulted by a commotion of male voices rounding the motel building. She turned to see her cousin leading two other men in the direction of the screened porch.

"Layla me love, there are a couple of gents I wanted you to meet, my two closest friends in the whole, wide world." The redhead focused on the two men, both appearing to be a few years older than her cousin, and both carrying open bottles of beer in one hand. "First, this is Perez, my oldest friend, going all the way back to my days in Lowell." She smiled and nodded to a man of her approximate height with dark, suntanned skin and graying hair.

"It's nice to put a face with the name," the man said politely.

"Aye," she responded, thinking back to the story of these two men during her visit to New Hampshire and their interesting collection techniques.

"And this is Bobby, my friend from Maine and our youthful days of unemployment: skirt chasing, more unemployment, bikini chasing at Old Orchard Beach, and, yes, still more unemployment. We literally met in the unemployment office."

"Brian, I'm sorry to break this to you, but little red here clearly got all the looks in her wing of the family, and half of the looks in yours," exclaimed Bobby while his eyes took in every inch of the young, Irish girl. Layla returned the man an uncomfortable smile. Bobby, like his partner, was suntanned and significantly shorter than Brian. His hair was long, extending well over his shirt collar. His narrow face sported a three-day-old beard.

"Cousin, you look absolutely stunning. And I'm sure the last thing you want is for us three fossils standing around your place when your date is due to arrive." Brian's words were punctuated by the sound of a car engine being turned off at the rear of the cottage. "Oops, too late I think." A car door slammed shut and in the next instant Philip appeared from around the building. His eyes, initially drawn to the circle of men surrounding the porch, quickly shifted to Layla who sprang to her feet.

"You found me house," she said softly, her blue eyes already trained on his handsome face.

"The line of potential replacement dates was already forming, in case you were a no-show," joked Bobby. Trask ignored the man's words and moved toward the porch.

"I'd like you to meet me cousin. Brian Kelly, this is Philip Trask." Brian stepped forward and shook the man's hand. Trask returned the handshake and smiled politely, showing Brian more respect than his friend Bobby. "And these are his friends, Bobby and Perez." The men gestured but made no attempt to shake the sculptor's hand. Sensing an uncomfortable moment brewing, Brian reached around his two friends and playfully directed them away from the cottage.

"Why don't we leave these young and semi-young people to each other's company," said Brian as he moved with his buddies back toward the main house.

"No funny business tonight, Phil. We'll be getting a full report from red, and we know where you live," hollered Bobby from behind the motel and halfway back to the office. Trask extended his date an astonished look and shook his head in disbelief.

"And sure he's just coddin' with you," assured Layla, slightly irritated by the man's deportment. "Would you like the grand tour?" She gestured him toward the door. He followed her inside, his eyes immediately scanning the small, eleven by eleven foot room.

"It's cute, with all the creature comforts," he commented. "And you've got a great view from the porch." She flashed him a grin.

"And sure the view from the porch is nothing compared to me view from the bedroom." She directed his eyes upward to the sleeping loft. "You're dressed too nice to be climbing up there tonight, and I'd show you how easy it is to get up to me bed but then you'd be seeing me knickers." Philip smiled. "And I'd prefer to have you guessing about the color of me knickers and not seeing them," she added, patting him playfully on the cheek and returning to the door and out onto the porch.

"I know your cousin from somewhere, but I can't remember where," said Philip, rejoining his date on the screened porch. "Shall we be off?" asked the man, his arm resting casually on his date's shoulder. She looped her arm around his waist and squeezed. He let out with a groan.

"Are you hungry?" Philip asked as they deposited themselves in his car.

"I could eat an old man's arse through a blackthorn bush," blurted out the redhead. He chuckled.

"We'll have to see if it's on the menu," he came back dryly.

Philip did not follow the direct route to his destination point for dinner, Kennebunkport. He turned the car right at a traffic light on Route 9 and directed the vehicle toward the beaches at Kennebunk. Layla sat back and took in the meticulously maintained homes and perfectly manicured lawns.

"You know, you're the first, bona fide redhead I've ever gone out with," he confessed. She reached across the front seat and cupped his chin in her hand.

"Poor baby, they all turned you down."

"No, nothing like that. I mean, I've never been attracted to redheads. I've just never found them particularly appealing."

"And does that mean when you sat down and watched *The Quiet Man* you couldn't see what *John Wayne* saw in that ganky *Maureen O'Hara?*"

"No, I'm not talking about movie stars and celebrities. I'm talking about everyday people on the street. I've never found myself that stimulated by females of your type. However, you are clearly the exception to the rule. Oh, that golf course to our left, that's where former President Bush plays when he's staying at the house on Walkers Point." Layla leaned forward, taking in the expanse of fairway and a foursome lining up their putts on a green close by. Thirty seconds passed and the vehicle approached the crashing surf on a small beach largely void of people.

"Will we walk the beach after dinner?" she asked.

"If that's what you'd like to do...absolutely."

For the next mile the roadway traced the edge of the coastline. Layla was again struck by the difference between the shoreline here in southern Maine versus her own coastline back in County Donegal.

"Oh, I think I remember why your cousin looked so familiar to me. Last summer I kept seeing him with this absolute knockout. I mean, this woman looked like a model right out of a magazine. I kept seeing these two at Billy's on the weekend.

"'Tis his wife, Margaret. I spent the weekend with them at their house in New Hampshire a couple of weeks back." She glanced over at the man just as his eyes shifted to her. He smiled and shook his head.

"You know, I had already been talked out of making contact with you again when we came by Billy's a few days ago."

"Oh really. And who would have talked you out of that?"

"The usual suspects, Deidre, Eric, Jonathan."

"Deidre...so that's the little witch's name."

"And there I was sitting with them at lunch, and all everyone's doing is gossiping about this one or that one. I thought back to those three days you came over, and how the conversation was nothing like that. You're very funny, you know." She played with the idea of doing her *Joe Pecci* impersonation from *Goodfellas*, the 'do I amuse you' routine, but decided against it.

"It was just me, being meself."

"That's what's so great about you—the way you're so comfortable just being yourself. May I make a confession?"

"And does it involve some kind of physical deformity that's going to impair me appetite?"

"No, I'll save that for after dessert. Layla, I was sure you'd be all bent out of shape when I came over to you at Billy's the other day and asked you out. I was sure of it. And there you were, just shrugging it off." The pretty redhead smiled over at him innocently, masking thoughts of her crying fit at Mr. Johnston's table and the wisdom of her cousin's advice.

"And for sure, I may not be like any other woman you have ever known. Be careful around me, I make me way into men's blood and you'll pay a brutal price trying to get me out." He turned his head from the road, bringing his hand up slowly and tenderly pushing strands of red hair back from over her eye. He grew silent. From that silence she knew inroads were being made. She was penetrating his thoughts, feelings, and to some extent, perhaps even his heart. She was entering into the arena of human emotion, a place where men and women have waged war for centuries. At stake would be her complete happiness. At risk, the possibility of becoming a casualty of this magnificent war, and the prospect of a painful recovery from the wounds which affairs of the heart, gone wrong, will exact.

Layla sat quietly while the vehicle passed over the narrow neck of water separating Kennebunk from Kennebunkport's Dock Square. It was her second visit to this attractive township with its clustered shops set amongst majestic inns and exquisitely maintained, historic residences. Brian had taken her here more than a month before, but now the sidewalks and grid work of 'ONE WAY' side streets were filled with strolling visitors. Philip carefully motored the car through an opening between buildings, finding his way into a parking lot that sat along an interior body of water.

"Don't move," he said, bounding from the driver's seat and circling the car to open the door for his date. He escorted her across the parking lot and through a wooden walkway between the dated seaside buildings replete with retail shops. Exiting the alleyway, he directed her into Alisson's Restaurant.

"If we have to wait for a table, it shouldn't be a long one," he assured her.

There was no wait on this evening. The hostess walked them by the bar toward a small table in the lounge. Their entrance was accompanied by the turning of heads, Layla's radiant red hair and perfectly fitting silk dress commanding the attention of males and females alike. She felt the attention and her spirits soared.

"And sure Philip, you're turning more than a few heads, you are." The man reacted to her sense of humor, leaning over her shoulder and whispering 'thank you' into her ear as they approached the table for two.

For the next hour and between bites of their food, the couple provided each other with more detail of their respective lives. Layla learned that the primary market for Philip's art were individuals who wished to immortalize themselves or a loved one by having a life-size bust made in their likeness. The sculpture, it was theorized, would be passed down through the generations of the family. Some, Philip thought, also saw this as a way of stopping the aging process by freezing the individual in time. For this, he was paid handsomely. Layla, on the other hand, spoke little of her job at Billy's Chowder House or her quest to save money for the purchase of the family's home. Instead, she shared her remembrances of growing up in Glencolombkille and the considerable time spent roaming the mountainsides around her home.

"It would be grand if I could take you up to the mountaintops around

Slieve League with a lunch basket and we could spend the day lying in the grass and breathing in the fresh air blowing over us off of the bay. There's a waterfall far away from the main path where we could lie and gaze down at the glistening water as it falls hundreds of feet and out of sight." Philip listened to the young woman's words while the small candle on the table sent fluctuating rays of flickering light over her face.

"Do you have any idea how mesmerizing and hypnotically beautiful you are at this moment?" he asked. She placed her fork back on the table and reached over to him, her hand caressing his cheek. "Oh, and there's that special scent of yours," he added, commenting on her perfume.

"Careful now Mr. Trask, don't you be getting too carried away."

"My friends say I'm developing a Florence Nightingale syndrome, because of you nursing me those three days."

"And did you tell them where I threatened to put your thermometer or how I sat on me patient when I thought he was foosterin' around in bed?"

"No, I left those details out."

"Maybe that explains why those three eejits were blatherin' about this Florence Nightingale rubbish," she theorized as she carved a slice from her strawberry cheesecake. Philip interrupted a brief lull in the conversation by casually breaking off a small piece of his date's dessert and spooning it into his mouth.

"By the way, what's the story with your first name? That's not exactly a name you associate with the Irish," he observed.

"Me da is a big *Eric Clapton* fan. It was his idea to call me Layla, and he's quick to add that I'm named after the rock n' roll Layla, you know, by *Derek and the Dominoes,* and not the easy listening one," she explained.

"I can see that. You're not exactly an easy listening sort of girl," he concluded.

The room around them was alive with the sound of conversation when the waitress returned to the table and asked if they would like anything else. Philip ordered another martini, his third, and Layla requested a cup of coffee. She was thankful for the opportunity to extend her time in the restaurant. She truly felt beautiful, the subdued light in the establishment enhancing the comeliness of not just her, but every other woman in the room. Her spirit soared every time she turned her head and found someone's eyes trained on her.

Only seconds after the beverages arrived Philip excused himself and set off for the men's room. Layla took this time to glance deliberately around the room. The age makeup of the patrons reminded her some of the people she might expect to find in a pub back home. That is, anywhere from nine to ninety. She turned away when she caught sight of two men seated at the bar, both sets of eyes unquestionably focused on her. A few feet away, an elderly couple rose from their chairs and made their way in her direction. Stopping just over her shoulder, a woman with bluish-white hair leaned over to speak to her.

"Pardon me dear, but aren't you the Irish girl who works at Billy's Chowder House?"

"Aye, and this is me night off."

"See, I told you that was her," she snapped at the man. "My husband didn't think so. Oh, my dear, you look much prettier with your hair down like this," added the woman.

"Well, tis nice of you to say so. And I'm sure it helps not having to duck me head in and out of a one hundred degree kitchen every ten seconds." A second later her date rejoined her at the table, a little taken aback by the attention being showered on her. On his arrival, the elderly couple excused themselves and complemented the redhead a final time.

"My little superstar," he said before taking a sip from the martini.

"Tis nice to hear strangers flattering you once in a while." Philip ran his finger around the top of his glass, giving the impression he was running something over in his mind.

"Is there any chance you might come back with me to the house and spend the night? It's a beautiful evening and we'll have the ocean crashing at our doorstep. I make a hell of a breakfast for my overnight guests."

"I'd be thinking you have two chances for that to happen: slim and none." Layla cupped her hand around one ear. "And did you hear the sound of that train whistle in the distance? That'd be slim leaving on the eight forty-five train to Dublin. So, I guess that'd leave you with none."

"No Layla, seriously, I see something happening between you and me... long term."

"And is it a brasser you see me as? Your a fine thing, Mr. Philip Trask, and I too think this could be going somewhere... long term. Now I'd love to go back to that fine house of yours and watch and listen to the ocean come crashing in over the rocks. But, it'll be a goodnight kiss you'll be getting tonight and nothing like what I think you're alluding to."

"You can't be serious. Layla, we're grownups here, not a couple of high school kids."

"It's clear you have no idea what a goodnight kiss from a girl from Donegal, and a direct descendent of the pirate queen herself, Granuaile O'Malley, is like. I promise you, you've had nothing from the sad lot of American girls, like that geebag Deidre for example, to compare me goodnight kiss to," she declared. Layla looked across the table and thought she picked up on an attitude coming over the man. "Now don't you be putting on a long face. That shite's not going to work on me. You look around this room and into the face of every red blooded male here. I'm thinking there's not one of the lot who wouldn't trade places with you right now." Trask responded with a disinclined smile.

"You truly look beautiful tonight," he admitted. She reached across the table, running the tips of her fingers through his hair.

"And there's no one I'd rather be here with than you," she added.

Out in the parking lot Layla offered to drive, owing to the three martinis her date had with dinner. Philip vehemently refused. It was a beautiful night and the two decided to drive back toward Wells with the windows down. They had just crossed over the town line and into the lower village of Kennebunk when a couple signaled to them to cross the road. The man and woman, clearly tourists, were profoundly overweight. The two signaled thank you in unison and awkwardly scurried to the far sidewalk. Inside the vehicle, Trask snickered and rolled the car slowly forward.

"All you can eat buffet, two doors down guys," he called out sarcastically before hitting the gas and speeding up the road. Layla reached back and cuffed him on the arm.

"What's the matter with you? Why did you do that?"

"Did you see those two?"

"You malignant gobshite."

"I was only kidding," he explained defensively.

"It was a cruel thing to do." He let out a sigh and shook his head in disgust. "Me best friend at Billy's is overweight. Do you think that way about her too?"

"Oh please, Layla. Can you honestly tell me that you would be out with me tonight if I looked like that guy back there?"

"Yes, if you had a good heart and was good to me."

"That's absolute crap. We're out together because we're both physically attractive. Please don't insult my intelligence and tell me otherwise." Layla glanced over at Philip but withheld a response, sure his words were born of the alcohol in his system. Plus, there was none to be given. She knew, buried deep inside his cynical words was more than a grain of truth.

The conversation was guarded over the half-dozen or so miles back to the house on Moody Point. Layla broke an extended period of silence as the car crawled up the private driveway toward the oceanfront home.

"I'm sorry I smacked you on the arm back there," she apologized. "I lost me temper for a second."

"Aren't redheads supposed to be noted for that?"

"Aye, I think we are. But you disappointed me when you called that business out of the window. I have a much higher opinion of you than that."

"It was probably a stupid thing to do," he admitted, shrugging his shoulders and tossing her a flirtatious glance.

"And what I don't want you doing is getting all nervous and uptight thinking about the goodnight kiss. When it comes, it comes... and they'll be nothing you can do to stop it, and I have reason to believe you'll not want to be stopping it." His eyes widened as a befuddled grin spread across his face.

"So you weren't joking back at Alisson's when you talked about your goodnight kisses?" She blushed back at the man.

"If I like a lad, I have a problem holding back. Do you want to hear a story about how mad I can get?"

"You have me curious now."

"In sixth grade I developed me first crush on a boy. His name was Jimmy Cunningham and he had a gorgeous face, he did. The sisters organized a dance for us at the parish hall and didn't I dance with Jimmy five or six times. After the dance, a few of us were still waiting for our rides and didn't I coax Jimmy around to the side of the hall and out of sight of the nuns. I got so excited that I pressed me lips on his and must have kissed very hard. Apparently, our feet got tangled and didn't I fall on him, all the time keeping me lips on his mouth. Then, somehow me legs got wrapped around his body and I must have been squeezing pretty hard. I was so excited, kissing me first lad, that I lost control of meself. When the nuns heard the mayhem around the side of the building they came running and pulled me off of the boy. By this time Jimmy was hollering for someone to help him, and I swear there were tears in his eyes. Me ma and da got an earful from Sister Mary Patrick, they did." Philip stared into her eyes, taken in by the account from her days in junior high school. He followed up by looping his arm around her shoulder.

"Where does this zest for life come from? It's like being out with a high school kid."

"Tis only been a couple of years."

"That's right, I almost forgot. Would you care to see my studio here at the house?"

"I thought you did all that in Kennebunkport."

"I do a lot there, but I also have a studio here behind the house." Using his arm, he directed her around the porch and out behind the building. Behind the house and resting against the backside of the garage was another small, wooden structure. Trask pulled a set of keys from his pocket and opened a weathered, wooden door. A second later he managed to find a switch against a wall of darkness and the shop was illuminated.

"I don't meet with customers and clients here, and I certainly don't have anyone do any posing here, but some work's not as critical and doesn't require the subject in front of me, so that lets me work right here at the house." Layla strolled casually between a few benches, feigning interest in her date's occupation. He walked up behind the redhead, dropping his arm over her shoulder as he had done a few minutes earlier.

"May I make a confession to you?" he asked. She turned her blue eyes on him and gestured him to continue. "I entered last weekend with absolutely no intention of getting back to you or asking you out."

"Is that right," she purred back at him.

"And then, Sunday night rolled around and I was back at the house, just dubbing around, and I caught myself hoping that you'd show up at my door or even just call. The house was as quiet as a tomb and I just had this desire to see you standing in the doorway or chattering about upstairs with one of your crazy stories from home."

"Don't you be feeding me that rubbish. I think you missed having a girl come up to your room and jump on top of your carcass," she countered.

"Yes, I must admit that was quite interesting. I mean... you barely knew me."

"And sure I knew in the condition you were in I could have easily kicked the shite out of you. I'd grown a wee bit fond of you and wanted to see if I could lift your spirits." He shook his head and innocently planted a kiss atop her head, drawing in the pleasant fragrance from her reddish, auburn hair.

"Another confession; coming right up," he blurted out.

"Out with it."

"All my life I've been attracted to a girl..."

"And sure that's a relief," interrupted Layla.

"Let me finish. All my life I've been attracted to a girl, only to find out after a short while that I'm bored by her. I mean, I've dated a lot of beautiful girls, but more times than not I wind up dropping them because I've become totally bored."

"And sometimes, do they not, become bored with you?"

"Oh, I'm sure a few of them have, like the ones who dropped me before I got around to dropping them."

"So why are ye telling me all this, Mr. Trask? Are you preparing me for the inevitable?"

"No, not even close. I'm telling you this because I can honestly say I cannot imagine anyone becoming bored with the likes of you. You, young lady, are a remarkable woman, not to mention being physically attractive." Layla leaned into the man, her hand cupping the back of his head as she brought her mouth in contact with his ear. Applying moderate pressure with her teeth, she tasted his skin before shifting her attention to his mouth.

After securing the studio the two walked back to the front of the house. The tide was advancing on the mainland, sending the surging ocean water up against and through the haphazard collection of boulders strewn along the adjacent shoreline. She asked him to take her for a walk. They strolled northward along Fisherman's Cove where the roadway almost taunts the sea to invade the line of houses rimming the tiny inlet. The road there is buttressed by a cement wall set behind a battery of huge boulders, placed there no doubt, by some civil authority to suppress the ocean. For the most part, the Atlantic obliges. However, on occasion, the sea storms against the will of man, causing the roadway and homes to be evacuated and resulting in a cleanup effort some time after the ocean has composed itself and returned to its normal self. Early on, Layla claimed the brim of the cement barrier, walking barefoot along the two-foot wide path, Philip on one side clutching one hand and the Atlantic on the other, the salt water advancing and retreating a few feet below her. On a couple of occasions the spray of ocean water reached the two, once drenching her feet and the second lightly spraying both and dampening their clothes. This second act of aggression by the sea prompted Philip to wrap his date in his arms and carry her for the remainder of the walk in the same manner a groom would transport his bride over a thresh hold.

The ocean was putting on a visual and audible show less than a stone's throw away when they arrived back at the house, the roar of the surf causing each to speak louder and listen more intently than usual. Layla glanced at her watch. It was a minute or so in front of ten forty-five.

"Tomorrow's a workday for us both and it's getting a wee late," she said, allowing a trace of regret to come though in her words. He glanced down at his watch but said nothing. "And now you'll have fulfilled your requirement of taking me out, being it is I nursed ye back to health and probably saved ye from an agonizing death." He leaned against the railing of the porch, looking out to sea and avoiding eye contact.

"I'm wondering if you might have reconsidered staying the night. With the surf the way it is, it's a hell of a romantic evening." Pulling him back from the edge of the wooden porch, the redhead deposited the man in one of three wicker chairs.

"I'll not be staying the night," she answered, standing over him and scanning every detail of his face with her suddenly intense eyes.

"Then I guess...," his words stopped in mid sentence as she climbed atop him, her mouth pressed to his and her knees pressed into the front of his torso. In a split second her fingers were gripping his hair, allowing her to manipulate the movement of his head. She kissed him with a reckless aggression, her legs and knees punctuating the streams of passion running through her.

"Me bloodline is one of aggression and strength and at no time do I feel it more than when me blood burns for the body of another. Tis another side of me altogether. But, this I'll be giving to only one man and not for any Joe Soap that shows up on me doorstep." She pressed the side of her face against his cheek and drew in a deep breath. Meanwhile, her strong legs pressed into her date's stomach muscles, causing him to resist. She brought her perform-ance to a close by returning her lips to his while raising her body upward over him, the force of her kiss pushing his head back against the chair and caus-ing it to topple backwards. A second later she came down upon him amid the crashing of the chair to the floor. "Sometimes I think there's a banshee pos-sessing me, and she comes out when the passion in me rises," she confessed as he lay matted under her.

"What the hell was that?" Philip asked, sensing the eye of the hurricane had passed.

"That was your goodnight kiss," she answered. He gazed up at her, a dazed expression stamped on his face.

"So that story about the boy in sixth-grade who you scared after the dance, that was not a crock."

"Aye, this is me nature. If I feel for someone, it comes out. Tis the O'Malley blood in me." She rose to her feet and assisted Philip to his. She brought her head to rest on his chest, her eyes dropping in a show of contri-tion. "You probably think I'm quite mad?"

"Exciting... unpredictable... incredible... but not crazy," he assured her.

"It will be an adventurous man who ties himself to Layla O'Malley in the end, it will," she announced, her warm breath delivering the words into his chest. "Tis a sign that I feel something for ye when I come off that way."

XV

THROUGH THE HUMID AIR of a Maine morning, Donna Pento's bicycle came into sight as she coasted down Mile Road and into the parking lot of Billy's Chowder House. By now, Wesley Wright had joined the two girls on their tri-weekly bike exercises around the area.

"I'm up for a ride all the way to York," called out Layla, her skin shining from the application of sun block covering it.

"Do we have time?" Donna asked.

"We'd be cutting it real close," chirped in Wesley.

"Okay, then what if we go as far as the Cliff House? That's only halfway between Ogunquit and Short Sands in York," reasoned Layla. The three agreed and set out along the coast.

"Oh, guys, are you ready for this? I got on the scale today, and it's another two and a half pounds! I've lost sixteen pounds already since I started this dieting and exercise," proclaimed Donna.

"Janey Mack! Me friend is going to turn into a raving beauty and I'll be losing her. And sure won't you and Vickie be spending all your time exchanging beauty secrets and putting down all the plain Janes you have to work with."

"I have you to thank, Layla, for everything. You got me going with this. And, of course, I still have a heck of a ways to go. If I can drop twenty-five more pounds I'll be down to about one hundred and twenty-five. Oh, and wouldn't my mother go nuts over that. She's coming up to visit in a couple of weeks. She won't believe what I've already done, losing sixteen."

The day was overcast but with no imminent threat of precipitation. The three bicycles moved along in single formation, passing Fisherman's Cove and taking the incline up to the high ground at Moody Point. Layla withheld comment as they pedaled past the Trask house, content to keep the detailed memories of her visits there to herself. They had just coasted down the hill that brought them back in direct touch with the blue, Atlantic water when Donna raced forward and pulled up aside Layla.

"I've got a big favor to ask of you," stated Donna. "And I don't want you to feel like you have to say yes." Layla glanced over to her friend and beckoned her to continue. "You know how those jerks in the next cabin to mine have been having regular parties for the last month and keeping me awake. Well, they're finally getting evicted on July first. That means two more days of noise all night and drinking and breaking beer bottles. I was wondering if you could put me up for the next couple of nights? I'd rent a motel room but it's in-season and it'll cost me an arm and a leg. Plus, I'm really scared of what these lowlifes might do before they leave."

"Hey, what are you two whispering about up there?" Wesley called out from ten yards back.

"And aren't we planning our attack on you and how we'll divide up all of your money," hollered Layla. The redhead turned back to Donna. "And wouldn't I be worthless as a friend if I couldn't put herself up for a couple of nights when she was in need. I'll give you your choice of sleeping on the bumpy convertible downstairs or next to me up in the loft."

"Layla, you're just the best," answered the relieved brunette.

Reaching Ogunquit Village, the threesome stopped in front of the pharmacy and decided on an ice cream soda to quench their collective thirsts. Donna was left on the sidewalk to guard the bicycles while Layla and Wesley stepped inside to place the order. Ten minutes later the trio were seated on the sidewalk bench, sipping on their cool beverages and observing the wide assortment of people passing by them.

"Layla, you haven't mentioned your savings program in a while. Where are you at with that?" Donna asked.

"T'irty one hundred dollars, and most of it safely in the bank. Me cousin made me open an account here when he heard I was hiding it under the mattress in the loft."

"You've saved that much already this summer!" exclaimed Wesley.

"Aye, and sure it doesn't hurt having me cousin give me the cottage for nothing and saving me t'ousands in rent," she said.

The three employees of Billy's Chowder House spent twenty minutes on the bench before Layla gulped down the last of her ice cream soda and proclaimed an end to their pit stop. The threesome then remounted their bikes and wove their ways through car and foot traffic to the shore road leading to Perkins Cove. They made good progress, the slope being largely in their favor, and turned onto the shore road linking Ogunquit to York ten minutes later. This narrow and twisting road proved more of a challenge, requiring them to pump vigorously on more than one occasion. The three were in tight formation on one of the few, level stretches when Donna tossed out a feeler.

"Is anyone as interested as me in going to see *The Truman Show.* It's playing right now in Wells." Layla glanced back at Wesley, hoping to prompt a reply from him. The redhead had precious little time to spend with Philip as it was and did not want to commit to anything she would regret later.

"I'm sorry, but it isn't me cup of tea," she answered. She turned back to Wesley a second time, attempting to nudge him into action. He pedaled on, muted by his own insecurity.

They had just navigated a particularly treacherous series of bends in the road when the redhead extended her arm outward, signaling the mini convoy to stop. To their right was a golf course, the smell of recently mowed grass filling the air.

"Herself is in need of a breather," she declared following a long, deep breath. The three dismounted their bicycles, balancing them against a crop of small trees that lined the roadway. They were only a few steps away from an expanse of deep, green grass, the likes of which only a meticulously maintained golf course could provide. Layla walked slowly into a shaded patch of perfectly maintained grass and turned back to her friends.

"Tis heavenly, this spot," she purred. Then, she approached Wesley, an angelic smile on her face. His mouth dropped open in amazement and wonder while his eyes remained fixed on his Irish friend. Her approach, simultaneously sweet and coy, left him partially hypnotized. Upon reaching the bewildered young man, she curled her leg through his and brought him to the ground in a thud beneath her. Sitting atop the stunned dishwasher, she called out to Donna to join her. Within seconds Wesley Wright's torso was supporting the weight of both young women.

"Now unless you want the next foursome to see you lying here like an eejit under two little girls, I think someone should be asking someone else out to the cinema," declared the redhead.

"I must have died and gone to heaven, cause here I am lying under not one, but two beautiful girls. Pinch me someone, I must be dreaming."

"Ah, the little bowsie's a glutton for punishment, he is." Layla shimmied higher onto his shoulders, pinning his arms and rendering them useless. Reaching down to the ground by the side of his head, she tore up a handful of grass and sprinkled it over the young man's face. Her actions caused Wesley to explode with laughter as he tried to blow the blades from around his mouth. "Me beautiful girlfriend here needs an escort to the cinema. Now stop being an eejit and ask her," demanded Layla. The lanky young man continued to resist.

"You're getting grass in my mouth and up my nose," he called out, albeit through continued laughter.

"And didn't me ancestors have to eat the same during the famine. You'll be getting no sympathy from me you miserable bowsie, you," she joked. "Donna, do you think someone's enjoying this treatment a little too much?"

"He doesn't seem to mind it at all," she responded, now staring down at the dishwasher.

"Donna, would you do me the privilege of going to the movies with me?"

"Wesley, this is so sudden. I'll have to think it over," she answered. A second later the three heard the sound of a golf ball make contact with the ground. Fifty feet away, a dimpled ball sat in the middle of the green.

"Incoming rounds!" Layla cried out. "And shall we free our captive before the golfers arrive or let him endure the humiliation of having two little girls use him for a park bench?"

"Maybe we should let him up," agreed Donna, hoisting herself off the lad and assisting her girlfriend to her feet. The boy remained on the ground for thirty seconds, gazing up at his two female friends.

"You girls are a lot of fun, do you know that?"

XVI

L AYLA FELT HERSELF drawn from a deep sleep by movement next to her in bed. Still far from awake, she reached over and made contact with a warm body. It was Tuesday morning, the last day of June. This marked the end of two months in Maine, two months away from her parents and County Donegal. She closed her eyes for a moment, a sense of tiredness trapped behind her eyelids. They had been up talking well beyond midnight, robbing her of normally early retirement. The redhead crawled to the bottom of the mattress, peeking down at the clock on the ground floor. It was after eight o'clock, considerably later than the usual time she would rise for the day. She let out with an extended yawn and descended the ladder.

Up in the loft, Donna remained silently asleep. Reaching for the kettle out of habit, she froze for a moment, then grabbed for the coffee stored over her head in the cabinet. Donna was her guest and deserved consideration. In all likelihood, her friend was a coffee drinker. Layla measured out the ingredients for four cups of coffee and clicked on the brewer. The redhead had just begun picking up the living area when a figure appeared at the door, visible through the curtains hung over the pane of glass. She quickly threw on a robe and went to the door. Squinting through the curtain, she made out Brian standing out on the porch.

"Brian, what a pleasant surprise," she whispered, not wanting to awaken her friend.

"Can you join me out here, please," he answered, a serious overtone present in his voice.

"Aye", she said, ducking through the door and joining him on the tiny porch. He sat down in one of the two chairs and gestured to her to join him. She did so, with growing apprehension. "Is everything all right?"

"I don't know. Is it?" While not angry, her cousin displayed an uncharacteristic temperance.

"I don't understand your meaning."

"When your folks let me bring you over here and sort of act as your guardian, I think they expected me to act on their behalf. When I pulled in this morning, Millie pointed out the small problem we seem to have."

"Would you be meaning me overnight guest?" she asked innocently.

"That's precisely what I mean."

"Tis only for a couple of nights, no more."

"I want this jerkoff out of here in an hour, along with his crappy car and its 'Born to be Wild' and 'If you don't like my driving call 1-800-EAT SHIT' bumper stickers. What the hell were you thinking Layla? Would you pull this crap around your parents?" Tears welled up in the girl's eyes as she stared across at her cousin.

"I should have asked for permission. Tis my fault for that. But I've done nothing like you might think." At that instant Donna appeared in the doorway, a sheet wrapped around her like a toga.

"She was just helping me out, Mr. Kelly. The car belongs to my brother who's stationed in Germany until March. He's letting me use it but he's told me not to remove or change anything. I'm assuming he means the bumper stickers too." Brian's eyes moved from the stranger standing in the doorway down to his cousin. Layla sat quietly, unsuccessfully trying to hold back the tears that were welling in her eyes. Visibly shaken himself, the man let out a sigh, closed his eyes, and rose from the chair. Taking a couple of steps toward the door, he halted and placed his hand on Layla's shoulder.

"I am so sorry about this. I hope you can forgive me for being so stupid."

"Aye," she replied, wrapping her arm around him and pulling their bodies together. He planted a kiss on her head and disengaged himself.

"I'll go tell Millie. She's equally stupid on this count." He gestured his regret a final time before disappearing behind the motel building.

Sometime after ten-thirty the girls locked up the cottage and headed for work. They piled into Donna's sedan, both head's of hair still wet from showers. Donna circled her vehicle out from behind cottage fourteen and started toward the driveway and Route 1. They stopped to allow a guest to back out of his parking spot only to be hailed down by Millie from atop the stairs to the office. Layla opened the passenger door and planted one foot on the pavement, her head extending above the roof of the car.

"I hope you'll accept an apology from an old biddy who should have known better," the gray-haired woman called out.

"I would, if there was an old biddy on the premises. Tis already forgotten," Layla called back, a wide grin creasing her face. The redhead fell back into the car and it pulled away.

Billy's Chowder House was organized bedlam on this day. The summer heat was upon the region and the Fourth of July loomed over the coming weekend. Shortly after noontime a line developed by the front door and waitresses found themselves assigned additional stations. It was on days like this that the girls would lend each other a hand, sensing if another was falling behind or possibly becoming rattled. In the kitchen, the temperature was approaching one hundred degrees, causing tempers to flare at the slightest provocation. The spiraling temperature on this day was particularly hard on the expediter, Dave Newcombe, the extra pounds he carried acting as an anchor in carrying out his duties. For this reason, Adam Dillon had instructed Billy Sousa to join him and lend a hand to the obese man. Ninety minutes into this blitz of activity, Layla came through the swinging doors to check up on the status of one of her orders for a table of six. She was covering the dining room on this day. Her inquiry brought her into close proximity to Sousa. It was then that the wisecracking, assistant cook picked up on the scent of her perfume, no doubt a welcome break from the steady parade of seafood aromas wafting up from the customer's plates.

"Jesus paddy, you actually smell good today. What do you have on?"

"Me manky knickers, you mangy gobshite," she blurted out, sending Adam and Dave into spontaneous laughter.

"What did she say?" asked Sousa, still not accustomed to the girl's Irish jargon.

"She says you seem to be drawn to a pair of her dirty underwear," explained Adam. Sousa looked up to see the redhead stopped in the doorway, her eyes locked on him.

"And sure it's a pathetic creature you are, Billy Sousa," she added before disappearing behind the doors with her tray full of food.

The lunchtime rush continued through two o'clock before any sign of slowing. At two-thirty Layla emerged from the kitchen and spotted William Johnston seated at one of her small tables. She brought her tray of food to the waiting customers and snuck up behind the lobsterman, tugging twice on the back of his shirt.

"And what are you doing letting them sit you anywhere but the back bay. I know that's your favorite of the rooms."

"They sat me here," he growled back at her.

"I think someone asked to be seated at his favorite waitress's table. She'd be the one with red hair who knows enough not to take any of his malarkey."

"The devil you know is better than the devil you don't know," he explained without lifting his eyes.

"Shall I bring ye a menu?"

"A large bowl of chowder with extra crackers and a Bushmills and ginger."

"And have you rung your sister back home yet and told her you were coming home for Christmas?"

"I have not."

"Are you going to make me write her meself and get this terrible situation sorted out?"

"Oh, and wouldn't she be delighted hearing from a total stranger, telling her to call her brother and invite him home for Christmas."

"We're not going to know until we try. All right then, I want you to give me her address and I'll drop her a line. If you don't, I'll be haunting you like the ghost of Christmas past. I'll give you no peace."

"If it'll get you off my back, I'll give it to you. But then, leave it alone."

"All right then, I'll put in your order. A fish sandwich and a Guinness it was, right?"

"Off with you," he barked, recognizing her sense of humor and letting her heckling go.

The mid-afternoon slowdown in customers was short lived. By five-fifteen a line had reformed and the staff again was pushed to the limit. Donna was working the back bay and the two friends would only catch glimpses of each other entering and leaving the kitchen. Layla had only spent a couple of hours with Philip over the weekend. She was hoping to see him over lunch, at a minimum, but neither he nor his friends made an appearance on this day.

Donna was seated on the bench, her head tilted back from exhaustion, when Layla cashed out her last customer and joined her by the front desk. The redhead walked up to her friend and extended a hand.

"Take me home before I collapse right here on the floor," said Layla.

"Oh, thank goodness I have one more night with you and I'm not going back to my place. I'll bet they'll be drinking until sunrise tonight," she predicted, lifting herself up from the bench and walking toward the door.

Donna steered the sedan through the entrance as the vehicle rolled slowly through the complex. There was a light on in the office but Layla had already decided to make it to bed early on this night. The car had just passed the main house when a light from her cottage grabbed her eye. Upon closer scrutiny she was able to determine that the porch light was on in cottage fourteen. This piqued her curiosity. When the vehicle lurched to a stop behind the cabin, she jumped from the car and made her way toward the porch. On arrival, her eyes focused on a bouquet of flowers propped up in front of the door. Opening the porch door, she snatched the card resting atop the collection of white, pink and red roses. "A token of my regret for doubting what I already knew about my Irish cousin...Brian."

"Is it from Philip?" Donna asked when she reached the porch.

"No, it's from me cousin."

"There's something stuck in the door," added Donna. Layla lifted her eyes and spotted the pink slip wedged in the door. She snatched it down. Her tired eyes widened reading the message: 'Philip called. Can you join him on

Thursday night for dinner and some time walking the beach?'

"Tis been a grand day," she sighed, pushing her key into the lock and nudging open the heavy, wooden door.

The two young women slipped out of their working clothes, sitting side by side on the couch in their underwear. Layla pulled out her leather tote, her receptacle of choice to carry around her working cash and, at the end of the evening, her accumulated tips. She reached in and pulled out a fistful of paper currency. Donna crossed the room, pulled her day's gratuities from her pocket, and rejoined her friend. With childlike enthusiasm the two friends counted out their stockpiles.

"Janey Mack! Me tips came to one hundred and sixty-one dollars!" exclaimed Layla. "I don't believe it."

"One hundred and forty-three," countered Donna, holding the bills up in front of her and spread out like a fan.

"And sure you don't have one hundred and forty t'ree," disputed her friend. Layla reached over to the brunette's stack. "And won't I be taking eighty dollars for rent, and ten dollars each for food, coffee, clean laundry, parking, the use of me shampoo, and lastly, the privilege of fetching me clothes from the clothesline this morning. I think that comes to one hundred and forty dollars," she clowned, plucking the money out of the pile. "Ah, the joys of being a landlady." She tossed the cash back into her friend's lap and stared up at the pine boards above her head. "Tis been a grand day, it has."

The young women did not retire to the loft immediately. With the television on for nothing more than background noise, they prepped themselves for a night's sleep, taking turns applying skin cream in front of the bathroom mirror and discussing the day's happenings. They clicked off the evening news just as it was being introduced and climbed the ladder up to the loft. They had barely settled in on their halves of the mattress when Donna rolled onto her side and addressed her friend.

"In three and a half months you'll be going home and none of us may ever see you again. Will you miss us and aren't you going to miss Philip?" Layla did not respond for a moment, perhaps considering how much of her true feelings she was willing to share with her new friend.

"The question of Philip Trask and how I can ever bear to leave him behind has already begun to haunt me. I'm not lying when I say I've never felt anything like how I feel for that man. I'm afraid I love him so much it hurts," she confided, rolling onto her side and away from her bedmate.

"Do you think he feels the same about you?"

"He feels something for me, but I don't know if he's even capable of the feelings I have for him," she admitted.

The young women slept in the next morning, neither stirring until Donna began playfully running her fingers through her Irish friend's long hair. When Layla punched at her pillow Donna broke the long night's silence.

"I love the color of your hair," she admitted. The redhead rolled onto her side and faced her guest.

"And you're getting lovelier every day, me swan, me work in progress." The brunette stretched her arms and yawned, setting off a chain reaction from her friend. Layla edged slowly toward the bottom of the bed.

"Last one down loses her tips," she called out, scrambling down the ladder and pulling it away from the loft.

"Come on Layla, put it back," insisted Donna from her perch seven feet above the room.

"I'll be putting on a kettle for us and pouring us out some cereal," announced Layla, turning on the cold water and filling the yellow kettle resting atop the burners. A few seconds later, she was maneuvering the ladder into place and allowing her houseguest to descend from above.

The young women were seated at the small table by the front windows, eating corn flakes and sipping on their warm beverages.

"Just think, by now those hooligans are out of the other cottage and you can go back to living in peace."

"I guess," she responded unenthusiastically. "You know, I wish there was some way I could stay with you here. I'd be willing to pay you rent." Layla's eyes dropped down to the rim of her cup and she grew serious.

"Donna, having you here has been grand, but it's not really me cabin to start with, and I'd be out of line to be extending it to someone else when me cousin is giving it to me for no charge in the first place." The brunette nodded, indicating she understood, but made it known by her expression that she would prefer to stay. "Oh, and when are you and Wesley going to the movies? Have you set a day yet?" The question was asked more to change the current subject of conversation than by any nagging curiosity on her part.

"Friday night. I have the whole day off and Wesley's getting out of work early so we can make the show at nine-fifteen," reported Donna disinterestedly.

"Did you know that he went out of his way to thank me for pushing the issue? He told me how he's been noticing all the weight you've been losing and what a pretty girl you're turning into." Donna smiled dimly.

"I probably shouldn't be telling you this. Do you know who I think is kind of handsome?" Layla shook her head and beckoned for a name.

"You're cousin, Brian…for an older guy I mean."

"Now don't you be batting those pretty, brown eyes around me cousin, and talking him into giving you me cottage, and tossing me out to sleep in the storage shed with the field mice." The brunette laughed and walked across the room to the medicine cabinet mirror just inside the door to the bathroom. There, she stared at her image for a few seconds, admiring it as if for the first time. The matter of allowing Donna to permanently move in to cottage fourteen was dropped with not a word spoken on the subject in the days and weeks to come. Although she chose to not comment on the issue, Layla felt a certain proprietary attachment to the tiny place that she was not willing to share, even with a devoted friend. However, when she was honest with herself, and these moments of honestly largely arose on those occasions when she sat alone within the confines of these four, knotty pine walls, she recognized the value of her cousin's attention and guardianship. This she saw as a blessing, and something she was unwilling to share with anyone, no matter how close.

XVII

SUMMER HEAT TEMPERED by cool, evening breezes off the ocean was the order of the day as the July pages were torn from calendars and the last full month of summer began. The beginning of August also marked the start of Layla's fourth month in the United States. She was scheduled to leave Maine in mid-October, meaning she was more than halfway through her work stay. Layla's cash savings topped five thousand dollars, meaning she was on schedule to return home with her goal of eight thousand dollars. Long working hours by both her and Philip Trask somewhat stunted the growth of their personal relationship. Over the preceding weeks the Thursday night date had become a foregone conclusion. In addition to this regularly scheduled time together, Layla would bicycle down to the house at Moody Point after work, totally unannounced, at least once a week and on two occasions she found the sculptor waiting in the parking lot for her at the end of her shift.

Wesley and Donna by now had grown closer, their connection adrift somewhere between platonic and romantic. By August, the brunette had shed an astounding thirty-one pounds and was beginning to draw attention from a variety of males who frequented the restaurant. In addition to the three bike rides per week logged by the trio of friends, Donna had taken up jogging and was frequently spotted running along the beach in the early morning hours just after sunrise.

It was Tuesday morning and Layla decided to have breakfast over at the main house with her cousin, or Millie, or both. She crossed the yard and skipped up the stairs leading to the office. Inside, both Brian and Millie were milling about, attending to details involving the complex.

"I'm not here to make a nuisance of meself, but instead thought I might be of some help to someone. I've barely had a moment to speak to you two for the last couple of weeks and I've missed ye," announced the redhead.

"Make me some porridge you mangy, little bogtrotter, and toss some more peat on the fire," roared Brian from the kitchen door.

"'Tis already seventy-five degrees out there and you'll be wanting a fire?" Layla asked, plopping herself down on the couch. "It's just that I'm in particularly good form today."

"And why is that sweetheart?" questioned Millie.

"Last night when I left work, who do you think was leaning against me bicycle?"

"Whose bicycle?" Brian injected.

"Who do you think was leaning against me handsome cousin's bicycle?" He peeked around the corner from the kitchen.

"Handsome, huh? Don't fall for me kid; I'm nothing but trouble."

"Those are not me words, but Donna's. I think you made an impression on the girl when she stayed with me at the cottage a little while back."

"So let me get this straight. Your little boyfriend was standing by my bicycle hoping to get a glimpse of me, no doubt having heard the glowing reports from Donna about your handsome cousin." Layla let out a howl.

"Millie, and how can you put up with this one's madness?" she called out. "The man was waiting on me by the bicycle because he said he couldn't go another day without laying eyes on me face, and hearing me speak to him."

"How old is this guy?" Brian asked sarcastically. "He sounds like a lovesick teenager. Miss O'Malley, what have you done to this pillar of the community, or at least the artistic wing of it?" She smiled up at her cousin who was now propped in the kitchen doorway. "Hey red, where's my porridge?" The girl sprang to her feet and scurried toward the kitchen.

"I didn't think you were serious," she blurted out, ducking under her cousin's arm and making for the cabinet.

"Millie has me working on our linens all morning, meaning I'll be down in the basement feeding the washers and dryers until noontime, if not later. I need my energy." By now familiar with the Atlantic Coast Lodge kitchen, Layla found the ingredients and a pot and began preparing the man his breakfast.

"And you won't mind if I make a little extra for meself and Millie, your grace?"

"No, go ahead. I have a long history of showering my subjects with acts of kindness," he joked back. The young woman flitted around him while he worked at the table, using a small calculator to run a series of numbers and scratching the results on a piece of paper in front of him.

"Do you know that I've been in the states over three months now and I still haven't met Jenny and Brendan yet?" Brian stopped in mid-calculation and looked up at her in astonishment.

"Really? That's absolutely insane," he commented. "That's right, they were hiking when you visited and now they're both working full-time back home."

"You'd think they'd want to stay at the beach house some weekend or something," reasoned Layla.

"Okay, we'll set a goal for ourselves here. By hook or by crook we'll get you to meet them before you have to go home."

"It would be lovely speaking to Jenny. Didn't she spend a summer in number fourteen like I'm doing?"

"Yeah, she did. But she wasn't staying there alone like you. A girl named Trudy Abrams stayed with her. I rescued them from some jerks down in Ogunquit and moved them up here." Layla stood over the stove, watching over the breakfast as it simmered.

"Have you been keeping up with your phone calls home?" her cousin asked.

"Aye. I've yet to miss a week and they always send their best wishes to you."

Brian cleared away a small stack of paperwork from the table as his cousin prepared to ladle out his oatmeal. The slim redhead placed down two additional bowls and proceeded to fill each vessel to half capacity.

"Where's me brown sugar," squawked the man, deliberately adopting his Irish cousin's habit of abandoning the possessive pronoun.

"Don't you be barking at me," she snapped back, giving his shoulder a shove with her hand. She fumbled through the cabinet and came up with a covered dish containing individually wrapped packets of brown sugar.

"And where's me milk?" he added sarcastically.

"Sweet Jaysus! You're turning into a regular Cromwell, you are," she cried out, opening the refrigerator and delivering a plastic gallon of milk. "Millie, I've poured you out a bowl for yourself. Can I bring it to you?"

"No child, that won't be necessary," she called out from the front desk. "I'll be in in two shakes."

A minute after dishing out the warm cereal, Millie joined the two at the kitchen table.

"So kid, what do you have on the agenda this week?" Brian asked, closing out a pause in the conversation.

"Philip has said he'll be taking me out for a fancy dinner on Thursday night. He's keeping it a secret but I told him it'll have to be somewhere we haven't been to because I only have that one good dress and I'll be wanting to keep up appearances."

"Why don't you just spring for a new dress?"

"I'll not be doing anything of the sort. Every pound has to be going toward the house back home."

"Now there's a refreshing thing to be hearing from the younger generation, someone who can practice a little thrift. Most of the young people in this country act like their money's burning a hole in their pocket," added

Millie. The girl looked up from the table, giving the woman an appreciative smile.

"Oh, and Donna's mother is supposed to be coming by Billy's today or tomorrow to see her daughter and to meet me. She hasn't seen Donna since May, and she doesn't know about her diet and exercise program."

"How much weight has she lost now?" Brian asked.

"Over t'irty pounds. She's not just bicycling with Wesley and me t'ree times a week but jogging on top of that. She's turning into quite the beauty she is."

"And all this just to impress me," mused Brian, reaching over the table and giving Millie a squeeze on the arm.

"And sure I should never have said anything to you about Donna," confessed Layla, shaking her head in regret.

"What is this business all about?" questioned Millie.

"It seems that our Layla's little friend, Donna, thinks that I am incredibly—*incredibly* handsome," reported Brian.

"Stop the lights! And where are you getting this whole *incredibly* thing? She said that you were slightly good-looking, and didn't she qualify it by saying...*for an older man.* I seem to remember that."

"Oh God, me world is crumbling," he answered dramatically, clutching at his heart.

"And, come to think of it, she was quite bollixed at the time and talking all sorts of rubbish."

"Someone shoot me. I have no reason to live anymore," he whimpered. His cousin reached over and playfully grabbed for his hair.

"I'll be missing this lovable eejit when I go home," she confessed to Millie, grabbing her cousin's hair and good-naturedly tossing it about.

The warm air and humidity covered Route 1 like an oppressive blanket when Layla turned her bicycle down Mile Road and coasted toward work. The only movement of air on this day was a mild breeze from the west, and that was as warm as the inland ground from over which it came. Her red hair blowing behind her from the movement of the bicycle, she reached the middle of the wildlife sanctuary and Billy's Chowder House in less than three minutes, thanks to the favorable incline and the pumping of her legs. Her bike secured by the side of the building, she cleared the front door and made for the time clock, waiving at Donna who sat by herself on the bench. After punching herself in, visiting a few seconds with Wesley, and tossing Adam a wave from across the room, she exited the kitchen and joined Donna Pento on the bench in the front hall.

"Did you actually run in this heat this morning?" Layla asked, depositing herself next to her friend.

"Yeah, but I scaled it back to a couple of miles, and I took it pretty easy," she answered, extending her tanned legs out from under the seat and in full view.

"Sweet Jaysus, Donna. I swear you're beginning to look like those girl tennis players on the television. You've done a brilliant job with your dieting and exercise." Donna smiled at her friend and shot her a curious smile. "Is everything all right with you?"

"My mother's coming by later today...for lunch or dinner. She wasn't too specific."

"Oh, and wait till she sets her eyes on you. She won't be believing what she sees." Again, Donna responded with the same, unusual smile.

"I'm in the lounge today. You're working in the back bay with Lori." Layla shrugged her shoulders, gesturing that it made no difference to her.

"But you'll be sure to bring your ma over to meet me, won't you?"

"Oh sure. I've told her all about you over the phone. She's dying to meet you." In the next instant, Layla hopped to her feet and bounded back into the kitchen. She returned to her friend a few seconds later carrying a list of specials for the dinner menu. The redhead handed the brunette a copy before scanning over her own.

"Do you and Wesley have anything special planned for Friday?" Her eyes still trained on the menu, she waited on a response. Finally, she looked up at Donna when no reply came to her question.

"If I let you in on something, do you promise not to tell it to anyone?"

"Aye, I'm your friend and I wouldn't gossip on you behind your back."

"Billy Sousa's asked me out on Friday. He's only working half a day and he wants to take me down to Portsmouth for the evening. There's a club there he's really high on and he wants to show it to me."

"And how does Wesley feel about this?"

"Wesley doesn't know, of course, and the last thing I want to do is hurt his feelings. I'm going to come up with some kind of excuse why I can't see him Friday, and go with Billy. We'll be out of town, so there's no chance of running into him." Layla looked into her friend's face, staring intently into her eyes. "I hope you won't be judgmental, Layla. I mean, it's all well and good for you to preach from your high horse, dating one of the best looking guys on the planet."

"Did I say anything judgmental?" answered the twenty-year-old, her voice just above a whisper. Donna shrugged her shoulders and looked away. "I almost wished you hadn't said anything to me. I'm afraid it could put me in a bad position later on," she confessed.

By eleven-thirty customers had begun trickling in, sending Layla and Donna to different parts of the restaurant. On two occasions when the paths of the two young women crossed in the kitchen, the redhead gave the brunette a playful pinch on the rear end, showing she was not harboring any sort of bad feelings for her friend. Donna responded both times with a silly face, she too, not wanting the situation to cause any animosity between the two young women.

At approximately one forty-five Layla, laboring under the weight of a well-stacked serving tray, returned to the back bay and spotted William Johnston out of the corner of her eye. The redhead maneuvered her way to the table of five, slipping behind Lori Schofield who stood nearby attending to her own customers, and brought her tray of seafood plates in for a successful landing. The next two minutes were spent in conversation, assuring herself that the lobster eaters were all versed in the art of dismembering the crustacean and making sure everyone's meal met with their satisfaction. Once convinced her attention was not needed for the moment, she strolled up to the lobsterman's table from behind.

"And sure, this man cannot seem to get enough of me," she proclaimed, wrapping her arms around his neck and giving a squeeze. "And did you ever think of getting the smell of brine off of ye before you came a courting?"

"Sweet Jesus, now I'm expected to put on a shirt and tie just for her. A little demanding, ain't you?"

"I'm afraid to change a thing, Mr. Johnston, you like me so much the way I am."

"A bowl of fish chowder with extra crackers...and a Bushmills and ginger," he called out. Withholding comment, she turned and made for the bar and kitchen.

Layla returned a short time later with the lobsterman's lunch. After placing the drink and bowl of chowder down, she paused for a moment, then dropped a half-dozen bags of crackers on the surface of the table. Johnston looked up at her in surprise.

"Are you quite done now?" he asked.

"No, I am not," she answered, producing another bag of crackers from her pocket and dropping it in front of him.

"Are you done now?"

"No sir, I am not." Reaching into her opposite pocket, she removed two additional bags and dropped them onto the table. "You asked for extra crackers, and the customer is always right."

"I take it you're quite done now?"

"Are ye asking for more crackers?" she questioned, a mischievous look in her eye.

"And what if I am?" he asked defiantly. The redhead slowly reached inside her starched, white blouse and produced another bag of crackers, tossing it to the edge of the table and ultimately into his lap.

"Now Orangeman, would you like to be calling me bluff and asking for more crackers. However, be advised, you may not be too happy with where the next bag of crackers will be coming from," she warned, her angelic face reflecting a trace of madness. The usually stoic man burst into laughter, causing heads in the room to turn in his direction. She reached down and affectionately tossed his hair, much like she had done to her cousin only hours before. "When you're done with your lunch, there's something a little more serious I need to be updating you on." She left the man to his lunch and newspaper, returning fifteen minutes later.

The room was largely clear of customers when Layla ambled up to William Johnston's table and took a seat across from him.

"Your sister answered me letter but I think she misunderstood a lot of what I was trying to say," she blurted out. The man's eyes widened, seemingly dumbstruck by her statement.

"You actually wrote to Sarah? You wrote to her about me?"

"Aye. But she clearly mistook me for some geebag who was out to take your money and was just trying to endear themselves to your family," she explained.

"Seriously, you wrote to Sarah, in Portrush, about me?"

"Aye, and didn't I tell you I was going to?"

"I thought that was just more of your Irish blarney."

"I'm not one who peddles the blarney. You should know that by now. Anyway, I've already written back to the woman and explained, in much greater detail, me relationship with you and what I hope to accomplish." The man stared across at the girl, temporarily speechless. "This second letter should do the trick," she announced confidently.

"How, missy, is my life any of your business?"

"Me friend's general happiness and well-being is me business," she answered matter-of-factly. A hand came down on her shoulder at that moment. She looked up to see Lori Schofield standing over her.

"When you have a free moment, there's something that you should be aware of," she said, her tone indicating that the matter might be of some importance. The redhead rose immediately, intent on being updated on the matter in question.

"William, don't you be worrying yourself about anything. We'll have you home for Christmas and visiting me in Donegal at the same time. It'll be grand," she concluded. Johnston shook his head in disgust, tossed a few bills on the table, and made his way from the room.

Lori brought Layla to the far corner of the room by the window, away from the ears of others. Outside, two canoes passed by in the blue, estuary water, crossing under the bridge and northward toward the harbor.

"After work tonight, there's going to be a fight. Wesley challenged Billy Sousa to a fight."

"Wesley did! Is he mad?"

"Billy was shooting his mouth off about you and Philip Trask. I didn't hear exactly what he said but I guess it wasn't too nice. Wesley overheard it and told him to shut up. Then, you know how men get, one thing led to another. Now, they're going to duke it out after work tonight."

"And it's all over me—and what was being said about me?"

"That's the way it sounds," answered Lori, a look of concern etched on her classically pretty face. The Irish girl thanked the woman and walked slowly back to Mr. Johnston's table, picking up the small stack of folded bills. Largely alone in the dining area, she walked back to the row of windows along the far wall. Deep in thought, she said a short prayer for strength and guidance, turned, then marched toward the kitchen.

Layla cleared the kitchen's swinging doors and was immediately struck by the oppressive heat and the sight of Billy's Sousa's impudent grin. Returning his grin with a glare, she walked the aisle to the back of the room where she found her friend hunched over a sink, his face awash with perspiration.

"What's this shite I heard about a fight tonight?"

"Billy Sousa and me—in the parking lot."

"There'll be no fight tonight, or any other night."

"Layla, it's on for tonight."

"Wesley, you'll not be fighting because if you do I will never speak to you again—no biking, no friendship, no nothing."

"You don't understand. I have to fight now. I can't back down."

"There'll be no fight, and no talk of a fight, from either of you. You will not fight because I know you value me friendship. Do you not value me friendship?"

"Of course I do. You know that."

"And Billy will not fight for another reason. That'll be between him and me. Now, do you understand? When your shift ends you just go home. There'll be no fight or talk of a fight. Am I clear on this?"

"I'll look like a coward," he exclaimed.

"There'll be no one standing out in the parking lot. I'll see to that. Have I made meself clear? No one will look like a coward."

"Okay, no fight."

"And we'll, us t'ree, meet and bicycle tomorrow morning?"

"Absolutely."

"Now get back to work before Dick comes down here and eats your head off for loafing on the job," she warned. She turned from him.

"Thank you, Layla," said the teenager in a hushed voice. She smiled at him and went in search of Adam Dillon. As it was, she found the head cook standing outside by the back of the building, crouched down by the edge of the water.

"'Tis a few degrees cooler out here than in the kitchen," she sang out, moving down an embankment toward the man.

"And how can I be of service to Maine's gift from Ireland?"

"I'll not be needing much of anything, just five minutes alone with your assistant cook."

"Are you sure you want to get involved in all this craziness?"

"Are you saying I can't have me five minutes with the eejit?"

"No, go right ahead. Be my guest," he conceded, throwing his arms up in frustration. "Maybe he'll listen to you."

"And for sure, his physical well-being depends on it," she answered back before turning and making for the back door.

Billy Sousa was in the act of guzzling down the last of a bottle of soda when a tap came upon his shoulder. He whirled around and came face to face with Layla O'Malley.

"Adam said I could steal you away for five minutes outside for a talk. I'd be lying if I said me heart was not pumping with excitement." The sarcasm was lost on Sousa.

"I've got a pretty good idea what you're going to be asking me, and the answer is no."

"Billy boy, you haven't the faintest idea of what I'll be asking you. If you did, you wouldn't be acting the eejit and wasting our time here." A smug, cocky smile ever present on his face, he took a moment to think, then gestured her toward the back door. They met Adam Dillon on the way out.

"Don't you crazy kids go and elope on us," he joked, reentering the kitchen and a wave of hot air. Layla led Sousa around to the far corner of the building where an arm of the estuary connects with the main artery. Without warning she stopped in her tracks and turned back to the man.

"I'm not sure why I'm doing you this favor, but I am."

"No doubt you're gonna ask me to leave your little friend alone and not beat the shit out of him tonight," snarled the man.

"Oh, that's all been taken care of. I've asked Wesley not to fight tonight and he's agreed. I also told him that I'm expecting him not to even speak of the matter again."

"I'll bet you didn't have to twist his arm too far to go along with that."

"Actually, typical man that he is, he wanted to fight. I told him I'd never speak to him again if he went through with this nonsense and he agreed to go straight home tonight. And now Billy boy, this brings us to you. It seems that all this shite's been brought on because of things you've been saying about Philip Trask and me. Is this correct?"

"I've made a few jokes," laughed Sousa.

"Me first instinct was to tell me cousin about some of the things that have been said about his little cousin. Me cousin Brian stands a half a foot over you and would probably knock you into next week with a single blow. And sure, all I'd have to do is make up some things that a certain Billy Sousa has said about me, ruining his sainted, Irish cousin's reputation, and he'd be down here in thirty minutes. Then I asked meself if that was what I really wanted. Me God, you'd be out so fast you wouldn't feel a thing, not till you woke up anyway."

"This shit's not scaring me," he snarled.

"Then I thought of the two hooligans he chums with. White trash you call them over here in the states, but technically, I'm not even sure if they're both white. And I asked meself: What is handsome Billy most proud of? His straight, white teeth—that's what he's most proud of. What if I asked these hooligans to knock a few of these perfect teeth out? If I told them how you talked about me knickers in public and embarrassed me, and made me cry at work. They're the sort of people who might be experienced in such things, white trash bar fights and all. Do you see where I'm going with this?" Sousa folded his arms and stared coldly into her eyes. "So here's the deal, Billy boy: You go straight home tonight and never talk of the fight again, like it never was; you don't say a peep to Wesley or anyone else about the fight; and you never, ever, bring up me or me love life in a conversation again. You follow these few steps and your smile can continue to slay the ladies for heaven knows how long. But, if I hear you haven't, I will see to it that you get the shite brutally kicked out of you, and those pearly whites of yours will be me trophy. Bring them back to Donegal, I will, through customs and all. Am I making meself clear enough?" She stared intently at the young man and thought she detected a crack in Sousa's resolve.

"And how do I know Wright's not going to parade around tomorrow saying I backed out of the fight?"

"Because he's been told not to, by me." Sousa looked over her shoulder toward the restaurant.

"Yeah, okay, I can live with that," he relented, turning away and walking back toward the kitchen.

"And Billy, use this episode as a life lesson, and how you don't have to have muscles and strength to have influence. In the end, even sweet and innocent little things like me can be behind a lot of mayhem."

The dinner traffic descended on Billy's Chowder House like a tidal wave on this day. Dick Varano, the owner, was called down to greet at the front desk, freeing up Vickie for waiting tables. Layla and Lori remained stationed by themselves in the back bay. Layla was busy clearing a table when a tap came on her shoulder. She turned and saw Donna standing beside a heavy set, middle-aged woman.

"Layla, I know you're as busy as hell but my mom couldn't leave without meeting my best friend. I told her so much about you."

"It is so good to finally put a face with the name. My daughter's been very good with keeping in touch this summer. Thank you, especially, for putting her up at your house during that terrible time last month with her neighbors."

"And what are friends for," responded the redhead. "And do you believe what me little swan has accomplished these past couple of months?" Layla asked while stepping forward and applying a hug on her friend.

"Incredible, absolutely incredible. I swear I didn't even recognize her at first. She had to literally walk up to me to get my attention."

"She's worked hard she has."

"It was Layla who pushed me all the way. I don't know what I'm going to do when she goes home."

"It'll be brutal saying good-bye, it will," confessed the Irish girl.

"I think I'd better be letting both you hard working girls get back to work," exclaimed the woman. Layla reached out and clutched the woman's hand.

"And you'll come back and visit us again, when we're a wee bit less busy?"

"I promise," came back the heavily made-up woman before turning and leaving the room with her daughter.

The wonderful thing about an obscenely busy night is that time appears to literally pass at light speed. So it was, when Layla glanced down at her watch and saw it was nearly nine o'clock, she had to look twice, unwilling to accept what her eyes told her on their first pass.

"You know O'Malley, I had no idea how disruptive a force you are out on the floor. Maybe I should work out here more often," voiced Dick Varano from behind the front desk.

"And what exactly would ye be referring to?" asked the twenty-year-old as she approached the man.

"No exaggeration, I've had a half-dozen people come in and ask for one of the Irish girl's tables. I've had to shuttle these people into the back bay all night. It throws me off, and screws up my system."

"And sure I never hear Vickie or Lori or anyone else who's been greeting complain of it. You know Dick, maybe it's your system that's pure shite and nothing to do with a simple little girl from Donegal trying to eke out a living?" The man laughed and shook his head.

"You've always got an answer. You people have it, the gift of the gab."

XVIII

THE FIREBIRD ROARED out of the driveway, across Route 1, and into a line of traffic. Layla was quick to fasten her seat belt as the vehicle roared southward.

"At this time of year, he who hesitates is lost—in traffic anyway," quipped Philip from the driver's seat.

"Well, it's good to see we're heading south, seeing that Kennebunkport has already seen me in this dress," added Layla. He glanced across the front seat, looking her up and down as if laying eyes on her for the first time. "And are you going to tell me where we are going on this glorious evening?"

"It's a surprise." They motored past the shopping mall, prompting the redhead to fill the front seat with conversation.

"I thought I saw you in Ames Department Store the other day," she said. "I ran over to say something but the bloke turned and looked nothing like you."

"I don't shop in discount stores," he answered curtly.

"I bought me a pair of purple knickers there on Monday," she confessed, turning sideways in her seat. Her movement caught his attention. He reached across the cabin of the car, brushing her reddish hair from off her face.

"Do you have any idea how wonderful it is to have you all to myself this evening?" he asked.

"In case you haven't noticed, I've been keeping me only night off all week open for one person, and one person only," she replied. He reached over to her again, kneading the back of her neck with his fingertips.

"That's a sure way of bringing the banshee in me to the surface. Of course, that may have been your intention all along."

"Ah yes, the dangerous—and unpredictable—Layla O'Malley," he mused.

"I'd be interested, how many people have you told about me?"

"I'll have you know, I told my mother about you just the other day," confessed Philip. "She will actually be coming down to visit in a few days."

"And will you be introducing me?"

"Possibly…possibly." She sat up straight in her seat, the introduction of Mrs. Trask into the conversation piquing her interest.

"And how is it that a woman with a beautiful house, right on the ocean mind you, doesn't spend more time there and instead lets her lazy, sickly son have it to himself?"

"She has a place in the White Mountains where she hangs out most of the time…at least in the summer and winter anyway."

"Sweet Jaysus! How many houses do the Trasks own?"

"My mother has part ownership of the one here at the point, the one up in Randolph—that's in New Hampshire—and the primary back in Winchester. My dad is down to his one condo in Boston and half of Moody Point. Mom did very well in the divorce." Layla gestured with a smile but did not press the conversation any further, slightly embarrassed by the differences in family backgrounds, at least in the area of real estate holdings.

Reaching the intersection at Ogunquit, Philip nudged his way through the line of northward traffic on Route 1 and headed toward Perkins Cove.

"Me friends and I come down here on our bicycles occasionally," tossed out the redhead.

"Oh really, on your way to where?"

"Sometimes the cove, and sometimes to take the coast road and up by the golf course."

"Do you play golf?"

"Go on with ya, no. We went as far as the golf course once. We planned on visiting the Cliff House but talked ourselves out of it. That's a truly fancy place and we thought we might get tossed out like a shower of savages."

"I'm sure that wouldn't have happened," said Philip as the vehicle proceeded eastward between brightly colored shops and pristine, well-maintained motel buildings. "You're wearing that perfume you wore the night you attacked me on my sick bed."

"And a pitiful excuse for a man you were on that evening." Trask burst out laughing, responding to his date's irreverent sense of humor.

The car traversed a series of undulating twists and turns carved into the landscape that closely bordered the edge of the Atlantic Ocean. Layla peered out the passenger window, taking in the same countryside she had seen from her bicycle only a few weeks before. It was not long before they were rolling by the recently mowed fairways of the golf course.

"It was along here me friends and I stopped and rolled in the grass," she reported.

"Rolled in the grass? You *rolled* in the grass?"

"Aye. Donna was looking for some company to go to the movies, and Wesley was not picking up on the hint. So we took it upon ourselves to wrestle him to the ground and, with our body weight making him one with the grass, point out all the positive things about going to the movies."

"It sounds like it might have gotten quite physical."

"And didn't he laugh it up with the two of us looking down on him like the helpless boyo that he was. Right there it was," Layla proudly announced, pointing to a patch of grass between the roadway and a perfectly, manicured green. Within seconds the car turned from the road and onto the driveway to the Cliff House. The redhead let out with a giggle as they proceeded up the shaded lane, the vehicle finally reaching the parking lot overlooking the front entrance to the resort thirty seconds later.

Philip circled the car and assisted his date from the passenger seat.

"I do hope I don't make an eejit of meself here tonight... in front of you and these people with their grand manners."

"Relax. Look at you, fitted perfectly in that white dress and with a face to melt the heart of the harshest critic," he added. Passing through the front door, they made their way toward the far side of the building, eventually stopping by the lectern guarding the entrance to the dining room. Behind the stand stood a meticulously groomed man of about forty.

"Trask, reservation for two," stated Philip nonchalantly. The man glanced down through a pair of reading glasses at a sheet of paper on the stand in front of him.

"This way," he responded, stepping out from behind his station and walking in the direction of the far wall of windows. Philip reached down and took Layla's hand, lacing his fingers through her own. Stepping off behind the distinguished looking gentleman, the twenty-year-old was first conscious of the feel of the carpet beneath her feet. The expansive dining room, perhaps two-thirds full at the moment, was circumscribed in glass affording all those present a view of the open ocean along with a splendid panorama of the rock formation outside. With Philip walking only inches behind her, they continued to follow the gentleman as he sauntered between tables, all the while moving steadily closer to the far wall. Layla felt herself literally draw in a deep breath when their host strode up to the table in the far northeast corner of the room and placed down the leather bound menus.

"Oh me God," she whispered back to Philip as their greeter pulled out one of the four chairs surrounding the table and beckoned her to be seated. From behind she picked up on Philip Trask chuckling under his breath.

"Gunther will be your waiter," the man announced before returning to his station and another party standing patiently by his desk. Layla leaned forward over the table, peeking down at crashing waves as they exploded over the marbled ledge of rocks below.

"Tis a lighthouse a few miles out to sea," she observed, her voice displaying a childlike quality. The man swiveled his neck and gazed out toward the

Atlantic.

"Ah yes, the Boon Island lighthouse."

"And is it manned or is it automated too?"

"Automated, of course. I think they all are now. If I remember correctly, it's sort of famous, but not for a good reason."

"And what would that be?" she inquired, her curiosity piqued.

"I'll tell you after dinner."

"And sure I can't be waiting all that time. You can tell me now. I'm not one of your dainty, little Boston girls. I'm descended from a pirate queen for God's sake. Now, what's the lighthouse famous for, a murder?"

"Worse."

"Sweet Jaysus, worse than murder, he says. Is it a child molestation and then a murder?"

"Cannibalism. I don't remember the exact circumstances but I do remember the cannibalism."

"Uh-hummm," came a sound from someone clearing his throat. They looked up to see a fair-skinned, blond young man standing over them. Clearly, Gunther had made his way to their table. Philip ordered beverages for him and his date after pleading with her to have something alcoholic. She declined. "I'll be back in a few minutes to take your order for dinner," Gunther added before turning away.

"I can only imagine what that bloke will be saying about us once he gets back to the kitchen. He'll be talking about the two bogtrotters out at the corner table jawing about cannibals, and what a waste it is giving that wonderful table to a couple of eejits like them." Trask let out with a hearty laugh, extending his hand across the table and folding it over hers. "By the way Mr. Trask, I think I failed to tell ye that you look very handsome tonight." He responded with a broad smile, his perfectly aligned, white teeth lending themselves to his facial features. "I'd say there's a good chance that a place like that is haunted. Do you think you might take herself out to visit the lighthouse someday?"

"I thought you were a good Catholic. Catholics aren't allowed to believe in ghosts, are they?"

"What sort of rubbish have you been listening to? Of course we can believe in ghosts. Tis proof of life after death. Ireland is crawling with ghosts, it is. How could we not believe?"

"Don't talk about Ireland, Layla. Because, when you talk about Ireland, I'm reminded that you'll be going back in a few months." The redhead closed her eyes and frowned for a moment, a physical reaction to the thought of separation.

"Me trip here to the states has made herself fall in love with a new place, and grow very fond of people who were strangers to me only last spring, but it's also made me miss me parents and Glencolombkille." Staring across the table, Layla thought she detected a certain melancholy etching its way onto Philip's face.

"It's really quite painful only being able to spend time with you one night a week," he confessed. He appeared to be fumbling with his thoughts, unable to address a specific sentiment.

"Which is why I peddle down to see ye a couple of times a week after work. It couldn't be any further out of me way." He smiled his response, a timid, halfhearted smile that, no doubt, masked his true feelings. Their waiter reappeared from between the adjacent tables carrying their drinks, reminding them that they were no closer to choosing their entree than they were ten minutes earlier.

"We'll need a few more minutes before we order dinner," announced Philip. Gunther acknowledged the man's words and made his way over to another of his patrons. Layla glanced down at her menu, then out toward the sparkling seawater. From the north and about two hundred yards out to sea, a sailboat was making its way past this elevated neck of rocky shoreline. Two individuals, a man and a woman, were quite visible on deck.

"When our food arrives I want you to eat very, very slowly. I want this meal to go on forever, and never end. And do you know why that is, Philip Trask?" He smiled and shook his head in the negative. "Because at this moment, there is nowhere I would rather be—and there is no one I would rather be with."

Layla and Philip were ninety minutes into the meal and waiting on the arrival of their individual desserts. Outside their window, the building was casting an extended shadow out over the gray, craggy rocks below. Over the preceding few minutes, swells had developed offshore and brought forth a series of spectacular waves, some producing sprays of up to twenty-five feet.

"Will you escort me down to the breakers after dinner?" she asked.

"Absolutely," he responded. "Oh, before I forget, when we were driving down earlier you said something in passing about going bicycling with your friends. Are those friends all female?"

"Well first, there's only two: one female and one male."

"Friends from work?"

"Aye. There's Wesley. He washes dishes and busses tables. And there's Donna, who waitresses along with me."

"Is Donna the relatively new one with the nice tan?"

"She's not that new. She started just after me, but she's lost a great deal of weight over the last two months and looks like a different girl."

"I guess. When we were in for lunch last week I was looking at her with her back turned and I thought to myself how Vickie had developed really nice, athletic legs. Then she whirled around and I saw it was this different girl and not Vickie. She's very pretty, too."

"Aye, she's me swan."

"Is she seeing that Wesley guy?"

"Aye, they've been going out and having a few laughs together for a while now. But she told me the other day how she's planning on seeing this bowsie who works in the kitchen. The man's a real gobshite but I've learned from experience not to be meddling in matters of the heart. I just pray Wesley doesn't get his heart broken from all this." The words barely out of the red-head's mouth, Gunther approached the table with their desserts. The golden-haired young man asked if there would be anything else, prompting Layla to order a pot of tea for the table.

"Now remember biffo, I want you to take your sweet time with that piece of cake; no gulping it down," she insisted.

"Yes ma'am," he answered behind a tender smile.

"I can hardly wait to tell me ma and da about me evening. It's me night to call them."

"I've never heard you talk about your parents, at least not that much."

"Oh, they're just a pair of hard working people. We don't have a lot of money but there's a lot of love in our house."

"Which one do you take after, you know, appearance wise?"

"Well, me da has the red hair and I'm much taller than me ma, more like me father's side of the family."

"And that's the side of the family with the pirate woman."

"Aye, and she was a queen, not just a woman."

"Excuse me, your majesty."

The two lovers lingered over their Black Forest cake while the sky on the eastern horizon slowly darkened. When Philip commented on the number of visible aircraft this night, Layla was reminded of her flight home and its early evening departure time. In slightly more than two months, it would be her aboard an Aer Lingus aircraft passing by the Cliff House restaurant along the distant horizon.

"Look there," she exclaimed, pointing southeastward out the window. "The beacon from the lighthouse is on." Philip barely moved his eyes, content to stare long and hard at the youthful female seated across the table.

"You know Layla, there is an exuberance and freshness about you that is rare these days."

"Go on with ya. I think you've just been spending too much time hanging around with that crowd of yours, and not enough time around real people."

"I mean, you have this wonderful innocence about you and a wide eyed exuberance. Not only that, you're twenty years old but you could easily pass for sixteen."

"Sixteen! Oh no, is me acne coming back?" she clowned.

"No, I'm serious. There is almost a guilty pleasure being with an adult who you can easily fantasize about as a minor." She laughed and shook her head in mock disbelief.

"Philip...me dear, dear Philip. Don't you go and get too carried away here," she cautioned.

"May I be totally honest with you?"

"You may, but first I want you to look behind you and across the room. Who does the man in the white suit and gray hair look like to you?" Trask swung around and glanced behind him. Meanwhile, Layla took the opportunity to carve a generous slice from his cake and put it into her mouth.

"I don't know, James Woods?"

"No, I was thinking more of Jimmy O'Day."

"Who's he?"

"That sheep farmer from Carrick who made such an eejit of himself at the Christmas dance last year." Trask stared at his date, knowing he was being played the fool on some level.

"May I get serious, please?"

"Go on, if you must."

"Before you came to my rescue that day at Billy's, I had seen you at the restaurant, and I knew that you had taken some kind of interest in me. It was obvious. But *I* wasn't interested. It was only when you were with me at the house, and nursing me back to health, that I felt myself being drawn to you. Part of it was probably the whole nurturing thing. My mother wasn't exactly big on nurturing or caring for me as a child. She had too many outside interests. But, in those few days at the house you exposed me to something that I've lacked all my life...an attentive female who cared deeply for me in a totally unselfish way."

"And sure, I was your Florence Nightingale."

"But then it became more than the nurturing thing. The way that you joked with me, like about the thermometer, and wound up pouncing on me in bed. All these psychological ploys of yours started screwing with my head. My friends pointed out how you were playing mind games on me but I wound up coming back for more."

"You must believe me when I say I'm not for playing games with people. I am just being meself. This is who I am: a product of me parent's upbringing, me faith in God, and all the desires boiling up inside of me." Philip leaned forward across the table, taking hold of her hands.

"Layla O'Malley, I am falling deeper and deeper in love with you with every passing day, and I just keep falling." A sad smile came to the girl's face as tears appeared in the corner of both eyes.

"Philip Trask, I love you so much it hurts, and I'm afraid I'll never be able to love anyone like this again for as long as I live."

They left the restaurant fifteen minutes after professing their love for one another. At Layla's insistence, they descended a series of staircases and walked out onto the uneven plateau of ocean-smoothed rock separating the resort building from the omnipotent Atlantic Ocean.

"If I close me eyes I can almost imagine meself back at the beach at Glencolombkille," she called out over the sound of the pounding surf and swirling ocean breeze.

"I hope you'll take me there someday, and up into the hills of Donegal to picnic."

"Oh Philip, I've already taken you to me beach so many times in me head." With the couple locked in an embrace, a wave crashed to their right, spouting foaming seawater into the air, the mist from which reached the lovers.

"Stop the lights! I think it's time to retreat to higher ground," she called out. They scurried back toward the set of cement stairs and safety. Forty feet above their heads, the lights from the restaurant continued to shine brightly out over the dark Atlantic.

A peaceful quiet occupied the car as the two cruised southward along the ocean road toward Short Sands and the town of York. From there they would rejoin Route 1 and make their way to Portsmouth. It was still relatively early and Philip thought a couple of hours of jazz might top off the evening. Reaching the New Hampshire port city, it was immediately clear to Layla that her companion knew the city well and had probably visited it before on countless occasions. Trask found his way into a parking garage and within minutes the two were strolling through an alleyway and ultimately up a flight of stairs. After paying a cover charge they entered a large, darkened room where a quartet was holding court on an under-lit stage. At the back of the room they settled in at one end of a vacant couch. As Layla's eyes adjusted to her dark surroundings she learned the room was only two-thirds full. Within seconds Philip had ordered two drinks, allowing the pair to sit back and relax. Layla, her shoes already removed, rested her body along Philip's, an arm draped comfortably over him. They spent over two hours together in this manner, allowing the hypnotic rhythms and the other's physical presence to transport their spirits to another plane. By the time they made their way through the eighteenth-century streets and back to their vehicle they were high on life and intoxicated, each with the other.

Again, Layla marveled at her date's knowledge of the traffic scheme for the city of Portsmouth. Two minutes after leaving the parking garage, the car was cruising up Route 95 toward the Maine Turnpike. Trask glanced over at his companion as they rolled across the bridge linking New Hampshire to Maine, high above Portsmouth Harbor.

"I swear you become more beautiful with the passing of every hour," he said.

"And if you had downed one more martini back there, I'd be Miss Ireland by now...at least in your eyes."

"You know, I've been wrestling with the question of whether to ask you something all night. Now, I'm figuring...what the hell." The redhead turned sideways in her seat, intrigued by his admission. "I'm not sure how much longer I can last just seeing you here and there. I've given it a lot of thought and I'm ready to make a real commitment. I'd like you to move in with me down at the point, at least until you have to go home to Ireland."

"Philip, I think you know I can't be doing that."

"Why, because of your religion?"

"Aye, and also because I'm opposed to that sort of thing morally."

"It's two months, and then you could go back home and go to confession, or whatever it is you people do."

"No."

"It's not a sin if we both love each other."

"Don't you be feeding me that rubbish, and don't think that I'm not flattered, but the answer to your question is no."

"Layla, I think you're losing sight of the fact that I'm making a commitment here," he argued.

"A commitment is it? Is it anything like the commitment you made to that Barbie Doll you lived with a couple of summers ago?"

"Where did you hear about that?"

"And do you think that this town does not have its wagging tongues?" He turned his face squarely back to the road, unable to completely conceal his exasperation. "You've given me one of the most wonderful nights of me life. Please don't go and spoil it now over this."

"Damn it, I'm in love with you."

"And I swear, as God is me witness, that I love you, and that before you I didn't even know the meaning of the word. I care that much for you, Philip Trask."

"So how can you keep us separated this way with all this old world garbage?"

"And that's what you think of me faith? Tis just so much rubbish?" The man shook his head in disgust, not answering her question.

Trask exited the highway just before the toll, returning to Route 1. The cabin of the vehicle held within it an uncomfortable silence, and had so for a couple of minutes.

"So, where do you see this whole thing going?" he asked, his voice slightly tempered.

"And what whole thing is that?"

"Our relationship; the sculptor and the waitress."

"It goes where it goes. Tis nothing more to be said."

"You're throwing away your youth," he argued.

"As opposed to throwing away something else," she countered.

"Okay, so how do you see things playing out—the saint that you are?"

"I think I've told you this before, but apparently you were so distracted by me beauty, you failed to pick up on it. The man that I marry gets me...all of me. I'll marry in the church and I'll marry for life, the way the church teaches."

"Catholics can divorce nowadays. Our senators back in Massachusetts, Kennedy and Kerry, they're both Catholics and they both got divorced and remarried in the church."

"And don't you be using your malignant, gobshite politicians as examples for me. I've had a bellyful, me, of your bleedin' politicians and their dealings with the church! I'm just saying that the man who marches down the aisle with me will not just be getting a direct descendent of the great Granuaile O'Malley but also a woman possessed with a burning passion—a banshee locked within her as I see it. It will be a lucky man who first lies with me. I just hope the poor creature can survive what I have in store for him and make it to middle age. Of course, in your case, that wouldn't have to be too many years, would it?" Layla asked, shooting him a devilish smile. Philip let out with a sigh.

"You know exactly how to screw with my head," he said. "Tell me, are banshees supposed to be good or bad?"

"Very, very bad," she answered, delivering her words behind an evil glare.

The Firebird rolled deliberately over the speed bumps, crawling quietly across the complex and toward cottage fourteen. The main house was in complete darkness.

"I probably won't even be putting me head on the pillow for a while. I'll be calling me parents in about an hour," explained the girl. Philip nodded his head but reserved comment. "Now don't you be moving from your seat," she instructed as she stepped from the car. Circling around the back of the vehicle, she reappeared standing over him by the driver's door. "Open the door," she commanded. He snapped open the lock and swung the door outward. In an instant she was straddling his lap. "Now, I'm putting your fate and well-being in your own hands. Do you, or do you not, want a goodnight kiss? And, before you answer, let me tell you in the interest of full disclosure: the banshee feels particularly alive inside me at the moment." He looked into her blue eyes and gave a nervous laugh.

"What the hell...I'll take the goodnight kiss."

Philip Trask walked gingerly over the next few days, nursing sore ribs on both sides of his torso and a bruised lip. His mother joined him for dinner

Sunday night. She questioned him on the condition of his lip and on the pain evidenced in even the most basic movements of his body. He explained it away by relating a story about a fall from the front porch.

XIX

LAYLA STOOD ON HER BICYCLE propped up against a light pole in the parking lot of the Wells Shopping Center, waiting on the arrival of her two friends. It was a few minutes past eight o'clock on a Monday morning. August was drawing to a close. In addition to the hard, numerical facts provided by her wall calendar, there was also the matter of the cool breeze that made its way through her loft window overnight, sending her reaching for the blanket rolled up at the foot of the mattress. She felt her time in Maine quickening its pace. Later in the week she would be visiting the bank and depositing funds that would bring her balance to over six thousand dollars. She glanced up toward Route 1 and spotted Donna turning down the entrance to the mall and coasting toward her. Within seconds her tall, well-tanned friend was upon her, applying the brakes to her bike.

"Still no sign of Wesley," called out the redhead.

"He won't be joining us this morning," answered Donna.

"Ah, the lazy good-for-nothing," joked Layla. She looked up to see her friend gesturing to her. "What?"

"I had a falling out with Wesley last night after work. I explained to him how I was seeing someone else and that it made me uncomfortable having him around, particularly when I might want to be discussing personal matters with you." Layla stood in front of her friend, straddling her bike, her face now reflecting the shock from the news.

"Is all this coming from your thing with Billy Sousa?"

"Of course. What else could it be?"

"And how did he stand up to the news?"

"He acted childish. I may not have been as diplomatic as I could have been. But I read somewhere that it's best for everyone involved if you just lay it on the line—to be truthful even if it comes off as a little harsh."

"What did you tell the poor creature?"

"I told him that there have been a lot of changes in my life—my slimming down and getting in shape and all. When he tried to lay some kind of guilt trip on me I just told him that I was too good for him now, and that I was looking to get into a serious relationship."

"You actually said that? You said you were too good for him?"

"I told him the truth! I didn't exactly enjoy doing it, you know," explained the brunette defensively.

The morning ride was unusually quiet on this Monday. The two young women peddled north, visiting Drakes Island beach. It was Donna who did the majority of the talking, sharing stories from her private time spent in the company of Billy Sousa. Following a two-mile ride amid summer tourist traffic and sandy shoulders by the roadside, they turned eastward and coasted a mile through marshland and eventually arrived at the hamlet of Drake's Island. They biked over to the primary parking lot that guarded one side of the entranceway to Wells Harbor, alongside the northern of two, parallel jetties. Standing atop the elongated expansion of giant rocks, they watched a small craft sail by their position, navigated by a boy who appeared to be no more than ten years of age. Donna challenged her friend to a race to the eastern end of the finger of giant granite boulders, a distance of a few hundred yards. Layla reluctantly accepted the challenge and was promptly shocked by the pretty brunette's speed and dexterity. Although close for the better part of the run, Donna pulled ahead in the last fifteen yards and won by a couple of body lengths. While strolling back toward the bicycles, they were asked by a carload of boys to join them on the beach. The girls declined and, shortly after, retraced their route back toward Mile Road and the Atlantic Coast Lodge.

Layla arrived back at her cottage slightly before ten o'clock, still slightly unnerved by her friend's news about Wesley and from a perceived change in Donna's disposition. Reaching the front door she was surprised to see an envelope tucked in above the locking mechanism. She pulled it free and scanned the postmark. Her eyes widened at the sight of Portrush, Northern Ireland stamped in the right-hand corner.

Her hair still partially wet from a hot shower, Layla left the cottage for work early on this day, hoping to catch a free moment with her cousin at the main house. She got as far as the door to the office before realizing he was busy with two groups of tourists. With no assurance that he would be free anytime in the next fifteen minutes, she pushed off on her bicycle and headed for work.

Layla pulled open the restaurant's front door and was confronted with a vacated front area, no doubt she being the first of the waitresses to arrive this day. Without hesitation, she pushed her way through the doors to the kitchen and went in search of Wesley Wright. Purposely avoiding any eye contact with Billy Sousa, she walked to the far end of the room and found the teenager bent over a tray of dishes.

"I missed you this morning," she said softly. The teenager turned and looked up at the redhead.

"I missed riding this morning…the company mostly," he responded sadly.

"Donna told me what happened. I'm sorry Wesley. I want you to know that if you could use me ear to bend, then I'm here for you. You're me friend, just like Donna, no more and no less." The young man let out an exaggerated sigh and slumped back against the chrome face of the dishwasher.

"I sort of had the feeling that my relationship with Donna wasn't really going anywhere, but you know how you can always hold out hope?"

"Aye, I think we've all been through something like that," she consoled.

"My problem is that, outside of my dates with Donna, that riding in the morning was pretty much my whole social life."

"Now, she's pretty much dead against you joining us in the future, but I'm thinking why don't you be joining me a couple of days a week and I'll cut back a little on me time with her."

"You wouldn't mind?" he asked, appearing astonished.

"I'm hoping I'm wrong on this, but it's almost like the girl is getting a little full of herself lately. I think I liked her better when she was a doorful of a lass. You'll be making for better company."

"I'm not looking forward to seeing her ten times a day. I like my job here at Billy's more than the last place I worked, and I'd miss seeing my little Irish friend every day if I left." The redhead reached over and guided Wesley to his feet, then applied a long, affectionate hug.

"Just don't go moping around like a constipated greyhound. Why don't you come by me cottage tomorrow morning? Do you know where the Atlantic Coast Lodge is?"

"I think so," he answered.

"Across the street from Congdon's Doughnuts, you bogtrotting eejit," she joked.

"I can find it now."

"Oh really, then which cottage would I be in, biffo?"

"Oops, you'll have to tell me."

"Fourteen biffo, fourteen."

"Thanks Layla, for everything."

"And sure I'll leave you with an Irish blessing," she announced, placing her hand on the top of the young man's head. "May the road rise to meet you; may the wind be always at your back…and may you never die until I shoot you." She ended her spiel with a toss of his hair and made her way out of the kitchen and back toward the front desk.

On this day Donna was assigned to work the lounge along with Vickie. Meanwhile, Layla, Betsy Chase and Lori Schofield were stationed in the main dining room. For the first two and a half hours, the redhead caught herself eyeing the entrance with heightened interest. She had not seen Philip in over a week, largely due to him canceling their Thursday night date at the last moment. Reportedly, he had been called back to Massachusetts on family matters. Now, it was after two o'clock and neither he nor his regular companions had showed their faces. Finally, the door opened and William Johnston stood by the front desk.

"You can send the biffo over to me here, Susanne," called out Layla, her voice carrying to the next room. The blond directed the lobsterman into the oldest part of the building and seated the man down in front of Layla.

"I'm not from Offaly," grunted Johnston while snatching the menu out of his waitress's hand.

"Aye, but sure, everything else fits you like a glove, it does."

"I see your tongue hasn't softened over the weekend. A bowl of chowder with extra crackers…and a Bushmills and ginger," he barked.

"Mr. Johnston, I don't want you leaving here without me seeing you out. I'll be taking me afternoon break with you out in the parking lot."

"What are you up to, missy?"

"You'll see in good time, biffo. You'll see in good time."

The crusty sixty-year-old kept to himself over lunch this day, content to engross himself in his Biddeford paper. He surprised Layla by opting for dessert, the strawberry shortcake, which arrived at the table and prompted a child seated nearby to demand one herself. With Johnston on the last stages of his meal, she slipped back into the kitchen and retrieved her mail from earlier in the day. Returning to the front of the restaurant, she eyed the back of William Johnston's head and heavily soiled work shirt descending the stairs.

"And where do you think you're off to?" she called out, scurrying toward the exit.

"I left my money on the table. The extra is yours," he growled back.

"I told you I'd be joining you outside on me break. Now don't ye be driving off on me," she demanded. She signaled to Lori to cover her station and hustled down the short set of stairs and out the door. Turning left, she picked up on the man as he lumbered across the parking lot. The redhead sprinted up to the hulking man, grabbing him by the shirt.

"Mr. Johnston, now don't you be acting all cold and ornery with me. I know you too well for this kind of foolishness. I've got something I want to share with you. Now will you just cool your jets and let me read something to you? It's from your sister." The man froze in front of her, staring sternly over her head and back in the direction of the harbor.

"Just give me the letter and be off with you. I'll read it at my leisure."

"I will not. Tis me letter, and I'm afraid you'd just throw it in the rubbish and not read it at all," she answered. He shook his head in frustration and pointed her toward a rusted, weather-worn pickup truck parked a few yards away. Reaching the rear of the vehicle, he reached for the tailgate, releasing a catch and causing it to drop down horizontally. Layla hopped up and seated herself, causing the suspension to let out with a mechanical groan.

"Tis quite the piece of shite you drive around in. And what's a rich man like you doing driving around in this bucket of rattles and moans? You won't be attracting any pretty widows driving around in the likes of this time bomb."

"Get on with the letter, will you," he growled back.

"Aye. As I said before, the letter is from your sister in Portrush. 'Dear Miss O'Malley, I fear I owe you an apology on account of my last letter. I made an improper assumption about your relationship with my brother. I hope you will forgive me for that. Now, on the matter of William's return home for a visit at Christmas, I would certainly have no objections to that and would expect him to stay here with me in Portrush and not at some costly hotel. I can honestly say it would be a joy having him here, sitting across the table from me just like in the years we grew up in this house. I suspect that he would have no knowledge of my Harry's passing a year and a half ago and I hope you will forward that news along to him. I know there was no love lost between him and his brother-in-law but I miss my husband terribly. My two boys both work in London, Harry junior is married and Robert is still a bachelor. They didn't make it home for Christmas last year and I don't expect them this year either, but I can always hope. Will you also tell my brother that I have put the whole matter of our mother's death behind me. That is something that he must live with. That's between him, mother and God. Thank you for your interest in this family business and assure William that if he should visit or pick up the phone and call, there will be no bad blood coming from my end of the phone. Very truly yours, Sally Johnston-Neal.'" Layla folded the letter, tucked it back in the envelope and handed it to the man. Johnston stood frozen in his tracks, his eyes trained on the activity in the harbor a mile away. Studying his face for a moment, she thought she detected a trace of moisture building in his eyes. "She's put her phone number at the bottom of the letter, in case you've forgotten it."

Layla jumped down from the back of the pickup and brushed the remnants of debris from the back of her skirt.

"Now, Mr. Johnston, I don't want to be seeing you or talking to you again until you call this good woman and make peace at home. If you come by the restaurant, I'll not be waiting on you until you've mended these fences." She looked back towards the man who by now was moving toward the cabin of the truck.

"I'll be going home to Donegal in a month and a half, and it'd make it a wee bit easier to leave knowing that I'd be seeing at least one of me Maine friends at Christmas time. You will drive over and see me when you visit your sister, won't you? It can't be more than two or three hours by car," she called out to him.

"We'll see, missy. We'll see," he answered before seating himself in the truck and slamming the heavily dented door behind him.

XX

LIKE EVERYWHERE ELSE, there is a changing of the seasons in the vacation communities along the southern coast of Maine. However, it comes two or three weeks before the calendar's transference of summer to fall. At this time there is reclaiming of the beaches, restaurants, and shops by the World War II and baby boomer generations. Largely gone is the noise and exuberance of grade school children. Instead, the region is overrun by titanic tour buses and recreational vehicles. The oversized vehicles needle their way through narrow, harbored streets with their cargo of aging yet enthusiastic visitors from some faraway place. For the period between Labor Day in early September and Columbus Day in the second week of October, the weather gods seem to smile down on these summer season stragglers, blessing them with an end to the blistering humidity of July and August and replacing it with simple warmth, clear and dry, during the day, and nighttime skies illuminated by countless stars. This was again the case in 1998. Like the return of swallows to Capistrano, Layla observed the changeover in tourists the day after Labor Day. The holiday came late this year, falling on the eighth of the month. As if gathered up by some mythical army of enforcers, all children of school age magically vanished, leaving the region at this glorious time of the year to those old enough to have earned this time in utopia, perhaps as a reward for the accumulation of their life's works.

Layla lay on her back in the sleeping loft, the knotty pine boards a few feet above her head now familiar to her. Her time left in the states was better measured in weeks, five, and no longer months. In her phone conversation the prior week, she picked up on her father's excitement. He was now able to report to friends that his daughter would be returning home to Glencolombkille next month. No doubt, the words, 'next month,' had a wonderful ring to him. Her savings account balance was approaching seven thousand dollars, meaning, barring tragedy, she would return home with something in excess of the eight thousand she set out to bring back for the down payment on the house. She had not heard from or seen Philip since their date the previous Thursday. This concerned her and she planned on a surprise visit to his house after leaving Billy's that night. At work, Donna had lost an amazing forty-four pounds to date and now rivaled Vickie for the unofficial honor as the most attractive female on staff at Billy's Chowder House.

Unexpectedly, a cool breeze from the east came up, causing the window curtains just above her head to flutter. She took in a deep breath and thought she detected the clean scent of autumn. Rolling over onto her stomach, Layla looked out toward the distant Wells Harbor. She thought of William Johnston. Approximately two weeks had passed since the letter from Portrush had been passed along to him. She had not seen him since. He had not contacted his sister, no doubt, and was heeding her words about staying away from her and the restaurant. The refreshing current of air continued to blow in through the window. She thought about how wonderful it would be having Philip beside her in bed at this moment. Layla peered down at the swimming pool. It was still open and the crystal clear water glistened beneath the morning sun, but nary a person ventured into it these days. Summer had passed, she thought. The summer of 1998 had passed and would never be again. She desperately needed to speak with her cousin.

A full hour passed before Layla summoned the energy and the inclination to kick off the bed covers and descend the ladder to the living area. When her bare feet made contact with the hardwood floors at the edge of the room she was reminded of mornings back home in Glencolombkille. She proceeded to the sink and fumbled around until a kettle was on for tea. Donna had backed out of bicycle riding this day, leaving Layla the entire morning to do what she pleased.

It was nearly nine o'clock when the redhead locked the front door to her cottage and made her way toward the main house. Approaching the steps leading to the office she picked up on the sound of Millie's voice. Layla pushed in the door and saw the woman behind the front desk waiting on an elderly couple. Glancing to her left toward the community room she spotted Brian seated next to a woman. Her cousin looked up to see her frozen in place near the entrance.

"Oh Layla, please come over and let me introduce you to someone," he called out. Layla was disappointed to find Brian occupied with someone else but masked her feelings and strolled into the next room. "This lovely lady sitting next to me here is Linda Turcotte. She is not just a dear, dear friend but just happens to be Brendan's mother."

"Your Brendan?" asked the slightly confused Irish girl.

"Our Brendan," corrected the stranger. She stood and extended her hand. She was older than Brian, perhaps fifty years of age. Layla grasped the woman's hand and studied her for a moment. She had an attractive face, not classically beautiful but appealing, with smooth skin and a youthful smile. The woman's hair was salt and pepper in color and perfectly groomed.

"Did you know that I've been here in the states for four and a half months and still haven't met me cousin, Brendan?"

"I live in Kennebunk. He's coming up for a visit next week. I will insist on him coming down to see you, do you understand?"

"That'll be grand."

"Look at his pretty, little cousin here... and he hasn't found time to come visit," observed Brian. "What kind of a jerk did you raise?"

"Don't blame me. It's his poor blood line, that's all," countered the woman, applying an affectionate hug on Brian. "Well, I've got to be off. Off to Boston and a day of shameless shopping in the big city."

"Watch out for the *Big Dig*. If you've been away from Boston for a while, you're in for a shock." She nodded, grabbed her pocketbook, and applied a kiss to Brian's cheek.

"Next week, with Brendan up, maybe the three of us for dinner or something?"

"I'll make it work," he answered before applying a second hug. Layla watched as her cousin accompanied Linda Turcotte out to the reception area where Millie exchanged a hug with the woman.

By the time Brian rejoined his cousin in the community room, Millie was busy attending to two middle aged, female guests.

"You know, I'd feel guilty about doing all this socializing while my assistant manager does all the work, but I've been carrying that woman for years now... just so much dead weight," he chimed out, his voice raised loud enough to be overheard in the next room.

"That's me all right. I come to work every morning with nothing but my sunscreen and a descent book to read," shouted back the woman to the amusement of the guests. Layla stood by quietly, smiling weakly back at her cousin.

"I'll be needing to bend your ear... and in private," she confessed.

"It's been way too long since you bent my ear. What if we go out in the kitchen or back to your cottage for a spot of tea?"

"We could sit out on the porch of me cottage and I'll put on the kettle," she suggested.

"Mill, I'm just going over to fourteen for a bit. Ring me on my cell phone if things get too hectic."

"Why don't you two just go off and have a nice chat, like you did before things got so darn busy around here."

Layla removed two cups from the cabinet and whisked them to the porch while the water heated on the burner. She collapsed into the vacant chair beside her cousin and let out an exaggerated sigh.

"In less than a month I'm going to be losing my Irish cousin and the complex isn't going to be the same," he confessed. She looked over at him sadly and shook her head.

"You'll be getting rid of a busybody and be better off for it."

"Okay, what's getting you so down on yourself?"

"I'm just beginning to question everything I am and starting to wonder if me parents haven't raised an eejit."

"And speaking of your parents, how are they doing?"

"Ah, they're grand. Me da is all excited at the prospect of me getting home. Me ma too."

"Okay baby girl, so what's all this that's got you so down and needing to talk with your idiot cousin?" Layla fidgeted in her chair for a moment before speaking.

"Where do I start? Okay, thanks to the fact that I'm a busybody and can't mind me own business, Mr. Johnston's stopped coming to Billy's because I told him I didn't want to see his face if he didn't call home to Portrush and mend fences with his sister. Since when is it me business to stick me nose in everyone else's life and meddle."

"You do things like that because you give a shit... I'm sorry, shite. You give a shite about other people and you're willing to make an effort on their behalf. I'm sorry kid, but I don't see this as a vice. It's one of the reasons that I love my cousin."

"I may never see Mr. Johnston again."

"But, then again, you may. You did what you thought was right. You cared. There's nothing wrong with you." The redhead looked into her cousin's eyes, processing his words.

"And what color would your eyes be?"

"Hazel—and never mind my eyes! Stay focused," he ordered, reaching over the small, porch table and giving a shove to her arm. From inside came the sound of the kettle water coming to a boil. Layla bounded to her feet.

"I'll prepare the tea," she said, entering the cottage.

It only took two minutes for the twenty-year-old to return with the cups of tea. Carefully placing them down on the table, she added sugar and milk to both and resumed the discussion.

"Me friend Donna is changing right before me eyes. She's not the sweet girl I made friends with in the spring."

"And why do you think this is?"

"I'm thinking is has to do with her losing all this weight and becoming more popular with the boys."

"Are you jealous?"

"Not at all, really. I only have eyes for Philip and so she can find a million boys and it wouldn't bother me. I think it's bothering me because I'm losing me friend, and I'm really responsible for her losing the weight and changing her whole personality."

"Once again, you did something for someone else's own good, and if she isn't handling it well…well, it's out of your hands. Then again, she may be pulling away from you a little because she knows you're leaving in a few weeks and it makes it easier if you're not so attached." His words caused Layla to pause and ponder, visibly considering her cousin's observations. She balanced her saucer in the palm of her hand and drew a sip from the cup. "I've got to be honest here. So far, I see no reason for a certain gorgeous redhead to be hanging her head and moping," declared the man.

A prolonged silence fell upon the porch. Intuitively, the man knew his cousin was not through discussing the pressing issues in her life and took no steps to leave. Amid the quiet and before Layla moved on to the next topic, a pair of monarch butterflies flitted above the lawn in front of the cottage then disappeared behind the motel building.

"I'm feeling a great deal of pressure to make love with Philip," she blurted out hastily, as if uneasy to bring up the subject.

"What kind of pressure?"

"From him, mostly. He's great for reminding me that he's an adult, being in his thirties, and I'm acting like a juvenile. He knows I'm a virgin."

"And how do you feel?"

"I'm starting to feel like a bleedin' holy joe, I am. What's more important is I'm beginning to worry about losing him if I don't go all the way. Do you hear what I'm saying? I could lose him if I stick to me guns. You're a man, Brian. Tell me if it isn't true."

"You could lose him if you *don't* go all the way, and you could just as well lose him if you *do* go all the way. There's this thing called the thrill of the chase, and once you get caught, you're caught. Maybe I'm the wrong guy to be talking to."

"No, you're the right guy. I absolutely believe in you."

"Okay, let's talk it through. If you decide to go all the way and he dumps you after, you wind up with nothing and the realization that you probably screwed up. If you don't go all the way and that causes him to dump you, there's the realization that you probably screwed up, but you still have something for the right guy when he comes along."

"He says that he loves me."

"There're a lot of guys who'll say they love you if they think that it'll get them in your pants. That *I love you* and a buck and a half will get you a cup of coffee at Congdon's. Then there are the guys who just can't say the words… can't get it out of their mouths. They're even more pathetic than the others."

"Okay, let me ask you a personal question. The girl you told me about that day by the pool, the one whose grave you visit every year up in Quebec, didn't you say she was a good Catholic?"

"Yes, she was."

"Did you sleep with her?"

"Yes, a few times."

"So you thought it was okay?"

"First of all, we did that after knowing each other for five years. She was only fifteen when we met. We loved each other and were getting married after her graduation from college... right after."

"Would you have waited for her if she insisted on it... until you were married I mean?"

"Yes, absolutely. I didn't want to live without her under any circumstances. I think that's what love is all about," he said quietly. Layla lifted her cup back to her lips, running her cousin's words over in her mind. "You do realize you make a great cup of tea, right?" She rose from her chair and embraced him.

"More than anything else in the states, I am going to miss you," she confessed.

Layla and Donna were stationed together in the lounge on this day, Tuesday, the fifteenth of September. Behind the scenes in the kitchen, Donna and Billy Sousa made no attempt to hide their romantic relationship. Since her talk with the cook a few weeks back there had been no conversation or banter between the two. Layla's cheerful disposition and whimsical brogue by now had built a following among regular patrons, causing her tables to be frequently requested. For this reason she was only moderately surprised to hear a customer was waiting on one of her tables for lunch while other girl's stations were only half-full. She was in the process of helping Wesley clear a small table by the far end of the bar when she glanced up to see William Johnston approaching, his newspaper tucked under one arm.

"Mr. Johnston, does this mean what I think it means?" Layla called out.

"Yes, I suppose it does. I'll be in Ulster for three weeks later in the year. I'll be flying back to Boston on January fifth."

"And will you be including a trip over to Donegal and Glencolombkille when you're there?"

"That was not part of our deal!" he insisted in a loud voice.

"And why wouldn't you want to come over? What do you think, that I'm inviting you over so I can hand you over to the IRA for ransom money?"

"I wouldn't put anything beyond you," he replied.

"You're coming to the house and having lunch with us. We'll do it on a Saturday and make a day of it." The man shook his head in mock exasperation but could not mask his amusement.

Earlier in the afternoon Layla asked Vickie to let her know if Philip stopped by. Vickie was working the back bay and Layla knew there was a chance she might miss the sculptor and his friends for that reason. As the days passed and there was no word from Philip she grew more concerned. As it stood at the moment, there was no confirmation of their Thursday night together. For this reason she felt entitled to drop down to the house at Moody Point, unannounced, and inquire into their plans for the week. All this she worked out in the back of her head as she flitted from table to table, charming customers and earning gratuities.

William Johnston spent an unusual amount of time over his meal and reading the newspaper. Catching a free moment, Layla tiptoed up behind the man.

"So why did it take you so long to come back and see me? Did you not call your sister first thing?"

"I did not. It took over a week for me to muster up the nerve to make the call. But, in the end, I did."

"And don't you feel better having it out of the way and behind you?"

"Yes, I guess I do. Now I've got that long plane ride to worry about from now until I touch down over there. I hate flying."

"I suppose you'll be flying into Dublin, seeing that there seems to be no planes flying directly from here to Belfast."

"That's right, flying into Dublin."

"I'd be more concerned about having to drive out of the airport and sharing the road with all those bleedin' jackeens, the uppity gobshites that they are." Johnston responded with a hearty laugh.

"I'll be missing you missy, when you're gone that is."

It was nearly ten o'clock before Layla finally punched out her time card and hurried toward the front door. Outside the restaurant, the partial moon and a million stars provided the better part of the light along Mile Road. Armed with a measure of anxiety, the redhead hopped on her bicycle and pedaled eastward on the roadway leading to Moody Point. A month earlier she could have expected shouts from a passing car of teenagers as she traveled the mile and a half to the Trask family's home. However, summer was over and the number of cars occupied by cruising teenage males was at a minimum. On this September night the girl encountered little in the way of traffic and pulled into the Trask driveway less than fifteen minutes after leaving the parking lot of Billy's Chowder House.

As the bicycle rolled up the gravel driveway, Layla noticed the absence of any illumination from within the residence. But, beside the venerable, old house was parked Philip's Firebird, seeming to indicate that the sculptor was home. Laying down her bike by the front steps, she walked to the front door and listened for any sign of life. The building, silent and blanketed in darkness, seemed in a deep sleep. Perplexed, Layla moved around the stately wooden structure, glancing up to the second story and the two bedrooms. It was then, from peripheral vision, she picked up on a sliver of light escaping from the workshop at the rear of the property. Layla stepped through the thick, plush grass and up to the partially open, wooden door. Hoping to remain unobserved, she deliberately pushed in the door, causing a moaning squeal that prompted the man to turn abruptly from his work.

"I didn't mean to startle you. It's just that I began to worry after not hearing from ye," she confessed.

"Layla, you must have gotten the message."

"And what message might that be?"

"I spoke to your cousin about an hour ago. He said he'd tack it to your door."

"No, I haven't been back to the cottage. I came here directly from work." Trask let out a sigh and collapsed back onto a shopworn bench. In the next second he gestured to her to join him. She complied, seating herself next to the man and draping her arm over his shoulder. He lifted his head and gazed at a bust perched atop a working pedestal.

"I just can't seem to finish this monster. I want it to be… it has to be perfect." The bust was of a distinguished looking gentleman sporting a handlebar mustache and rather long sideburns.

"It looks quite good to me," she said while tenderly massaging the back of Trask's neck.

"No, there's something missing, some small detail that I'm not capturing." The twenty-year-old stared back at the bust for a moment before training her eyes back on the man.

"And what does the note say?" she asked apprehensively. He leaned forward and shook his head.

"Last week I got the idea in my head that I could just cut myself loose from this relationship and go on without you. I went so far as to think that I hated you… hated you for making me feel this way and disturbing my otherwise carefree life. I wanted to hurt you, and so I decided to just end things without saying a word. I'd just leave you dangling, not knowing what the hell happened or what the hell you did. I actually did this."

"Is this why I haven't heard from you?"

"That's right. That was until an hour ago when I just needed to see you, and be with you. I called your cousin at the lodge and asked him to jot down a message and deliver it to you. It's supposed to read: 'Thursday? Thinking about nothing but you.'"

"You asked Brian to do that for you?"

"Yes. God, he must think I am an absolute idiot." Layla affectionately wrapped her arms around his neck.

"Brian's not like that." Philip let his neck and shoulders go limp, allowing him to literally fall into her embrace.

"I know part of my problem is this goddamn thing here. I've got to put this thing to bed, but not until it's right."

"Is it for an important customer?" she asked.

"The whole family's important. But the grandfather here is quite ill with only a little time left. The family wants him to see this before the end."

"It looks like a grand bust to me," she injected.

"That's to the untrained eye. I just know that I'm not capturing something. It's there in the photographs I'm working from but it's not in the work."

"And isn't it too bad you're not an abstract painter. Then you could just slop any old shite on the canvas and tell your customer it was done, and absolutely brilliant," she blurted out. Her words brought a chuckle from the man.

"My problem right now, besides this damn thing, is that I don't see enough of you. One night a week and a glimpse of you here and there is not enough."

"And sure there's a remedy for that," she stated.

"What?" She flashed him a sad smile and pointed to the ring finger of her left hand.

"I know, I know. Don't think I haven't been wrestling with that question for a while. Why do you have to be so old world?" He turned his head back toward the unfinished bust. Layla rose from the bench, planting a kiss on the top of his head.

"Me darling, I'll let you get back to work but take comfort in knowing that you'll be the last thing I think about before I drop off to sleep tonight and the first thing I think of when I open me eyes in the morning."

"Thanks Irish girl, it's nice to hear something like that every once in a while."

"And I'll say a prayer to St. Jude, the patron saint of hopeless cases. It seems you have your own hopeless case here in the person of old mister sideburns."

"Any assistance will be gratefully accepted. Do you want a ride back to your cottage?" She waived him off, leaving him with an innocent kiss on the lips.

The bike ride back to Route 1 and the cottage gave Layla time to mull over the events of the evening. She was buoyed by Philip's admission of the strong need to share her company. There was little traffic to share the road with at this hour. It was not quite eleven o'clock when Layla pedaled her way up the driveway of the complex.

"There's a note tacked to your door, biffo," called out Brian from the porch of the main house. He was standing in the shadows.

"Aye, I spent a wee time with Philip earlier. He says he feels like an eejit for bothering you with that." Brian stepped forward into the moonlight. He held a coffee mug in one hand.

"Yeah, I can understand that. Is everything okay?"

"And sure it's grand. I'd say I'm in good form at the moment," she answered.

"You know cuz... and this is only my amateur observation, I'd say you have this guy sort of where you want him. If that wasn't love I heard at the other end of the phone line tonight, then it was a pretty, damn good imitation."

"I'd like to think so, I would."

"You asked for my advice earlier. Here's an update. This guy is in love with you—really in love. And why shouldn't he be? You're the whole package. Don't do anything stupid that you might live to regret. Okay?"

"Aye." She pushed off on her bike and coasted toward her cottage.

"And Layla, tonight I'll be thinking about nothing but you," he called out, parroting Philip's words in a wimpy, lovesick fashion.

"That'll be enough from Maggie May's slave boy, it will," she sang back, revisiting the running joke from the Bedford weekend three months earlier. She heard her cousin break out in a deep, earnest laugh before stepping back inside the office and out of earshot.

XXI

L AYLA WAS JOLTED FROM a sound sleep by the droning wail of the alarm clock perched only a few inches above her head. She swiped at it twice before making contact with the alarm button and silencing the harsh noise. The face on the digital clock read 1:30. The redhead rolled herself off the couch and stumbled to her feet. From above her head descended the sound of raindrops making contact with the cottage's skylight. It had been two weeks since she last spoke with her parents and she was not about to let any more time pass between phone calls. Still fully dressed from her night at Billy's, she nonetheless pulled an Aran sweater on over her uniform and stepped out onto the screened porch. It was a cold rain falling on this night, the chilly, wet air causing her body to shiver as she bolted across the yard and to the office. Moments later the twenty-year-old was punching the familiar string of numbers into the telephone and waiting on the other end.

"Good morning me darling—and didn't I know you'd be calling this very morn," sang out her father.

"Good morning Da, and how would everyone be?"

"Oh we're grand, just grand. Do you realize what day this is?"

"Tis the twenty-ninth or t'irtieth."

"The t'irtieth it is, making tomorrow October and the month of your return. Your mother and I can hardly wait for the day. We've decided to both hop work on the fifteenth and meet you at Shannon. Are you getting excited yourself?"

"Aye, I am. And I'll have you know that me savings topped eight t'ousand this past weekend. We've done it. We'll have the money for Mr. Connolly and the bank."

"Not we, Layla...tis all your doing."

"And is Ma anywhere nearby?"

"She is. Let me put her on." There came the sound of the phone passing hands before the voice of Finula O'Malley came through the wires.

"Two weeks it is, two weeks and we'll have you back here in your own bed," the woman exclaimed.

"Yes, and you'll both be down to pick me up at Shannon I hear."

"We will, and won't that be a grand drive home from County Clare with our daughter in the back seat with stories of the United States and all the new friends she's made."

"Aye, it will Ma, it will."

"And have you been keeping up with going to mass and receiving the sacraments?"

"I have, and wasn't I about to ask the same thing of you two," answered Layla, recognizing her mother's clumsy way of checking up on the specific nature of her romantic life.

The phone call was restricted to a reasonable twelve minutes on this night. The O'Malleys agreed not to speak again until a day or two before her return, and to use that time to iron out all the details of her return flight and arrival time. Her spirits elevated by the voices of her parents, she returned to the cottage and prepared for a shortened night of sleep. She was scheduled to meet with Donna Pento at eight this morning for breakfast and a bike ride. In truth, she would have preferred to sleep in on this Wednesday and forego the meal and exercise. However, her friendship with Donna had grown increasingly fragile and she did not want to do anything to strain the relationship. Peeling off her clothes, she glanced around the tiny cottage, the exposed, knotty pine roof boards and stained wooden walls now seeming like old, familiar friends. She would miss this place, she thought. Finally, she maneuvered the ladder into place and climbed up to the loft. A mild state of melancholy descended on her, knowing that in a mere two weeks this cottage would become nothing more than a fading memory.

Layla sat astride her bicycle close by the entrance to Ames Department Store, waiting on the arrival of Donna Pento. She covered her mouth through an expanded yawn and glanced down at her watch. It was nearly twenty minutes past eight o'clock and still no sign of her friend. Dismounting the bike, she carefully laid it down on the sidewalk and took a seat with her back against the exterior to the store. With her long, reddish auburn hair in full contact with the department store's wall, she closed her eyes.

The noise from a vehicle passing by on the roadway within ten feet of her position brought Layla out of her unscheduled nap. Mildly flustered, she looked down at her watch. It was after eight-thirty and there was still no sign of her friend. Layla remounted her bicycle and pedaled back to her cottage, a distance no more than a quarter of a mile away. Back in cottage fourteen, the redhead grabbed another nap before showering and changing for her eleven o'clock shift at Billy's Chowder House.

Layla was seated on the hallway bench, reviewing that day's specials, when she was joined by Wesley Wright. The teenager appeared more upbeat on this morning, plunking himself down beside his friend and playfully fiddling with her menu.

"Oh, if you wouldn't mind, I wondered if we could limit our time together tomorrow morning to breakfast... maybe nine-thirty at Congdon's?"

"Dragging arse, are we?" replied the young man while mimicking the Irish girl's jargon.

"Aye, that's pretty much it. And what are you so rapid about this morning?"

"Oh, it's just that I have this bad habit of getting off on the misery of others."

"And whose misery would this be?"

"Billy Sousa's out in the kitchen, bitching and moaning about getting dumped by Donna," he reported. Layla's eyes widened as she turned and faced the dishwasher.

"Oh, and I'm sure that's put a spring in your step," said Layla, her mind already trying to piece together this information with her friend's no-show performance the same morning. "I'm glad to see she's finally smartened up."

"He was out there calling Donna a little whore before Adam made him shut up and focus on his work."

"Has she said anything to you?"

"No, as far as I know we're still not on speaking terms anymore," he confessed. "Well, I've got to get back to work. So, if we don't talk again, nine-thirty at Congdon's tomorrow morning, right?"

"Aye, and maybe we'll know more about this whole mess by then."

Donna Pento arrived late for work on this morning. She searched out Layla, collapsing onto the bench beside her and letting out with a sigh.

"Layla, would you be a dear and go out in the kitchen and punch me in?" she asked. "I have no desire to set eyes on Billy this morning or for the rest of the day for that matter."

"I'll punch you in but there's no way you'll be avoiding him all day. It's not like you can be staying out of the kitchen," answered the redhead, rising to her feet and walking through the swinging doors. She rejoined her friend a few seconds later in the hall.

"And where were ye this morning at eight o'clock. I sat there for over thirty minutes."

"I was wasted. I slept in."

"Well, it would have been nice if you had called and let me do the same," snapped back her friend.

"Jesus, don't make a federal goddamn case out of it. It was a goddamn bike ride for Christ's sake," sniped back Donna.

"I guess I looked at it all wrong then. To me it was committed time with me friend," she answered. The attractive brunette shook her head in frustration and turned away. The two were joined by Lori Schofield seconds later, allowing Layla to jump into a conversation with the woman. When two male customers appeared in the doorway, Donna unfolded her long, tan, athletically defined legs out into the aisle, prompting Lori to raise her eyebrows and gesture to Layla to take a peek. The redhead did and reacted with a faintly audible groan.

On this Wednesday Layla was stationed in the back bay along with Betsy and Susanne. Vickie had put in for this day off back in August. Staffing was a little thin, requiring each of the girls to work a little harder than usual. Layla was entertaining a table of Irish-Americans from South Boston when a tap came on her shoulder. She turned to see Philip standing behind her, appearing ill at ease.

"I hate bothering you while you're working but I'm wondering if you could be ready earlier than usual tomorrow. I'll break from work in the afternoon and maybe pick you up at three-thirty. Will that work?"

"T'ree t'irty it is," Layla answered. "At me palace."

"Great, it'll give us a little more time together," said Trask before whirling around and attempting to leave the room. The redhead clutched him by the forearm and pulled him back.

"And this is me boyfriend, folks. I know you're thinking that the bloke's old enough to be me da, but he's not. He's just the man who won me heart," she explained. "Philip, these good people are the Ryans from South Boston... by way of Tipperary." Philip fidgeted nervously as the table full of strangers gazed up at him.

"I've got a half-dozen nephews who I can fix this little doll up with if you should let her get away," called out an overweight woman from across the table.

"Three-thirty," he stated again.

"T'ree t'irty it is," she repeated, deliberately flaunting her brogue. "And why didn't you ask for one of me tables? Vickie's got the day off."

"Oversight," he explained bluntly, then made his way away from the twenty-year-old and her customers.

A short time after her unexpected visit from Philip, Layla scurried across the building to the lounge to place an alcoholic order. She was about to return to the kitchen when an outburst of laughter from the corner of the room captured her attention. There, at a table at the far side of the bar, sat Philip and his usual entourage. Philip, his back to the remainder of the room, had no way of knowing that Layla was twenty feet away. However, she was spotted by Deidre, the black-haired girl who made no secret of her dislike for her. Of particular interest to Layla was the animated behavior from their waitress, Donna Pento. She looked on as the trim brunette stood between two of the males at the table, her hands placed in a familiar fashion on the shoulders of Philip and one of his friends. Frozen in place for an extended moment, she abruptly regained her wits and made her way back to the kitchen.

The Ryan family lingered at their table well after the last dessert plate was removed from their table, caught under the spell of their Irish waitress. Layla was in the midst of an animated story from home when a hand clutched at her sleeve. She whirled to find Philip standing behind her.

"I just needed to see that face one more time before I left," he explained.

"Oh, you've got this guy but good," called out a woman good-naturedly from the table. Layla looked up into the man's face and thought she detected a trace of embarrassment.

"Oh no… tis he who has me… and from the first moment herself set eyes on him," she whispered back, just loud enough for the table of onlookers to hear. The two exchanged innocent pecks to a chorus oohs and ahhs from the Ryan family and the man made haste toward the door. The perky redhead replayed the short visit over in her mind throughout the afternoon and into the evening. There was a tenderness about it that brought her warmth and comfort. Meanwhile, in the back of her mind, the image of Donna Pento's arms draped familiarly over Philip and his friend's shoulders that afternoon in the lounge kept resurfacing. She was grateful that he had extended himself to make contact with her before returning to work.

Billy's Chowder House was almost empty of customers as the waitresses and busboys scurried around to clear tables and return every dish and piece of silverware to the dishwashers. Just prior to punching out Layla found herself alone with Lori Schofield by the front desk.

"Lori, weren't you hosting during lunch today?" she asked.

"Yeah, but I was back on tables for dinner."

"Do you happen to remember if you seated me Philip and his eejit friends?"

"Distinctly. I was a little surprised when he asked for Donna and not you, but then I figured you had some kind of an understanding about that," she answered, looking up at Layla and seemingly waiting on a clarification.

"Aye… tis an understanding we have about things of that sort," she replied without further comment or elaboration.

XXII

WITH HER FEET PROPPED UP on the railing surrounding her, Layla sat out on the porch of her cottage and looked down at the marshland and harbor spread out below. Oranges and yellows had begun to bleed into the expanse of green that was the Rachel Carson Wildlife Sanctuary. Earlier in the day from her perch in the sleeping loft, she had watched as a flock of migrating birds had risen in a unified cloud and headed southward toward warmer weather. The mornings had grown noticeably cooler, prompting her to add a blanket or two to her bed. No longer were the pleasure boats pushing southward from the harbor and into the arm of the Webhannet River as they had in the spring and summer. However, not only was the landscape changing, everything was changing in the life of Layla O'Malley. On this morning she had begun thinking about the prospect of saying good-bye to her cousin Brian. It was true. Her time in the states was growing short. Even more importantly, her time with Philip Trask was drawing to a close.

On this afternoon she was dressed for the season. She wore a pair of perfectly fitting designer jeans, a present from Margaret Kelly back in New Hampshire. She took inventory of her time spent in New England. She had seen far too little of Brian's family. With two weeks remaining in the country, she still had not set eyes on Brendan or Jenny. Without a doubt, her time had been dominated by work. Her thoughts of a more serious nature were interrupted in that instant when Brian rounded the corner of the cottage and invited himself onto the porch.

"I carry here the largest cup of hot chocolate in the world," he announced, holding up a gigantic, white and red mug. "Would you care to help me drink it down while you wait on your suitor?"

"Thanks, but I think I'll pass on the generous offer."

"Hot chocolate, Layla…nature's anti-depressant," he reasoned.

"Well, that I could certainly use."

"Five months is a heck of a long time. You've made friends and developed some attachments," Brian added. He offered her the cup and she accepted, putting it to her lips and taking a dainty sip.

"Make sure you tell your wife how much I loved the jeans she sent me. Sweet Jaysus, they caress me body like a lover. I'm sure there's not a jackeen in all of Dublin with a finer pair of pants."

"She took a liking to you, my Maggie May. She doesn't do that with a lot of people."

"Tis only because I'm a blood relation to the man she loves," offered Layla.

"No kid, it's more than that. You're a special, young lady, and I'm going to miss you something terrible when you're gone," the man confessed, taking back the cup.

"And sure you barely saw me for weeks at a time over the summer."

"I know, I know. But I always knew you were there over behind the motel. I always knew that if I wanted to, I could go over and see my cousin. In a way, I think I squandered a lot of the time you were here, and I'm really going to miss seeing you bicycle by the office, and come over to hassle me on occasion."

"You know, it makes me sound like a complete eejit, but I consider this little place me home in America."

"Your folks must be excited about you coming home."

"Aye, and aren't they both driving down to Shannon to pick me up in two weeks."

"How are you getting to Logan the day you leave?"

"Philip's offered to take me down and see me off," she reported.

"Ahh, replaced I am by a younger man." She reached over the small table, putting her hand to his cheek.

"No Brian Kelly; there'd be no replacing you." He took a long, thoughtful sip from the mug and stared out over the estuary below.

"Has he popped the question yet… or alluded to it?"

"He's talked around the subject and gotten real emotional about me leaving. But to answer your question, no."

"Do you expect him to?"

"Two weeks ago I was thinking that it was only a matter of time. But lately, I'm picking up on different feelings and emotions."

"Like what?"

"Tis hard to put into words. It makes me feel uncomfortable just thinking about it. But I'm starting to wonder if he might not be sharing his time with someone else."

"And why is that?"

"I don't know. Partly a woman's intuition and partly…"

"Yeah?"

"Partly because he hasn't been dogging me lately about having sex. I'm not complaining, mind you, but it is a wee curious."

"Listen to me young lady. If you have no basis for not trusting the man, then don't think that way. If you don't trust the man or woman you love, then you give them cause to deceive you." Layla shot her cousin a curious look and gestured for the mug.

"Nature's anti-depressant you say?"

"Absolutely," he answered. "But you might want to brush your teeth again before your date pulls up and sees little miss brown teeth." The twenty-year-old bolted to her feet and raced inside the cottage.

The autumn shadows from the buildings lining the crest of the hill on the complex were just beginning to lengthen when Layla heard the sound of a high performance engine idling behind the cottage. Brian rose from his chair and motioned to his cousin.

"I believe your laddie has arrived," he said, stepping to the side and allowing her to exit the porch.

"Good luck tonight princess…on all fronts." She gave the side of his face an affectionate clatter and headed around the building to the car. Philip had stepped out from behind the wheel but immediately reentered the vehicle upon spotting his date.

"This may look like I'm dressing down for the evening but I have a feeling these jeans came with a hefty price tag," called out the redhead at the sight of Philip lowering his sunglasses and taking her in.

"If I ever questioned your feminine curves, those questions have been answered," he joked, apparently pleased with the lines of her body brought out by the form-fitting outfit. A few seconds passed before the vehicle turned toward the entrance and cautiously maneuvered its way over two speed bumps before brashly accelerating onto Route 1 and speeding northward in the direction of Kennebunk.

"You appear to be a man who knows where he is off to," observed the girl from the passenger seat.

"Portland for a night of drinking and dancing…Kennebunkport for an evening of quiet dining and a walk among majestic homes…"

"The girls at work asked me if I'd seen Parson's Way and the Bush compound yet. I told them that I hadn't."

"Then why don't we start there. If the tide is right we'll sit you on spouting rock and give you a real thrill," he exclaimed. "The water temperature is probably down to fifty degrees by now. That should tune you right in." With that said, the car sped by the long line of antique shops and finally the Maine Diner before turning right onto Route 9 and a direct line to Kennebunkport.

After winding through streets lined with a succession of trendy shops and artist's galleries, Trask motored his Pontiac Firebird by the majestic Colony Hotel, pulling his car off the roadway and onto the grassy shoulder.

"What do you say we walk for a bit, maybe as far as George Bush's house at Walkers Point?"

"George Bush, the ex-president?"

"Yeah, this is Kennebunkport, remember?" Stepping from the car, Layla threw her arm around Philip's waist and they scurried to higher ground. Above and beyond the dark blue water immediately below them was an extended expanse of Maine coastline that took in the beaches of Wells and Ogunquit.

"Where will we find this spout I'm supposed to sit on?" she asked.

"Up the road a ways. Don't worry, we'll be there soon enough," he explained, his arm now encircling her slender waist. Over the next few minutes they passed couples seated on many of the dozens of benches laid out along the rocky shoreline. They passed a church seemingly built from nothing but stones.

"I know the Bush family goes to church here when they're up," reported Philip to his auburn haired companion.

"Never mind the church biffo, where's the spout I'm supposed to set me bum down on?" asked Layla with childish enthusiasm.

"Hold your horses now. We'll be there soon enough." They followed a sidewalk for the next few minutes before Trask pulled her over a path columned with sharp, protruding rocks and up onto a rise. There, they sat down on one of two benches and looked out to sea. The ocean had grown choppier, the action of the waves smacking noisily against the wall of rock constituting the shoreline.

"Where's me spout?" she demanded, shaking his arm and clutching the material of his jacket.

"It's just not here at the moment, but if the tide is coming in then it should be putting on a show right over there in a short while," he explained, pointing over her shoulder to the right of their position. She let out with a disappointed moan and lay her head on his shoulder. Fifty yards north of them and extended out on a small neck of land was an impressive residence constructed largely of rocks that appear to have been excavated from the surrounding terrain. There was a wonderful, moody semblance to the structure, causing Layla to stare at it at length.

"Philip, will you buy me that house for me twenty-first birthday?"

"Ahh, Layla, a girl of such simple wants and needs," he mused. They looked on in silence as a formation of birds winged their way into sight, less than thirty feet above the ocean water, and proceeded to follow the line of the Kennebunkport coast until they disappeared behind a cluster of oceanfront homes. Meanwhile, an invigorating breeze blew in off the Maine water, causing the redhead to pull her boyfriend closer for warmth. They sat together without a word exchanged, appreciating the time together and the beautiful surroundings now solely available to them. She leaned forward and kissed the man on the side of the face.

"I'm going to be asking you something and I'm already hating meself for it. But I need to put me mind to rest." He turned toward her, curiosity evident on his face. "There's been a change in you for a time now. Not a bad change, but enough to raise questions in me head. The other day at work, when I was in the lounge and fetching a drink for one of me customers, I noticed me friend Donna at your table and her hands on you and one of your friends in a manner that was...unusually friendly. It just seemed a little...unusual, seeing that you people generally never get the girl to wait on you, that being Vickie's very own honor."

"I'm not sure what you're alluding to Layla?" he answered defensively.

"It's just that the girl has just dumped her boyfriend for no apparent reason and here she is acting the brasser at a table of strangers." Trask paused and took a deep breath.

"I'd appreciate it if you didn't share what I'm about to tell you with anyone, okay?" Layla nodded in the affirmative. "Your friend has begun going out with my friend, Eric. This is something that's been in the works for a short while, and for the time being they'd like to keep it secret. Do you understand, Layla?" The twenty-year-old let out with a sigh of relief.

"I can't begin to tell you how much better that makes me feel," she admitted, placing her head back on his shoulder. They sat together silently for another length of time, each watching the swells in the water just off shore.

"Your perfume is quite effective this afternoon. I do love that personal scent of yours. And I can't believe what those jeans do for your figure," he admitted.

"Me figure is all me. Me jeans just do nothing to mask the exquisite form God has given me," she explained. At that moment, prompted by a succession of swells reaching shore, spouting rock, at a distance of fifty feet from their position, began to spurt water up into the air. Layla sprang to her feet, pulling Philip up from the bench with her.

"Escort me over to the spout so I can park me behind over it," she ordered.

"You're not serious, are you?"

"And sure it is I am." Wrapping an arm around her flabbergasted date, she drove them in unison in the direction of the natural, oceanic geyser. They were only a few feet from the break in the rocks through which the seawater had jetted upward when she abruptly twisted the man's arm behind his back.

"What are you doing? That hurts. You're going to break my arm," he called out. The words barely out of his mouth, Layla pushed the two forward, directly into the path of the spouting water. Beneath their feet, the force of the incoming swell of water roared through a labyrinth of rocks and sent saltwater upward, spraying over them.

"You're certifiably insane," he called out, ocean water streaming down his face.

"Aye, quite mad I am." Layla, her red hair glistening from the spray from the rock, jumped up, wrapping her legs around Trask's body. "And the banshee I carry within me cries out for you, Philip Trask. You, the man I love." With that said, she brought her lips to his and kissed him with the same intensity that she had on that fateful night at the house on Moody Point.

"Do you think they'll even seat us at Alisson's in the state we're in?" quizzed Philip good-naturedly.

"Who could turn away the most accomplished sculptor in all of Kennebunkport? And there we'll be, leaving a wet spot on our chairs like a pair of toddlers," she mused.

Layla and Philip were reasonably dry by the time they presented themselves at the door of Alisson's Restaurant in Kennebunkport. The Dock Square establishment by now had taken on a nostalgic feel for Layla, having shared dinner with both Philip and her cousin Brian since her arrival in May. Seated at a small, window table overlooking the square, the mood was jovial. It was as if both were avoiding the reality that hung over them like a dark cloud: Layla's departure in two weeks time. Finally, it was the girl who broached the subject of her return home to Ireland.

"I'm thinking that in a month's time I'll be standing back on the beach at Glencolombkille with thoughts of me love dancing through me head," she said sadly, hoping to engage the man in talk of their future plans.

"I know I should be coming up with a game plan regarding you and me, and the future. But, the truth is, I'm out straight at the studio and I've got to have some down time to work out a blueprint for us. There's a lot to consider."

"We're two people in love with each other. To herself, the blueprint couldn't be more clear." Philip fidgeted uncomfortably with his utensils.

"You can't believe the sort of garbage I've had thrown at me since we hooked up. Deidre's convinced you're pushing for marriage so you can stay in the country and don't have to go back."

"And are you saying you're even considering such rubbish?" she asked, an edge showing up in her voice.

"Of course not, not seriously anyway."

"So, you are considering the possibility that your poor, bogtrotter of a girlfriend might have some devious scheme in the back of her head?" He reached across the table, pressing his hand affectionately to her cheek.

"By the end of the month, things will have seriously slowed down. I'll fly over to Ireland and see you, and meet your parents. Did you hear that? I'll meet your parents! We'll map things out then. Just give me these few weeks." She responded with a tender smile.

"Aye, if it's what you need. We'll do that. I'll take you down to me beach at Glencolombkille." Trask ordered a second martini and scanned the room in search of any familiar faces.

"Oh, while I'm thinking of it, I won't be home Monday night. I'm going to be down with my dad in Boston and I'll stay with him that night. I wouldn't want you biking all the way down to Moody Point after work on one of your unannounced visits for nothing."

"Nothing wrong I hope?"

"No, just a little family business."

"Now, does the man even know about me?"

"Oh, he does. I don't think he realizes how serious we are, but he knows about you, the redheaded ancestor of a pirate queen." His answer brought a giggle from the girl as she added butter to her baked potato.

The complex was shrouded in darkness as the Firebird idled behind her cottage and Philip stood with Layla by the front door.

"I'm only working the dinner shift on Sunday but I'll be staying down with the Kellys on Atlantic Avenue on Saturday night and spending the morning and part of the afternoon with them on Sunday. It'll be the last time I get to see Colleen."

"Is Colleen Brian's hot wife?"

"I'll be sleeping with Colleen if I'm not mistaken."

"You're sleeping with your cousin's wife?"

"No, you eejit. Colleen's his four-year-old daughter, and I don't like hearing you talking about other women that way," she exclaimed, putting her face directly into his. "I told you, when we're finally together and we've tied the knot, in front of a priest and in the sight of God, I will show you sexual passion the likes of which you've never dreamed of. Me good night kisses, as out of hand as they can get and hard on your ribs, they be nothing compared to what's in store for you. Philip Trask, I'll make you the happiest man on earth, and I'm not just coddin' with you." The handsome bachelor shook his head and let out with a guarded chuckle. "Now me banshee feels like she might be even a wee bit more active than usual tonight. Would you be wanting to skip the kiss, for your peace of mind?"

"What? I took spouting rock up me arse this afternoon, thanks to you, and not even a goodnight kiss?" Philip asked, going so far to even adopt her pronunciation.

"Herself is thinking you look extremely handsome in this moonlight," she added with more than a hint of mischief in her voice.

"Where's my goodnight..." Layla hopped up on the man, encircling his waist with her legs and causing Trask to fall sideways against the cottage. They hit the grass together a moment later with Philip on the bottom and taking the brunt of the fall. Already his head was in her hands and their lips locked together.

"Oh Christ, my ribs," he called out.

"Quiet, you baby. You'll wake the renters," she ordered, taking only a moment's respite from the kiss. "Me blood is boiling for ye, and when we're married I'll take you to places your cultured girlfriends from Boston never dreamed of," she promised while unlocking her ankles and releasing him from her hold.

"You really know how to screw with my head, Layla." The redhead lifted the man to his feet and brushed his back of loose grass.

"Our honeymoon will be legendary. What kind of a honeymoon is it for these mulchies who've already been living together for two years? What kind of excitement is that? Just think Philip, I'll be letting the banshee out of me on our honeymoon and you'll see for the first time what I've been promising you." Trask stared deep into her eyes, her words evidently heightening his imagination.

"Say hi to the Kellys for me," he said, turning from the twenty-year-old.

"Say hi to that geebag Deidre for me," she answered, opening the screen door and stepping onto the porch. Layla was struggling to open the front door with an uncooperative house key when she caught sight of Philip through the porch screen standing a few feet away.

"You're still here?"

"Before I left I wanted you to know that I love you for more than the sexual intrigue and games you put me through," he admitted.

"And I should hope so."

"Layla, you are the most vibrant, and exciting, and most joyous woman I have ever come in contact with. The fact that you're also gorgeous is just a bonus. I don't know what I'd do if I ever lost you." She took a step forward and placed her open hand up on the screen. He followed her initiative and did the same, their hands only separated by the thin, iron mesh.

"You won't lose me Philip; I'm yours."

XXIII

WHEN LAYLA LEFT WORK on Saturday she had to remember to point her bicycle toward the ocean and not Route 1. She would stay with the Kellys on this night at their beachfront house on Wells Beach. It was nine-thirty when she rounded the corner past the Beachcomber, a landmark gift shop dating back to the early twentieth century, and headed down Atlantic Avenue. The road was quiet on this evening. The redhead picked up a head of steam on the initial slope and barreled northward the half-mile to the house, passing by darkened houses that, only a month before, were ablaze in artificial light. Turning into the driveway, she hopped off the bike and discreetly guided it up a short flight of stairs and onto the building's two-sided porch. She barely had time to reach the back door when the sound of a latch being thrown was heard.

"Layla's sleeping with me – Layla's sleeping with me," called out an overly enthusiastic Colleen through the screen door.

"We let her stay up and wait for you," explained her mother standing directly behind her. The Irish girl entered the kitchen carrying a small overnight bag.

"Thank God you came tonight. She kept creeping down from her bedroom last night and we finally had to let her sleep with us," called out Brian from the nearby living room. "Moira's got another date this weekend so she's back in Bedford."

"Did Jenny and Brendan come over by any chance?" Layla asked.

"I'm afraid not," answered Margaret. "They have these friends at school, a regular Algonquin Round Table to hear them talk. I'm sorry Layla." The twenty-year-old shrugged her shoulders, plainly disappointed by the couple's absence.

With the four-year-old dozing beside her on the couch, Layla sipped tea and politely joined the Kellys in conversation for the next half hour. Their one hundred year old house was smartly decorated, exhibiting no signs of the

215

presence of a preschooler. On the east side of the room was a picture window that looked over the outside porch and Atlantic Ocean. Margaret Kelly dominated the better part of the discourse as she outlined her and her guest's shopping plans for the following day. In the end, it was decided that Brian, Colleen and Layla would rise early the next morning and head out to seven o'clock mass. They would return to the house for a hearty breakfast, after which Margaret and Layla would head out to Portland for some serious shopping. Layla was only scheduled to work the dinner shift on Sunday, leaving her the better part of the afternoon to spend with her cousin's wife. With Layla's departure date drawing near, the two women decided to work on picking up presents for the Irish girl's parents. Margaret assured her guest that Portland's 'Old Port' district was the perfect place for such an undertaking.

The kitchen clock was chiming eleven while Layla climbed the narrow stairwell up to the second, then third floor of the oceanfront home. On her back rode Colleen, her arms draped about the redhead's neck. On the second story she passed through the Kelly's combination sitting room and study. The impressive room, with its knotty pined walls and dominant window looking far out to sea, was flanked on the west by the master bedroom. With her blond-haired charge gradually regaining consciousness, the twenty-year-old started up the next, even narrower stairwell. Halfway up this next flight of stairs, she was forced to lower her head and shoulders, the roofline constricting the height of the stairwell. Ultimately the two arrived on the third story and entered one of the two, attic bedrooms. Layla deposited her rider on the full-sized bed of the eastern room, a small bedroom with inclined ceilings dictated by the roof and with a small, solitary window. However, that single window with its extended elevation prompted the young woman to pause at the edge of the bed, staring out at the expanse of ocean water illuminated by moonlight. From this lofty perch she could almost see back to County Donegal, she thought. Her meditative state did not extend beyond a few seconds, thanks to her tiny cousin's lunge into her arms and a cry for attention.

"Down to bed and under the rugs with you," commanded Layla playfully. The little girl complied but with a rush of giddiness.

"Don't you be keeping Layla up all night," called out Margaret from two floors below. Colleen giggled and tugged at her cousin to join her under the covers.

Layla lay still in bed, comforted by the sound of crashing waves no more than fifty yards away. She had not pulled the window shade, happy to stare out at the starry sky on this night. So close to her was the four-year-old that the warmth of the child's breathe could be felt on her neck.

"It is so good to have you here with me tonight," confessed Colleen following a few minutes of silence.

"And sure you have to get over being afraid of the dark, you do."

"Oh, I'm not afraid of the dark. Moira can tell you that."

"Then why did you go downstairs and bother you're ma and da last night, and make them let you sleep with them?" The girl tightened her embrace of her cousin.

"Last night I dreamed that bad men came into the house, and I heard them killing daddy and mommy, and then they started climbing the stairs to kill me," answered Colleen, her voice registering a measure of fear even after twenty-four hours.

"That's from watching too much rubbish on the television. Your da wouldn't let anyone hurt him or your mommy, and he certainly wouldn't let anyone hurt you. Your daddy's a big, strong man and he wouldn't let it happen," declared Layla with absolute certitude.

"Even against monsters?" asked Colleen.

"Even against monsters."

By any standards, Layla and Margaret Kelly enjoyed a good day of shopping on Sunday morning and afternoon. Over and beyond their goal of finding gifts for the O'Malleys back in Glencolombkille the two found themselves sharing personal matters with the other. Layla learned of the great satisfaction Margaret Kelly had derived from initiating her husband's genealogical study and the ultimate locating of the former Finula Kelly in County Donegal. She had always sensed a void in her spouse stemming from a lack of any known, living blood relatives and felt a great feeling of accomplishment with the locating of kin in Glencolombkille. Layla, in turn, shared with the woman many of the details of her relationship with Philip Trask, including her fears, hopes and expectations.

It was one-thirty on a mostly cloudy afternoon when the two sat by the window of a homey coffee shop in Portland, a tiny pastry shop not unlike the many back in Ireland, and looked over the items purchased this day. Layla was particularly proud of the choices for her parents: a strong, hand held telescope for her father—an immense upgrade from the piece he presently used—and a simple, jeweled necklace for her mother—an item selected specifically by Margaret and for which she insisted on and paid half the negotiated price. On the lighter side, Layla came across a doll in a collectibles and antique shop. The doll was that of a banshee and sported long, red hair, fiery crimson eyes, and a wild, devilish smirk. She would surprise Philip with this reminder of his Irish girlfriend's inner self. She hoped it would serve as a constant reminder of the excitement ultimately in store for him in their future life together.

It was almost four o'clock on Sunday afternoon when Layla extended good-byes to Margaret and Colleen Kelly. Layla and Colleen exchanged teary hugs, the little girl asking her cousin not to leave and instead to return with her to New Hampshire. Margaret, too, embraced the girl but in a more reserved manner, insisting that they would soon be together again, one visiting the other. Brian, enjoying the better part of a day off, invited his cousin to drop by the office after work for a cup of tea. Layla promised she would as she pushed off on her bicycle and started her mile-long ride to work.

XXIV

On Monday Layla was again scheduled for dinner hours only, giving her the morning and the better part of the afternoon off. Donna drew the luncheon schedule on this day, meaning Layla would only catch a quick glimpse of her friend at the changing of the shifts. After some reflection and an extended talk with Wesley during their bike ride to Parson's Beach this day, she decided to speak to Donna and see if she could iron out the recent development of cracks in the friendship. She saw this as critical, given her imminent return home. She figured, if there was something she had done to alienate her closest female friend she wanted to know about it. This way, hopefully, things could be resolved before her trip home. They were scheduled to ride together on Wednesday morning and the redhead was resolved to bring up the issue early on that day and talk it through. As she saw it, Donna had allowed her newly found fitness and attractiveness to alter her heretofore-warm disposition. However, she also realized that there might be other factors at play, health or personal, of which she had no knowledge. Plus, there was also Donna's budding relationship with Philip's friend, Eric. Layla could never resist the lure of a little romantic intrigue, and her friend's budding romance was no exception. It would be an interesting bike ride on Wednesday, she thought, interesting to say the least.

Fog had silently made its way inland on Monday night, past Billy's Chowder House and up the gentle slope to Route 1. After wishing Betsy Chase and Lori Schofield a good night, Layla unlocked her bicycle and made her way into the fog toward Moody Point. Philip would not be home this night but she carried with her his present. Strapped inside the bike's carrying case was the banshee doll she had picked up in Portland the day before. The plan was for her to leave the doll propped up in the doorway to greet him on his return, a humorous 'welcome home' from his Celtic girlfriend. The air was cold and extremely damp on this evening with visibility no more than fifty feet. As a precaution she rode facing the traffic, allowing herself to spot the approach of an errant vehicle as early as possible. Traveling at a slower speed than usual, she managed to reach Moody Point by ten o'clock. Turning onto the gravel driveway, the surface of the roadway gave off a crunching sound under her tires accentuated by the dead still of the neighborhood. Predictably, through the horizontal movement of thick fog, the house sat in darkness and quiet, the parking space by the porch empty of Philip's Firebird.

Layla reached the house and laid her bicycle down in the damp grass. She moved cautiously, the heavy fog not allowing much light to filter in from the road a hundred feet away. Stepping up onto the porch, she leaned the doll against the base of the front door and smiled down upon the sight, albeit barely visible. She turned away from the house and quietly hopped down to the wet grass. She breathed in the moist air. Her eyes were adapting somewhat to the darkness and fog. Turning to leave, she thought she picked up on a woman's voice. The redhead remained still, almost questioning her ears. Then, seconds later, the voice came out of the quiet again. It seemed to be coming from above. Walking a few steps away from the house, she gazed intently up at the second story. She remained silent and still. Then, a second voice was heard, lower in tone and evidently male. This voice caused the female to laugh. Layla felt her stomach churn as she walked toward the far side of the building, her eyes picking up on the faint outline of two vehicles parked on the grass there, out of sight from any passersby on the road. With each breath of air coming in quick sequence, she walked up to the first car. She peered downward and read the inscriptions: *Born to be Wild* and *If you don't like my driving dial 1-800-EAT SHIT.* She closed her eyes and took a deep breath. She feared the worst. Advancing a few steps to her left, she was able to identify Philip's Firebird.

Layla let out with a scream and it carried with it the intensity of the pain that ripped through her, cutting through the moist, silent air. Scrambling back over the driveway, she grabbed her bicycle and sped off toward the road. Instinctively, she pedaled frantically toward home, ignoring the danger posed by poor visibility. The bike continued to accelerate around Fisherman's Cove as she moved the vehicle by the retaining wall separating herself from the Atlantic Ocean. The tide was in but the ocean calm on this night. After flirting with a collision with no less than three telephone poles flanking the road she reached a stretch in the roadway lacking illumination. Disregarding caution, she headed the bike toward the light above the distant Crescent Beach ramp. It was then that her front tire struck a large rock by the road, no doubt thrown up from an earlier high tide, sending her sailing over the handlebars.

In mid-air and conscious she had left the bicycle behind her, Layla found herself momentarily suspended above ground until her right hand, left elbow and both knees made contact with the graveled road shoulder and tarred pavement, in that order. A burning sensation in these extremities ensued, albeit numbed somewhat by the confusion and anguish whirling within her head from the discovery of the past few minutes. She cried out again, this time from the utter frustration of her predicament. Using her arms to push herself up from the ground and onto her feet, she attempted to survey her physical condition. Limping forward a dozen steps, she arrived under the street light at the beach ramp. There she saw blood running from the puncture on her right hand and swelling already beginning to show on one elbow. Shifting her eyes downward, she could make out the knee of one pant leg shredded while a biting pain radiated up her thigh from the other. The redhead let out with an instinctive whimper and hobbled back toward the bicycle. Using only her left hand, she raised the bike and mounted it. Incredibly, it rolled forward in a normal manner, the wheels and mechanism undamaged from the accident. With pain shooting up and down her body, the twenty-year-old gingerly pedaled herself all the way to Mile Road and ultimately to the gentle slope leading up to Route 1. Dismounting the bike, Layla pushed it and herself the four hundred yards to the grounds of the Atlantic Coast Lodge.

Dropping the bicycle on its side by the main building she hobbled up the short set of stairs and pushed open the office door. Inside, Brian sat in front of the computer, his eyes glued to a column of numbers projected on the screen. It took a moment before he nonchalantly glanced across the room towards the doorway. It took only a split second for his eyes to focus on the image of his cousin, her face streaked with blood and her slacks ripped open at one knee.

"Who did this? Are you all right?" Brian shouted, bounding to his feet and scrambling out from behind the desk. Layla's first response was to break out in a fit of uncontrolled weeping. Reaching his cousin's side, he clutched her by the shoulders. "Are you all right? Did someone do this to you?" asked the man in a roar, his temper out from under his control. Layla shook her head no.

"I…I hit a rock with the bicycle and landed…landed on the road. They were together, at the house," she said, managing to force the phrases out between sobs and stunted losses of breath.

"Who were together? Where are you coming from?" Layla burst into a fresh series of sobs and stumbled in the direction of the couch. Collapsing onto the thick cushions, she turned over her hand and examined her wound for the first time under adequate light. Brian, too, dropped down onto the couch, getting a meaningful look at the cuts and abrasions for the first time.

"Okay, into the kitchen. I'll get out the first aid kit and we'll get this damage cleaned up," he instructed, hoisting the young woman to her feet and assisting her toward the next room. "Do you have a pair of shorts at the cottage?"

"Aye."

"Where?"

"They'd be in me set of drawers—second drawer down."

"Do you mind if I go over there and bring you back a pair?"

"No, not at all," she answered while surveying the gash on her knee."

It only took Brian a few minutes to return to the kitchen and produce a pair of shorts. Layla had already peeled off her slacks and sat with her legs hidden from sight. Within minutes her cousin was cleaning her wounds with a warm, soapy cloth. She sat in silence, allowing him to bandage the deep cut on her hand and apply a disinfecting agent to all open wounds.

"I'm finishing up the season the same way I started it, as white as a sheet," she blurted out, no doubt self-conscious of her alabaster skin and the amount of her exposed flesh within full view of her male cousin.

"You're a magnificent, physical specimen, regardless of the pigmentation of your skin," he answered, his eyes coming up to meet hers. "Now what happened tonight leading up to all this? And this time, say it slower and without the bawling." She threw her head back in a show of anguish and tried again to recount the details of her findings back at Moody Point.

"I decided to bring Philip the present I'd picked up for him in Portland on Sunday. He told me how he wouldn't be home Monday night but I thought it would be a bit of fun to leave the banshee I'd bought for him on his doorstep, for when he came home. So I bicycled down to his house after work and placed it there on his doorstep. The banshee is our own personal joke. I was about to leave when I thought I picked up on voices coming from upstairs in the house, up in the bedrooms. When I stood still outside and listened real hard I picked up on a woman's voice, then a male's. Then, I made me way to the far side of the house and saw the two cars parked out of sight, from the road, that is. One was Donna's car."

"Not the Donna you let stay here with you?"

"Aye, the same. And the other car was Philip's."

"Maybe he let someone else use his car," suggested Brian.

"There'd be no chance of that. Philip's not for letting anyone drive or use that car. I'm thinking of last week and he telling me not to visit the house on Monday because he'd be in Boston with his da. Already planned, it was. That brasser, she's been working on this scheme for a while, I'm thinking."

"Probably, but don't go and cut this lying scumbag, Philip, any slack. It takes two to tango." The redhead closed her eyes and let her head drop forward. It took only an instant for her to break into a second crying fit.

"It hurts so much it's making me stomach ache. Brian, how could these two do this to me? I've never done anything to them to make them do such a thing." Her cousin rose to his feet and stood beside the twenty-year-old. Layla rested her cheek on his side, her tears making contact with his shirt and moistening the fabric.

"It happens kid. It happens all the time."

"Me heart is breaking. For the first time I can say I know what the words mean. Me heart, it hurts so bleedin' much."

"I know what you're going through. It happens to all of us."

"To you? It's happened to you?"

"Yes, and more than once."

"What did you do?"

"You just do the best you can. Pick yourself up and do the best that you can. What else is there?"

"I want them dead, I do. I'd like to put a knife through them."

"Well, we know that's not going to happen. But, you're going to have to deal with these two dirtbags for another week and a half before you go home. Do they know you've got the goods on them?"

"Aye, they have to. I let out a scream after I saw the two cars. And there's also the banshee I left on the porch. Sweet Jaysus! I feel like such an eejit." The man reached down and stroked her auburn hair, attempting to comfort her as best he could.

"If my memory serves me right, you won't be getting a very good night's sleep tonight."

"And who was it, this woman who hurt you like this?" she asked, happy to linger on someone else's pain, if even for only a moment.

"Maggie May," he answered.

"Mrs. Kelly!"

"You know Layla, this doesn't mean that he's absolutely walking away from you. We men can be loathsome, weak creatures, and he may wake up tomorrow morning wondering what the hell he's done. You're head and shoulders over Donna Pento."

"I'm not so sure of that. With all her working out and dieting and losing weight, she's got men panting after her now."

"You've got looks too, but a whole lot more. Trask is no jerk. Actually, come to think of it, he is a jerk. But even a total jerk like Philip—and by the way, why does it have to be Philip and not Phil? God, people who insist on their proper names are usually such anal retentive jerkoffs. Anyway, don't be too surprised if that pretty boy scumbag doesn't come crawling back before too long. And if he does, you'll have a tough decision on your hands."

"Brian, I love him so much it hurts."

"Nonetheless, you'll have a very tough decision to make." The redhead took a deep breath and rose to her feet.

"I'm thinking I have another crying fit coming on and maybe I should go back to me cottage and let you finish your work and get to bed."

"It hurts more when you're alone. Are you going to be all right?"

"Aye." Brian leaned down and kissed the young woman on the top of the head.

"Don't stay up all night. At least try to doze off," he suggested. She stepped gingerly out of the kitchen and toward the office door.

"'Tis only nine days till I go home, and I'm going to miss me American cousin more than he knows." She stole a peek back at Brian and, awkwardly favoring one leg, made her way down the porch steps and across the yard.

It was midnight before Layla climbed the ladder up into her sleeping loft. She had hoped that the eleven o'clock news and the opening monologue from the *Tonight Show* would distract her from the events two hours earlier, and moreover, dull the ache in her heart. Instead, she was reminded of how fond she had become of *Jay Leno* and how she would miss him back home in Glencolombkille. The ache, however, was still very much with her. Falling forward onto the mattress, she lapsed into another outburst of tears. She struggled with the heartache, as it seemed to gnaw at her stomach lining, the emotion literally bringing on physical pain. She had never experienced anything of this magnitude in her twenty years. For the first time she was able to grasp heartbreak's almost bottomless depth. It explained, she thought, the crazed reactions it sometimes drew from those passed by or discarded from affairs of the heart. Wiping moisture from the side of her face, Layla rolled onto her side. She closed her eyes as pain radiated up from her elbows, hand and knees. Then, in spite of her best efforts, she tortured herself by conjuring up images of the two coupled in his warm, comfortable bed.

Layla opened her eyes and scrutinized the knots that pockmarked the pine boards constituting the roof directly over her head. This wooden overlay, her bedtime tapestry, had become as familiar as her parent's loving faces over the past months. She found herself totally awake at this hour. Raising herself up, she scrambled to the bottom of the mattress and glanced down to the clock below. It was ten minutes past two. It struck her that, as Brian predicted, she would get little sleep this night. She fell back onto the mattress and considered her shift at Billy's on Tuesday. Her shift was only for lunch and she would be off at four o'clock. That would bring her in contact with Donna when she reported for the dinner shift. Layla considered how she would approach this unpleasant situation. She reasoned that, in the end, she would let her former friend's behavior dictate her plan of action. If Donna Pento approached her with a contrite heart, then possibly, only possibly, something might be worked out. She did not know what, but there was always a chance that some form of reconciliation could be brought about. If, on the other hand, the brunette arrived at Billy's Chowder House with a measure of the same cocky insolence that had dominated her personality in recent weeks she would get a quick lesson in why her people were referred to as the 'fighting

O'Malleys' back in Ireland. As for Philip, she had a strong feeling that it would be a few days before he could muster up the courage to face her.

It was after three-thirty when Layla back-stepped her way down the ladder and turned on the television. Rolling her body into a snug, little ball on the sofa, she glued her eyes on the undersized screen while an infomercial heralded the astounding properties of the latest in exercise apparatus.

The redhead's eyes fluttered open, accompanied by the sound of the morning news from the television across the room. Groggy, she rose up onto unsteady legs and was immediately reminded of the bruises and abrasions carved into her extremities. She stepped to the window and turned the Venetian blinds. The sun was just rising through the houses lining Atlantic Avenue a mile away. Layla reached out for the ladder through a drawn out yawn and sluggishly made her way up to the loft. She would be sound asleep less than a minute later and would not be roused from her unsettled slumbering until the sound of pounding at the front door shocked her back to consciousness. The pounding fist on the door below belonged to her cousin Brian. It was ten o'clock. She called out to the man, assuring him she was awake and would soon be preparing herself for work. Slowly descending the ladder, the twenty-year-old was struck by the lack of any impulse to cry. For the time being, that urge had been suppressed. However, the gnawing pain in the pit of her stomach remained, immune to the passage of eight hours or the bright, October sun beating down on southern Maine. Layla pulled the ladder back from the loft and returned it to its daytime resting place, snugly lodged against the far wall and overhead ceiling beam. She had no way to know that she would not be returning to that familiar sleeping loft, not that night or any time in the near future.

XXV

THANKS TO RESTRICTING HER SHOWER to less than five minutes and dashing about the cottage like a madwoman while dressing herself, Layla was able to punch in her timecard on the hour at eleven o'clock. She grabbed a menu to study and returned to the front hall where she joined Nicole and Lori sitting quietly at the far end of the bench. On the bike ride to work this morning she was abruptly struck with the notion that Philip and Donna's relationship might be public knowledge with herself, the Donegal bogtrotter, the only employee at Billy's Chowder House not privy to their sexual relationship.

"Ladies, could I ask you both for a wee bit of information, and I'd hope you'd be honest with me." The two women looked up from their menus and searched Layla's eyes for a clue to the purpose behind her uncharacteristically sober questioning.

"Of course, sweetie. What's on your mind?"

"What have people been saying about me relationship with Philip Trask? I mean, when I'm not there to hear. Of all the girls I work with here, you two fall on the side of the ones I trust." A confused expression broke out on both women's faces.

"Do you mean what people think are your chances of getting a proposal from the guy?" Nicole asked.

"Aye, and anything else they might be talking about?" The waitresses stole a look at each other, both appearing slightly bewildered.

"Are you concerned about anything Billy Sousa's been saying lately? If you are, then you can put your mind to rest. It's Donna and no one else but Donna on the receiving end of his foul mouth these days. Is that what you're worried about Layla?" questioned Lori.

"Aye, it'd only be that. It sounds like the bleedin' eejit has taken up spreading his rubbish about a new lassie, and I'm all the better for it," she exclaimed, satisfied word of Philip's affair had not reached her fellow workers.

It was a Tuesday luncheon crowd in October and by one o'clock the restaurant's tables were half occupied. Layla was returning from the lounge balancing a tray of beverages when she caught sight of Brian and Dick Varano standing by the front desk. Approaching the two men, she picked up on their serious demeanors. Both sets of eyes were focused intently on her.

"I think you better go grab your coat and come with me," suggested Brian calmly. Dick stepped forward and relieved her of the tray.

"Brian, you're scaring me here, you are," she muttered, a look of overwhelming concern spreading across her face. Her cousin came to her side and directed her back toward the kitchen and her jacket.

"I'll fill you completely in on the way to the truck," he assured her, guiding her through the swinging doors and into the kitchen. "Everything's going to be okay but you've got to do as I say." Layla snatched up her coat and punched her time card out for the day. The room filled with a chorus of voices, each inquiring into the nature of the unfolding drama. Dick halted the cousins at the door.

"Layla, I'll take care of everything at this end, with your pay and all," the owner assured her. The redhead lifted her eyes to his, her blue eyes awash in tears. She reached out for the man but was whisked out the door and down the stairs before any physical contact could be made.

"Your father suffered a stroke at work back home. He's been rushed to a hospital. Your mom called and asked for you. She wants and needs you back home. I've already called Aer Lingus about getting you on a flight tonight, and that's what Millie's working on right now, getting you on that flight." Layla let out with a solitary, wailing sound while her body collapsed against Brian's. Her cousin's arms enveloped the girl and deposited her in the front seat of his Ford. "No one is sure exactly how serious the stroke is but they can't take any chances. If and when your mom gets any more definitive word she'll be calling us at the office. Until then, we've got to get you ready to fly out tonight. We have to assume that Aer Lingus will get you on that flight out of Boston this evening. I believe it's leaving around eight forty-five or so. In the meantime, you've got to pack this afternoon and we've got to get you to the bank to draw out your savings."

"Did me mother say if she was at the hospital with Da?"

"I believe she said she was, but I'm not sure. She did say she would be driving down to Shannon Airport overnight and pick you up in the morning when you arrive." The man glanced across the cabin of his vehicle as he turned onto Route 1. His cousin stared blankly through the windshield while suffering from shortness of breath. Conscious of being observed, she looked back at him, her eyes seeming to implore the man to wake her from this horrible dream. "He's going to be fine. It's precautionary. It's more of a case of your mom needing you now, for support. Your dad will be fine," he reassured her. Brian coasted the pickup to a stop at the rear of the main building and hopped down from behind the wheel.

"Layla's booked on the eight-forty flight this evening out of Logan, on Aer Lingus. I just got confirmation of that," reported Millie from the top step of the porch.

Brian helped his cousin down from the pickup and guided her in the direction of her cottage. She said nothing, content to follow the directions of the man without comment. Reaching the tiny cabin, he pushed in the unlocked door, his eyes immediately scanning the exposed area above the bathroom for luggage.

"Why is God doing this to me?" exploded Layla in a sudden emergence from her trancelike state. "I don't deserve any of this," she argued aloud to anyone or anything listening within the universe.

"I don't know baby girl, I really don't. But, we all seem to get our turn eventually. Yours just seems to be coming a little too close together. Now as far as that crap that Philip and that fat girl pulled, that doesn't have anything to do with Him."

"She's not fat anymore, thanks to a certain eejit from Donegal."

"Maybe not this second, but I'm sure there's a two gallon tub of triple chocolate ice cream sitting out there somewhere with her name and fat rear end carved on it." The man watched as his cousin's eyes noticeably softened.

"Would the tub of ice cream have a huge glob of extra fattening whipped cream sitting at the top of it?"

"Indeed it does. And in that huge glob of whipped cream is the imprint of Donna's fat face, put there in her anxiety to eat that chocolate blob and not willing to even wait for a spoon." The redhead let out with a weak chuckle.

"And sure it'll be a doorful of a woman she'll become again," Layla predicted. Brian reached for the girl, drawing her tightly to his side.

"Your mom and dad's gain will be my loss," he confessed in a heartfelt tone. "Now, get that luggage down and start packing. I'll go back to the office, call the bank, and explain your circumstances. Maybe they can do something at their end to speed your withdrawal up."

The pickup turned into the driveway just as the four-thirty headline news flashed over the radio. In her handbag Layla carried a cashier's check for over eighty-two hundred American dollars, something slightly in excess of her goal. Sitting in the grass at the back of the main house were her three pieces of luggage, one more than she had arrived with just over five months earlier.

"Make sure you thank Millie for everything," Brian counseled his cousin.

"Aye, but I'd like to make a last visit back to me cottage." The man nodded but pointed at his watch, reminding the girl that they had to leave extra time for possible delays. Layla hopped from the vehicle and trotted across the grass to cottage fourteen. Standing on the small, screened porch she pushed open the door and stared into the darkened studio that had been her home for five months. The familiar clock on the far wall read just after three-thirty, telling her the batteries powering the imitation 1950's wall clock were running down, much like her remaining time in America. Entering within the knotty pine walls, she hastily pulled the ladder across the room to the lip of the sleeping loft and scrambled up the wooden steps. Moving forward over the mattress she pulled open the miniature, blue curtains and looked eastward, out over the swimming pool, marshland, Wells Harbor, and distant Atlantic Ocean. The blue water in the distance caused her to think of her father, battling his infliction back home, far beyond the horizon line. She was reminded of the conversations with him over the summer and the enthusiastic way he reminded her of the steadily dwindling number of days before her return. She longed to hear his voice again and began to cry. Amazingly, Layla remembered a morning early on when she awoke before dawn and followed the movement of car lights along distant Atlantic Avenue as they repeatedly appeared and vanished behind the closely aligned homes along the roadway. It seemed so very, very long ago. Finally, following a last look toward Kennebunkport and the white dot that was the Colony Hotel a number of miles away, she pulled the curtains back over the window and closed a chapter in her life.

Entering the office, Layla was greeted by Millie who hopped to her feet and rushed to her.

"I want you to know that I already have a large number of women from church praying for your father's quick recovery," she said while applying an affectionate hug.

"And I'm sure that after the Big Guy recovers from the shock of hearing from all the prayers from those Congregationalist heathens he's got to act on it," chirped Brian returning from the kitchen with beverages for the drive to Massachusetts. Layla glanced toward her cousin who playfully winked his eye.

"I'll be the one gloating someday at the great banquet in heaven when it's us Congregationalists sitting up front at the good tables and you Catholics up somewhere in the nosebleed section," she answered. "All except you honey, you'll be up front with me by special invitation," added Millie. The gray-haired woman pulled the girl against her a final time before turning and taking her place behind the front desk.

"Millie, try to keep your money stealing activities to a minimum while I'm gone," he joked, before leaning over to the woman. "And thanks for coming in with no notice like this," he whispered. She gestured him to leave and he noticed she was visibly withholding tears.

"We'll hold your cottage for you for next year," she called out as Layla and Brian made their way from the building.

They were cruising southward on Route 1 a few miles south of Ogunquit when Brian observed his cousin staring blankly through the windshield and biting on a fingernail. He reached across and flicked her hand from her mouth.

"Let's keep those hands perfect for when your dad first sees you," he suggested, introducing a positive thought into the girl's head. A dim smile came over her face. "And won't it be nice seeing your mom at Shannon tomorrow morning?"

"It'll be grand, it will."

"And think of how your father's face will light up when you come waltzing into his room later in the day."

"Aye," she answered. "Aye." The redhead looked to her right out the side window. "'Tis the road to Bedford," she observed, albeit listlessly.

"We'll be joining the turnpike soon and heading due south to Boston," explained her cousin.

"I will probably never set eyes on Philip again," she said in a quiet voice.

"Worse things could happen to you, kid, but you never know."

"I don't see him coming to Glencolombkille, now that he's got his Donna."

"Oh please! If that model you told me he was hooked up with couldn't hold him down, do you really think that Donna Pento's going to be able to?" Layla smirked.

"And maybe it's a doorful of a woman he's set his eyes on now?"

"And in Donna Pento's case, a garage door," he quipped to his cousin's amusement. The man was doing everything in his power to keep his cousin's spirits up.

"Oh cuz, there is one more piece of bad news I was holding back from you, but there's no point keeping it from you any longer." His cousin's eyes widened in anticipation.

"Those two hooligans you met at the airport in May, you know, the ones you were talking to when I came and picked you up. Well, I asked them if they wouldn't like to meet up with us tonight and see you off. Unfortunately, they both have choir practice this evening and can't make it. But, they were heartbroken they couldn't." Layla laughed and slid over the front seat to her cousin, resting her head on his shoulder.

Brian directed the Ford up the incline and into the parking lot for Terminal E. They had arrived at Logan Airport before six-thirty. Pulling the luggage from the back of the pickup, they began the walk toward the section of the international building allotted to Aer Lingus. They both sighed aloud at the multitude of passengers cued up in line for flights on the Irish airline. Brian pointed his cousin toward a ticket window where an attractive, young female with black hair worked alone at a computer terminal. They approached the woman porting Layla's luggage and waited on her to pull herself back from her work. Following ten seconds of quietly standing in place, the woman lifted her eyes. Brian immediately went into an explanation of his cousin's circumstances. She listened intently and then, with great confidence, instructed them to inquire at a specific office close by. She assured Layla that her ticket would be in the possession of one Mr. Hurley and she could purchase the ticket directly from him.

With her luggage already checked in and her boarding pass in hand, Layla stepped to the side of the hallway and gestured to Brian to do the same. There, he stood beside his cousin in the shadow of the 'Passengers Only Beyond This Point' sign.

"And God haven't I been dreading this moment," voiced Layla as she stared up at Brian Kelly.

"The place is not going to be the same without you," he admitted, placing his hands down on the girl's shoulders.

"In a way, I think it'll be you that I miss most."

"After Philip you mean."

"No, Philip's lost I believe."

"Any regrets?"

"Aye, one that comes to mind. I didn't spend enough time with me cousin and too much with me friends."

"I'm from a different generation. You would have been bored silly. No, you did the right thing. Oh, do you want to hear something pitiful?" Layla gestured yes.

"Jenny and Brendan were coming up this weekend to surprise you down at the house. They were going to go to Billy's first, ask for one of your tables, and jerk you around without telling you who they were." The redhead nodded in disbelief and rested her head on the man's chest.

"I just don't know how to say good-bye to you," she admitted before bursting into tears. "There aren't words enough to thank you." She drew in her breath and gazed up at the man. There were tears in his eyes.

"Find some cousin, because I'm beginning to come apart here."

"I love you, Brian, and I'll make sure me ma and da know how good you were to me. I only wish I knew when I'd be seeing you again."

"How about this: I ask Maggie May to plan on joining me right after tax season for two weeks in Ireland, after her busy season and before mine. If she says no then I go by myself over the winter. I'll spend all my time in Donegal, with my relatives."

"And sure you'll be bored, you will," she predicted.

"Not a chance."

"We'll put you up in our new house."

"If that's an invitation, then I accept." Brian reached forward, pulling the redhead into an extended embrace. It ended with individual kisses to each cheek and a final peck to the bridge of the nose. "Call me collect, at the office." The words said, he turned and walked in the direction of the exit. No doubt, he heard his cousin's weeping until he disappeared into the crowd of travelers making their way toward the departure gates.

XXVI

T HE MAN TURNED THE KEY and pushed the heavy, wooden door into the cottage. A week had passed since Layla O'Malley had vacated the cabin and returned to Ireland. Minutes earlier he was struck with the thought that the baseboard heat and water heater might have been left on inadvertently, prompting his visit to the tiny cabin. He stepped inside the shady room, the interior darkened by the drawn Venetian blinds. He reached back and flicked the switch, illuminating two lights on the far wall. The interior of the cabin was in perfect order right down to the thick carpet under his feet that still retained the effects of the swirling action from a vacuum cleaner. He walked to the far side of the room and ran his hand over the baseboard unit. He found the long, metal unit cold and the temperature dial turned off. Stepping into the four by nine foot bathroom, he swung open the fuse box and saw that the water heater had also been turned off. Even in the face of turmoil it seems his Irish cousin had remembered to shut down the cottage before vacating the premises.

Brian moved back into the living room and fell backward onto the couch. He drew in a deep breath while his eyes scanned the knotty pine walls and simple furnishings. Surrounded by the silence, he revisited the increasing chapters of his life touched by events played out within these four walls. He considered how a quarter of a century had passed since he first set eyes on this tiny cabin. The teenage Brian Kelly survived his first summer of heartache here. It was the lingering aftermath of his shredded relationship with Maggie May Keogh. Incredibly, it was eighteen years later when these four walls provided sanctuary for Jenny Keogh, herself in need of protection from the dangerous, cruel world. And now, the recent memories of Layla O'Malley seemed to occupy the interior of the cabin, the echo of her lilting brogue seemingly loitering between the walls and overhead in the eves of the building. Outside, the complex prepared for winter. Soon the water would be drawn from a majority of the units, including this one, sending them into a long, winter's sleep. Brian's thoughts shifted to the O'Malleys back in County Donegal. He was still awaiting word on the condition of Layla's father. Glancing up toward the ceiling and sleeping loft, he was reminded of a summer long ago when the teenage Brian Kelly found refuge and a summer job here. It was in that loft where that same young man fought his demons. Demons created by a certain Maggie May Keogh, and demons no different from the ones his Irish cousin, no doubt, found herself battling with these many years later.

Brian sprang to his feet, preparing to exit the building. Reaching for the door, his eyes were distracted by an object trapped against the wall, pinned there by a leg of the table. Frozen in his tracks, he plucked what appeared to be a photograph from the floor and held it up to the light. It portrayed the image of his cousin, Layla, seated on a porch, a hesitant smile on her face. His eyes poured over the photo. The location of the photograph was not clear to him, causing him to theorize it was snapped sometime over the summer at the Trask house. Tucking the picture into his shirt pocket, he left the cottage and returned to the office.

His chair rolled backwards from the desk, gliding effortlessly over the polished, hardwood floor. Alone in the building at the moment, Brian let out with a loud cheer nonetheless. He had just rented sixteen of his cottages in a block over a long weekend period in early May of 1999. The organizer of a family reunion in nearby Sanford had remembered the Atlantic Coast Lodge from a personal vacation a few years earlier and contacted him. Now, following thirty minutes on the phone, a reservation was made and a deposit would be mailed promptly. Celebrating his accomplishment, he jumped to his feet and pumped his fist triumphantly. Off-season rental activity of this magnitude was rare and not in the budget. As he saw it, this was found money and would allow him to bring some of his people back to work early next year. He glanced over at the photograph of his cousin, Layla, propped up against the library lamp at the front of his desk. He addressed the photo.

"Biffo, huh. No biffo could have pulled that off...cuz." He flashed the photograph a sad smile. The night before he had glanced over at her cabin and, momentarily, thought he saw light emitting from the building's skylight. On closer scrutiny it proved to be reflection from the moon. Across the desk the phone rang through the quiet, office air.

"Atlantic Coast Lodge," he answered routinely.

"I want to speak to the bloke who owns the place. I'd be looking for a refund, I would." The caller's voice belonged to Layla.

"Is that me little bogtrotter?" came back Brian in a poorly orchestrated brogue.

"Tis. And grand it is to hear me favorite cousin hasn't forgotten me yet."

"Never. God, I was just over in your cottage a couple of hours ago."

"Mine is it? And how soon can I be expecting the paperwork on that purchase?"

"Never mind that—you silly article. How's your dad?"

"And wasn't that what I was calling you about? As of today he was declared completely out of danger. We start outlining his physical therapy program tomorrow."

"Oh, that's great. I mean, everyone's been praying for him back here."

"I knew you would be—you and Millie."

"Okay, catch me up on everything. When are you taking your dad home?"

"Not for a while. It's been decided to have his therapy here in Letterkenny, so we'll be staying at me uncle's house."

"Well, that's convenient, having relatives close by."

"Oh Brian, tis convenient but little else."

"What? Don't you guys get along with your uncle?"

"Uncle Jack is fine. Tis his wife—me aunt. She's not a joy to be around under the best of conditions, and now here we are under her roof."

"What's so bad about her?"

"Oh Brian, for starters she's as tight as the bark on a tree."

"She's letting you guys stay with her. That doesn't sound like a penny pincher to me," said Brian, coming to the defense of the woman.

"First of all, we'd be paying the O'Malleys room and board, so don't you be placing any halos over their heads."

"Not as generous as your American cousin, huh? Okay cuz, exactly how tight is tight?"

"Tight enough to draw a line on the milk bottle at night to make sure no one gets up and drinks anything overnight."

"Couldn't you just get up and drink some milk, then refill the bottle back to the line with water?" His suggestion brought a fit of laughter from the girl.

"And what, tell her it was a miracle? Regular milk changing to skim milk overnight?"

"Who's the patron saint of watery milk? Anything else?" Brian asked.

"I think she's counting the corn flakes every night before she goes to bed," stated Layla.

"Now you're just jerking me around, baby girl," he scoffed. "I hope you know how much we already miss you?" Brian had turned serious.

"And don't I miss you too."

"As I started to tell you a few minutes ago, I just came from your cabin. I was checking to see that the heat and hot water was turned off. Anyway, I found something on the floor."

"And what was that?"

"It was a picture of a little, Irish girl sitting on someone's porch." His statement spawned an extended pause.

"I was wondering what happened to that photograph. It was taken just a few months back and doesn't it feel like another lifetime, it does," she answered wistfully. "And have you heard anything from the crowd down at Billy's?"

"Layla, I've been home with the family in Bedford for the past four days. I'd have no way of knowing if anyone called. However, if I were a betting man I'd bet that they had. By the way, are you calling from your uncle's house?"

"Sweet Jaysus, no. I bought a calling card."

"Well, you're going to have to keep us appraised of your father's progress. Is there a number I can reach you at?"

"We're going to be in Letterkenny for at least another month. Tis better if I make it a point of reaching you." Brian let out with an exaggerated sigh.

"I'll keep Millie and her friends down in York praying for your dad and I'll do the same. We won't settle for anything short of a complete recovery."

"Tell Millie I miss her—and you know how much I miss me cousin. Oh, and Brian, drop me a line if you hear from anybody else," she requested sheepishly.

"By anybody, I assume you mean Trask."

"Aye, Philip."

"Is it possible to send you an e-mail?"

"I'm not sure where you'd have to send it. Me uncle has no internet connection at the house."

"What year is this? What planet am I on?" bellowed Brian into the phone.

"I'm just a poor girl from Donegal, I am. I only have me sheep and me wildflowers on the hillside. I'm nothing like me rich cousin from the states, biffo that he is."

"You know you can always call me collect."

"You've done enough for me. I'll stay in touch. Tis a promise," she stated emphatically. With those words the line went quiet, the calling card expired or the connection lost.

Brian returned the receiver to its cradle and glanced down at the photograph of his cousin. He was happy to have heard her voice and the encouraging news. However, the girl's voice also caused a painful sadness to descend upon him. He spent the remainder of the day directing his mind toward other matters than his Irish cousin's well being.

XXVII

L AYLA SAT ALONE in the living room, gazing blankly through the front window out onto the road. In less than a week it would be December. This year would bring another happy Christmas, happy but bittersweet. It was Wednesday and she would have the house to herself for two days. Following six weeks of physical therapy away from Glencolumbkille, Eoin O'Malley would return home Friday night. Finula would accompany him and serve as driver. Layla had come home in advance of her parents to begin the task of cataloguing and packing personal belongings. For the last month and a half the O'Malleys had been staying under the roof of Eoin's relatives on the other side of the county. The twenty-one-year old gave out with an extended sigh and ran the tip of her finger along the living room table, leaving a visible line in the accumulation of dust. Unable to motivate herself to begin the chore of packing, she leaned her head back on the couch. She had just closed her eyes when the telephone rang out from the kitchen, slicing through the silent house like a knife. Hopping to her feet, Layla scrambled into the next room and lifted the receiver.

"Hello," she sang out in her usual breezy voice.

"I don't frigin' believe it! There's actually someone there," roared Brian Kelly from the far end of the phone line.

"Brian, I just got home, I did, and me folks won't be joining me till Friday."

"No e-mail address to communicate through. No fax machine. Not even a bleedin' answering machine. We got one lousy message here saying your father was recovering, and then absolute silence. Oh, and by the way, Millie and all her Protestant friends in York took credit for that." The comment brought a chuckle out of the redhead.

"Like I had said on the phone, we were staying with relatives, and not terribly sociable relatives at that. It was hard."

"You've got people over here wondering about you."

"And haven't I been thinking about all of you over there."

"Well red, grab a comfortable chair and catch me up on things."

"I'm in the kitchen so there's nothing terribly comfortable. But I'll make do. Let's see, me da is coming along so well that he's been cleared to go back to work right after New Year's. Ma, she lost the job at the laundry on account of missing so much work, but she'll be starting her search next week. And me, I'll be going in search of employment right after the move. In the meantime, packing will be me top priority," Layla explained.

"You're not buying the house?"

"Aye. We lost too much ground with me dad recuperating and all, and me ma wanting to be right by his side."

"Exactly how far behind did you fall?"

"I didn't want me parents going through their life savings so I paid for all of our expenses and put the down payment on the family's new car, because both of the old ones died."

"Layla, how much of your savings is left?"

"Less than a thousand pounds," she answered, sounding almost ashamed. Her cousin let out with a groan.

"And you guys could still buy the house if that money was still there?"

"That's what they say. Me da will be back to work again in five or six weeks."

"Well, listen, let me give this some thought for a short while. In the meantime, I want to catch you up on all the people who keep asking about you and calling the office. Of course, you know the family in Bedford has been on me to contact you. A short while back I heard from Wesley Wright from Billy's. He was pulling up stakes and leaving Wells and wanted to know if I had an update on you and your father. I told him your father was coming along fine but had no word on you. Dick Varano asks about you whenever I see him at the restaurant or on the street. I've gotten a couple of calls from Bill Johnston asking about you and wanting your address so he can mail you something. I think it's a Christmas present."

"Isn't he coming over to visit his sister?" blurted out Layla.

"Yeah, he said something about that but he was afraid you guys would get your wires crossed and wanted to be sure you got something from him." Brian picked up on a pregnant pause at the County Donegal end of the line. "Philip has dropped by to inquire about you... twice."

"And what about his little girlfriend?"

"Little?" Layla laughed, remembering their banter concerning Donna Pento's former physical stature. "Donna Pento is no longer working at Billy's and no longer with Philip. I'm pretty sure she's moved on somewhere."

"You said he inquired about me?"

"Yes, the second time was just a few days ago. I was a little rough on him, particularly the first time. This last time he was actually talking about flying over to see you." Brian waited on a response. Following an extended period of dead air, he continued. "Layla, what do you want me to tell him? Do I tell him to kiss off or what?"

"Tell him I had nothing to say on whether he comes over or not."

"Okay, so that makes me think you are not totally against seeing him again."

"Me life is so upside down right now, I'm not sure what I'm for or against," she admitted.

"Cuz, let me toss something out there for you to consider. What if I send you over eight thousand dollars to replace what was lost from your dad's health problems? Now, this would be strictly to be used to buy that house, and for nothing else."

"Brian, I can't."

"What do you mean, you can't? I have money sitting in this bank account and that bank account's not doing much for anyone but the banks. Why can't I send it over to my extended family? I want you guys to get that house. I mean, you grew up in it, didn't you?"

"Aye."

"I would like one thing in return, though."

"And that would be what?"

"I want my cousin to come back next summer and work one more year here in Maine."

"And pay you back the eight t'ousand dollars from me earnings?"

"Absolutely not! I just want you back here, staying in cottage fourteen. I want you to stay with us one more year and go back under better conditions. Everything you earn and save, you keep."

"It would be grand seeing you again but herself would have to sort that out with me ma and da."

"Just try, okay? Oh, and by the way, Maggie May is not up for going back to Ireland after tax season like I wanted. She says she'll be too busy working on the Atlantic Avenue house. So, that means I'll be over in January or February, and I'd like to think I'll be staying in your Glencolumbkille house."

"Me parents are going to go mad with excitement over this."

"Tell them to get the couch ready for their American relative this winter."

"Are you mad? Tis me they'll be putting on the couch."

"Okay Layla, that's the plan. I'll make sure everybody gets the word from Donegal over here, and you make sure your parents don't have any qualms about the gift. Do we have a deal?"

"We do Brian, and God bless you," she added. "Good-bye, and I'll talk to you soon."

"Take care kid."

Hanging up the phone, Layla called aloud with a giddy exuberance missing since her return to Ireland. "Thank you God. Thank You so very much," she cried to the walls of the empty house. She lifted the receiver and punched in the numbers to her aunt's house. Seconds later she was delivering the news of Brian's offer to her folks who, after an initial period of shock, embraced their cousin's generous gesture. In the interests of keeping the conversation brief, Layla volunteered to prepare an elaborate dinner at the house on Friday, celebrating her father's return home. It was with a true sense of joy that the twenty-one-year old walked to the grocery store that afternoon and picked up the foodstuffs for the next two days. Her one-half mile walk was interrupted no less than five times by locals welcoming her back home and inquiring into her father's progress. She turned down all offers for a lift to the store but comically left the door open for any like-kind offers for her trip back to the house. On reaching the store, she decided upon curry chicken for the Friday night meal, an accommodation to her limited experience in the kitchen.

At six o'clock a heavy rain blew in over the choppy waters of Donegal Bay and washed clean the streets of Glencolumbkille. Layla sat alone in the warm, quiet house, an open book balanced on her chest. By her side on the coffee table rested a half-finished cup of tea and the empty plate from her dinner meal. From overhead the sound of raindrops striking the house's slate roof provided calming, hypnotic background noise. This peaceful, meditative moment was interrupted by the telephone. Placing the book aside as not to lose the page, she hustled out to the kitchen and caught the intrusion before the third ring.

"Greetings from the O'Malley residence," she answered whimsically.

"God, it is good to hear your voice again," sounded a male voice. It belonged to Philip Trask. "I know I may be the last person you wanted to hear from right about now but I'm going to take that chance."

"Hello Philip. And where would ye be calling from?"

"Killybegs. I'm staying at a bed and breakfast at the edge of town. Ocean View. Have you heard of it?"

"Is it the one by Kitty Kelly's?"

"Yes, but the restaurant's closed for the season."

"Aye, not enough tourists to support it. And what would it be that brought you up to Donegal?" Layla asked, as if unable to fathom a reason.

"Just keeping a promise I made to someone a couple of months ago." She did not respond to his words, causing him to become noticeably flustered. "I was happy to hear your father was on the mend. I can't imagine what you must of been feeling back then, with everything happening the way it did."

"The worst days of me life, they were."

"Your cousin, Brian, wasn't the most cooperative fellow on the planet when I inquired about you and how to possibly reach you."

"I'm sure you could have gotten the information from him if you had tried hard enough."

"He's a lot bigger than me so beating it out of him was not going to happen. Layla, I'm not even going to try to apologize and say I'm sorry. I made a terrible error in judgment. I ruined a friendship, and I know I did something that I'll regret for the rest of my life."

"And when did you come to that conclusion, the moment she slipped her knickers back on and bid you a fond farewell?"

"I think we both knew it was over when I found that doll on the porch the next morning," confessed Trask.

"And how many more rides did you two have before you knew it was really, really over?"

"Please Layla, meet with me. Don't send me away without seeing you after I've flown all the way over here and traveled the length of the country just to set eyes on you. I still love you, and I'm here to try and prove it."

"And where are you now?"

"I'm in a pub in Killybegs."

"And you have a rented car?"

"Of course."

"Then I'll meet you tomorrow at eleven o'clock at me beach here in Glencolumbkille."

"That's the place you talked about all the time."

"Aye, it's me favorite place in the world."

"You told me more than once about wanting to take me there. I hope this is a good sign."

"It's not a sign at all. Tis where we'll meet and nothing more."

"And they'll be no problem finding it?"

"There's a heritage center directly across the street from the parking lot. Follow the signs to there."

"Eleven o'clock tomorrow; I'll be there. And Layla…"

"Aye."

"It's been wonderful just hearing your voice again."

"Goodnight Philip."

The conversation over, Layla hung up the phone and walked deliberately back to the living room. Outside, the wind had intensified and sent a series of gusts against the front door, the rainwater pounding on the wooden exterior like an angry landlord in pursuit of his rent. Layla collapsed back onto the living room couch, her mind as unsettled as the weather outside her window. She would have much to consider before retiring upstairs later that evening.

XXVIII

A STREAK OF MORNING SUNLIGHT broke into the bedroom, slipping in between the edge of the shade and the window panel. Layla opened her eyes to her first morning completely home in Glencolumbkille in nearly seven months. It felt good to be finally home, she thought. Glancing over to her alarm clock, she saw it was after seven. She had slept well. It was only an instant before her stomach began to swirl in anxious anticipation of her meeting with Philip. She had not set eyes on him in almost two months and she wondered how she would react in the presence of that handsome face. It was the face and smile that had prompted her to overlook shortcomings and personality flaws time and time again. He had always held the trump card, a smile capable of leaving her lightheaded. Still and all, he had betrayed her, robbed her of a friend, and lied to her barefaced in doing it.

She lifted herself from the mattress, placing her bare feet down on the cold, wooden floor. Walking to the closet, she pulled open the door and saw her slippers neatly standing at attention before her. Prodding them out with one foot, she slipped them on, wrapped herself in a robe, and headed for the stairs. The redhead paused as she passed her parent's bedroom, the bed undisturbed for too many nights. How grand it would be rising on Saturday morning with Eoin and Finula O'Malley back in the house with her, she thought. She descended the stairs, walked to the kitchen, and put on a kettle. She checked the clock there. It read seven twenty-five. She had spent the prior evening and up until the moment she nodded off to sleep wondering what Philip Trask had on his mind. She would not stew over it anymore, she decided. After flicking on the radio she went in search of the canister holding the porridge. She was coming off of six uninterrupted weeks of corn flakes at the home of relatives and a break was long overdue.

The O'Malley's home was approximately two-thirds of a mile from the beach at Glencolumbkille and Layla gave herself nearly a half an hour to arrive there. It was a cool, crisp morning and she dressed warmly in jeans and an imitation leather coat with a fur-lined, hooded collar. Her heart was beating rapidly as she made her way into the wind and down the roadway toward the beach. Overhead the sky reflected a deep blue with a few incidental swirls of white clouds providing some contrast. Arriving at the parking lot, she observed a solitary vehicle. Her eyes scanned the bumper and back windshield and came up with an Avis decal. It was a rental and it was, no doubt, Philip's rental. With her auburn hair blowing frantically about her head, Layla walked past the vehicle and closer to her rendezvous. Stopping at the edge of a collar of land that broke sharply away, she peered downward and saw Philip Trask standing with his hands in his pockets and looking out to sea. She glanced down at her watch. It was eleven o'clock. Coincidentally, the notion of time must have also struck her American visitor in that he looked down at his own timepiece and then over his shoulder toward the parking lot. His head lifted slightly as his eyes focused on the form of Layla O'Malley staring down on him. To him, she must have seemed like some mystical, Celtic goddess with her red hair waving wildly about her face and her slender form silhouetted by the grassy hillside beyond.

Philip gestured to her and Layla turned and made for the steps. Descending the familiar stairs at a measured, steady pace, she reached the beach and started toward the man. There was no enthusiastic quickness in her steps. As he watched her move toward him, perhaps Trask's thoughts went back to the afternoon spent together in Kennebunkport and out at spouting rock. Two months time and a foolish indiscretion on his part had drained the effervescent spirit from this young woman at the moment, at least when it came to anything associated with him.

Layla stepped methodically through the sand and toward the water's edge where the sculptor waited on her. Behind her she left a trail of foot impressions, a straight line toward the man she had sought out that same summer a continent away. Philip walked forward to meet her as the two converged. Tentatively, he leaned forward and kissed her on the cheek. She smiled and looked up at him.

"Well, it's not exactly how we planned it back in Maine but here we are together at your beach. All we're missing now is our picnic on Slieve League," he suggested.

"'Tis a wee cold up there this time of year, and we might be blown off to boot." Trask fidgeted in place, his eyes darting from hers to the surrounding hillside and back.

"I'm here… Thanksgiving Day. Did you know that? It's Thanksgiving Day back home. My folks are pissed as hell at me for coming over at the holidays to visit my 'little Irish girl.' I'm supposed to be with mother today up in Randolph for turkey dinner and back in Boston at eight for some kind of charade with dear old dad and his trophy girlfriend. Instead, I'm over here in this little town I can't even pronounce asking to be forgiven."

"You shouldn't be spending time away from your family on important days when you could be visiting here next week and accomplishing whatever you need to do," she answered. "And yes, I forgive you, Philip." She watched as his eyes widened. He took a single step toward her and applied a loving hug. They remained silent through the embrace. "And there it is, the scent that I have longed to inhale for over a month but had to travel across the Atlantic to experience."

"And sure you could have saved yourself a lot of time and money and gone to New Hampshire to do the same. I gave Mrs. Kelly a bottle of me cologne over the summer. You could have paid herself a visit and smelled her," suggested Layla.

"Oh sure, the guy's just been looking for an excuse to take a poke at me and you're suggesting I search out his wife so I can smell her!" exclaimed Philip, sending both into a burst of laughter and helping to put both more at ease. The surge from a single wave sent a rush of foaming seawater to within inches of their feet and they stepped back in unison from the surf. "I brought something over with me and…" His words were interrupted by her fingers as she put them up to his lips. She cupped his face with the palms of her hands.

"Before you say anything more I want you to kiss me the way you kissed me at Moody Point. Remember Philip, on those nights I came over after work and we sat on the porch and shared our hopes and dreams." He stepped forward and pressed his lips to hers, exploring her mouth and hungrily grinding his body against hers. They remained in the embrace until she pushed him back, returning him to arm's length distance. Layla looked up at the man sadly, her blue eyes growing moist as a look of apprehension took shape on his face.

"Please don't say what I'm afraid you're going to say," he asked.

"Tis that obvious, is it?"

"You said you forgave me. Have you just stopped loving me?"

"A part of me would kill to have it back, that lightheaded madness you brought out in me. For certain it was love." She closed her eyes and let her head slump down onto his chest. "I needed to know if the magic was there, if the banshee that possesses me would rise up as it always did in the past. Me love, you see that it did not."

"So, it's all come to this… nothing," he concluded.

"I'll not have you think anything of the sort," she shot back, clasping her hands behind his neck and peering deeply into his eyes. "You were me first love, Philip Trask, and you brought me joy I never believed possible. People older and wiser than me say you never forget your first love. Me cousin says no man ever fully gets over his first love, and why should women be any different. No, anything with this much pleasure and pain attached to it can't be called nothing. But, clearly, it wasn't meant to be."

The star-crossed lovers spent well over an hour walking the length of the beach at Glencolumbkille recounting and reliving the summer of 1998 and the role each played in the other's life. Their steps methodically traced and retraced the sandy edge of the inlet, one arm slung around the other's waist. There was a certain finality about the interlude, the last, dying breaths of an improbable relationship that conquered nationality, age differential, education and social class distinction, only to tragically crash and burn on a foggy, Maine night at Moody Point.

They had reached the near end of the beach when Philip shot a glance at his watch. Nearly two hours had passed since he descended the stony steps down to this quarter-mile of sand and waited on Layla O'Malley.

"I probably should be going." She acknowledged his statement with a subtle squeeze of her hand. "I'm booked for one more night back at Ocean View. My flight home isn't for another five days. I had hoped that things were going to work out a little differently."

"And I'm thinking they worked out about as well as we could have expected. Everything's been forgiven and we can move forward as friends." Dropping his hands on her shoulders, he stared directly into her face.

"Do you think you'll ever come back to Maine again?"

"Funny you should ask. I'll be sorting out me plans on that very subject on me walk back to the house," she said.

"So you don't want a ride?"

"No, I'll be needing that time to think."

"So, this is it?"

"Aye. Tis." He reached down and kissed her good-bye. She did not resist. Trask drew in a deep breath as their lips separated. He turned and started toward the steps,

"Good-bye me love, and take care of yourself," she called out. Stopping in his tracks, his body folded forward. She watched as Philip wrestled with his emotions, his body shaking slightly as he held in the effects of his disappointment. Layla ran forward to him.

"I'm sorry about this," he called out, extending his hand out to her. He was breathing deeply, tears visible.

"No, tis nothing to be sorry about. Long overdue it is."

"I must look pathetic."

"Nothing of the sort. And don't the Irish men cry all the time, and there's nothing weak or pathetic about them. There's something in the air over here that brings this out in everyone." He laughed and straightened up.

"You always had a way with words, the right words at the right time." He winked and started for the steps.

"If you're smart you won't be flying home until it's time. If you're smart you'll take that rented car of yours to Dublin and find yourself a lonely jackeen to share some black stuff with. There's a lot of thirsty girls in Dublin I hear, and you're a fine bit of stuff, Philip Trask, you are," she called out. He looked back at her a final time, flashed his choreographed smile, and walked from her life.

XXIX

Layla's spirits soared as she set the kitchen table for three. Within hours her mother and father would be returning home and the anticipation of that long awaited, happy event had her as giddy as a schoolgirl. Inside the refrigerator, wine was chilling and her ambitious experiment in making homemade bread for the occasion of their first meal together, at their own table, in over six months seemed to be working. She stood back in the corner of the kitchen and took in everything. All was perfect, she thought.

Picking up the telephone, she punched in the long sequence of digits required for her international call and waited.

"Atlantic Coast Lodge," answered a familiar voice.

"Brian. Tis Layla," she announced joyously.

"Are you calling from the Glencolumbkille house?" he asked.

"Aye."

"I'll call you right back. It'll save you a few bucks. So hang up the phone, muttonhead," he ordered. The redhead chuckled and put down the receiver. A minute later the phone rang in her kitchen.

"Muttonhead, Muttonhead, Muttonhead and O'Malley, Solicitors at Law," answered a female voice.

"Give me Muttonhead, Muttonhead or Muttonhead. Just don't give me O'Malley," insisted Brian.

"And sure I can't do that, the Muttonhead brothers are all out on the links. I can give you Miss O'Malley," said Layla.

"Very well, put her on. I'm sure she'll be married into that Muttonhead family eventually. She's got all the qualifications."

"And how's me cousin on this grand day?" she asked.

"Fine, fine... and you?"

"Grand. Me da and ma will be coming in t'ree hours or so."

"Well, I'm glad you called. This'll give me a chance to update you on everything."

"And everyone is well?"

"There're fine. It's good you called because I really wanted to update you on something that literally blew me away yesterday."

"Aye?"

"I had a visitor come by with a package he wanted sent on to you. Would you like to venture a guess who it was?"

"Dick Varano?"

"No, but you're warm. Think of Dick but with a much, much stronger smell of brine."

"Mr. Johnston?"

"Ah yes, William Johnston, and the face that hasn't smiled since the Carter administration."

"And what was he up to now?"

"As I said, he came by with a package he wanted to mail to you. He wanted the right address from me. Anyway, we started talking while I hunted for your address and I told him about how a lot of your money got used up covering expenses while your father recovered and went through therapy. Oh, before I forget, he wanted me to let you know that he'd be over from December fifteenth to January fifth. He says he'd like to come over and visit on the nineteenth or twentieth, over the weekend."

"And I'm sure that'll be fine it will. And won't it be grand to see Mr. Johnston again," added Layla.

"He's sending the package just in case things can't be worked out with the visit to Glencolumbkille."

"And why couldn't they be worked out? The man talks so much rubbish," she added.

"Anyway, brace yourself for this. When I told him about how you folks were going to be able to buy the house in spite of all this bad luck, and how I was putting up the eight thousand dollars to close on it, he said he wanted to do something. Are you listening to me?"

"I'm listening."

"He said he wanted to foot half the bill. Four thousand dollars!"

"Stop the lights!"

"I'm not kidding you. When I tried to waive him off and said it wasn't necessary, he got goddamn belligerent."

"Mr. Johnston's very good at that, he is."

"He starts hollering about how his money is as good as anyone else's. Thankfully, there were no guests around. I was a baby's breath from tossing his nasty ass out of the office when I realized the guy was about to save me four grand. So I let him run his mouth off. He wrote me a check for the four grand on the spot. What did you do for that guy?"

"I always gave him extra crackers. Tis nice that he didn't forget."

"I gave him your phone number so you'll probably be hearing from him in the middle of December."

"We'll have him for dinner. I'll have Da buy some Bushmills. Mr. Johnston will like that."

"You know, Layla, I'd ask you how you do it, but I know how you do it. You could charm a life preserver from a drowning man."

The second phone line in the office sounded and Brian excused himself for a moment. When he returned his tone of voice grew more serious.

"So kid, have you made a decision yet on my proposal about coming back for one more year?"

"I have," she answered.

"And?"

"If you'll have me and Dick will let me come back to Billy's... aye, I'll come back for one more summer."

"All right!" cried out her cousin. Oh, cuz, one little detail: Yesterday I rented out your cottage to a Canadian family of six, so you'll have to be sharing cottage fourteen next summer with them."

"Janey Mack! There'll be seven of us sharing that wee place with one bed?"

"*The Three Stooges* used to share a bed like that all the time. Don't be so fussy," mused Brian.

"Are you still coming over to visit in January?"

"That's right kid. Two weeks of sleeping on my relative's couch in Glencolombkille... now that's a vacation I couldn't get from a travel agent."

If you enjoyed reading

Miss O'Malley's Maine Summer

By

Thomas E. Coughlin

Look for his other works of fiction

Maggie May's Diary

Brian Kelly: Route 1

Obscene Bliss

The Odyssey of Sheba Smith

Scott Brooker

Artist & Photographer

New York City born & trained

(603) 232-3237

Resides in Manchester, NH

About the author

Thomas E. Coughlin is the author of the best-selling *Maggie May's Diary*. He is a practicing certified public accountant and former radio announcer. He was born, raised and educated in Lowell, Massachusetts. Mr. Coughlin resides in Chester, New Hampshire.